P9-DZY-062

A Wicked Gentleman is also available as an eBook

Also by Jane Feather

Almost a Lady
Almost a Bride
The Wedding Game
The Bride Hunt
The Bachelor List

JANE FEATHER

A
WICKED
GENTLEMAN

POCKET STAR BOOKS

New York   London   Toronto   Sydney

An *Original* Publication of POCKET BOOKS

 A Pocket Star Book published by
POCKET BOOKS, a division of Simon & Schuster, Inc.
1230 Avenue of the Americas, New York, NY 10020

This book is a work of fiction. Names, characters, places and incidents are products of the author's imagination or are used fictitiously. Any resemblance to actual events or locales or persons, living or dead, is entirely coincidental.

ISBN-13: 978-1-4165-2551-6
ISBN-10:   1-4165-2551-3

This Pocket Star Books paperback edition April 2007

10 9 8 7 6 5 4   3 0646 00185 7758

POCKET STAR BOOKS and colophon are registered trademarks of Simon & Schuster, Inc.

Front cover design by Lisa Litwack; front cover illustration by Aleta Rafton

Manufactured in the United States of America

For information regarding special discounts for bulk purchases, please contact Simon & Schuster Special Sales at 1-800-456-6798 or business@simonandschuster.com.

A
WICKED
GENTLEMAN

Prologue

H E DUCKED INTO THE SHADOWS of the yew hedge bordering the square garden and held his breath, listening. He could hear nothing but he knew they were behind him somewhere in the darkness. They were as skilled at pursuit as he was at eluding it. He slipped his hand inside his shirt and felt the small, hard shape taped securely beneath his right arm. They mustn't find it on him.

No lamplight shone from the row of tall houses across the street. Even the servants were in bed at this unfriendly hour of the night. A fitful moon illuminated short flights of honed steps that led up directly from the pavement to the immaculate front doors with their gleaming brass knockers. Neat black railings enclosed the area steps that led down to the kitchen regions.

Behind him something crackled . . . a squirrel rustling through the fallen leaves . . . but no, he knew it was them. He was unsure how many there were, but guessed at least two. He stroked the hilt of the short blade in its sheath at his waist. He could make a stand here, if there were only two of them. But if there were more they could come at him from all sides in the shadowy gloom of this cold February night.

He was in motion almost before his mind was aware of it, breaking cover and racing across the street. And now he could hear them, feet pounding behind him. In the flickering moonlight he made out a carriage rounding the corner of the square, the four-in-hand at a near gallop under the direction of a whip-cracking young man and his two companions, swaying drunkenly on the box, their raucous laughter demolishing the quiet.

Bent double, inches from the flailing hooves, he dived for the far pavement. The leaders, already panicked by the shrieking laughter and the out-of-control hands on their reins, lunged and reared at the thing suddenly rolling beneath them. Laughter gave way to shouts as the team lurched sideways and the carriage hung on two wheels, before losing purchase on the road and toppling over.

The man paused for barely a second, assessing the noisy chaos behind him in the middle of the street. The horses struggled in the traces, their reins twisted. One of the leaders was on its knees.

Mayhem enough to hold off his pursuers for vital minutes. He held still, his eyes accustomed now to the semidarkness, scanning his immediate surroundings. The elegant well-maintained facades of London's aristocracy lined the square on all four sides. For the moment no house light yet shone in response to the mayhem. Something brushed against his ankles. He started and there was a protesting squall. A cat leaped between his feet and down the area steps immediately in front of him. He stared down into the black depths of the tiny yard. A pair of eyes gleamed as the cat jumped onto a low windowsill. Then it vanished.

Instinct took him down the steps, feeling his way. Above him the sounds of chaos intensified. He pressed himself against the wall at the bottom of the steps and saw the cat's eyes glaring at him from the windowsill. But this time they were inside the window, looking out. The window sash was raised about twelve inches, more than enough for a cat to wriggle through, but not for a man. He was a skinny man, to be sure, but no contortionist.

He put his hands beneath the window and pushed. It rose infinitesimally. But it *had* moved. The cat jumped down with a protesting meow. The man pushed again. A foot and a half would do it. He was calm even though every sense was stretched to catch the slightest sound, smell, the merest whiff of his pursuers. The window creaked, stuck, creaked again—then shifted just enough.

He slithered through the space on his belly, kicking his legs like a novice swimmer, and fell to the flagstone floor, bracing himself on his flattened hands.

There was a smell of damp, of kitchen detritus left

overlong. The ashes in the range were cold. The flags beneath his feet were sticky with refuse. A rat scampered behind the wainscot.

Harry Bonham ran his hands over the horse's fetlocks. He had coaxed the terrified animal up from its knees, and now it stood, lathered and panting distressfully, head lowered, eyes still rolling. "How are the others, Lester?"

"They'll do, sir," his companion stated, spitting onto the cobbles with an expression of disgust, as he added, "By some miracle."

"Aye," the other said, straightening to regard the dispossessed coachman. "What of you, man? You hurt?"

The coachman was surveying the tumbled carriage and his distressed horses with an expression of confused dismay. "No . . . no, sir. Thank'ee. Thank God, you were 'ere, sir. It weren't my fault, sir. Them tosspots put a pistol to my head, snatched the reins. It was all I could do to 'ang on up there. Thank God you were 'ere, sir," he repeated with the same bewildered defensiveness.

Harry Bonham's eyebrows flickered. As far as he was concerned, nothing could have been less fortuitous than the timing of this encounter. He glanced around. The three young men who'd been driving the carriage were picking themselves up from the cobbles. Their movements were uncertain and when they managed to stand they swayed like saplings in a gale. Their extravagantly high cravats and violently colored waistcoats identified them as aspirants to the Four Horse Club, Corinthians in the making.

Harry's lip curled. Idiot children of privilege, drunken sots with no more ability to drive a four-in-hand than to dig a ditch. And they had no idea what work their sottish prank had disrupted this night. A tongue of anger licked at his customary impassivity.

He bent down and picked up the coachman's long driving whip that had fallen to the street in the chaos. He flicked and caught the tip in his gloved hand, then advanced on the three youths.

Lester nodded as if in satisfaction, and said to the coachman, "Help me get these beasts out of the traces."

The man hurried to oblige, although his eyes darted over his shoulder at the scene unfolding behind him.

The three young men stared at the man coming towards them. He was impeccably dressed in black, and, if he'd been wearing the obligatory white waistcoat, could have been on his way home from Brooks's or some such aristocratic haunt. But his coat was buttoned to the neck and he wore a bicorn hat pulled low over his forehead. His eyes were cold in the faint white moonlight.

His hand flicked, the whip cracked, and the youths yelled more in bewildered outrage than fear or pain. It cracked again, and this time fear spurred their headlong flight. For a few moments that the coachman and Lester could only find comic, they blundered into each other, trying to find a route away from the fiery tip of the avenging whip, the relentless advance of the black-clad, cold-eyed avenger. None of it made sense. They'd done nothing wrong . . . nothing out of the ordinary. Everyone played such pranks, it was no worse than boxing the Watch.

The whip-wielding stranger, however, maintained an almost indifferent silence as he went about his work, and finally, as pain penetrated the alcoholic anesthesia, they fled towards the darkness of the square garden, their pursuer in leisurely fashion flicking them on their way.

Harry's nostrils flared as they disappeared into the shrubbery. He caught the tip of the whip and coiled it neatly, turning back to the toppled carriage and the now-released horses. "Any serious damage?"

"Off-side leader has a strained fetlock, sir," the coachman said, stroking the animal's neck.

"Yes, I noticed." Harry reached inside his coat and drew out a card. "Take them here. My head groom's a wizard with fetlocks."

The man took the card and cast a questioning look at the man who had given it to him. "I can lead 'em there all right, m'lord, but what about the carriage?"

Harry shrugged. "An expensive toy for spoiled brats. It's no concern of mine. But the horses are." He turned away, then said over his shoulder, "Giles makes an excellent rum punch . . . tell him I say you've earned it."

The coachman touched his forelock. "Aye, m'lord. Thankee, sir."

"And if I were you, I'd choose my employers with

more care," Bonham said. "I'll tell my agent to expect you tomorrow. We need a coachman." He raised a hand in farewell and stepped out of the road onto the narrow pavement.

"We lost him," he stated, looking along the row of elegant houses fronting the square. Anger flickered again behind the cool green eyes. "Those damned drunken louts . . ."

"Aye, sir," Lester agreed, keeping his tone neutral. His master's fury, cold and all but tangible in the frosty night, was as much directed internally as it was against the follies of misguided youth. The viscount had allowed his focus to blur. But Harry Bonham was incapable of ignoring one downed horse and three panicked ones plunging in their traces in imminent danger of broken legs.

"So where did he go?" It was a considering murmur as Harry scanned the houses. "He didn't double back to the square."

"You're sure of that, sir?" Lester looked uncertainly across the street. "In that mess, anyone could have gone anywhere."

"No," Harry said definitely. "I knew who was on the street." He stroked the knuckles of one hand, frowning in reflection. "Light the torch, Lester. Let's see what we've got here."

There was no longer any need to rely only on moonlight. The cacophony in the street had brought lamplight to a dozen windows around the square. No one had ventured into the street, however. It was the Watch's business to deal with a midnight fracas. A cat circled Harry's ankles, purring like Cleopatra. He looked down at it. Golden eyes gazed back. The animal arched its back coquettishly and sniffed his boots. Harry liked cats almost as much as he liked horses. He bent to scratch its neck and inhaled a musty, damp smell from its fur.

"So where did you come from?" he murmured.

As if in answer, the cat leaped away from him and shot down the steps to a basement area a few feet away.

Gut instinct stirred. Long ago Harry had learned to trust it. He could almost smell his prey. "Douse the torch," he instructed in a bare whisper. Instantly they were in semidarkness, the only light from the occasional lamps in the adjoining houses and the first faint gray of the false dawn.

Harry moved as silently as the cat down the steps into the area. He saw the slight opening in the window and pressed himself into the darkest corner of the tiny yard, certain now that his quarry had gone to ground through that window. He didn't hear Lester but felt him scrunched into the opposite corner of the yard in the shadow of the steps. There was no point going in after the man. Blundering around in a dark and unfamiliar house would do more harm than good. The man had to come out sometime and logic dictated that he use the same route. If he slipped out through a door, he'd be unable to lock it behind him, and he couldn't afford to leave any sign at all of his intrusion. Not if, as Harry suspected, he was going to leave something behind for later retrieval.

They waited. The darkness even in the basement area diminished shade by shade. The light was almost gray when they heard the faint scrape of the window. Saw the slithering shape. They waited until the shape materialized, rose slowly from a crouch. And as it did so, realized that he had company.

Lester jumped on him, and the two went down in a scuffling heap. There was an instant when Harry, drawing his pistol, couldn't distinguish Lester from their quarry amid the tangle of limbs. Then something flashed bright in the confusion and Lester gave a cry of mingled pain and surprise. He released his grip on the man, who was instantly gone like a wraith up out of the darkness of the area, up the steps to the street.

"Dear God," Harry muttered through his teeth, torn for the barest second between chasing after the fast-moving shadow shape of his quarry and tending to his injured companion.

"Go after him, sir." Lester pressed his hand to his chest. "'Tis but a scratch."

"Nonsense, man," Harry said brusquely. "It's too late, he's long gone, and that's no scratch." His voice filled with concern as he knelt beside Lester, tearing open his shirt. "You need a surgeon." He unbuttoned his own coat and pulled a pristine cravat from around his neck. Wadding it, he pressed it against the wound. "Hold it there, and I'll be back in five minutes."

He ran to the corner of the square where the first hackney carriages were emerging to face the new day. Within minutes, Lester, swearing with reassuring vigor at every jolt, was ensconced in the carriage and the coachman instructed to take him immediately to 11 Mount Street.

Harry remained where he was, looking up at the house towering above him, its lightless windows facing the street. Somewhere in there was what he sought, and if he couldn't put right this night's work, God only knew how many people would die. He needed reinforcements, and quickly. He strode off in the direction of Pall Mall.

Chapter 1

"ABSOLUTELY OUT OF THE QUESTION." The emphatic statement was accompanied by an equally emphatic palm slapping onto the cherrywood table.

There was silence. The four elderly men sitting along one side of the table regarded the woman seated opposite them with expressions of serene confidence. Judgment had been pronounced by the patriarch, there was nothing more to be said.

Cornelia Dagenham looked down at the deeply polished surface of the table, thoughtfully examining her companions' bewhiskered reflections. They all radiated the pink-cheeked untroubled certainty of those who had never faced a moment's opposition or an instant of want in all their privileged years.

She raised her head and gazed steadily across the table at her father-in-law. "Out of the question, my lord?" Her voice held a note of faint incredulity. "I don't understand. A short sojourn in London is hardly an outlandish proposal."

It was the old earl's turn to look incredulous. "My dear Cornelia, of course it is. Never heard such an outlandish proposal." He glanced to either side, seeking confirmation from his peers.

"Quite right . . . quite right, Markby," murmured his immediate neighbor. "Lady Dagenham, you must see that it would be quite improper for you, a widow, to set up house in town."

Cornelia twisted her fingers together in her lap to keep them from drumming her impatience on the tabletop. "I was not suggesting setting up house, Lord Rugby, merely visiting London with a close friend and my sister-in-law for a few weeks. We would put up at Grillons Hotel, which you must admit is the height of respectability. We are all past the age of discretion, all perfectly capable of chaperoning ourselves without causing a raised eyebrow, even if we were interested in taking part in the season, which we are not. It will be educational for the children—"

"Nonsense," the earl of Markby interrupted, slapping the table again. "Utter nonsense. You and your children belong here. Your place is to supervise the care of Stephen's son and heir, my heir indeed, until he's ready to go to Harrow. And that care is to take place at Dagenham Manor as his father would have wished."

Cornelia's lips tightened, and a tiny muscle in her cheek jumped, but she kept her voice quiet. "May I point out, my lord, that Stephen left the sole guardianship of our children to me. If I consider a trip to London to be in their best interests, then that is my decision, not the family's."

The earl's pink complexion darkened to a deep red, and a vein stood out on his temple. "Lady Dagenham, I will brook no opposition in this matter. As his trustees, we are responsible for Viscount Dagenham, *my* grandson, during his minority—"

"You are mistaken, my lord," Cornelia interrupted with an upraised hand. She was very pale now, and her eyes, usually a warm and sunny blue, were bleached with a cold anger. "*I* and only *I* am responsible for my son during his minority. That was a decision my husband and I made together." She placed her hand in her lap, holding herself very still, her eyes never leaving the earl's.

He leaned forward, and his own gaze was narrowed as he stared at her. "That may be so, madam, but your trustees hold the purse strings. You can do nothing without funds, and I promise you, ma'am, those funds will not be released for such an irresponsible jaunt as this."

"Indeed, Cornelia, do but consider." A new voice joined the confrontation, but with a conciliatory edge to it. "You have no real experience of town. A single debutante season cannot give you the sophistication, the town polish you would need for such an excursion."

Gray eyes twinkled, a soft hand reached across the table to pat her arm. "Be sensible, my dear. Three inexperienced women, country mice all of you, would be eaten alive. You could not possibly manage to get about town . . ." A hand waved expressively. "Just think of all the little details, all the financial issues of hotels and carriages . . . matters that you have never had to trouble yourself about. You cannot make such a journey without a man to advise you."

Cornelia rose from her chair. "You mean well, Uncle Carlton, and I thank you, but believe me, my lords . . ." Her cold gaze swept their faces. "You underestimate these particular country mice. I intend to take my children to London for a month, whether you release the funds from the trust or not. I bid you good afternoon."

She bowed, a mere inclination of her head, and swung away towards the door, ignoring the earl's outraged rumble of expostulation, the scrape of chairs on wood as the trustees came hastily to their feet.

She took satisfaction from closing the door very gently behind her, but then all pretense of calm left her. She stood still, drawing several deep breaths, then swore softly but with all the fluency of a mariner.

"I take it matters didn't go your way, coz?" A soft voice spoke from the shadows beneath the curving staircase.

As the man stepped into full view, Cornelia regarded her late husband's first cousin with a rueful half smile. Tall and gangly, with a loose-limbed athleticism, Nigel Dagenham was an attractive young man straddling the line between boyhood and manhood. His present costume of violently striped waistcoat and impossibly high cravat made him look a lot younger than he realized, Cornelia reflected, closing her eyes for a second against the dazzle of puce and purple. He would do a lot better to revert to the casual country styles he had worn before going up to Oxford.

"How did you guess?" she said with a shrug.

"Your admirable command of expletives," he returned. Then he grinned, looking even younger than before. "My uncle has a carrying voice, and I confess I was a little close to the door."

Cornelia couldn't help but laugh. "You had your ear pressed to the keyhole, you mean?"

"Not quite," he said. "But surely it comes as no surprise that the trustees would refuse to let you take Stevie out of their jurisdiction?" His slate gray eyes were sympathetic. He had experienced the family curb bit himself often enough to understand how Cornelia felt.

"It's just for a month," she stated with some vehemence. "For God's sake, I wasn't suggesting I take him to Outer Mongolia."

"No," he agreed with the same sympathy. "I'd offer to intercede for you, but I'm not exactly in the earl's good books at present."

"Outrun the carpenter again, Nigel?" she inquired, noticing that his eyes were somewhat shadowed, his expression a little drawn. Her cousin-in-law was always in debt, and she guessed that his general tendency to extravagance was exacerbated by running with an expensive crowd at Oxford, one a lot plumper in the pocket than he was. And one with a deal more interest in cards and horses than the pursuit of elusive Greek and Latin texts.

"Creditors are a little pressing," he conceded. "In fact . . . in fact a few weeks of rustication was . . . uh . . . suggested." He flipped open a snuffbox and took a leisurely pinch with an air of sophistication that somehow didn't convince Cornelia.

"So this rustication was not exactly of your own choice?" she said. "You were sent down by the college?"

He shrugged ruefully. "You have it, coz . . . and for the rest of the year too. But the earl doesn't know that little detail. He thinks I'm in debt only until next quarter day and that I decided for myself that I needed to be away from the fleshpots of the dreaming spires for a couple of weeks. So mum's the word."

"Of course." Cornelia shook her head in mock reproof. "You can butter him up, though, Nigel. You know you can. Just play the prodigal nephew as well as you always do and the earl will come round."

"Funnily enough that's exactly why I'm here. I'm escorting the old misery everywhere he goes," Nigel said with another irreverent grin. "Offering my services as his aide-de-camp, if you like." He adjusted the highly starched folds of his cravat, winked at her, and turned to enter the library where his elderly relatives were still congregated.

Cornelia dismissed Nigel's concerns as her own loomed large again. She crossed the stone-flagged hallway to the great front door of the earl of Markby's ancestral home. A leather-aproned servant set down the coal scuttle he was carrying and hurried to open the front door for her.

"Cold out there, m'lady," he observed.

Cornelia gave him a nod of acknowledgment as she walked out, drawing a deep breath, shaking her head vigorously as if to rid herself of something distasteful. She barely noticed the sharp February air, bare tree branches bending under the gusty wind as she marched across the graveled sweep in front of the house and headed out across the frost-crisp lawn.

She paused at a once ornamental fishpond, now looking neglected and uninviting beneath the leaden skies, and bent to pick up a sizable twig blown down from one of the tall beach trees that lined the driveway. Her defiant declaration of intent had been just words. Without funds, she could not possibly leave Dagenham Manor, with or without her children.

Making no attempt this time to moderate her voice, Cornelia swore a barnyard oath and hurled the stick into the green, stagnant waters of the pond. It relieved her feelings somewhat, at the same time making her realize how cold she was in her flimsy muslin and thin sandals. The cloak she'd arrived in was still in Markby Hall, but she couldn't face going back for it . . . not until that smug, patronizing quorum of trustees had broken up. She'd borrow a pelisse from Ellie for her two-mile walk home, back to Dagenham Manor.

She strode around the pond towards a break in the privet hedge that separated the formal gardens from the home farm. Beyond the fields of the farm stretched the gorse-strewn heath of the New Forest, which in turn gave way to the richly wooded acres that had been hunted by the kings of England since before William Rufus the Red, the son of William the Conqueror, lost his life to an ill-aimed arrow. Or maybe it was a well-aimed arrow, legend was uncertain on the matter, but the Rufus Stone a few miles away over the heath, still marked the spot where he'd died.

Cornelia hiked up her skirts as she picked her way across a damp pasture towards a stile that gave access to the narrow village lane. Once over, she headed, half-running against the cold, towards the village green and a pretty red-brick manor house set back from the lane. The house that had been her own childhood home. An idyllic childhood in many respects, in this village sandwiched between the Forest and the blue waters of the Solent. But rustic pleasures could pall eventually, and she was more than ready for a change of scene she reflected with a grimace as she raised her hand to the brass knocker.

"Eh, Lady Nell, catch yer death you will," the housekeeper scolded as she opened the door to the imperative knock. "Comin' out like that . . . might as well be in yer shift."

"Is her ladyship in, Bessie?" Cornelia hugged her arms across her chest.

"In the nursery, ma'am."

"Good." Cornelia hastened towards the stairs. "One of your sack possetts, Bessie, *please.*"

The other woman smiled with obvious satisfaction. "Right away, m'lady."

Cornelia ran up the first flight of stairs, then hurried down a passage to the nursery stairs that led to the top floor. She could hear the voices of her sister-in-law and the nurse interspersed with the high-pitched stream of words pouring forth from Aurelia's four-year-old daughter. Despite her cold and her fury, Cornelia smiled. Little Franny was a force to be reckoned with when it came to holding the floor. The young Lord Dagenham had quickly learned that discretion was the better part of valor when it came to words with his younger cousin.

Cornelia pushed open the nursery door and was greeted with the blaze of the fire, and the wonderful smell of hot irons as the nursery maid went about her pressing.

"Well, Nell?" Lady Aurelia Farnham demanded instantly, disentangling her daughter's fingers from her pale blond hair before jumping to her feet. Her brown eyes shrewdly assessed her sister-in-law and made a fair guess at her mood.

Cornelia shook her head. The wind had snatched her hair from its pins, and she pulled them out as the honey-colored braids, almost long enough for her to sit on, fell from the once-neat coronet around her head.

"They refused?" her sister-in-law said, her head tilted slightly, her fair eyebrows lifted.

"Yes, Ellie, they refused," Cornelia confirmed bluntly. "I obey a peremptory summons to Markby Hall to discuss my request . . . it was *not* a request; it was a declaration . . ." Her voice rose a little with her rekindled anger, and her blue eyes glittered.

"In my letter I'd stated my intention and merely said I would need an extra sum released from the trust to fund the trip, as has always been the case when unusual circumstances have arisen . . . and what do they do? They treat me like some errant schoolgirl, and refuse point-blank to entertain the idea . . . and they'll say the same to you, so I wouldn't bother asking," she added, pacing agitatedly in front of the fire.

"Carlton Farnham could probably have been persuaded, so you might try an appeal directly to him since he's more your trustee than mine, but you know what influence the earl has over them all."

"Why did the earl refuse . . . on what grounds?" Aurelia asked, and instantly wished she hadn't, as her sister-in-law's expression became yet more ferocious.

"Ah, yes, the grounds," Cornelia said, bending to warm her hands at the fire. "Well, it would seem that we are country mice, lacking in sophistication, quite incapable of managing to conduct ourselves in town without male advice and support, and our one and only purpose in this life is to nurture our late husbands' children so that they can be educated to take their places in their fathers' world."

"But we have guardianship, Nell," Aurelia pointed out. "You did tell them that . . ." She saw Cornelia's expression. "Oh, yes, of course you did."

"I did," Cornelia agreed. She straightened and rubbed her upper lip before saying a mite defensively, "However, I told them that we were going with or without the funds." She shrugged. "We can't, of course, but it felt good saying it."

"Pompous bores," Aurelia said, then cast a quick guilty look at her daughter. The pompous bores in question held the purse strings for herself and her child just as they did for Cornelia and her offspring. It wouldn't do for the ever-babbling and always indiscreet Franny to repeat her mother's judgment in the middle of a family get-together.

"Let's go to my parlor." She linked arms with Cornelia and urged her out of the nursery.

The housekeeper bearing a tray had just reached the top of the nursery stairs as the two women appeared. "Oh, the sack posset," Cornelia declared. We're going to Lady Ellie's parlor. I'll take the tray, Bessie."

The housekeeper, panting slightly, relinquished her burden with obvious relief. Cornelia sniffed hungrily. "Spice cakes . . . you are a wonder."

Bessie merely nodded, accepting it as her due. "You drink some of that, Lady Nell. You're chilled to the bone."

"I intend to," Cornelia said with a warm smile as she headed down the stairs, followed by Aurelia. They went into a pleasant, slightly shabby room that overlooked the garden at the rear of the house. It had been Cornelia's mother's parlor, and Cornelia still felt as at home there as in her own parlor in Dagenham Manor. More so, if she was willing to admit it.

She set down the tray and poured the fragrant possett into two cups. She passed one to Aurelia, then deposited herself gracefully in a faded chintz armchair by the fire. She took a bite of spice cake and sipped from the dainty Sèvres cup, her frowning blue eyes fixed upon the fire. Her thick honey-colored plaits fell forward over her shoulders, making her look much younger than her twenty-eight years.

Aurelia regarded her over the lip of her own cup, her soft brown eyes probing gently. "Are you sure they can't be persuaded to change their minds?"

"Uncle Carlton perhaps, as I said," Cornelia mused. "But his voice doesn't count, and the earl won't budge."

Aurelia started to respond just as rapid steps sounded along the corridor outside and the door flew open to admit a whirlwind, bearing the fresh February cold in her pink cheeks and tousled blue-black hair. Even her thick black eyebrows seemed wind tangled.

"Do either of you have relatives you don't know you have?" Lady Livia Lacey demanded, flourishing a sheet of vellum, heavily inscribed.

Cornelia raised her eyes from the fire and turned in her chair. She exchanged a brief grin with Aurelia. Livia was not always overly logical. "If we did, Liv, we wouldn't know it by definition."

"Ah, no, I suppose not," Livia agreed. "Oh, is that

sack posset? I'll borrow your cup, Ellie." She helped her-self liberally and took a sip with an exaggerated groan of pleasure. "Pure heaven . . . it's like an ice house out there." She glanced at her friends, taking in their expres-sions. "Oh, the trustees wouldn't be persuaded?"

"No, in a word," Cornelia said shortly.

"So what's this about relatives you don't know you have, Liv?" Aurelia prompted, tucking a fine strand of her pale hair into its pins as she firmly changed the sub-ject.

"Well, it seems I have . . . no had . . . an Aunt Sophia, some distant cousin of Father's," Livia said, flinging her-self into a corner of the sofa. "Father's very hazy about the relationship . . . Lady Sophia was related to some half brother of his uncle's . . . something like that."

She waved the vellum at them. "Anyway, this is a let-ter from her solicitors. Apparently she died a few days ago and left me this house on Cavendish Square." She opened her hands. "Isn't that amazing? Why me?"

"Amazing," Cornelia agreed, sitting up straight in her chair. "A house on Cavendish Square is going to be worth quite a bit, Liv."

"Exactly," the other woman said with satisfaction. "And since at the moment I don't have two farthings to rub together . . ." She cocked her head like an inquisitive sparrow. "The solicitor says he's already been ap-proached with an offer for the house, a good one, he says."

She bent her eyes to the vellum. "A Lord Bonham is

interested in buying it apparently. This Mr. Masters, the solicitor, doesn't say how much he's offering, but if I sell the house, then I can invest the proceeds and that will give me an income . . . maybe even a dowry," she added.

"The spinster daughter of an impoverished country clergyman, however well-connected, doesn't have much in the way of marriage prospects. Breeding is no substitute for a portion," she continued with a melancholy sigh that was not in the least convincing.

"There's not much in the way of suitors in these parts," Cornelia pointed out with a touch of acerbity.

"No, you two got the only two possibilities," Livia agreed. "And now they're both dead . . ." She didn't complete her thought. "Sorry," she said. "Did that sound insensitive?"

"From anyone else it might have done," Aurelia said. "But we know what you mean."

"Anyway, Ellie and I have been resigned to our loss for nearly two years now." Cornelia turned her gaze back to the fire for a moment. Marriage to Stephen, Viscount Dagenham, had not been exactly a firework-filled union of passion, but they had liked each other well enough, had known each other from childhood, and she supposed they would have grown old together in solid companionship. Not an exciting prospect, certainly, but infinitely preferable to the dead end of widowhood.

She raised her head and met Aurelia's steady gaze and knew that her sister-in-law shared her thoughts. Ellie had been married to Cornelia's brother. Another safely solid marriage of convenience between family acquaintances, brought like her own to a violent end at the Battle of Trafalgar.

Of course, they both had their children. Her own two, Stephen at five and three-year-old Susannah, were her joy and delight, just as Franny was for Aurelia. But the joy and delight of children were no substitute for adult companionship and the pleasures of the bedchamber. She and Stephen may not have reached the heights, but there'd been some substantial satisfaction in the regular gratification of physical need. Her life, like Aurelia's, was now a dreary wasteland, the years stretching ahead in the stultifying comfort and financial dependence of trustee-controlled bereavement.

The prospect of a short visit to London had enlivened that future: the bustle of town, a social scene whose highlights were more than just hunting, whist parties, country dances, and the interminable gossip of an incestuously close-knit community insulated from the outside world.

A prospect that those damned trustees had dashed without a moment's hesitation.

Except . . . Her blue eyes swung towards Livia, a gleam in their depths that her friends recognized.

"What?" Aurelia demanded, leaning forward in her chair.

"I was just thinking," Cornelia murmured. "If we didn't have to pay for accommodation, perhaps we could scrape by in London for a month or so. My allowance is not lavish, but with care . . ." She raised her eyebrows, a slight smile now hovering on her well-shaped mouth.

"Mine too," Aurelia said, needing no further explanation. "If we pooled our resources . . . we'd only need one nurse for the children. Presumably there's a staff in this house, Liv? This Lady Sophia would have had a housekeeper, a cook, at least."

"I don't know, but I'd guess as much," Livia said, catching on just as readily. "And I really ought to go and inspect my inheritance, don't you think? I should have some idea of what it's worth, particularly since there's already a prospective buyer. It must be rather desirable if someone's interested in it so quickly."

"Absolutely, you should inspect it," Cornelia said firmly. "And you can't possibly go unchaperoned. What more respectable chaperones could you have than your widowed cousin and her widowed sister-in-law? And what more respectable residence for us all than the late Lady Sophia Lacey's house on Cavendish Square."

"True." Livia nodded, grinning broadly. "I might even decide not to sell the house. Maybe it would make better sense financially to keep it and hire it out. I have to consider all my options, don't I? The rental would give me a regular income, and it's in a good part of town. Plenty of people like to rent houses for the season."

"Of course that would depend on the condition of the house," Aurelia said. "No one of substance is going to hire a house that's falling to pieces."

"And I know nothing of this mysterious relative's circumstances," Livia mused. "She could have been destitute, living on crumbs in a collapsing attic."

"You're letting your romantic imagination get the better of you again, Liv," Cornelia stated. "I doubt she was destitute. She was a Lacey, when all's said and done."

"And Laceys are notorious penny-pinchers," Aurelia said. "With the notable exception of Liv." She chuckled. "For all we know, this distant relative could have been living on crusts while the house fell apart around her ears."

"Except that this Lord Bonham is so keen to buy it," Cornelia reminded them. "Unless he's simpleminded, he wouldn't be rushing to buy a pig in a poke." She reached over and took the letter from Livia's loosened grip. "Viscount Bonham," she murmured. "Never heard of the family."

She folded the sheet carefully. "Yes, I think it definitely behooves us all to go and inspect the property and . . ." Her eyes gleamed, chasing away all residue of her previous anger . . . "*And* the prospective buyer. I confess to being somewhat intrigued by this unknown gentleman. Who knows, Liv, he might be a prospect for you."

"A house *and* a husband," Livia declared, flinging up her hands in mock astonishment. "I doubt I could be *that* lucky."

"Well, you never know," Cornelia said cheerfully. "But first things first. You should write to the solicitors,

Liv." She held up the letter to read the masthead. "Masters & Sons on Threadneedle Street . . . and tell them you're not interested in selling until you've considered all the options."

The gleam in her eye intensified. "Who's to say what those options might be."

Chapter 2

"Turned down?" Harry Bonham frowned at the stiff-backed gentleman sitting behind the massive desk in the lawyer's office on Threadneedle Street. "Why, man? Was it not a fair offer?"

"Oh, yes, my lord. I considered it to be more than fair . . . considering . . ." The lawyer meticulously adjusted the papers on his desk so that every edge was neatly aligned. "Considering the condition of the property," he concluded, raising his eyes to meet his visitor's steady green gaze. "I explained that to your own solicitors, my lord."

He coughed into his hand. "I have to say that I expected to be dealing with them rather than yourself, my lord. It is customary to conduct such affairs through the solicitors of the parties concerned."

"I prefer to conduct my own business," his lordship declared with an impatient toss of his hand. "It's a damn sight quicker for one. All that middleman nonsense. As to the condition of the house, I don't give a fig." The vis-count frowned at Masters. "I told you that already. Is it more money they're after?" His eyes narrowed, and he leaned back in his chair, crossing one buckskin-clad leg over the other, regarding the lawyer closely.

Mr. Masters fussed a little more with the papers. "There's no mention of that, sir. No counteroffer has been made at this point."

"Mmm." Harry, still frowning, tapped his booted foot with his riding whip. "So who owns the house now that the old lady's gone?"

The lawyer hesitated, wondering about the ethics here, but Viscount Bonham did not strike him as a man it would be wise to obstruct, and there were no confidences in the lady's letter. He selected one of the papers in front of him and pushed it across the desk. "A Lady Livia Lacey, my lord."

Harry picked up the paper and read it. The hand was elegant, the vellum plain and unscented, the message unequivocal. It seemed that Lady Livia Lacey wished to inspect her inheritance for herself before making any de-cision as to its disposition.

"And who exactly is the lady?" he inquired, returning the letter to the desk with an air of finality.

"I believe her ladyship is distantly related to the late Lady Sophia Lacey, although I'm unsure of the exact connection." Masters took the letter and returned it to its place in the sheaf of papers with yet more care over the alignment of the edges.

"Lady Sophia was not specific, but she was most insistent that the property be left to a female relative who bore her name. Lady Livia was the only one who fitted the specifications."

"Some old spinster biddy, I presume," Harry said without any particular malice in the description.

"Well, as to that, my lord, I'm not sure," the lawyer said. "The handwriting is not that of an elderly lady."

"No, but she probably has a young companion, a charity-case relative, to walk her pugs and see to her correspondence." Harry held out his hand. "Show me the letter again, Masters."

With a barely concealed sigh, the lawyer disturbed his neat pile to extricate the sheet of vellum and passed it over.

"Ringwood, Hampshire," Harry murmured. "A nice sleepy little village in the New Forest. Now just why would some maiden lady living in peaceful country retirement want to trouble herself with a trip to London to inspect a deteriorating property for which she's already received a more than handsome offer?" He shook his head. "Beats me."

Masters cleared his throat. "It's always possible, sir, that the lady's circumstances are not what we think."

Harry uncrossed his legs with an energetic movement that made the lawyer flinch reflexively. "Maybe so. Do what you can to discover the circumstances, Masters. And offer another three thousand." He uncoiled himself from his chair, rising to his feet with the same energy as before.

The lawyer gazed at him in consternation, then blurted, "Indeed, my lord, in all honesty I must tell you that if I were your solicitor I would most earnestly counsel against such a move. The property is not worth your original offer. Another three thousand would be a reckless expenditure . . . in all conscience, sir . . ." His voice trailed away.

The viscount regarded him with a degree of sympathy. The poor man was clearly caught on the horns of a dilemma. On the one hand, he was obliged to advance the interests of his clients, in this case the Lacey ladies both late and present, but his conscience obliged him to tread an honest path.

"I appreciate your advice, Masters, don't think otherwise," he said equably, drawing on his driving gloves. "And I fully understand your difficulties in offering it, but I will take the liberty of declining to act upon it. Please relay my new offer to this Lady Livia Lacey, and do what you can to discover her circumstances." He gave the man a nod as he went to the door, flicking his riding cloak off the coatrack as he passed. "I bid you good day, Masters."

The lawyer hastened to accompany his august visitor down the narrow stairs to the front door. A sleety rain was falling. Harry drew the cloak tightly over his shoulders as he looked up and down the street. Beside him, his companion shivered in his black coat and britches.

"Go inside, man," Harry instructed. "My groom's

walking the horses, he'll be back any minute, there's no need for you to catch your death."

Gratefully Masters shook his visitor's hand and retreated within.

Harry stamped his feet, clapped his hands across his body, and cursed his groom, but without much conviction. He'd instructed the man to walk the horses to keep their blood moving, and he'd need to go farther than the end of the street and back to do that. Soon enough the two horses appeared around the corner of Cornhill. The groom, astride a sturdy cob, saw his master immediately and urged his own horse and the raking chestnut he was leading to lengthen their strides.

"Devil take it, Eric, I thought you'd headed for the nearest tavern," Harry said, taking the reins from the groom and swinging himself into the saddle. "It's cold enough to freeze the balls off a brass monkey."

"Aye, m'lord. Sorry to have kept you waiting," the man returned stolidly. "Is it home now?"

"Yes, but have a care, the road's slippery."

"Aye, m'lord," the groom muttered. "I had noticed it meself."

Harry shot him a quick glance and grinned. "Off your high horse, Eric. I know you had." He clicked his tongue, nudging the horse's flanks with his heels, and the chestnut moved forward, his neck arched, nostrils flaring against the cold.

Harry left the horse to set his own pace on the slippery cobbles and concentrated on the considerably more than irritating news he'd just been given. If he couldn't enter the house on Cavendish Square legitimately, he would have to resort to more devious means. There was no time to waste in this race to retrieve the package.

Whoever was responsible for the original theft, either the French or Russians, or indeed both if they were co-operating with each other in this instance, knew that the key to the code was hidden somewhere in that neglected house on Cavendish Square. It had been a week since the theft and the debacle that had led to Lester's injury and he knew they were as frantically trying to retrieve it as he himself. And they had the advantage of knowing exactly where to look, although they wouldn't evade the surveillance of the Ministry's watchers who had been in place in Cavendish Square since the dawn fracas.

Neither it seemed would they get legitimately past the eccentric guardians of the gates. Despite his anxiety he couldn't help but smile grimly at the recollection of his own reception at the hands of Sophia Lacey's three retainers. After the lady's death, he had knocked on the door with what he thought was a perfect pretext to enter and search. He was to value the contents for probate.

His reception had been dusty to say the least. An elderly man in stained leather britches and jerkin, bent almost double but with fierce if rheumy eyes, and two severely black-gowned women, both with a greenish pallor that made them look as if the earth of the cemetery had just opened to disgorge them, stared at him in forbidding silence as he'd explained his business.

The gentleman, whom he took to be a butler of sorts, turned to his companions and stated, "One of them, again, Ada. Not a furriner this time, though." And he had closed the door in the visitor's face, locking and bolting it with a vigor that belied his age.

Somehow he had to get into the house, and his first thought had been that the easiest way of doing that was to own it. But thanks to Lady Livia Lacey, the house didn't look to be his in the foreseeable future.

However . . . however . . .

A slow smile spread across his face. Maybe he didn't need to own the house to gain access; maybe cultivating its new owner would do the trick. He had the perfect excuse for introducing himself . . . he was still a prospective and most eager buyer for her property, hoping to persuade her to sell.

He gave a nod of satisfaction and urged his horse to increase his pace. The Ministry would keep the house under observation until Lady Livia Lacey came to town, then he'd pay a social call and see what he could see.

But despite this logical plan he found it impossible to sit on the sidelines during the next few days and took his own part in the surveillance of the house on Cavendish Square even though he knew the Ministry's observers were more than capable.

It was several days later on a moonless night when the long hours of cramped and frozen watching were rewarded. A figure approached the basement steps . . . a darker shadow in the shadows of the night, with his black cloak drawn tight about him, a black hat pulled low over his brow.

The prospect of action warmed his blood. Harry crept out of his observation point behind the hedge in the square garden and moved soundlessly to crouch behind the railings on the pavement while he waited for the intruder to reemerge safely in possession of the package, if the gods were on the side of the angels. If he himself couldn't catch him, there were four other men strategically positioned along the street and around the square who could pick up the pursuit if necessary.

But Harry was grimly determined to retrieve himself what had been stolen from him . . . the fruits of hours of complex mathematical calculations and intricate mental gymnastics . . . personal issues quite apart from the theft's vital significance to the bloody struggle that engulfed the Continent.

The massive explosion sent him leaping to his feet, the months of painstaking training vanquished by the sheer magnitude and unexpectedness of the sound on this genteel, quiet piece of Mayfair. Windows flew open, shrieks rent the air, and up the basement steps came the shadowy figure of a man, his cloak in tatters, hatless, his hair standing up around his head like a halo.

Harry hurled himself at the man's ankles as he leaped onto the pavement from the top step and brought him down to the hard ground in a tangle of limbs that winded him as much as his quarry.

"It's all right, sir, we've got him." Hands reached down and pulled him to his feet, while others hauled his breathless quarry upright.

Harry brushed off his hands demanding, "What the hell was that?"

"Haven't a clue, sir." The man who'd helped him to his feet looked around as if a clue might materialize from the gloom. "Never heard its like."

Harry shrugged. "Well, it scared the wits out of our friend, and I doubt that did us any favors." He regarded the sagging figure with a frown. "He might not have had enough time to retrieve what he was after."

"Like as not, sir, but we'll take him anyway. No knowing what we might get out of him." The speaker put two fingers to his lips and sent a piercing whistle into the square. An unmarked carriage appeared almost immediately, and Harry's thief was bundled inside, his captors following, before anyone really understood what had happened.

"That'll larn the bugger." A rasping Yorkshire accent that Harry immediately recognized as belonging to Sophia Lacey's rusty butler came from the area steps behind him. He spun around to face the mouth of a blunderbuss wielded by the gentleman in question, clad on this occasion in a purple-striped dressing gown and a somewhat lopsided nightcap.

Harry regarded the ancient weapon in dawning comprehension. A blunderbuss fired in a confined space. The violent explosion now made perfect sense. "How the devil did you manage not to hit him?" he asked with a degree of awe.

The butler peered at him myopically in the semidarkness. "I weren't aimin' to, sir. If I 'ad been, 'ed have felt it."

"Yes," Harry agreed with a grin. "I'm sure he would. Good night to you."

"Good night to 'ee," came the response and the butler and the blunderbuss returned whence they'd come via the basement steps.

It was safe to assume that no other attempt would be made on the house tonight, Harry decided. If the thief had anything to give, he would give it up before the night was over.

Chapter 3

THE IRON WHEELS OF THE CARRIAGE clattered over cobbles, and the city noise rose in increasing cacophony from outside the dim stuffy confines of the vehicle. Cornelia leaned forward to move aside the leather flap that served as a curtain over the grimy windows. The children's nurse had insisted the curtains be kept in place throughout the journey to protect her charges from the light that might damage their eyes and whatever sights of debauchery that might damage their souls. Not that there had been much of the latter to enliven their tedious journey, Cornelia reflected wearily.

She looked out now with renewed interest. It was early afternoon as the carriage turned into a quiet square, leaving the lively bustle of the streets behind. The garden in the center of the square was winter-bare and had a slightly desolate air, but it would give the children some freedom. The carriage creaked to a halt, and she felt her shoulders tighten in anticipation.

"Are we here, Mama . . . is this the house . . . can we get out . . . ?"

"I want to be first, Mama . . . move, Franny . . ."

Cornelia closed her eyes for a moment as the childish voices rose around her, joined belatedly by Susannah's as the little girl awoke and realized that things were going on that she was about to miss.

Cornelia opened her eyes and exchanged a glance with Aurelia. *Journey's end.* Whatever they found here it had to be a welcome change from the long jolting journey in the company of three fractious children.

"Courage," Aurelia said. "We're here."

"So we are." Cornelia grabbed Stevie as he was about to plunge out of the just-opened door and set him firmly on the seat. "Wait with Linton, *all* of you."

Ignoring the rising protests, she stepped down onto the pavement and looked around her. Aurelia and Livia joined her, and the three of them scrutinized the tall substantial house in front of them, long windows on either side of double doors in the center of the facade. Peeling paint, scraped railings, unhoned steps, grimy windows all set it apart from its neighbors.

"I thought we were expected," Aurelia murmured, as they gazed at the firmly closed front door.

"We are," Livia announced. "I wrote two days ago. This is *my* house, in case anyone's forgotten." She stalked up the stairs and raised the tarnished knocker and banged it several times.

"Linton, would you and Daisy take the children into

the square garden until we sort things out?" Cornelia
spoke to the nurse, who was gathering her charges, all
the while shooting slightly disdainful glances at the dilapidated house. "Let them run off some of their energy,
they've been cooped up all day."

"Yes, my lady." It was said a mite stiffly, but Cornelia
decided she didn't have time to worry about Linton's
less-than-favorable impressions at this point. Time
enough when they were installed. She mounted the
steps with Aurelia to stand just behind Livia, who was
about to raise the heavy knocker for the third time.

Bolts creaked, and the door opened slowly; a pair of
slightly rheumy eyes were at first all that was visible in
the crack. "Aye?"

Cornelia hid a smile as she felt Livia stiffen. It was a
foolish person who mistook the bubbly, pretty young
woman for an easily intimidated featherbrain.

"I am Lady Livia Lacey, and you, I take it, are my em-
ployee," Livia announced. "Kindly send someone to
help the coachman unload the coach and bring our lug-
gage inside." So saying, she swept the door wide open
and stepped past the man into the fusty gloom of a large
square hall.

Cornelia and Aurelia followed her, and the three of
them looked around with ill-concealed dismay. It was
cold and damp, the parquet beneath their feet grimy and
slightly sticky, the long windows on either side of the
front door so covered in grime that very little daylight
leached through. A horseshoe staircase, admittedly

handsome, rose from the center of the hall, its upper reaches vanishing into impenetrable gloom. A chandelier, again probably a very beautiful piece when it was cleaned, hung from the center of the high-ceilinged hall. There were a few candle stubs in its branches.

"Well, we didn't expect nirvana," Cornelia said bravely. "We guessed it would need work."

"But *this* much?" Aurelia murmured. "If these are the public rooms, what is the rest of it like?"

"We shall find out," Livia stated. She turned to the man who had let them in. "I don't know your name."

"Morecombe, ma'am," the man said. He had clearly once been a big man, but the broad shoulders were now hunched, and his legs had a distinct bow to them. His manner, however, was less than conciliatory.

"I worked for Lady Sophia, God rest her soul. I don't know nuthin' about this 'ere Lady Livia," he declared, digging out a checkered kerchief from a pocket of his calico knee britches, whose original color was a mere memory. He wiped his watery eyes with a degree of vigor.

"Did Lady Sophia's solicitors not talk to you, Morecombe?" Cornelia asked incredulously. "Surely when the will was read some provision was made as to your future."

He shook his head. "Not as I 'eard, ma'am. Lady Sophia told us, our Ada and our Mavis, to 'ave a care for 'er things, an' that's what we done. She'd 'ave a care fer us, that's what she said."

"And your Ada . . . your Mavis . . . are they here?"

"Aye, where else would they be?"

Obviously the finer points of employer/employee discourse were not going to apply here, Cornelia decided. "I'm sure Lady Livia would like an introduction."

"Oh, aye, like as not," he said with a careless nod. He walked to the rear of the hall. "Eh, Ada . . . our Mavis, come on out . . . t'new mistress is 'ere."

The two women who emerged through the shabby baize door were clearly twins. Hair scraped back in vigorous buns, long black gowns, angular faces with a strange greenish tinge to their pallor, crumpled aprons, and identically fierce and suspicious brown eyes.

They regarded the three younger women without expression and offered the sketchiest of curtsies.

"Beggin' yer pardon, m'lady, but we 'ave to unload the carriage. The 'orses need their oats." The interruption came from the coachman, who now stood, cap in hand, in the doorway.

"Oh, yes, I'm sorry." Cornelia abandoned the scene in the hall and hurried over to him. "Ask the outriders to help you unload. I'll . . ." She fumbled in her reticule.

"Not our job really, m'lady." He twisted his cap.

Cornelia found a shilling piece and drew it out, trying not to think what it would buy the household in terms of general supplies. But clearly the resident retainers were not going to unload the postchaise and she and her companions couldn't.

The coachman crammed his hat on his head and

went outside shouting orders. Within fifteen minutes the hall was a sea of bandboxes, hampers, portmanteaux. Sophia Lacey's three retainers stood watching the proceedings with an air of mild indifference.

Cornelia paid off the coachman and the outriders and crossed the square to the garden where the children were playing some form of hide-and-seek with Daisy while Linton watched from a bench.

"Shall we bring them in now, Linton?" she asked, aware of how tentative she sounded. But she knew Linton would be up in arms if the nursery quarters did not come up to expectations, and Cornelia was fairly confident that they wouldn't. Linton had been her own nurse and still had the power on occasion to reduce her confidence to that of a fumbling child.

"It's high time, Lady Nell," the nurse declared, standing up and smoothing down her black skirts. "Lady Susannah is liable to get a chill in this damp air. London," she muttered. "Such an unhealthy place for children."

Thank goodness the earl hadn't consulted Linton, Cornelia reflected. She'd have given him ample ammunition in his fight to keep them at home. They'd all have been sequestered for life among the oaks of the New Forest.

Her courage failed her a little when she and Aurelia, with nurses and children in tow, followed one of the twins, our Ada she thought it was, up the elegant sweep of the main staircase along a drafty corridor and up the narrow nursery stairs at the rear. The children were for once silenced by the gloomy shadows that Ada's candle barely penetrated. The nursery quarters looked as if they hadn't been occupied for several generations. Linton inhaled and did not appear to exhale until she had marched the length and breadth of the four-room suite, examining the bed linen, peering up the chimney, running a gloved finger over tables and chests and finally across the grime-encrusted windowpanes.

Cornelia and Aurelia stood just inside the door, the children clinging to their skirts. Ada stood impassively in the middle of the day nursery waiting. Finally, Linton dusted off her hands and pronounced, "No child in my charge is going to sleep in here, and that's my last word, Lady Nell."

"If we light a fire, air the bedding, clean up generally, it will be fine, Linton," Cornelia said. "Ada . . . it is Ada, isn't it, I'd like you and Mavis to clean up in here before you do anything else. Morecombe must bring up coals, and we'll light fires in all the chimneys, and bring up hot water. You'll see, Linton, in an hour we can work wonders."

Her tone was cajoling even as she drew off her own gloves. "Lady Aurelia and I will deal with the bed linen. We'll air it out in front of the fires as soon as they're lit . . . come, Ellie." She strode energetically into the night nursery, and Aurelia, with a slightly raised eyebrow, followed her.

"Do you think you're going to convince her, Nell?"

"The trick with Linton is to sweep right through

her," Cornelia explained, tearing off coverlets from the four little beds. "She'll huff and puff, but if we don't take any notice, she'll come round in the end." She shook out blankets in a cloud of dust. "But sweet heaven, Ellie, this is worse than we could ever have imagined."

"An understatement," Aurelia said a shade grimly, pummeling pillows. "I dread to think what the rest of the house is like."

Harry frowned down at the sheet of hieroglyphics he'd just transcribed, then he gave a little nod. A nicely devious piece of misdirection if he said so himself. When this code fell into enemy hands, as it was designed to do, it would give them hours of headache until they finally found the clue he'd embedded in the code to enable them to break it, then they'd be off running like headless chickens on a fool's errand while the real agenda unfolded under their very noses.

He reached for the sander, reflecting on the sheer joy of an occupation that so suited his talents and his temperament. Give him a good juicy code to break, and he would forget all about food, drink, or sleep for days on end. And the same applied to encryption. Nothing was as satisfying as coming up with a code that would defeat the cleverest encrypters in the French, Russian, or Austrian secret services.

He dusted the ink on the parchment and shook the sand into the wastepaper basket, then folded the document. He was just warming the stick of red wax in the candle flame when someone scratched at the door.

He'd been locked in his own world of mental gymnastics for longer than he could calculate, and at first he didn't recognize the sound. No one disturbed Viscount Bonham when he shut himself up in the attic chamber of his house on Mount Street.

"Who is it?" he called, slipping the parchment into the top drawer of the desk where he worked.

"Lester, m'lord."

"Good God, man, come in." Harry pushed back his chair and got to his feet, aware as he did so of the crick in his neck. "What are you doing up and about, Lester? The sawbones said another four days in bed."

Lester made a disgusted sound in the back of his throat. "He's an old woman," he declared. "And besides, I couldn't stand another minute of Mrs. Henderson flapping around me like a broody hen. Another mouthful of that stuff she calls a tonic would be the death of me."

Harry laughed and shook Lester's hand heartily before pushing him into a chair. "Well it's good to see you. I don't deny I've missed you."

The other man nodded and gestured to the desk. "Been working, sir?"

"Aye." Harry stretched and rolled his shoulders. "What's the time?"

"Just afore noon, sir. Hector said you'd been up here since late yesterday afternoon."

"Then I suppose I have," Harry said with indifference. He went over to the narrow attic casement and peered out at a clear blue sky, the vista punctuated with the smoke-spewing chimney pots of London town.

"I brought a message for you, sir. A man came from the Ministry."

Harry's tired green gaze sharpened. "Don't tell me they got anything out of that thief we apprehended?"

"Not what we're after, sir, not as yet, but I understand he's given 'em a few crumbs about other matters of interest. But the real message is that the new owner of the house has taken up residence . . . arrived yesterday afternoon, according to the blokes on watch. Quite a party, they said. Several ladies at least. Children too. The Ministry wants to know what you want them to do about it."

"Just keep the watch going, nothing else," Harry pronounced. "I'll take it from here myself." He rubbed his chin, grimacing at the stubble. "I can't pay a social call looking like this."

"You could do with a mutton chop inside you," Lester observed, well aware of his master's eating habits when he was working. "And a pint of good claret, I daresay."

Harry considered this, taking stock of his body for the first time in a day and a half. "I believe you're right, Lester. Tell Hector to serve me in the breakfast parlor and I'll be down in half an hour." He took the parchment out of the drawer. . . . "Oh, and have someone take this immediately to the War Office." He dropped wax on the folded parchment, pressed his signet ring into the wax, and handed the document to Lester before leaving his office with an energetic step that belied his fatigue.

Half an hour later he was addressing a mutton chop and boiled potato and making inroads into a decanter of claret. Plain fare certainly, but Viscount Bonham had little time for the delicacies when dining alone in his own house. Food and drink merely served a purpose, and right now he was starving.

"You're going to call on this Lady Livia Lacey then, sir?" Lester said, more of a statement than a question. "Will I be coming with you?"

"Yes, and no," Harry said succinctly. "You're looking positively whey-faced again, man. When I *do* need you, I'll need you in full fettle, so get some rest this afternoon. I don't need a bodyguard to pay a courtesy call on some old spinster biddy." He wiped his mouth and threw down his napkin. "Well, I'll be off." He strode to the door, calling to his butler, "Hector, I'm walking round to the mews."

"Aye, m'lord." The butler stood ready beside the hall table, the viscount's riding cloak over his arm, beaver hat in his hand. He handed both to his master, then passed him his riding whip.

Harry nodded his thanks and went out of the front door, held by a footman, and paused on the top step to draw a deep breath of the cold air. It felt wonderfully refreshing after his hours of stuffy incarceration, and his head cleared immediately, his fatigue dropping away from him.

He walked around to the mews and waited patiently while his horse was saddled, inhaling the sweet fragrance of the hay overlaid with the stable smells of leather, manure, and horseflesh. He recognized his sense of slightly heady euphoria as an old friend, the natural result of his long hours of work and the utterly satisfactory conclusion of that work. Later would come exhaustion and a dreamless sleep. But for the moment he was running on nervous energy.

Eric led the chestnut from the stable and held him while the viscount mounted. "I'll fetch the cob, shall I, m'lord?"

"Yes, I'll need you to walk Perseus while I pay a call. It's too cold to leave him standing." He sat the chestnut, murmuring softly to him as the animal shifted impatiently on the cobbles, threw back his head against the bridle, and showed every sign of wanting to be on the move. As soon as Eric appeared on the sturdy cob, the chestnut needed no encouragement and plunged forward towards the arched entrance to the mews. Harry checked him with a sharp word, and the animal obeyed, high-stepping onto South Audley Street.

It was early afternoon when Harry arrived outside the house in Cavendish Square. He looked up at the dilapidated facade, frowning. Why on earth wouldn't the new owner, a country dweller with presumably no interest in town life, jump at the chance to sell her inheritance at an inflated price? It made absolutely no sense at all. Then he remembered what Masters, the lawyer, had said. *Perhaps the lady's circumstances are not what we think.*

True, he knew nothing about her, and it mattered little. But where did the children come in? He was sure Lester had mentioned children. A husband could complicate matters since presumably he had charge of his wife's affairs. But it was the lady herself who'd written to her solicitor.

He swung down and passed the reins to Eric. "Walk them; I doubt I'll be above twenty minutes." That was the appropriate duration of a first call even if this was more business than social.

He ran lightly up the steps to the front door and raised the tarnished lion's head knocker. There was no response to his first politely discreet knock, so he tried again. This time the clang resounded in the quiet street. He tapped his whip impatiently against his boot. Somebody had to be in. Apart from the three retainers in the house that he already knew about, Lady Livia had brought women with her, a lady's maid and presumably a companion of some description, or a nurse for the children.

At last he heard the creak of an unoiled bolt on the far side of the door. It opened and a woman stood on the threshold regarding him with a questioning air in her piercing blue eyes. Her hair was invisible beneath a headscarf, her figure swathed in a none-too-clean apron. A smudge of dirt adorned a straight nose.

"Yes?" she said.

The black cat twined itself around her ankles before leaping, tail erect, down the steps between Harry's booted feet.

Harry was for a moment disconcerted by the whirlwind of fur and took a step backwards to the second step. This left him looking up at the woman in the doorway, a position that for some reason he immediately resented. He stepped up again and proffered his card, saying distantly, "Viscount Bonham presents his compliments to Lady Livia Lacey."

Cornelia took it and read it. So this was the mysteriously eager would-be buyer. She glanced up at him. Quite attractive if one liked the lean and hungry type. A very broad, domed forehead, of the kind that usually denoted intelligence. An impression borne out by a pair of wide-apart and very deep-set green eyes. There was a cool distance in his gaze that was rather unnerving, as if he observed the world from some Olympian peak. Arrogant seemed a good description on first observation.

Harry did not care to be kept standing on a drafty doorstep in the middle of winter by anyone, let alone a mere servant who seemed to be subjecting him to an impertinent scrutiny that unless he was much mistaken found him wanting in some respects.

"My good woman, I would be much obliged to you if you would carry my card to your mistress immediately," he stated. "You will find that Lady Livia will recognize my name, and she will know my business. Kindly go about yours without delay." Having issued his order, he turned his back on the woman and gazed off into the distance towards the square, still tapping his boot with his whip.

Mistress! Good woman! Cornelia opened her mouth to protest, indignation sparking in her eyes as she stared at his insolently turned back. Then a smile touched her mouth. Viscount Bonham was in for a few mortifying surprises. "Begging your pardon, my lord," she said humbly, "but my Lady Livia is not receiving at present."

"Ah." He turned back to her slowly, his gaze still cold, his tone crisp. "I daresay she's resting after her journey?" He didn't wait for confirmation, merely continued, "Present my card with my respects and inform her that I will call again tomorrow when I trust she will have recovered her strength." He swung away, saying over his shoulder, "My business with your mistress is urgent. Convey that, if you please."

Cornelia stared at his retreating back, her mouth ajar at his breathtaking arrogance. What made him think Livia was so feeble she couldn't manage a two-day journey without needing to rest? What the devil gave him the right to make any of the disparaging assumptions that had poured from his mouth in the last three or four minutes? She looked down at the card in her hand and for a second was tempted to tear it in shreds and send them flying after their owner.

But no. She could imagine a much more satisfactory revenge. She stepped back into the hall and closed the door with a slam.

Harry had only just reached the pavement when the door slammed behind him, and he started at the sound, spinning around to look behind him. Flakes of paint from the door, dislodged by the violence of its closing, fluttered onto the steps. The new servants seemed on a par with the old, he thought, shaking his head with a flicker of reluctant amusement. But at least he hadn't been driven away by the old man's blunderbuss. One should be thankful for small mercies. He took the reins from Eric and mounted his horse. He'd know what to expect on his return.

Chapter 4

RIDING THE TIDE OF HER INDIGNATION, Cornelia
stalked into the kitchen, where she knew she would find
the others.

"Who was that at the door, Nell?" Livia asked, back-
ing out of the inglenook where she'd been examining the
chimney, directing Morecombe to push a broomstick up
as a high as he could to dislodge any birds' nests.

"That, my dear, was Viscount Bonham," Cornelia informed her. "And a nasty piece of work he is." She exhaled noisily. "Arrogant, insulting, presumptuous. He
informs you that he will be calling upon you tomorrow
to discuss a matter of urgent business."

"Dear me," Aurelia murmured, coming out of the
pantry with a dusty armful of jars of preserves. "Lord
knows how long these have been there." She set her burden on the now-scrubbed deal table and dusted off her
hands. "So you didn't care for the gentleman then,
Nell?"

"Is it that obvious?" Cornelia said with a sardonic smile. "He took me for a servant, addressed me as his 'good woman,' and demanded to see my mistress!"

Aurelia went into a peal of laughter and was joined by Livia. "Look at yourself, Nell," Livia said. "You look like a servant. We all do."

Cornelia examined her friends, both of them dusty, swathed in grimy aprons, hair tucked away beneath protective scarves, faces smudged with, in Livia's case, soot, in Aurelia's, cobweb residue. She glanced down at her apron, put a hand hesitantly to her headscarf, then burst into laughter. "You're probably right. But even so he had no right to make assumptions. And no right at all to his manner. People should be polite, and most particularly to servants."

"What d'you want done with these, mum?" One of the twin retainers gestured to a box of china she'd just put on the table.

Livia peered at the contents of the box. "They're all mismatched, but look at this." She lifted out a sauce boat. "It's Sèvres, look how lovely it is." She carried it to the wide sink and poured water over it from the jug. "I wonder if there are any more pieces."

Aurelia went to examine the box. "Where do they come from . . . uh . . . Mavis?" she hazarded.

"It's Ada, mum," the woman corrected stolidly. "And they're all bits o' broken sets. Lady Sophia wouldn't throw any of 'em away, but she'd never 'ave an unmatched set on her table neither."

"That explains it." Livia came back to the table. "Let's see what else we've got. Oh, look, there's a paper knife at the bottom here." She took the slender knife out and held it up. "It's bone I think . . . oh, my goodness." She peered closely at the blade. "Look at the engraving." Her eyes were wide as she held the object out to her friends. "It's positively indecent."

Cornelia took it and gazed closely at the engraving. "It's scrimshaw, I think they call it. The kind of carving that sailors do to pass the time on long voyages. But, oh dear, this poor sailor must have been feeling very deprived of some of the comforts of home. The mermaid seems to be engaging in some very friendly activity here." Her voice trembled with laughter as she showed the paper knife to Aurelia.

"What on earth is such an object doing in a spinster's kitchen?" Aurelia murmured as she examined the cavorting figures. She glanced across at Morecombe and the twins, who maintained a steadfast silence. "I think we should put it back where it came from. I'd hate to have to explain what's going on to Franny, and you know she'll ask if she sees it."

"I'll keep it in the desk in my room," Livia said, taking the knife from her. "I think it's ivory not bone."

"Well, *please* keep it away from the children," Aurelia begged, shaking her head with amusement, as she returned to her preserves.

The kitchen was beginning to look usable again, Cornelia reflected, but it was still cold. There was a draft coming through the window that was opened at the bottom, and she went across to close it.

"Eh, madam, don't you be shuttin' that," Morecombe declared. "Tis fer Lady Sophia's cat. She needs t' come in an' out like. Her ladyship insisted on't."

"Well, maybe she did," Cornelia said firmly. "But I'm still closing it. If the cat wants to come in, she can jump on the sill and let us know." She was about to slam the window closed when the cat jumped like a shadow from the dank darkness, through the narrow aperture, and into the kitchen.

"Too cold for you? I don't blame you," Cornelia said, bending to stroke the cat. "What's her name, Morecombe?"

"Oh, Lady Sophia jest called 'er Puss," the man responded. "But I tell you straight, ma'am, that window stays open at night. She likes t' go ahuntin'. 'Tis agin nature to expect a cat t' stay in at night."

"We'll worry about that later," Cornelia said pacifically. "She's in now anyway." She closed the window firmly and turned her attention to an ancient pottery flour barrel that could be put to good use again. She peered into it with a grimace of disgust. "This flour's full of weevils."

She hefted the barrel and upended it into the sink. Something chinked against the porcelain. "What's this?" She delicately sifted the flour through her fingers, closing her mind to the wriggling grubs. "Well, would you look at this. This kitchen's full of surprises." She held up a thimble. The light from the now-clean window above the sink caught and held a sparkle of silver through the flour dust. She wiped the thimble on a corner of her apron and held it up again. "It's most unusual. Look at the design." She chuckled slightly. "It's fascinating but not as much fun as the engraving on the paper knife."

Aurelia and Livia abandoned their china treasury and came over to her. They examined the thimble in turn. "It's obviously silver, and the design is such an intricate piece of engraving. A very skilled silversmith had a hand in this," Aurelia commented.

"But what's it doing in a flour barrel?" Livia asked.

"Well, the flour's been in there since the last century, judging by its condition," Cornelia said, taking the thimble back. "I'd guess some long-ago maid forgot she was wearing it when she delved into the barrel for a cup of flour or something and it just slipped off."

"It doesn't look like something a maid would use," Livia said doubtfully.

"Well, perhaps the lady of the house was doing some baking of her own," Cornelia said with a careless shrug. "Anyway, you may as well ask what a lewd paper knife is doing in a box of rejected china."

"Fair enough," Livia agreed. "Let's see what else we have in the way of china."

"I'm going to explore the cellar," Cornelia said, slipping the thimble into her apron pocket. "Do you have the key, Morecombe?"

"Aye, mum. Haven't been down there in a while," he said, pulling his broomstick out of the chimney, bringing a fine cloud of soot with it. "Lady Sophia weren't much fer wine. She took a small glass o' port of an evening, but that was about all."

"Is there anything worth drinking down there?"

"Oh, aye, reckon so." He pulled a ring of keys from the pocket of his britches and fumbled through them, holding each one up to his eye for closer inspection. "The old earl, Lady Sophia's brother that was, kept a good cellar."

"How long ago did he die?" Cornelia asked somewhat doubtfully.

"Oh, twenty year at least," the old man said, and shuffled across the kitchen to the door that led down into the cellar.

"Ghoulies and ghosties," Cornelia said with a mock shiver. "If no one's been down there in twenty years, what do you think I'll find?"

By evening they had the kitchen functioning, cooking fires lit, and the twins were engaged in some form of cooking although Cornelia and her companions had little confidence in the outcome of their efforts. But at least the children had been given a supper that met with Linton's approval, and they were ensconced in the nursery suite in relative warmth.

"Fire's lit in Lady Sophia's parlor, Lady Livia," Morecombe announced, coming into the kitchen where the three women were taking stock of their achievements.

"And I've opened a bottle of that burgundy you wanted brought up, m'lady." He nodded towards Cornelia.

"Did you fill the decanters too?" she asked.

"Aye," he said.

"There was a butt of quite passable sherry down there," Cornelia said, as they left the kitchen. "And a pipe of port, barely breached, and another cask of Madeira. The old earl knew what he was about. At least we'll be able to warm the cockles even if we don't get anything palatable to eat."

"I wonder what they cooked for Aunt Sophia," Livia commented as she opened the door to the only room in the house that had borne any signs of recent habitation. "I don't think she left this room in years."

It was an overstuffed, shabby parlor at the rear of the house, and that morning it had had the rather unpleasant aroma of old dusty fabric, overlaid with an odd stale flowery perfume, candle wax, and ashes from the cold grate. A day with the windows open had freshened the air, and the grate had been black leaded, the furniture polished with beeswax, and the carpets and upholstery subjected to a vigorous carpet beater. It was not a room one would ever call elegant, or even warmly comfortable, but it was a tolerable refuge.

Cornelia poured sherry, and the three of them sank down into sagging armchairs with small groans of relief. "I don't think I've ever worked so hard in my life," Livia remarked. "I ache from head to toe."

"I would love a bath," Aurelia murmured, taking a

long sip of her sherry. "But it'll take far too long to heat the water, then who's going to lug it all the way upstairs. Morecombe doesn't look as if he could carry a tray, let alone enough water for a bath."

"We'll tackle that issue tomorrow," Cornelia said, kicking off her shoes. She stretched her feet to the fender and wriggled her toes in the fire's warmth with a little whimper of pleasure. "And talking of tomorrow, Liv. Will you receive the uncivilized viscount? I wouldn't," she added. "I'd send him off with a flea in his ear."

"Don't you want to know why he's so keen to buy the property?" Aurelia asked, fetching the sherry decanter to refill their glasses. "He must have some reason . . . to offer all that money, and for what?" She gestured liberally at their surroundings. "Putting this place in shape will cost a small fortune."

"Well, I might as well receive him," Livia said comfortably, holding out her glass towards Aurelia. "Just to see what a barbarian he is. Oh, and Aunt Sophia's solicitor, Masters, the one who first wrote to me, he's going to call as well. Some papers I have to sign apparently."

"Well, you'll be busy," Aurelia said. "What'll we do, Nell?"

"Oh, you have to be here as well," Livia said, sounding alarmed. "This is a joint enterprise . . . and particularly when it comes to the viscount."

"Nell, what are you thinking?" Aurelia demanded seeing her sister-in-law's flickering smile. "You're up to something."

"Well, I was just thinking . . ."

The arrival of Morecombe and one of the twins carrying trays prevented her finishing her thought.

"There's potato soup," Morecombe announced, setting his tray on a gateleg table in the bow window. "An' bread and cheese and a bite o' ham." He stood aside as the twin set down her own tray of china and cutlery. "Should I pour the wine, m'lady?"

"Yes, please," Cornelia answered since the question was clearly directed towards her.

"Thank you, Morecombe." Livia rose from her chair and came over to the table. "You and Ada and Mavis have done wonders with so little. We're really very grateful."

"Eh, as to that Lady Livia, we do what Lady Sophia told us. Take care of the house an' all her things. An' that's all . . . jest doin' our duty." He stepped to the sideboard and took up the bottle of burgundy.

"Could I ask . . ." Aurelia said hesitantly. "Ada and Mavis are sisters, I believe."

"Aye, that we are," the present twin agreed. It was unusual for either of the twins to volunteer a comment, and Aurelia was emboldened to continue.

"Have you worked here with Morecombe for long?"

"Eh, bless you, ma'am, Morecombe married our Ada thirty year ago," Mavis, it was now clear that it was Mavis, declared. "An' where our Ada goes, I go too. Always been like that."

"I see." Aurelia smiled. "And did you marry too, Mavis?"

The woman shook her head with an expression of disgust. "Men," she stated. "Never could abide 'em. Dirty, messy things stompin' their mud all over the house." She tossed her head with something approaching a sniff and left the parlor.

Morecombe, apparently untroubled by this wholesale condemnation of his sex, nodded to the women in a semblance of a bow and followed in Mavis's wake.

"So, as I was saying," Cornelia continued as the door closed, "I was thinking it might be amusing to teach our viscount a salutary lesson in manners." She dipped her spoon in her soup.

"What do you have in mind?"

"Give him the opportunity to treat me as a servant, let him get in really deep, and then introduce him to the Viscountess Dagenham." She smiled wickedly over the lip of her glass. "What do you think?"

Chapter 5

IN THE MORNING ROOM OF HIS HOUSE on Mount Street, Viscount Bonham was breakfasting before the fire and contemplating his upcoming interview with Lady Livia. Apart from his rather fearsome great-aunt, the duchess of Gracechurch, his experience with elderly ladies hitherto had been confined to his grandmother and two maiden aunts. Since they had all doted upon him in his boyhood, very little effort had been required to persuade them to do anything for him. He could reasonably expect that Lady Livia would not give him this advantage. But there must be some lever he could pull.

He cut into his sirloin. If he knew a little more about her and her circumstances, it would help, but Masters had had almost no information beyond the address on the letter. He'd somehow fixed upon a mental image of the lady as an elderly, reclusive, country spinster, but what of the children? They didn't fit the image at all. But surely, if there was a husband on the scene, Masters would have known of it. Could she be a widow?

He reached for his coffee. Presumably all would be revealed at his first meeting with the lady, and he would adapt his approach according to the circumstances he found.

He finished his breakfast and went upstairs to his bedchamber. His valet was brushing specks of lint off a coat of dark green superfine. "Nasty weather, m'lord," he observed, gesturing with the clothes brush towards the dreary prospect beyond the window. It was a typically filthy English winter morning, rain sheeting down from leaden skies that bled all light from the day.

"A few spots of rain could ruin this coat," he added almost sotto voce. "I'd be taking a hackney m'self."

Harry hid a smile. His valet knew perfectly well his master would never take a hackney except in the direst emergency.

"I'm driving, Carton," he said gently. "I'll be wearing a driving coat."

"That won't protect your boots," the man muttered. "Spent hours polishing them, I did."

"A little rain never hurt anyone," Harry declared, slipping off his brocade dressing gown and putting his arms into the sleeves of the coat that Carton held for him.

The valet closed his lips tightly and smoothed out the set of the shoulders. The coat fitted like a glove as the tailor had intended. Light gray doeskin britches and gleaming top boots completed the viscount's ensemble.

Harry checked his reflection in the long cheval glass and nodded. There was nothing about his appearance to remind the old retainer of the somberly clad man with a muffler up to his ears, a hat pulled down over his eyes, and a hoarse voice, who a week or so ago had come to inspect the contents of the house for probate. And been turned away empty-handed for his pains. But this time he would at least gain entrance to the house . . . as long as that insolent maid or companion or whatever she was had taken his card to her mistress and delivered his message.

He dropped a dainty jade snuffbox into the pocket of his coat, took the voluminous driving coat and hat proffered by Carton, and went lightly down the stairs, almost relishing the prospect of a confrontation with the blue-eyed guardian of the gate.

"Send to the mews for my carriage, Hector," he instructed the butler, and turned aside into the library.

"Now, let's see what we can find to dazzle the viscount with." Livia bounded energetically to the armoire in Cornelia's bedchamber. A sullen fire in the grate did something to take the damp chill off the air, but not enough to render the room welcoming. "You mustn't look remotely like the woman he mistook for a skivvy yesterday."

"That won't be difficult," Cornelia remarked. "I only need to look clean to achieve that." She chuckled suddenly. "I've thought of an interesting twist to this little plot of ours."

"Oh?" Livia turned from the armoire to look at her.

"You've got that look of the devil in your eye, Nell," Aurelia accused with a tiny laugh. "What are you plotting?"

"Well, I just thought that it might be more amusing if the viscount is initially led to believe that the woman he insulted yesterday was actually Lady Livia Lacey herself," Cornelia said. "He'll ask for Liv at the door, and Morecombe can simply show him into the parlor where I'll be waiting, and he'll assume I'm Liv, which is bound to embarrass him even more. I'll let him dig his own pit for a few minutes, then at some point introduce myself." She grinned. "What do you think?"

"I think I'd be very careful not to put your back up in future," Aurelia said.

"Exactly," Cornelia agreed with some satisfaction. She stood beside Livia and peered into the armoire. "The problem is I don't have anything that isn't most dreadfully countrified. When did we last look at any of the fashion magazines? I don't even know what's modish these days, but I'm sure it's changed in the ten years since our last and only foray on the town."

"Your bronze silk is quite elegant," Aurelia suggested.

"It's probably the best I can find, but is it suitable for the morning? I only ever wear it in the evening at home," Cornelia protested.

"I'm guessing that what's suitable for an evening in

the country is suitable for a morning in town," Livia stated, drawing out the gown. "Depressing as that may be when and if we venture forth upon the town." She held up the dress. "It is very pretty, Nell."

"It's also the best we can do," her friend observed with a resigned shrug. "I could wear the cashmere shawl with it. That *is* elegant . . . besides which it'll keep me warm," she added, picking up a fold of the gown. "This silk is so thin. I'm not going to make much of an impression on the viscount if my lips are blue, and I can't talk for chattering teeth."

"It's not that cold in the parlor," Aurelia said. "And you can wear those silk mittens, they're perfectly acceptable for morning wear, even in the town."

"Here's yer 'ot water, mum." One of the twins appeared in the open doorway with a copper jug. It was as if she'd wafted there on some current of air, Cornelia reflected. The twins moved around utterly soundlessly, and none of the three women could get accustomed to their sudden materializations sometimes but not always accompanied by a monosyllabic explanation for the appearance.

"Thank you." She smiled warmly in lieu of addressing the woman by name. It seemed rude after two days not to be able to tell them apart.

The twin set the jug down on the dresser and wiped her hands on her apron before casting a glance around the room, rather as if she'd never seen it before, then glided out into the drafty corridor.

Cornelia poured water into the basin and, shivering, cast aside her dressing gown. She sponged herself rapidly. "What I'd give for a bath."

"Maybe this evening we could fill a tub by the kitchen fire and take it in turns," Livia suggested. "We could give Morecombe and the twins the evening off."

"I don't think they ever leave the house," Aurelia said. "Judging by Morecombe's reluctance this morning even to go to the shop for the children's chocolate. He sounded as if just venturing onto the street was the equivalent of a trip into enemy territory."

"Well, living with a recluse probably rubbed off." Cornelia dropped her chemise over her head. "Now which drawer did I use for my stockings?"

"This one. Do you want silk or wool?" Livia held up two pairs.

"It had better be silk with that gown, but I'd be much more comfortable in wool," Cornelia responded with another shiver as she reached for the silk stockings. "Ellie, will you do my hair? You're so clever at it."

"One of my minor talents," Aurelia agreed with a slightly smug smile. She gave her sister-in-law a shrewd glance. "You seem to be going to a lot of trouble for this pompous viscount. You must want to make an impression on him."

"It's not so much that as erase the one I made yesterday," Cornelia replied, but a slight touch of pink tinged her cheekbones as she buttoned the wrists of the long sleeves of the gown. She wanted to think that thoroughly erasing that impression would drive home to him the realization of his rudeness. But honesty obliged her to admit, at least to herself, that injured pride played its part. The viscount had presented an impeccable appearance, which made his arrogant, insultingly pompous assumptions all the more unbearable. This time she was giving him no advantages.

"Do they wear jewelry in the mornings these days?" Livia was trawling through Cornelia's jewel box. "You need something for that neckline, I think. It looks very bare."

"It is very bare," Cornelia said, peering down at her bosom. "I could wear a fichu?" She sounded doubtful.

"Too matronly," Aurelia pronounced. "Just because you're the dowager mother of two doesn't make you matronly." She reached into the jewel box, saying with authority, "The amber beads are perfect. It's not done to wear precious gems before sunset in the town or the country, but amber, topaz, amethyst, they're all quite acceptable."

She clasped the amber beads around her sister-in-law's long neck and stood back to examine the effect in the dresser mirror. "Yes, much better. Now for your hair."

Her fingers went to work and within five minutes she had braided the luxuriant honey-colored mass into a neat coil around Cornelia's head and teased ringlets to fall about her ears. "How's that?"

Cornelia tilted her head from side to side. "Pretty,"

she said, playing with one of the ringlets. "Let's hope it doesn't come tumbling down at a crucial moment."

"Did he say what time he would call?" Livia asked.

"No, but the usual time for morning visits is around eleven. Or at least it used to be." Cornelia glanced at the clock on the mantel. "It's only ten now. I'm going up to the nursery."

She spent the next hour with the children, planning their day with Linton, and just before eleven descended the stairs in search of Morecombe. Livia had asked him to clean the tarnished silver that was littered around the house, and Cornelia found him in the butler's pantry muttering to himself as he polished.

"Don't see no point t' this," he said, as she knocked on the open door. "'Twas good enough for Lady Sophia just as it were."

"Perhaps Lady Sophia's eyesight was not very good," Cornelia suggested. "Those cruets do look lovely now they're polished." She picked up one of them and held it to the light. "I'm sure it's Elizabethan." She was reminded of the thimble as she looked at the intricate designs on the salt cellar.

"Mebbe so," Morecombe muttered, not sounding convinced as he attacked a sugar caster.

"I'm expecting a visitor, Morecombe. When he arrives he'll ask for Lady Livia. Could you show him into the parlor. I'll wait for him there."

"Oh, aye?" Morecombe regarded her with his rheumy gaze. "An' where will Lady Livia be then, m'lady?"

"Oh, she asked me to see him for her," Cornelia said vaguely. "Just show him in. There's no need for you to explain."

"Oh, aye?" The lack of conviction was more pronounced, but he returned to his sugar caster, and Cornelia beat a prudent retreat.

Livia was waiting for her in the hall. "For a minute I forgot all about Mr. Masters. You remember he's supposed to call this morning too. Where shall I see him if you're in the parlor with the viscount?"

"The salon?" Cornelia suggested, opening the door onto that bleak chamber, where the furniture was still under dust covers, the curtains drawn tightly across the long windows to prevent any possibility of daylight, or, heaven forfend, sunlight from penetrating its dusty shadows.

She crossed the room and pulled back one set of heavy velvet drapes, releasing a cloud of dust. "Aunt Sophia's lawyer must know what condition the house is in," she observed, moving to another window. "He must have visited her on occasion. He won't be surprised at the state of this room, but at least we could let in some light."

"Not that there is much," Livia said, drawing back the third set of curtains and sneezing violently. "Even if the windows were clean. With all that rain, it's dark as a dungeon out there."

"And cold as charity in here," Cornelia added. She rubbed a circle in the grime on one long window and stared out at the rain-drenched street. "Oh, I think this must be our viscount. That's quite a turnout he's driving. He's obviously not short of a guinea or two."

"Let me see." Livia came to her side and peered through the cleared glass. "Oh, yes, I see what you mean. Beautiful pair of horses." She rubbed a wider circle in the grime. "I can't see much of the driver, though. He's all wrapped up. The collar of his greatcoat is turned up to his ears."

"It would be in this weather . . . fancy driving an open carriage," Cornelia said with a shake of her head. "Why didn't he take a hackney? Any sane man would."

"Perhaps he isn't," Livia murmured. "Sane, I mean. Would a sane man want to pay that kind of money for this wreck?" She waved a hand around the room.

"Money, enough of it, will put the house right," Cornelia said. "It has some very aristocratic lines to it. A noble house under all this neglect."

"Perhaps you're right . . . oh, he's drawing up. He's giving his reins to his tiger. You'd better go into the parlor before he knocks at the door. I'll wait in here."

Cornelia went swiftly into the hall and whisked herself into the parlor. She debated where to position herself to best effect when Viscount Bonham walked in. Before the fire? Over by the window, in an armchair deep in a book? No, not the latter, she decided. The chairs sagged too much for a graceful rise from their depths. The window seat was a possibility. She could be found there, her head bent over her sewing. But she'd left her workbox upstairs . . . no the secretaire. She would have her back to the door, apparently occupied with letter writing.

The knocker sounded as she sat down and picked up an ancient quill. It hadn't been sharpened in years, and she looked at its ragged tip with some dismay. But there was no time to change her position now. She aimed the pen at the inkstand, only to discover it dry as a bone. Now she could hear voices in the hall. The viscount's clipped tones, Morecombe's broad Yorkshire monosyllables. And then the parlor door opened.

"In 'ere, sir," Morecombe declared without embellishment, and departed, closing the door firmly behind him.

Harry stood for a second, hat in hand, torn between amusement and indignation at his unceremonious admission to the house. The man hadn't even offered to take his hat and his dripping driving coat.

The woman at the secretaire didn't turn around immediately, then she said in a soft voice that immediately brought his hackles up, "Forgive me, Lord Bonham, just one minute more." She reached for the sander and sprinkled it liberally over her page, then turned slowly in her chair, regarding him with a half smile, which only a fool would mistake as friendly, before rising to her feet.

"I believe we have already met, sir." She continued to regard him quizzically, but the glitter in her blue eyes was unmistakable, as unmistakable as the quiet, well-modulated voice he had heard the previous day.

Harry drew off his gloves one finger at a time. "It

would appear so, ma'am. I confess myself amazed at the transformation. You must forgive me for my error yesterday, but I'm sure you'll agree it was an understandable one?" An eyebrow flickered in a faint question mark. "Had you done me the courtesy of correcting the error, matters might have gone rather more agreeably between us."

Cornelia had been intending to bring the charade to a close immediately after the initial discomfort that she had been certain the man would feel. But now he was putting the blame upon her, looking not in the least discomfited. Indeed, there was a glint in his green eyes that seemed to be issuing a challenge to match her own. To her astonishment, she felt a stir of interest, a flutter of anticipation at the prospect.

"Your manner, sir, did not encourage such an introduction," she declared, drawing the cashmere shawl around her as she instinctively folded her arms and regarded him steadily. "I have no desire to prolong this interview, so perhaps you will state your business."

Harry tossed his hat and gloves onto the gateleg table. In the absence of an invitation to sit down, or even to remove his driving coat, he was obliged to stand dripping on the faded carpet. The magnitude of his mistaken assumption astonished him, and for an inconvenient moment he was hard-pressed not to laugh at the contrast between his preconception of an elderly lady wrapped in shawls with her feet in a mustard bath and the reality of this poised woman very far removed from her dotage.

Without volition he found himself taking inventory. She was tall, something he had failed to notice the previous day, and held herself erect. Her gown was hardly in the first style of fashion, but the bronze color suited her hair, which was, he thought absently, a combination of dark honey and golden butter. Her eyes, an intense and penetrating blue, were set beneath straight brown eyebrows, and her complexion, slightly flushed at present, was of the creamy variety.

Cornelia wasn't at all sure what to make of this silent and close examination. For some reason, it made her skin prickle. "Well, sir?" she prompted.

"Ah, yes," he said coolly, deciding it was time to take charge of this interview. He unbuttoned his coat but made no attempt to take it off. "I believe, ma'am, you are aware of my business. I am interested in purchasing this house. The lawyer who is handling Lady Sophia Lacey's estate has already made my offer known to you. I thought to make it in person."

"Mr. Masters has already been instructed to give you a response to your offer," Cornelia stated, choosing her words carefully. She was not going to lay verbal claim to Livia's identity. He was to labor under a misapprehension, not a direct lie. "That settled the matter, I believe."

He pinched his chin between finger and thumb, regarding her thoughtfully for a minute. In certain circumstances he could imagine enjoying a sparring match with the lady, but these were not they. The matter was too urgent for dalliance of any kind. "I would ask you to reconsider your response," he stated carefully. "I am willing to increase my offer."

"Do you generally misunderstand clear statements, viscount?" Cornelia inquired. "I had believed that the response to your offer was an unequivocal rejection. Could I have been mistaken?" She regarded him, her head tilted slightly to one side, with an expression of polite disbelief.

Harry frowned, considering his next move in this pas de deux. Nothing she had said could be considered discourteous—unhelpful certainly—but the words contained no insult. But everything about this woman, her posture, her expression, most particularly those expressive eyes radiated a challenge that he was finding difficult to ignore. But however tempting, he must not deviate from his path.

"I came here, ma'am, in good faith," he said, hoping to strike a conciliatory note of reason.

"On a fool's errand, sir," Cornelia stated bluntly. "It seems I have not spoken plainly enough so allow me to state the position in the simplest of terms. This house is *not* for sale."

He inclined his head slightly as if in acknowledgment of her statement, then he walked casually across the room towards where she stood beside the secretaire. She held her ground, meeting his steady gaze, her arms still folded beneath the cashmere shawl.

He stood close to her, close enough to smell the faintest hint of rosemary. An herb used with lavender when storing clothes not often worn. His eyes flicked to the secretaire over her shoulder. The sheet she had so elaborately sanded was blank. He reached around her and picked up the ragged quill.

"Dear me," he murmured, waving the dry pen with an air of incredulity. "I trust your correspondence isn't vital, ma'am."

He was rewarded by a conscious flash in her eyes, the sudden tightening of her lips. Then she observed, "I believe this concludes our business, Lord Bonham."

He smiled at her. "Perhaps so . . . at least for the present." He strode to the table and picked up his hat and gloves, then turned and bowed. "Your servant, Lady Livia." He spun on his heel and walked out.

Cornelia followed him to the door. As he crossed the hall the salon door opened, and Livia emerged with a stout, stiff-backed gentleman in the black cloth coat and britches of a man of business. He fussed with the sheaf of papers in his hands, his air that of a man who constantly expects an unpleasant surprise.

Lord Bonham stopped in his tracks. "Masters? You here?"

Masters looked astounded to see the viscount. "Why, yes, m'lord. I came to settle some matters with my client, Lady Livia," the lawyer said, gesturing to the young woman behind him. "I did not expect to see *you* here, sir? I was unaware that you were already acquainted with Lady Livia."

"It appears that I am not," Harry said dryly, casting a

glance at Cornelia, who stood a few feet behind him. "I seem always to be laboring under misapprehensions these days," he murmured.

He turned to Livia and bowed. "Ma'am. Allow me to present myself. Viscount Bonham at your service."

There was something so contained about him, something so intrinsically authoritative in his presence, that Livia began to have doubts as to the wisdom of their little game. She offered him an apologetic smile as she said in a rush, "Good morning to you, sir. I'm sorry I was not able to receive you. I had another engagement . . . Mr. Masters . . . Lady Dagenham offered to stand in for me. She knew what I . . ." Her voice trailed away as it became clear that the viscount's interest was elsewhere. His attention was once more focused on Cornelia.

"I see," he said slowly, beginning to draw on his gloves. "So I've been enjoying the . . . uh . . . pleasure, shall we call it, of Lady Dagenham's company."

"The Viscountess Dagenham," Cornelia said, her own voice cool and steady. "I don't believe I said otherwise."

His eyes narrowed. "No," he agreed. "I don't believe you did." He turned back to Livia. "Lady Livia, your servant. I trust I may wait upon you when you have no other engagement."

Livia murmured a somewhat incoherent response, glancing nervously between the viscount and Cornelia. The air seemed to be crackling around them.

Harry bowed once more and strolled to the front

door. He turned and looked again at Cornelia. "Tell me, Lady Dagenham, are you in the habit of playing scullery maid?" he inquired in a tone of mild inquiry.

Cornelia struggled for a second as her ready sense of the absurd threatened to get the better of her. It was clear as day that Viscount Bonham had no intention of leaving the house without evening the score.

"I only ask," he continued in the same mild tone, "because I fear that such an eccentricity might expose you to some discourtesy. And that would be a great pity." He smiled, offered a small nod in lieu of a bow, and let himself out into the rain.

Chapter 6

THERE WAS SILENCE IN THE HALL as the door slammed shut. Masters broke the quiet with a murmured, "Oh, dear me. His lordship didn't inform me that he wished to call upon you, my lady." He looked worriedly at Livia, twisting his gloves between pudgy hands. "Of course I would have insisted that I present any renewed offer to you myself. It would only have been proper since I handle your affairs in this matter. I do beg you will forgive me, ma'am."

"There's nothing to forgive, Mr. Masters," Livia said hastily.

"Indeed, it was for Lord Bonham to communicate his intentions to you. It is he who should be apologizing to you," Cornelia said calmly.

"Oh, my goodness, no . . . no, no, no," the lawyer exclaimed with a violent gesture that sent papers fluttering to his feet. He bent awkwardly to gather them up murmuring in some distress, "Lord Bonham is quite free to do whatever he thinks best. A gentleman of such standing, you understand . . . the Bonhams, such a well-connected family . . ."

"Indeed," Livia said in soothing tones, bending to help him with the papers.

"Too kind, Lady Livia, too kind," he stammered, straightening as he clutched his retrieved papers to his chest. He backed to the door, bowing every few steps. "Forgive me, your most obedient servant, my ladies. I must be going . . . I'll send you the papers, Lady Livia." He wrestled with the door for a few anguished seconds, then vanished into the rain-dark street beyond, still murmuring apologies.

Aurelia came running down the stairs, one hand lightly on the banister. "That was awkward," she observed. "I was listening on the half landing. Poor Mr. Masters, none of it was his fault, and he seemed to take all the blame . . . Well, Nell?" She looked expectantly at her sister-in-law.

Cornelia gave a little sigh. "I hadn't intended to keep up the charade, but he put my back up the minute he walked into the parlor." She shrugged, wondering how to explain the strange tide that had carried her beyond her intended point. "There was just something so . . ." She frowned. "I don't know what the word is . . . challenging, I suppose . . . about him. I felt on my mettle, as if I couldn't let him win a trick."

She shook her head. "Ridiculous, really. He's just a somewhat arrogant, self-satisfied member of the male species. Give him twenty years, and he'll be another Markby . . . or even worse."

"All the more reason to give him just what he deserved," Livia declared. "I didn't like the look of him at all. Such cold eyes, and his mouth's too thin. I shan't see him if he comes again." Having thus disposed of the insolent viscount, she dropped her voice to a conspiratorial whisper, "I have such exciting news. You'll never guess what."

Her friends turned at once towards her. "What?" they demanded in unison.

"Let's go into the parlor." Livia bounced ahead of them and closed the door once they were inside. She stood with her back against it, her black eyes glowing. "It seems that Aunt Sophia wasn't quite such an eccentric recluse as we thought. She did actually have a real plan when she left me this house."

She paused, waiting for a response, but when none came from her companions, who merely regarded her in expectant silence, she continued, "She left money to put the house in some kind of order if I decided not to sell. But Masters was not to reveal that clause in the will until I'd decided by myself what to do with the house. If I did sell it, then that was all I was to get, just the proceeds from the sale, and I'd never find out about the other part of the inheritance. But if I cared enough to keep the house, then she'd made financial arrangements. Isn't that astonishing?" She looked interrogatively between them.

"Somewhat whimsical, I would say." Cornelia

frowned. "If by happenstance you made the decision she wanted you to make, then good things would come to you. If not . . ." She gave an expressive shrug.

"But fortunately Liv made the right decision," Aurelia pointed out.

"Yes, exactly," Livia rushed on, her eyes still shining. "And the only stipulation is that Morecombe and the twins are to be kept on for as long as they wish. There's money for that, and small pensions for them when they decide to retire, if they ever do." She clasped her hands against her skirt. "Isn't that exciting? I have a real inheritance."

"That's wonderful, Liv." Cornelia hugged her. "I don't mean to be crass, but how much is there for repairs and such like?"

"About five thousand guineas." Liv turned to accept Aurelia's congratulatory hug. "It's plenty to hire a boot boy and a footman to help Morecombe with the heavy cleaning, and maybe a scullery maid to help out in the kitchen . . ."

"Well, that's good," Cornelia interrupted with a slightly sardonic smile. "At least I won't have to expose myself to further discourtesy. A great relief for Lord Bonham, I'm sure."

"You didn't really take any notice of that, did you?" Livia asked.

"No, of course I didn't. I was just funning," Cornelia said. "Go on about your plans, Liv."

"Oh, well, yes." Livia returned happily to the original subject. "There'll be enough to get new curtains, new furniture, and some fresh paint and, oh, I don't know, enough to make it habitable."

She did a little twirl, her sprig muslin skirts swinging around her ankles. "And then, ladies, once we can receive, we can burst upon society in fine fig."

"And you, my love, can find a husband," Cornelia said, exchanging a smile with Aurelia. They were both aware that five thousand, munificent though it sounded, wouldn't go quite as far as Livia had envisaged, but they weren't about to throw a damper on her excitement. There would certainly be sufficient to make the public rooms acceptable, and a few extra helping hands would go a long way to making life more comfortable even if they couldn't improve on the general condition of their private quarters. And if Livia's inheritance could catch her a husband of the right kind, then the main object of this expedition would be achieved.

Livia stopped in midtwirl. "I won't be able to find a husband if you two don't stay here with me," she reminded them. "Unlike you old married ladies, I have to have a chaperone."

"We have a month," Aurelia said.

"Yes, but it might take longer than that for me to find a husband," Livia pointed out. "However energetically I go about it. Don't forget we have money in the kitty now, enough to keep the household going for six months at least. And you have your allowances. The trustees won't stop paying those; they can't legally . . . can they?"

"Not without cause," Cornelia said thoughtfully.

"And as long as we don't give them that, they'll have to sit on their hands. We have enough money to carry us through, even if somewhat frugally, until next quarter day?" She glanced interrogatively at Aurelia, who nodded her agreement.

"Then it's settled," Livia declared.

Cornelia acquiesced with a smile, but her mind was elsewhere. Her friends had forgotten about Viscount Bonham, and she supposed he had become irrelevant, an irrelevant and now-dismissed nuisance. But he'd said he'd be back and what she'd seen of the man thus far gave her every certainty that he didn't make idle declarations of intent.

She was not at all certain that they had seen the last of Lord Bonham.

Harry drove through the rain, barely noticing it even though his horses shook their manes at regular intervals, sending raindrops showering all in their path. The events of the morning went round and around in his head. The Dagenham woman had certainly played him for a fool, and, in all honesty, she had some justification for taking offense over his manner the previous day. But then how was he to have known a viscountess enjoyed playing housemaid, as Marie Antoinette had enjoyed playing milkmaid? What kind of eccentricity was that?

He shook his head impatiently, exasperated as much with himself as with the viscountess. He had jumped to conclusions, just as he'd formed a mental image of Livia Lacey that was as far from the truth as it was possible to be. He'd made a fool of himself, and he didn't care for the knowledge one little bit. It was time to stand back and reassess the situation. The house was not for sale at any price, it seemed. So he needed another approach.

And one that steered well clear of the Viscountess Dagenham. Once burned was quite sufficient. Those blue eyes were amazing, though, startlingly luminous. And she had a most distinguished presence, composed and graceful. So what the devil did she think she was doing cleaning chimneys, or whatever it was that had covered her in grime and smudges? What had happened to the viscount-husband? She was young to be a widow . . . were there children . . . ?

No. He pulled himself up sharply. He had no interest in the viscountess. She was not going to help him resolve his present problem. He would devote his attentions to Lady Livia herself. He needed unfettered access to the house, and who better to provide it than the lady of the house. Lady Livia Lacey had seemed a very different character from her friend . . . or was Lady Dagenham another relative? Not that the exact nature of the connection mattered one way or the other.

Lady Livia Lacey had struck him as a soft, warm, young woman, one who would shrink from causing pain. She had sounded apologetic at the confusion. In fact, he would lay odds she hadn't had any notion of the mischief her companion had caused.

He was driving down St. James's before he came out of his reverie at the sound of his own name. Light from Brookes's bay window spilled onto the wet pavement, and a man climbing the steps to the front door waved at him.

"Harry . . . where've you been, man? I haven't seen you in days." He stepped back down to the street and came up to the curricle. "Devil of a day."

"That it is," Harry agreed, handing his reins to the groom as he jumped down. "Take 'em home, Eric. I'll walk back."

"Aye, m'lord." The groom took his place, picked up the reins, flicked the whip expertly, and the equipage went off at a smart trot.

"Nice pair, Harry," his companion said with an appreciative whistle. "Haven't seen those before. You always did have a good eye for cattle."

Harry laughed away the compliment and extended a hand to Sir Nicholas Petersham. "How are you, Nick?"

"Well enough, well enough. Where've you been hiding yourself?"

"Oh, in the country . . . family business . . . the usual," Harry said vaguely, as they turned up the steps to the club. His work for the War Office was a well-kept secret even from his closest friends and on the frequent occasions when he was closeted in his attic study and disappeared from circulation for a while, he usually employed an undefined family crisis as excuse. No one would dream of questioning him too closely, and since he was the oldest of the late Viscount Bonham's six children and thus considered the family patriarch, it seemed quite understandable that some minor issue with a sibling or his elderly mother would take him out of town for a few days.

"I thought you were going to drive right past me," Nick observed. "I hailed you twice. You didn't seem to know where you were."

"Oh, I was lost in thought, Nick, you know how it is," Harry said with a careless gesture. In truth the last thing on his mind had been a morning of wine and cards in his club, but the idea was suddenly appealing. A necessary diversion from his encounter in Cavendish Square.

The door of the club opened as the two men reached the top step. They nodded to the austerely clad steward who held open the door for them, and stepped into the cushioned masculine luxury of their own world.

"Morning, m'lord . . . Sir Nicholas." Two footmen helped the gentlemen out of their wet outer garments, took hats and gloves, and handed them reverently to their own juniors.

The men entered the front salon, where a muted murmur of voices, the chink of glass, the crackle of the fireplace greeted them.

"It's Bonham . . . Harry," a voice declared cheerily to all and sundry. "Come over here, dear fellow, we have a problem needs solving with that inestimable brain of yours. You too, Nick."

"I doubt I can be as useful to you as Harry, Newnham, if it's brain power you're asking for," Sir Nicholas said with an amiable smile as they strolled across the room to a table in the bay window. "A dullard, if ever there was one, I have to admit."

"A rattle, maybe," Harry corrected. "Dullard? Never say so . . . So what's the problem?" He deposited his lean length in an armchair and looked around for a flunkey. "First, madeira . . . what about you, Nick?"

"Oh, without a doubt, dear fellow. Madeira it is." Sir Nicholas raised a hand, and a waiter appeared with a tray of filled glasses.

"So, Harry, it's a matter of a wager . . ."

Harry smiled with a hint of resignation as he raised his glass to his lips. "Whenever is it anything else with you, Newnham? In your shoes I'd wait to make my wagers until I understood something of the mathematics behind the odds."

"Ah, but that's exactly what I'm doing," the other man said, beaming his triumph. "I've been sitting here for two days, isn't that so?" He turned for confirmation to his companions, who all nodded their solemn agreement. "Waiting just for you, m'dear fellow. Now, if I bet five hundred on the likelihood of it's raining tomorrow, hedge with another five hundred on rain Wednesday, and back it with three hundred on just clouds—"

"I don't want to know," Harry said, holding up his hands. "I'll untangle the odds on a horse for you, but I'm not entering the territory of the deity." He looked around the salon and encountered the fixed glare of an elderly man in an armchair by the fire.

The man, in an old-fashioned coat of plum-colored velvet, wearing a wig tied neatly at his nape, was florid of complexion. One hand held a glass resting on a substantial embonpoint, the other hand was fastened tightly around the silver knob of a cane.

"Don't mind Grafton, Harry," Nick murmured. "It's over."

Harry had gone very still, but his eyes didn't drop the older man's gaze. "Not for him," he responded distantly. He rose slowly and crossed the room, aware as he did so of eyes swiveling to follow his progress. The old scandal still had legs enough to engage the voyeur.

He stopped in front of the old man and bowed. "Your Grace." He waited, a thin smile hovering on his lips. Waited for the cut he knew was coming. The duke of Grafton turned his head and his shoulders towards the fire. He raised his glass and drank, then threw the goblet into the hearth, the sound of the shattering glass resounding in the dead silence of the salon.

Harry bowed again, turned, and walked back to his friends in the bay window.

"Why d'you do it, Harry?" Nick demanded in an undertone. "Why d'you let him do that to you?"

Harry shrugged and drained the contents of his goblet. "He thinks he has the right . . . maybe he has."

"I don't understand you, Harry. The inquest—"

"Oh, enough, Nick." Harry raised a hand in protest.

"I give the old man a little satisfaction once in a while. You could say it was the least I owed him. Let's play cards." He rose and walked briskly towards the card rooms, and Nick, after a minute, followed.

They walked through the series of candlelit card rooms, where groom porters called the odds softly, and the slap of cards, the rattle of dice were the only noticeable sounds. Harry paused at a macao table.

"Bonham, where've you been the last week? I swear it's been an age since we saw you." A gentleman in an impeccably cut black coat raised his quizzing glass and regarded the new arrival. "D'you care to take a hand?"

"Family matters," Harry said, pulling out a chair at the table. "And, yes, I will, thank you."

"Petersham?" The gentleman in black gestured to a second chair.

Nick shook his head with a laugh. "Oh, no, not I. Play with Harry, oh, no. I prefer to pluck chickens, not to be plucked." Waving, he went on his way.

"Calumny," Harry observed, genially taking up his cards. "As if I've ever plucked anything."

"Maybe not, but you're the devil's own player," the man who held the bank observed. "Hate playing with you, Bonham, though it pains me to say it."

The remark drew laughter. Harry merely smiled and played his cards. He was contemplating the odds of a five card onto his fifteen points when someone at a table behind said, "Dagenham, do you play?"

Harry continued to contemplate his odds, while he

listened. A youngish voice answered the question in the affirmative. Harry played two more hands, then excused himself.

"Premature for you, Bonham," the banker observed. "You don't usually leave the table until you've decimated the bank."

"Oh, the quality of mercy, Wetherby," Harry said. "Mustn't strain it." He wandered off in a seemingly random direction, but he was fairly confident that the young voice had come from the hazard table immediately behind him. He took a glass of Madeira from a waiter and strolled around the room, observing the play. At the hazard table he paused, sipping his drink.

"Care to join us, Bonham?"

He shook his head. "No, I thank you. I've had enough for one morning." He moved a little to one side, his eyes still on the table. He knew five of the seven players. The other two were both considerably younger than his own coterie. And they each bore the ravages of youthful excess in shadowed, red-rimmed eyes, drawn cheeks, and a grayish pallor.

It was common enough for young men of means in their first season to burn the candle at both ends and ordinarily Harry would have barely noticed these two, or if he had he would have merely cast a somewhat amused glance in their direction with the rueful memory of his own youthful indiscretions. These two would learn their lesson as had he and a thousand others. But one of them interested him mightily. One of them had some relationship with Viscountess Dagenham.

They both played lamentably, and he quickly identified the one who interested him. He seemed even more inexpert than his friend. There was no physical resemblance between this young man, who he reckoned must be in his very early twenties, and the viscountess, but that was hardly surprising since her title would have derived from her late husband.

After a while he tired of watching him lose hand after hand, the IOUs mounting beside the banker. He moved to the sideboard to refill his glass from the array of decanters. Petersham came up beside him.

"Tired of the play already, Harry?"

"My heart's not in it this morning," Harry responded, leaning back against the sideboard and surveying the room over the lip of his glass. "Who's the cub playing at Elliot's table?"

Nick's gaze followed his. "Which one?"

"The one in that absurd canary yellow waistcoat."

Nick frowned. "Dagenham, I think. He was only put up for the club about four days ago. If you ask me, the fellow who put him up was doing him no favors. Coltrain, I believe it was, the man with Dagenham is the marquess's son. Doesn't look as if either of the young fools knows what he's doing, but Coltrain's heir at least has good family credit. I only hope Dagenham's father has deep pockets. I doubt Markby will bail him out."

"Markby?"

"Mmm. Dagenham's a member of the junior branch of the family. You're probably not familiar with them. They none of them come up to town much, in fact I'm surprised this one's here. From what I hear, Markby holds the family purse strings mighty tight . . . rules the entire clan with a rod of iron. His son, Viscount Dagenham, died at sea . . . may even have been at Trafalgar . . . "

Nick frowned in thought. "Aye, that's it. It was Trafalgar." He beamed triumphantly. "Anyway, the present heir's no more than a babe in arms."

The child of Viscountess Dagenham, Harry reflected, absently stroking his mouth with two fingers. That explained the presence of children in Cavendish Square.

The hazard table was breaking up, and he watched as the banker stuffed IOUs into his coat pocket. Young Dagenham was watching the banker too, with a fixed expression akin to the desperation a rabbit might feel as the shadow of the hawk's wings darkened the ground ahead of him. Then he turned and walked away towards the salon.

Harry followed him. The young man stood at the sideboard filling a glass. He drained the contents in one, then refilled it. Harry strolled across to him.

"Drowning your losses, eh?" he observed with a light laugh. "That's one tried-and-true way to oblivion." He refilled his own glass and smiled at the young man. "I don't believe we've been introduced." He held out his hand. "Bonham, at your service."

"Dagenham . . . Nigel Dagenham," the youth said,

taking the extended hand. His smile was forced and did nothing to alleviate the strain around his eyes. "Your servant, sir."

"I haven't seen you here before," Harry observed, glancing idly around the room.

"No, sir, I'm newly put up," Nigel said, wondering what it was about this gentleman that made him feel very young and unsophisticated. There could be nothing wrong with his waistcoat, the color was all the rage he'd been told, and the snowy folds of his starched cravat tied high enough to support his chin were beyond reproach. And yet there was a subdued elegance to Bonham's green coat, plain waistcoat, and doeskin britches that made Nigel feel almost like a country bumpkin.

"Well, I look forward to furthering our acquaintance," Harry said, nodded pleasantly and strolled off to where a group of his own friends were gathered. *What a stupid thing to say.* He had no interest in a callow youth who was floundering in deep waters. It was never his practice to cultivate the ingénu crowd of either sex. The young women bored him to tears, not that their mamas would ever allow them to have a tête-à-tête with Viscount Bonham . . . not anymore . . . and as for the young bucks, the greatest service he could do any of them was to snub them sufficiently to ensure that eventually they would acquire some town polish.

So what the devil did he think he was doing furthering an acquaintance with young Dagenham?

Addlepated was the only answer that sprang to mind.

Chapter 7

W HAT DO YOU THINK of this straw-colored satin for the dining room chairs, Nell?" Livia fingered a bolt of material at a draper's warehouse on Goodge Street. "It's not hideously expensive."

Cornelia abandoned the crimson-striped damask that she'd been considering and came over to Livia. "I like it," she declared. "It will set off the cream wallpaper beautifully." She glanced around. "Where's Ellie?"

Livia looked up, frowning as she peered around the cavernous warehouse with its long tables, bolts of material, and bustling attendants flourishing draper's shears. "She's over there." She pointed. "She's talking to someone. She must have met someone she knows."

"I can't think who," Cornelia said with a note of surprise, then exclaimed, "It's Letitia Oglethorpe. I'd know that nose anywhere."

Livia stared and gave a little chuckle. "Oh, I see what you mean . . . Cyrano would be proud of it. Who is she?"

"We were all debutantes together," Cornelia informed her. "Letitia became engaged to Oglethorpe halfway through the season." She shook her head with a rueful laugh. "My mother said she'd done very well for herself, considering the size of her nose. It was very clear she was comparing Letitia's unlikely success on the marriage mart with my own lamentable failure to make a match. Ellie's mother said much the same to her."

"Should we go over?"

"I think we have to." Cornelia didn't sound too enthusiastic, but she could hardly leave Aurelia to hold the fort alone. Letitia had always been supremely irritating and unnecessarily condescending. She was bound to be even worse now since she'd have some cause. She was dressed to the nines, and enviably warmly, in a fur-trimmed velvet pelisse with a gypsy bonnet perched on top of her high-piled hair. Privately, Cornelia thought the bonnet a mistake. Its flat style accentuated the nose rather than diminished it. The catty reflection did nothing to lessen Cornelia's sense of their own outmoded dress, which approached shabbiness when compared with Letitia's outfit.

She sighed. "I'd hoped we'd be able to smarten ourselves up a little before making contact with the outside world. But needs must when the devil drives." She led the way between the tables.

"Cornelia . . . oh, goodness, I would never have recognized you," Letitia trilled, as they approached. "My dear, you look so . . . so mature." She tittered. "We've all changed, I'm sure. I was just telling Aurelia, I wouldn't have recognized her either." She took Cornelia's proffered hand in a limp hold before turning her gaze inquiringly on Livia.

"May I introduce Lady Livia Lacey, Letitia," Cornelia said smoothly. "She's just inherited a house on Cavendish Square, and we're doing some refurbishment." She gestured around the warehouse. "Liv, this is Lady Oglethorpe. An old acquaintance of ours."

Letitia's pale eyes had sharpened as she took Livia's hand. "Cavendish Square . . . why, my dear, such a good address. I was unaware there was any property for sale there. It so rarely comes on the open market."

Her gaze moved pointedly over Livia's cloth pelisse and down to her plain brown boots. "I take it this is your first visit to town?" She didn't wait for a response, but continued smoothly, "Aurelia was telling me you've been immured in the country for years, Cornelia. It shows, my dear. You won't mind my saying that, I'm sure. Such old friends as we are. You must be so glad for the opportunity to do a little shopping now. Why, I shall so enjoy bringing you up to date on all the fashions, I can tell you just how to go on . . . just who to go to . . . it's very different these days, and you'll be so out of touch with modes and such like." She waved an all-embracing hand.

"How kind of you, Letitia," Cornelia said, trying to avoid catching Aurelia's eye. Her sister-in-law was standing just behind Letitia and was struggling with laughter. "We shall be most grateful, I'm sure, of any little pointers you can give us. Won't we, Liv?" She winked at Livia, who was looking more than a little bemused.

"Well, no time like the present," Letitia declared. "You must all come at once to Berkeley Square . . . Oglethorpe has given me carte blanche for a complete redecoration of the house, and I can't wait to show you all my improvements. It will give you some ideas for your own refurbishment, Lady Livia. Everything in the best of taste, of course . . . now where's my maid . . . wretched girl, she's always wandering off . . . oh, there you are. Take my reticule, girl. It gets in the way. And don't forget those bandboxes . . . Come, ladies. My barouche is outside, plenty of room for four of us."

Aurelia cast Cornelia a desperate glance. How were they to prevent this kidnapping? Cornelia shrugged slightly and shook her head. It occurred to her that it would do Livia no harm to have news of her ownership of the house on Cavendish Square pass into the gossip stream, and Letitia would be the perfect conduit.

They followed Lady Oglethorpe out of the warehouse, attendants scurrying with packages and boxes in their wake. A handsome barouche stood at the curb, and the driver jumped down from the box to let down the footstep. He handed the ladies in and arranged his mistress's purchases in every available space before settling lap rugs over his passengers.

"Hetty, you must walk," Letitia declared to the maid, smoothing the rug over her knees. "There's no room for you with all these packages."

"Why don't you have the warehouse deliver them?" Livia asked bluntly. It was a bitterly cold morning and a long walk from Goodge Street to Berkeley Square.

Letitia looked at her in surprise. "Why on earth would I do that, Lady Livia? An unnecessary expense . . . they'd need to hire a hackney."

"Of course," Livia murmured, reflecting that now, thanks to this overbearing lady, her own purchase of the straw-colored satin would have to be made another day, necessitating another expensive hackney ride that they, unlike the countess, could ill afford.

Letitia prattled merrily as they drove to Berkeley Square, and her three companions, snug beneath their rugs, allowed the stream to flow over them. It was certainly a pleasanter method of travel than an ill-smelling, drafty hackney carriage.

The barouche drew up outside the handsome Oglethorpe mansion on Berkeley Square. The double doors opened before the ladies had set foot on the pavement, and both butler and footman stood in the hall as they ascended the short flight of steps.

"Have the boxes taken to my sitting room, Walter," the countess instructed, shrugging out of her fur-trimmed pelisse as she sailed towards the stairs. The butler caught it with practiced skill as it slipped from her shoulders. "I wish to see just how well the material will look on the window seat. And serve a nuncheon in the yellow room in half an hour. There will be four of us."

"Letitia, I'm afraid we cannot stay above an hour,"

Cornelia stated firmly as they followed their hostess. "It's very kind of you . . ."

"Nonsense," the lady interrupted, speaking over her shoulder. "There's so much I have to tell you about London these days. It's so changed, and you wouldn't want to be putting a foot wrong. Social disaster, my dear. Just for a start I have to tell you whom you may receive and whom you must not."

As they reached the upstairs hall, a footman hurried to throw open the doors to an apartment to the right of the landing. Cornelia stopped dead on the threshold. "God in heaven," she murmured in awestruck tones.

"Isn't it wonderful," Letitia declared, flinging her arms wide. "The *dernier cri* I assure you. Absolutely up to the minute. I dare swear no lady in London has a sitting room to match it."

Aurelia, who had come up short behind Cornelia, almost bumping into her, stared over her sister-in-law's shoulder in awed silence. "I wouldn't think so," she said finally, blinking as if to dispel the amazing riot of colors.

"Now, I have to tell you, the Indian style is all the rage," Letitia said, dropping her voice conspiratorially as if she were imparting some precious secret. She drew off her gloves, tossing them carelessly towards a drum table. They missed and fell unheeded to the turquoise rug.

"Believe me, Lady Livia, you won't go wrong if you choose an Indian motif for your drawing room. Don't you just adore the wallpaper?" She clasped her hands against her bosom, gazing in rapture at the vivid gold-

and-crimson flock that adorned the walls. Gold leaf adorned the molding, the mantel, the curtain rails, and the ornate mahogany scrollwork on the sofas and tables.

"Please, sit down all of you." She deposited herself gracefully onto a peacock embroidered daybed and gestured to the sofa opposite. "Walter will bring coffee."

Cornelia moved to an overstuffed gold velvet chair, debating what to do with an artfully draped length of silk embroidered with glittering beads that lay across the seat. It appeared to have no visible purpose. With an inner shrug she sat on it. Her gaze immediately fell on a pair of stuffed peacocks regarding her with dark beady eyes from alongside the fireplace. There has to be an elephant somewhere in here, she thought, her eyes darting surreptitiously. Ah, there it was. Not just one but a whole string of brass elephants marching along a shelf of the bookcase. A few urn-shaped lamps that looked as if they'd be more at home in the *Arabian Nights* were scattered around the room in apparently random fashion.

She studiously avoided looking at either Aurelia or Livia. "Do you have children, Letitia?"

"Oh, yes, two of them. Dear little things," the countess responded somewhat vaguely. "They're in the country. Oglethorpe thinks the country air is better for them, and I'm sure he's right. Besides, they make such a noise in town . . . Ah, thank you, Walter." She took a cup from the butler, who had slipped soundlessly into the room with the coffee tray.

Once he'd served them all and left, she leaned forward, and said, "So, I heard you had lost your husbands. How tragic for you both. But I could never understand why you were both so happy to retire to the country. How could you bear to live without the season?" She sipped her coffee.

"But now, I suppose, you're free to spread your wings a little . . . hmm?" A somewhat salacious smile licked at her lips. "I could perhaps put you both in the way of an eligible *parti* . . . there are a few suitable unattached gentlemen in town . . . not quite top drawer, of course, but . . ." She let a smile finish her thought for her.

But good enough for two dowdy widows who'd made less-than-stellar matches first time round, Cornelia thought. She said only, "I don't think Aurelia and I are in the market, but thank you for the thought, Letitia."

"Oh, just you wait and see," the countess said comfortably. "Once you start going out and about . . . once you've visited a dressmaker, of course. I must give you the name of mine, she can't be bettered . . . and Signor Salvatore . . . he's the genius behind the décor in this room, Lady Livia, I know you'll enjoy discussing your needs with him."

"You're very kind," Livia said faintly, taking a macaroon from a silver salver.

"So, now you must tell me. Whom have you seen since you arrived in town?" Letitia leaned forward again in her confidential manner.

"No one, actually," Cornelia said.

"Oh, that's not entirely true, Nell," Aurelia corrected,

finally managing to find her voice. She was growing tired of accepting the picture of friendless, pathetic drudges, and out-of-fashion country widows that Letitia seemed determined to paint. "We have been visited on several occasions by Viscount Bonham." She took a sip of her coffee.

"Oh, so you know Lord Bonham." Letitia's eyes widened. "Quite the charmer, isn't he? And such a prominent family. How do you know him?"

"We don't really know him," said Livia, who always had problems with gilding the truth. "We met him because he was interested in buying my house."

"Oh, I see. Just business then." Letitia couldn't hide her disappointment. Then she perked up. "I can't think why he'd want another house, though. He has a perfectly satisfactory town house on Mount Street. Very mysterious." She leaned forward again. "A word of advice though. He's very charming, but you'd do well to keep him at arm's length."

"Oh?" Cornelia hid a flicker of interest. "And why's that, Letitia?"

The countess's eyes gleamed and she licked her lips. "Well, there was some trouble, a scandal—" She broke off as the door opened to admit the butler.

"My lady, Lord Oglethorpe wonders if you would do him the honor of joining him in his book room," the butler intoned.

Cornelia seized the opportunity offered by Letitia's momentary hesitation. She jumped to her feet. "Indeed, one must not keep one's husband waiting, Letitia, and we really must be going. It's been delightful. Thank you so much for your hospitality . . . and of course the good advice. You may be sure we'll heed it."

"Yes, indeed," murmured Aurelia, gathering her shawl about her as she too rose to her feet. "Signor Salvatore, wasn't it? You must remember the name, Liv."

"Oh, I have no intention of forgetting it, believe me," her friend said firmly as she made her own farewells.

They escaped at last and managed to contain their laughter until they'd rounded the corner of the square. They walked the short distance to Cavendish Square on a tide of hilarity.

"I could almost feel sorry for Letitia," Cornelia said, as they let themselves into the house. "Except that she's so damnably self-satisfied."

"And damnably inquisitive," Aurelia said, pulling off her gloves. "She'll be knocking on the door in a day or two, mark my words. She always liked to be the first with any gossip."

"Just as long as she doesn't bring Signor Salvatore," Livia said with an involuntary shudder. *"That wallpaper."*

The blast of sound brought Cornelia out of a deep sleep mysteriously inhabited by oddly behaved elephants. Her heart thumped, and for a minute she fought nausea as her mind and body adjusted themselves to being so rudely awakened.

She threw off the coverlet and reached for her dressing gown. The embers in the grate still glowed but gave off little heat. There was light enough, however, once her eyes had adjusted to locate flint and tinder beside the candles on the dresser. Once the flicker of candlelight illuminated the chamber, she could see the clock face. Three in the morning.

Thrusting her feet into slippers, Cornelia went to the door. As she opened it, she heard the children crying from the nursery. Aurelia, carrying a candle, appeared from her own chamber across the corridor. "What on earth was that?" she demanded. "It sounded like the last trump."

"Sorry to be prosaic, but it was more like a blunderbuss than the end of the world," Cornelia responded. "It's woken the children."

"Hardly surprising," Aurelia said. "Linton will be up in arms." They both turned towards the nursery stairs.

"What was that?" Livia materialized in the darkness of the corridor, her white nightgown floating around her, her face visible as a pale oval beneath the cloud of black hair. "Ouch!" she exclaimed, stubbing her toe on an uneven floorboard.

"We don't know," Aurelia said. "Why haven't you got a candle?"

"Too much of a hurry," Livia said, moving fully into the circle of light from Aurelia's candle. "What was it?"

"Nell says a blunderbuss," Aurelia stated. "It's frightened the children . . . you go downstairs, Liv, and find out what's going on. We'll be down as soon as we've calmed things upstairs." She gave Livia her candle and hurried after Cornelia, whose own candle was throwing a path of light as she almost ran towards the cacophony emanating from the nursery.

Cornelia reached the nursery first. She dropped to her knees, catching her distraught children in her arms as she murmured soft reassurances. An ashen Daisy held little Franny, who was hiccuping sobs.

"Oh, my poor darling, it's all right." Aurelia rushed up to take the little girl.

"What kind of antics are these in a gentleman's house, I'd like to know?" Linton declared for the second time since Cornelia had arrived. The nurse, swathed in a thick robe, her hair in a gray rope down her back, was rigid with outrage. "Lady Nell, these children need to be back in their beds at home."

"It was just an accident, Linton," Cornelia said, stroking Susannah's hair as the child buried her face in her mother's shoulder. Of course she had no idea whether it was an accident or not at this point, but it seemed the easiest route to soothing the wrathful nurse. "It's quiet now. It's all over."

"What kind of accident, Mama?" Stevie demanded, wriggling out of his mother's embrace. His dark eyes . . . his father's eyes . . . were fixed round as buttons upon her face. "It sounded like Grandfather's gun when he's hunting."

"Morecombe was hunting mice," Cornelia said, ignoring Linton's disbelieving harrumph. "It just sounded so loud because it was inside not outside, and the house was very quiet too. It makes an echo, you see."

"I thought you hunted mice with traps," Stevie pointed out with a five-year-old's logic. "'Least that's what Nelson said." Nelson was the head groom at Dagenham Manor, and Stevie idolized him.

"Well, you can do it both ways," Cornelia improvised, not prepared to question the oracle. "Listen now, it's all quiet." She held up a finger, and the children listened intently.

"See," Aurelia said, wiping Susannah's eyes as the child's hiccuping sobs faded. "Aunt Nell's right, it's all quiet now." She stood up with the child. "Let's go back to bed."

It took fifteen minutes to tuck them back into their beds, with Linton muttering direly about what his lordship would say to these goings-on and Daisy still whimpering a little in shock's aftermath.

"We'll leave the lamp burning," Cornelia said, turning the wick down low. She bent to kiss her children. "Go to sleep now." She tiptoed out of the night nursery, Aurelia on her heels.

"They'll be all right now, Linton," she said. "I'm sorry you were disturbed."

"Well, that's as may be, Lady Nell, but it's not right," Linton declared, her arms folded, her expression implacable. "Poor little mites were scared out of their wits. That Morecombe ought to know better . . . hunting mice indeed." She snorted.

"We're really sorry, Linton, and we'll make sure it doesn't happen again," Aurelia said with a conciliatory smile. "The children are really all right now. There's not a peep from them."

Linton did not look appeased, but she said, "I'll bid you good night, my ladies," and stalked off to her own chamber.

"Oh, Lord," said Cornelia. "That's put the cat among the pigeons. We'd better find out what really happened. We'll take the back stairs to the kitchen."

They hurried down the narrow flight of stairs. As they got closer to the kitchen regions, they could hear the distinct sounds of furniture scraping across flagstones, and Morecombe's unmistakable Yorkshire burr raised in a stream of invective.

They emerged into the kitchen to find furniture overturned, Morecombe still flourishing an ancient but clearly functioning weapon as he righted toppled chairs with one hand, and the twins blinking in bleary-eyed indignation at a scene of disarray. Someone had been busy in the kitchen. And cooking had not been the object of the exercise.

"What on earth happened here?" Cornelia demanded.

"We don't know," Livia said helplessly. "Look at this shambles."

Cornelia shivered as a blast of cold air hit her. "Why's the window open?"

"For the cat, ma'am," Morecombe declared, finally setting down his blunderbuss.

"The cat doesn't need it wide open like that." Cornelia went to close it. The cat, tail bushed, back arched, ears pricked, was standing on the sill outside. "Something frightened you," Cornelia said. "But then that noise would raise the dead." She reached for the cat and brought it in side, then slammed the window shut.

"Someone came through that window." Aurelia put into words the obvious conclusion as she gestured to the chaos around them. China and glass had been taken from the shelves of the Welsh dresser and piled haphazardly across the floor, the flour barrel was upended, its fresh contents spilling across the table together with the contents of most of the storage jars from the pantry. Beans mingled with sugar that formed a paste with spilled oil and vinegar. The canisters containing coffee and tea lay on their sides.

"Why would a burglar break into *this* house?" Livia asked in bewilderment. "It must be the only house on the square that doesn't have much worth stealing in it."

"There's the silver, ma'am," Morecombe pointed out, sounding somewhat offended at Livia's comment.

"Is it still in your pantry?" Aurelia hurried out to check and returned almost immediately to report, "Everything's there, just as you left it, Morecombe."

"If you ask me, mum, it's just mischief makers," one of the twins stated. "Young ruffians with nowt to do wi' their 'ands. Jest lookin' for trouble, that's all."

"Aye, 'tis not the first time," her sister observed.

"What do you mean?" Livia asked.

"Oh, there's been some strange goings-on, m'lady," Morecombe said, with something akin to relish. "Ever since Lady Sophia . . . rest 'er soul . . . passed away, there's been bumps and bangs in the night. That's why I brought this up." He flourished his weapon. "Nearly caught one of 'em, I did, t'other night. Sent 'im packin' with more than a flea in 'is ear, I'll tell you for nowt. An' when I heard the cat sqawk tonight, I was ready for 'em."

"How strange," Livia frowned. "But maybe you're right. It's probably a gang of cutpurses, or some such, who thought they would find easy pickings in a house that . . ." She left the sentence hanging. She'd been about to say, *that no one seemed to care about,* but she had the sense that Morcombe and the twins wouldn't appreciate the sentiment.

"It certainly looks like the handiwork of vandals." Aurelia wrinkled her nose in disgust.

"Maybe," Cornelia said thoughtfully, looking around at the mess again. "Did you see them, Morecombe . . . before you fired?"

Morecombe shook his head. "Can't say as I did, m'lady. I fired an' he was gone quicker'n a will-o'-the-wisp.

"Was there only one of them then?"

"Far as I know, ma'am."

"Mmm." Cornelia looked down at the cat, still cradled in her arms. "I wonder if you know something that we don't, Puss."

"Well, whatever, or whoever, it was, there's nothing more we can do tonight," Aurelia said briskly. "Let's leave all this and deal with it in the morning."

"Yes, I don't think they'll come back again tonight," Livia agreed, going to the back stairs. "Come on, Cornelia." She yawned deeply.

Cornelia made to follow her. The cat wriggled in her arms, and she set her down. Instantly the animal jumped onto the windowsill with a demanding yowl.

"I told you, m'lady, she needs to 'ave the window open," Morecombe stated with some satisfaction.

"Yes, well she's going to have to learn," Cornelia retorted. "She can be inside or outside, but that window stays shut, Morecombe. Now, let's all go back to bed."

Sleep proved elusive, though. She tossed and turned, her mind refusing to let go of the conundrum. Why on earth would anyone want to break in repeatedly? The house looked derelict from the outside, and it wasn't much better on the inside. The only explanation did seem to be opportunistic ruffians on the look out for anything they could steal easily. Yet somehow she was not convinced.

Chapter 8

THE FOLLOWING MORNING Viscount Bonham was at breakfast when Lester joined him. "Something going on in Cavendish Square last night, sir," the man said without preamble. "Just had the report from the night watch."

"Have a seat, Lester." Harry waved towards a chair opposite his own. "This sirloin's excellent. Help yourself. Ale's in the jug."

"Don't mind if I do, sir." Lester cut a hefty slice of sirloin and poured himself a tankard of ale. "Seems that someone went in again last night," he said through a mouthful. "Our boys watched him go in, and they saw him come out in a hurry."

"The butler with the blunderbuss, I imagine," Harry said. "They caught him on his way out?"

Lester shook his head. "No, sir. 'Fraid this one slipped through their fingers. They went after him, but he dodged them somehow."

"*Damnation.*" Harry drummed his fingers on the table. "So we don't know if he got what he went in for."

"Well, our chaps took a peek through the window, once the ruckus died down." Lester slathered mustard on his sirloin. "Apparently it was a fine mess in there. Crocks and canisters all over the place. Our chaps reckoned whoever it was didn't know where to look, judging by the shambles. Fair took the place apart, he did. An' he was still looking when he was disturbed. It should have been a quick in-and-out job, instead . . ." He shrugged expressively.

"But he must have known where to look," Harry said frowning. "Maybe it wasn't where he expected it to be." He took a draught of ale.

"So someone's moved it then?"

"Maybe. But no one's gone into that house without our men knowing it." Harry set down his tankard with a thump. "If it has been moved, then it must have been by someone in the house already."

"They wouldn't know it's significance, though, would they, sir?"

"No." Harry tapped his mouth with his fingertips. "If someone in that house found it by accident, then they'll still have it . . . and that, Lester, could make our task a lot easier."

"How d'you mean, sir?"

He pushed back his chair, crossing one booted leg over the other. "Well, one of those women, or one of the servants, must have it. It narrows the search a little, wouldn't you say?"

Lester looked doubtful. "If you say so, m'lord."

"Well, we know three women with children are in residence. I've made the dubious acquaintance of both Lady Dagenham and Lady Livia." His lip curled at the memory of his encounter with the ladies.

"Presumably," he continued, "the third woman is a nursemaid. There are probably a couple of other maids, plus Lady Sophia's three retainers. We can discount the children and probably their attendants. They'll be restricted to the nursery quarters, and I doubt our thief would have ventured that far into the house. We need to find a way in, a legitimate way if possible, ask a few casual questions, and see if we can unearth anything. If we can discover which of them found it, assuming we're not barking up the wrong tree, then we'll know where to look."

"And how do we effect this legitimate entrance, sir?"

"You take the servants. I'm sure there's some pretty lass on the staff that you can persuade to invite you in." Harry grinned. "Right up your street, eh, Lester?"

"If you say so, m'lord," Lester repeated woodenly, but there was a gleam in his eye. "And you'll be taking on the ladies, I assume?"

"Well, one of them," Harry said a shade grimly. "It'll have to be Lady Livia. I don't fancy my chances with Viscountess Dagenham."

"Really, sir?" Lester looked interested. "How's that then?"

"She's something of a shrew. And if I'm going to turn

on my legendary charm, I might as well pour it on receptive ground." A slightly sardonic smile touched the corners of his mouth. "Although I imagine I'll have to try to mend fences with the viscountess." He got to his feet. "I'll see you later, Lester. Don't waste any time."

"No, m'lord." Lester rose and waited until the viscount had left the breakfast parlor before resuming his own repast.

Harry went into the hall. "Ah, there you are, Hector. I'm going out, but I'm expecting dinner guests this evening, so inform Armand would you. We'll dine at eight."

Hector proffered hat and gloves. "And how many guests should I tell Armand, my lord?"

Harry frowned as he drew on his gloves. "Not entirely sure. Four I think, but maybe five. I shouldn't make any difference to Armand."

"No, my lord," Hector murmured, well aware of exactly how much difference it would make to the excitable and irascible genius in the kitchen. He hurried to open the door for his master. "You're walking, sir?"

"Yes, I believe I am." The viscount stood on the top step and surveyed the winter street. A pale sun shone from a sharply blue sky, and the residue of the night's frost still clung to the iron railings to the steps. But it was an invigorating cold, and he set off with his long stride in the direction of Cavendish Square. He hadn't decided on how he was going to make his approach to Lady Livia, but maybe an opening would offer itself.

A brisk twenty minutes walking brought him to

Cavendish Square. Children's voices came from the square garden and, curious, he turned aside and entered the garden through the wicket gate. A ball, thrown with more enthusiasm than aim, landed at his feet. He bent to pick it up and looked around for its owner.

A small boy came running towards him. The frilled white shirt of his conventional skeleton suit had dirt on the cuffs, and one of the buttons that fastened his short coat to his nankeen trousers was undone. He came to an abrupt halt in front of Harry, scuffling the gravel with his black shoes. "Did it hit you?"

Harry tossed the ball from hand to hand and smiled at the child. "No, was it meant to?"

"No," the boy said, regarding him solemnly, rubbing the dusty sole of one foot against the white sock of his other, heedless of the black mark thus left.

Harry knew without a shadow of a doubt that this child belonged to Lady Dagenham. There was something about the set of the head and the very straight gaze that was unmistakable.

"Viscount Dagenham, I presume," he said, raising a quizzical eyebrow.

"Yes, sir." The child, impatient now with this conversation, held out an imperative hand. "Please may I have my ball back."

"Can you catch it? I'll throw it to you if you stand a little way back."

Stevie regarded the stranger with sudden suspicion. "You're not going to keep it?"

Harry laughed. "No, lad, why would I want to do that? I thought perhaps you'd like to play catch."

In Stevie's experience, grown men did not usually play catch. Daisy did, and sometimes Nelson could be persuaded to throw a ball once or twice for him, but his various grown-up uncles and cousins rarely seemed to notice him, let alone play with him. Cousin Nigel sometimes ruffled his hair, and once had tried to teach him to play cricket, but Stevie hadn't managed to hit a single ball, and Cousin Nigel had quickly remembered somewhere else he had to be.

"All right," he said after a moment's consideration. "If you promise not to keep it."

Harry had enough nieces and nephews to find nothing strange in this anxiety. "I promise."

Stevie ran back a few paces and then stood expectantly, his hands cupped in front of him. "Ready," he piped.

Harry tossed the ball gently, aiming it into the small cupped hands that showed no inclination to follow the ball's trajectory, instead waiting patiently to receive. It fell through his hands to the ground, and the child bent to scrabble it up.

"Stevie, where are you?" The quiet, mellow voice preceded the appearance of Viscountess Dagenham from behind a privet hedge. A very small girl had a firm hold of her hand.

Cornelia took in the scene in one quick glance, and her lips tightened. "Stevie, you know you're not to run out of sight," she scolded softly, going over to the child, leading Susannah. She bent to refasten the button on his jacket.

"I didn't, Mama," he protested. "The ball ran off. I had to follow it, and he was throwing it back to me." He pointed at the still figure of Viscount Bonham, demanding, "Tell Mama."

"The ball did appear to have intentions of its own," Harry said evenly. "Forgive me for intruding, ma'am." He bowed, watching as she bent over the child, smoothing back the hair from his forehead before pulling up the grubby socks with deft movements that indicated she was accustomed to caring for her children herself. It reminded him rather of his sister Annabel, who kept her hands very firmly on the reins when it came to her own large brood. But his bustling, matronly sister bore little resemblance to this slender, graceful woman. As she bent over the child, the curved fluidity of her posture put him in mind of a weeping willow yielding before the wind.

He dismissed the nonsensical fancy, and when she did not immediately respond to his apology, which had invited a denial, he said, "I would not have disturbed you for the world, believe me. I'm sure we both have pleasanter ways of spending our time."

Cornelia straightened and met his gaze. It was hard to tell whether he was being sarcastic. It certainly sounded as if he was, but there was a light in the green eyes that belied the seeming intent of the statement.

"Your courtesy overwhelms me, sir," she said, watching for his reaction.

He raised a hand in the gesture of a fencer acknowledging a hit. "Then I must be satisfied with that, my lady." He bowed again and turned to leave.

As he did so, a third child hurtled through the wicket gate with such single-minded purpose that she flew straight into his knees. She stared at him, for a moment stunned, then opened her mouth in a loud wail. Instinctively, he picked her up and she was instantly silenced, staring into his face with intent curiosity.

"Franny, darling!" The woman who hurried through the gate was a stranger to Harry. A very pretty woman of much the same age as the viscountess, but to Harry's presently prejudiced eyes a vast improvement. Pale blond hair caught up under a wide-brimmed bonnet and warm brown eyes that regarded him with hesitation. "What happened?"

"Your daughter . . . ?" A faint question mark lingered, and the woman nodded swiftly and held out her arms for the girl.

He handed her over. "She ran headlong into my knees. Fast enough to knock herself out," he added with a slight laugh.

"Oh, Franny," the woman said with a sigh. "She never does anything by halves, and she was in such a hurry to play with Stevie and Susannah. I'm sorry, Mr. . . . ?"

"Bonham," Harry said promptly. "Viscount Bonham." He saw the quick flash in her eye. "We have not met, ma'am."

"Lady Farnham," Aurelia said a little stiffly, aware of Cornelia standing immobile to one side, watching the scene. "Lady Dagenham's sister-in-law," she added even as she wondered why she was bothering to give him this information. The man was persona non grata in Cavendish Square.

"Ah, I see." He bowed. "Your servant, Lady Farnham." He turned towards Cornelia and offered her another ironic bow. "Servant, Lady Dagenham." With which he exited the garden.

Aurelia gazed after him, hitching Franny up onto her hip. "He's most personable, Nell."

"Nonsense," her sister-in-law declared. "Liv herself said what cold eyes he has."

"Not when he smiles," Aurelia said, regarding Cornelia with a shrewdly questioning air. She caught herself wondering if this was not a case of the lady protesting overmuch. But she wasn't prepared to get her head bitten off by advancing such a possibility. However, anger or something else had enlivened Nell's countenance quite powerfully. And her eyes had a militant sparkle that accentuated their brilliance. Aurelia knew herself to be pretty, but she often considered her looks to be insipid beside her sister-in-law's.

"Besides," Cornelia stated, interrupting Aurelia's reflections, "he was most abominably rude again." Then she shook her head in frustration. "Or at least, I think he was. It was hard to tell. What he said sounded discourteous, but the way he said it didn't."

"He was charming to *me,* and Franny seemed to take to him," Aurelia pointed out.

"Mama . . . Mama . . . will you throw the ball to me, just like the man did?" Stevie tugged at her hand.

"Stevie too, it would seem," Aurelia murmured mischievously.

Cornelia raised an eyebrow, then took the ball from her son. "Let's play on the grass, Stevie." She walked off with a child in each hand, and Aurelia, obeying Franny's insistent demand, followed.

Cornelia threw the ball for Stevie. It wasn't a very absorbing activity since mostly it involved Stevie hurling himself to the ground or into the bushes in energetic and not particularly efficient retrieval, with a shrieking Franny in hot pursuit. After a while she said, "So you're implying he's only discourteous to me?"

Aurelia, who was bending down at a flower bed searching for snowdrops with Susannah, glanced up with a comprehending smile. "Well, you haven't exactly been very polite to him. Any man worth his salt is going to give provocation for provocation."

"A gentleman would turn the other cheek," Cornelia said.

"Oh, Nell, you know you don't believe that," Aurelia scoffed, straightening up. "He was rude to you, and you got your own back in spades, I would have said. Can you blame him for being less than servile?"

"I don't want servility," Cornelia protested, half-laughing. "But civility. If he'd been civil this morning, I would have been too."

Aurelia let it go. "More to the point, what was he doing here?" she questioned. "I thought he understood yesterday that the house was not for sale."

"So did I," Cornelia said. "But he did say he would call upon Liv again. She'll refuse to receive him, of course, but he obviously intends to try again to persuade her to sell."

⤦⤦

Harry knocked on the door to the late Lady Sophia's house.

The door was opened by the old retainer in a baize apron. He looked up at the visitor in silence, his exprssion one of indifference.

"Is Lady Livia Lacey receiving this morning?" Harry asked, proffering his card.

"You was 'ere yesterday," the man stated, ignoring the card.

"Yes. Viscount Bonham. Please take my card to Lady Livia." Harry tried to conceal his irritation. Instinct told him it was not the way to gain favorable attention from this creaky old man.

"Well, I dunno about that." Morecombe took the card and held it up to his eyes for close examination. "I didn't 'ave no orders."

"You don't need orders to take a visitor's card to your

mistress," Harry stated with deliberate patience. It seemed that the only way to deal with this obstructive old man was on the retainer's own terms, step-by-step. He said again just as patiently. "Would you please present it to Lady Livia?"

"Wait 'ere then." The man sniffed, stepped back, and closed the door, leaving Harry standing on the doorstep.

Harry turned to look across the street to the square garden. He couldn't see the women or their children through the thick privet hedge lining the railings, but he could hear the occasional childish squeal of glee. He felt like a hapless batsman at a cricket match facing a fiendishly fast bowler; at each bowl the bail flew off the stumps before he could get close to the ball. His preconceptions about this situation were being knocked off in much the same inexorable fashion. Not one elderly lady but three young ones, none of whom resembled the kind of society women he was accustomed to either in manner or conduct. There were children and a tumbledown house run with all the efficiency of a Moroccan souk by an elderly retainer who had to be coaxed to do his job, and even then only if he was so inclined.

But still, he had to work with what he was given, Harry reflected with rueful resignation. He was used to adapting materials to his own needs.

The door creaked open a few inches, and his card was thrust at him. " 'Er ladyship said as 'ow she's not receivin'."

Harry took the card. Its unceremonious return was tantamount to a statement that he was not welcome in this house. It was a deliberate insult, and he couldn't for the life of him think what he had done to deserve it. To his knowledge he had not offended Lady Livia. He'd only met her the once, and they'd barely exchanged two words.

The door had almost closed on his fingers as he'd taken back the card, and he stood for a second in thought tapping it into the palm of his hand. *What now?*

He turned to stare again at the square garden. If Livia would not receive him, he could hardly work his charm upon her, but Lady Farnham was out in the open. If he could get her alone, maybe he could gain some leverage there.

As if on cue, Lady Farnham emerged from the garden, her only companion her daughter, whom she held firmly by the hand. They started to cross the street to the house, and the child suddenly dropped to her knees in the middle of the road, her eye caught by the iridescent gleam of a pigeon's feather.

"Look, Mama." She tried to pick it up, but a gust of wind caught it and sent it fluttering along the street. The child wrenched free of her mother's hand and chased after the prize just as a dray barreled around the corner from Wigmore Street.

"Franny!" Aurelia shouted, starting after the child, who continued her headlong pursuit of the elusive feather, her pigtails flying behind her.

Harry moved fast. He snatched the child up from the street and carried her kicking and screaming to the pavement. The cart horses pulling the dray clopped past, and Aurelia arrived, pale and breathless, on the pavement.

"Thank you . . . Franny, how many times must I tell you not to let go of my hand on the street?" She took the girl from Harry, and Franny instantly burst into a howling flood of tears.

"Feather . . . my feather . . ." She pointed at the feather that had come to rest again in the middle of the street. Her voice rose to a shriek. *"I want my feather."*

Harry retrieved it and brought it back. She took it, and, instantly, the tears dried.

"Thank you," Aurelia said again.

"I don't think she was in any danger," Harry said. "Not unless she changed direction suddenly."

"Which would not have been unusual," Aurelia said with a sigh. "She's a child of impulse, I'm afraid. But thank you again for such a quick reaction." She turned to go back into the house.

"Lady Farnham?"

"Yes?" She glanced back at him.

"I would like very much to discuss some business with Lady Livia, but it seems she will not receive me." He offered a questioning smile. "I'm not aware of how I might have offended her."

"Oh." Aurelia hesitated. "Lady Livia is not interested in selling the house, Lord Bonham. That's all I know."

"So I've been told. But I would like to hear her say that herself."

Aurelia glanced over his shoulder towards the square

garden. "We are all close friends, my lord," she said. "I wish you good morning." She went to the door. It opened at her knock, and Harry caught a glimpse of Livia Lacey as she opened the door to let in her friend and the child.

We are all close friends. A seeming non sequitur, he thought, but it wasn't. It was an oblique suggestion. If he wanted access to the house, he needed first to come to terms with Viscountess Dagenham.

Well, he'd always relished a challenge.

He strode across the street, back to the garden.

Cornelia heard the scrunch of feet on the gravel path that led through the privet hedge to the center of the garden. She was sitting on a stone bench to one side of the path and didn't look up from her scrutiny of her lapful of acorn cups and smooth brown conkers that Stevie and Susannah had gathered. She didn't need to look up. She knew exactly who was standing a few feet away.

Why has he come back? Not for another round of incivilities surely? She was actually getting rather tired of them herself.

"Lady Dagenham?" It was softly spoken.

"Lord Bonham?" She polished a conker with her handkerchief. "There you are, Susannah." She gave the nut to the child, and only then did she look across at the viscount.

For a moment they studied each other in silence, almost as if they were seeing each other properly for the first time, and, indeed, Cornelia felt that from her point of view that was the case. On their previous meetings, her impression of the man ahd been obscured by a fog of antagonism. She had thought him humorless and cold. Now she noticed with something of a shock that Aurelia had been right. When he smiled, his mouth had a rather delightfully humorous curve to it. And his green eyes, although grave at present, were not as stony as she remembered them.

Harry, for his part, was also revising his opinion of Lady Dagenham's personal charms. He had thought her cold, arrogant, and unfeminine compared with the other two women. But now he was not so sure. Without the angry glitter that he was used to, her blue eyes were more shrewd than shrewish, and her mouth, when it wasn't set in an uncompromising line, was both full and well shaped. She wore her hair caught up in a loose and slightly disordered knot, and the escaping tendrils seemed to accentuate that buttery honey color that he'd noticed before.

"We appear to have got off on the wrong foot," he said.

"I wouldn't dispute that, sir," she responded, scooping the nuts into her handkerchief as she rose slowly to her feet.

"Well, at least we can agree on something." His eyes became a little less grave, and the smile remained on his mouth. "But I confess I'm at something of a loss to know how it happened."

Cornelia looked at him in astonishment. "You're

what? My dear sir, I cannot believe you would be so disingenuous."

He held up his hands in protest. "Wait a minute. Let's not start again. Let us—"

He was interrupted by a voice from behind. "Lady Nell, it's time for Lady Susannah's nap. They've both been out long enough in the cold." Linton came down the path towards them, Daisy hurrying to keep up.

"Very well, Linton," Cornelia said. "Come, Stevie, Susannah . . . it's time to go in . . . Daisy, could you carry their treasure, please?" She gave the folded handkerchief to the nursemaid.

"Mercy, child, look at your socks," Linton exclaimed. "And those stains on your shirt. What have you been doing, Lord Stevie?" She addressed the child, but her accusing gaze was on his mother.

Cornelia's smile was contrite. "We were playing with the ball, Linton. But a little dirt doesn't hurt."

"How we're to get those stains off, I don't know," Linton grumbled, unappeased. "In that house . . . with no laundry maids, hardly any hot water. I don't know what's to be done." She tutted as she took Stevie's hand. "Come along then, both of you."

Her own children were no more inclined to question Linton's edicts than their mother and went off without protest.

"Oh, dear," Cornelia said, for a moment forgetting who she was talking to. "I'm in her bad books again. I'll have to find some way to mollify her."

"Rules the nursery with an iron hand, does she?" Harry asked, amused by the viscountess's discomfiture. She looked as guilty as a child.

Cornelia flushed a little at this inadvertent intimacy. "She was my own nurse," she offered in curt explanation. "Excuse me, Lord Bonham." She made a move to follow the nursery party from the garden.

Harry spoke swiftly, "Please don't go just yet. I'd like to see if we could get onto the right foot."

She paused, folding her arms as she drew her woolen shawl tighter around her. "I don't really see the point, viscount."

He regarded her thoughtfully. She was such a striking woman, despite the unfashionably plain round gown of dark blue worsted and a shawl that was clearly designed for warmth and comfort rather than elegance. She had regained her quiet assurance and stood now considering him, her head tilted slightly atop a neck that could only be described as swanlike.

"Don't you, ma'am?" he responded gently. "I find that I do."

"Ah." Cornelia couldn't come up with a more expansive response to this declaration. She was beginning to wonder if maybe she did see the point. The man intrigued her in some way that she couldn't put a finger on.

He proffered an arm clad in dark gray twill. "Will you take a stroll around the garden?"

She took the arm with a faint inclination of her head and waited with considerable interest for him to begin.

He began rather off the point. *"Nell,"* he said in a musing tone.

"Cornelia," she responded a touch sharply. "And I don't believe we have progressed to first names, Lord Bonham."

"No . . . no," he agreed. "But I was trying it out."

Cornelia decided to ignore this. "If you hope to persuade Livia to sell you the house, Lord Bonham, I can save you the time and trouble. She is not interested in selling."

"So you said." He nodded agreeably, as if the statement caused him no particular dismay.

"So what exactly is the point of this walk?" she asked, when it seemed as if he was going to remain silent for the length of the circuit.

"I don't like situations I don't understand. And I am at a loss to understand how I have deserved your incivility, Lady Dagenham," he stated roundly.

"My good woman," Cornelia murmured softly. "An infelicitous expression under any circumstances, I'm sure you'll agree, Lord Bonham."

He stopped on the path and turned to look at her. "If that's all, then I apologize unreservedly, and promise never to let such an infelicitous expression cross my lips again." He smiled. "Will that do, ma'am?"

"It might if I believed it was sincerely offered," she said.

"Oh, come, Nell." He took her shoulders suddenly, and his eyes were alight with laughter. "Don't be so niggardly. You know that we were both at fault. I suspect we both have a hair trigger in certain circumstances. Now, cry truce."

"Let go of me." She twitched her shoulders to free herself, but his hold merely tightened.

"No, not until you cry truce."

He watched the annoyance warring with reluctant laughter in her eyes until slowly her mouth curved in a smile even as she twitched her shoulders again beneath his hands. The smile was irresistible. He lifted his hands from her and fleetingly touched the curve of her mouth with a fingertip, a gesture so light it could almost have been an accident. But he saw in the sudden flash of her eyes that she knew it was not.

She spun away from him. "If you'll excuse me, I have matters to attend to in the house." She began to walk back towards the gate.

"Allow me to escort you." He stepped up beside her.

"I have no need of your escort, sir."

"No, but it pleases me to provide it," he said with an amiable smile. "A pleasant day, don't you think, ma'am? For the time of year, of course. I daresay the daffodils will be out in Hyde Park in a few weeks. Always a magnificent display. Do you intend to stay in town to see them?"

It was so absurdly inconsequential in the light of the last few minutes that Cornelia couldn't help a little bubble of laughter. "I can't imagine an existence so frivolous that watching daffodils bloom could provide the motivation for an extended stay anywhere, Lord Bonham," she said, trying to suppress the chuckle in her voice.

"So you have no time for frivolity, Lady Dagenham," he responded, raising a quizzical eyebrow. "Is there no opportunity in the country life for play?"

She looked at him startled. "What makes you assume I live solely in the country, sir?"

He shrugged. "I know through my dealings with Masters that Lady Livia lives in the New Forest. You're her friend . . . I drew a conclusion. Is it incorrect?"

"As it happens, no," she conceded. "This is my first visit to town for ten years." She continued with a sad little sigh, "I fear I live the life of a reclusive widow, Lord Bonham, concentrating on my children and my needlework. We're all three of us country mice. It's to be hoped the diversions of the town don't quite overset us . . . turn our heads . . . so unaccustomed as we are to anything beyond the diversions of our rural firesides."

He looked down at her, and she offered him a demure smile that made him laugh. "Fustian," he stated. "Utter nonsense. You and your friends are quite clearly more than capable of handling anything that comes your way, as I've already learned to my cost. And while you may well devote yourself to your children, ma'am, I'll lay odds you have a lot more interests than needlework."

"Perhaps so," she responded noncommittally, deciding the banter had gone on long enough.

He opened the gate onto the street and stood aside for her to precede him. "Do you and your friends intend to make your mark upon society, once you've established yourselves?"

"We haven't really given it much thought." She stepped past him, for some reason drawing her shawl more tightly arond her as she did so.

"Then I hope that you do. I hope that we will be able to further our acquaintance." Solicitously, he took her elbow to escort her across the street.

"The eternal optimist, my lord?" She raised her eyebrows in faint incredulity. "I fear your disappointment."

"Oh, do you? Pray don't put yourself to the trouble, ma'am. I am rarely disappointed," he said, delivering her to her doorstep.

"Don't be so sure," she said softly.

He cast her a quick sideways glance that held amusement and something else . . . something much more unsettling in its depths. "We shall see." He raised the knocker and let it fall, before lifting his hat and saying, "I won't trespass upon your time any further this morning, Lady Dagenham."

He bowed and turned to walk down the steps. At the bottom, he tossed over his shoulder, "Oh, by the way, Nell, my friends call me *Harry*."

Cornelia entered the house, drawing off her gloves, aware that her hands were shaking a little. Probably the cold, she decided, rubbing them vigorously as she turned towards the parlor. Then she changed her mind and made her way upstairs to her own bedchamber. She caught herself thinking about Stephen, about the morning he left to join Admiral Nelson on the HMS *Victory*. He'd kissed her and held her, and she remembered how she'd clung to him. Had she known then that he wouldn't return?

Was it really three years ago? Sometimes it seemed much longer, and sometimes as if it was yesterday. But Stephen had never known Susannah. Cornelia thought it likely the child had been conceived the night before Stephen's embarkation.

She went into her bedchamber and closed the door. A fire burned sullenly in the grate, and she bent to warm her hands. *Does Viscount Bonham have a wife?*

Chapter 9

"I DON'T UNDERSTAND WHAT YOU MEAN." The desiccated man behind the desk in the tall house on Gray's Inn Road tapped a paper knife on the scratched desk and fixed a cold-eyed stare on his visitor. "How was it not there, Victor? The English have not had a chance to search for it since you hid it there. We've been watching them as they've been watching us. We know the viscount has tried to get in, and once was admitted for a short time, but not long enough to search for something unless he knew where it was hidden. Besides, they are still watching the house. They wouldn't do that if they had already retrieved it."

"No, milord. Indeed," Victor said. "I do not know why it was not where I put it." He was small, thin, wiry, a man adept at inching through apertures in barely opened basement windows. He twisted his cap in his hand. The gentleman he was facing, one of Fouchet's most trusted lieutenants, was not one to understand, let alone forgive, failure. Victor had failed. The initial theft had been successful, but he had lamentably failed to bring the enterprise to its intended conclusion. His second attempt, which should have been effortlessly accomplished, had ended in a debacle of blunderbusses and chaos.

"Then think," his interlocutor invited, folding his hands over the paper knife. "It was not where you put it. Why not?"

"Someone must have moved it, milord," the unhappy Victor said, gazing at the dingy rug at his feet.

"Oh, get out. You're no further use to me." Milord waved a hand towards the door, and Victor scuttled out of the gloomy chamber, unable to believe his luck. Fouchet, the head of the French secret police, expected his lieutenants to be as ruthless in the pursuit of French interests as he was himself.

Victor's luck was short-lived. He didn't reach the street. The knife found his throat on the dark half-landing leading down to the narrow hall. He felt little, only a fleeting sense of loss before he slid to his knees against the banister.

The man in the gloomy chamber carefully set down his paper knife at the moment the agent paid for his failure. Someone in the house on Cavendish Square had found the tool. The good thing, the only good thing, was that they wouldn't know what it really was. Nighttime raids would no longer work, so he needed a new approach. A way into the house that would seem innocuous.

He reached for a small handbell on the desk and rang it, then reached sideways to fill a goblet from the flask that stood beside it. The scent of cognac perfumed the air as he swirled the contents of the glass, gazing reflectively into the amber depths.

"You rang, milord." A man slid into the room. Hatched-faced, he was thin enough to throw barely a shadow in the lamplight.

"Yes, Jean." Milord took an appreciative sip from his goblet before setting it down. "What do we know of the women who've taken up residence in Cavendish Square?"

"We have assembled a dossier, milord, but there's little of interest in it. They appear to have no secrets. If you'll pardon me . . . ?" Jean slipped from the room and was back in seconds with a sheaf of papers. "Will you read them, milord, or shall I give you the information?"

"Give it to me." Milord waved a hand towards him and picked up his goblet. He listened in silence as Jean described the quiet, uneventful histories of the three women from Ringwood in Hampshire who at present resided in Cavendish Square.

"There must be something . . . some leverage . . . someone . . ." he said as Jean fell silent. He snapped his fingers as he held out his hand for the papers. "No three people have no secrets." He scanned the top sheet. "Or no three people have no one in their family circle without secrets." He glanced over the top of the sheet. "Find me something, Jean. Something or somebody."

"Oui, milord." Jean backed towards the door.

"And quickly, Jean."

"Oui, milord." The door closed softly behind him.

The man behind the desk took another sip of cognac, then pulled the lamp closer to him and began to read the papers, a frown of concentration drawing his scant eyebrows together.

Harry strolled into Brookes's the following morning. He stopped to exchange pleasantries with a few friends, wandered around the cardrooms, and when he failed to locate his quarry, took his leave. He was taking his hat and gloves from the steward at the door when the duke of Grafton entered from the street.

Hat in hand, Harry bowed to the father of his late wife. "Your Grace."

The duke's nostrils flared. Deliberately, he turned his back.

Harry looked at the turned back for a second, then put on his hat and strode down the steps to the street. As always in the face of Grafton's cuts, his expression was unreadable. He had cultivated dispassion from the moment of his wife's death as the only way to maintain his honor. Four years ago, after the inquest into Anne's death, which had exonerated him, he had behaved as if the matter was behind him. Grafton's persistent refusal to accept the court's judgment merely made the duke look foolish, to all but the old guard who made up the duke's own family circle. For the rest it suited society to have a short memory, even when a man had lost his only child in somewhat dubious circumstances. There were too many fresh scandals to be played with. Society had lost interest, and the duke was left holding a card that had been long since played.

Except, of course, when it came to the mothers of society's eligible young maidens. The matrons were all smiles to his face but kept their daughters well behind their skirts. Viscount Bonham, wealthy widower in his prime though he was, would never again be an eligible suitor.

Not that he had interest in being so, which was fortunate, he reflected with a grim smile as he turned his steps up St. James's.

He ran his quarry to earth in White's. Nigel Dagenham was with a group of young bucks loudly disputing the results of a cockfight they had seen the previous evening.

"Bonham . . . come and take a hand." A voice from a whist table hailed him. "Alistair has deserted the four."

Harry shook hands around the table but declined the offer. He didn't want to be in the middle of a rubber when Nigel Dagenham left. He strolled around the rooms, greeting acquaintances, drinking a glass or two of claret, and waiting for the party of youngsters to break up.

Nigel was making his farewells to his companions before he became aware of Viscount Bonham. The viscount was standing casually by the sideboard, glass in hand, for the moment alone.

Nigel, on the strength of the viscount's warmth on their last meeting, went over to him. He held out his hand. "Dagenham, sir. I don't know if you remember . . ."

"Of course I do." Harry took the hand and shook it heartily. "You're making your way around, I see. Brookes's . . . White's. Watier's too?"

Nigel flushed with pleasure. "Oh, yes, indeed, Lord Bonham. Lord Coltrain . . . I'm his guest, y'know . . . put me up."

Harry smiled pleasantly even as he thought unpleasantly that Coltrain, when it came to gaming, was a notorious encourager, if not corrupter, of the young, not excluding his own son. But that family could afford it. Could young Dagenham?

"Do you leave now?" he asked with a distinct note of invitation.

Nigel couldn't help but be flattered. Established club members didn't ordinarily pay much attention to novitiates. "Well, yes, indeed, my lord."

"Then perhaps you'll give me the pleasure of your company." Harry's benign smile spilled sunshine over the youth. "I'm walking today."

"Oh, I also, Lord Bonham." Nigel followed his lordship out onto the street, grateful that he didn't have to explain that he had neither riding horse nor carriage in town. He could have brought his horse from home, but the stabling in London was prohibitive, and he could not expect his host to bear the cost.

"Just Bonham will do," Harry said casually as they set off down St. James's towards Piccadilly. "So where are you heading, Dagenham?"

Nigel had had no destination in mind, but he was so flustered by the intimacy bestowed upon him that he blurted, "Oh, to visit my cousin, Lady Dagenham. She's in Cavendish Square."

Harry nodded and cast aside his convoluted plan for oblique suggestions that would eventually have led them to that destination. Dagenham had made it so much simpler. "I believe I made her ladyship's acquaintance yesterday. She was with two delightful children."

"Oh, Stevie and Susannah," Nigel said. "Yes, they've all come to town, together with Nell's sister-in-law, Lady Farnham, and their friend, Lady Livia Lacey. They're setting up house together." Odd that such a nonpareil as Lord Bonham should be acquainted with them though. He asked rather tentatively, "How did you meet my cousin, sir?"

"Oh, by accident," Harry said carelessly. "I happened to be passing when Lady Farnham's little girl ran from the square garden into the street in front of a dray. I was able to help, and met Lady Dagenham, who was with them at the time." He shrugged. "I'll accompany you, if you have no objection. I'd like to reassure myself that the child has suffered no ill effects from her adventure."

"Oh, not Franny, sir," Nigel said with a laugh. "Nothing upsets that one. A regular scrapper, she is." Then he recollected himself. "But I'd be delighted if you'd bear me company, sir. I'm sure Ellie would be very happy to give you news of Franny."

Ellie would provide the entrée perfectly well. Harry murmured a platitude, then asked what the odds had been on the cockfight Nigel and his friends had been so heatedly discussing.

It was sufficient distraction, and they had reached Cavendish Square before Nigel had completed his bloody description of the battle.

"I own I'm interested to see the house, sir," Nigel confided as he banged the knocker. "Liv suspected that her Aunt Sophia had been a penny-pinching hermit."

Harry made no comment but took a step backwards so that he was not immediately visible to whoever opened the door. He intended to ride in on Nigel Dagenham's coattails.

As it happened, it was the rusty butler who stuck his head through the aperture and demanded, "Yes?"

Nigel, not having his companion's previous experience with the retainers, was taken aback. "Lady Dagenham?" he said haughtily. "Is she in?"

"Aye, reckon so." The man continued to peer through the crack he'd opened.

Nigel was aware of the viscount at his back and wondered what the devil the sophisticated man of the town could be making of this rough reception. He squared his shoulders and said in the same lofty tones, "Inform her, if you please, that her cousin, the Honorable Nigel Dagenham, has come to call."

The man made no response, merely shut the door.

"What the . . . ?" Nigel reached for the knocker again.

"Oh, he'll come back," Harry said cheerfully. "He lacks the niceties, I'm afraid, but he does what's necessary in his own good time and in his own inimitable style."

"Oh. I daresay you encountered him yesterday then?"

That was certainly true, and Harry agreed with a clear conscience. Despite his opinion, however, Nigel loudly plied the knocker once again.

This effort was rewarded in minutes. The door was opened wide and Aurelia stood smiling in the doorway. "Nigel, come in . . . Nell's upstairs with Stevie, he's just lost his first tooth, would you believe, and he's rather upset . . . oh . . . ." She noticed Nigel's companion for the first time. The smile that came naturally to her wavered a little with her uncertainty as to how Cornelia would view this visitation. "Viscount Bonham."

"The very same, ma'am." He doffed his hat and bowed. "I came to inquire about your daughter. I trust she suffered no ill effects from her adventure with the dray."

Aurelia, on familiar territory now, laughed. "I don't even think she knew it was there," she said with a frank smile. "But you're very kind to ask." She could not possibly invite Nigel in and leave Lord Bonham standing on the doorstep, particularly when his errand was such an impeccably courteous one. Cornelia would just have to put up with it.

"Do come in," she said, opening the door wider. "Our accommodations are a little primitive, I'm afraid, but we are already making improvements."

"Good God, Ellie," Nigel exclaimed as he stepped into the hall and took in the general air of neglect. "What was the old lady doing in a place like this?"

"We don't think she lived in much of it," Aurelia said, leading the way to the parlor. "Just in here, and her bed-chamber. Liv has that now, but it's not really much of an improvement on any of the others."

The men followed her into the parlor. Harry was familiar with the shabby room. His eyes darted towards the secretaire where he'd disturbed Lady Dagenham at her counterfeit composition. There was no sign today of assiduous correspondence.

"Please, gentlemen, sit down." Aurelia indicated the only sofa that had relatively intact springs. "May I offer you sherry or Madeira? Nell . . ." She cast a glance towards the viscount, and continued, "Lady Dagen-ham . . . found some forgotten treasures in the cellar."

"Sherry, if you please," the viscount said, and Nigel, who would have preferred a bumper of Madeira, hastily concurred.

Aurelia poured two glasses and perched carefully on a Chippendale chair with a rickety leg. "Are you enjoying being in town, Nigel?"

"Oh, famously," he said, tipping back the contents of his glass. "You wouldn't believe, Ellie, how high the fellows play."

A quick frown crossed Aurelia's eyes. She was aware of the viscount, impassive in the corner of the sofa, one leg crossed casually over the other, his glass resting on the arm, and she swallowed the anxious query that would have come naturally in the family informality of the country.

She was spared further difficulty by Cornelia's arrival. "Did I hear the door knocker?" She breezed in, a workbox under her arm, then paused as she took in the visitors. "Oh, it's you." Her eyes were on Harry, then she turned aside to set down the workbox.

"That's no way to greet a cousin, Nell," Nigel protested, assuming the ambiguous greeting was directed at him. "I told you I'd call upon you as soon as I was in town. I have to say I've a much more comfortable billet than you, coz. Regular funeral parlor this is." He held out his glass.

"We're improving on it gradually," Cornelia said, fetching the decanter from the sideboard. "And Lord Bonham, I did not expect to see you." She'd been about to add, *so soon* but checked herself. She filled Nigel's glass and offered the decanter to the viscount.

"I happened to run into your cousin at White's," Harry said, accepting a refill. He couldn't help noticing that her gaze was unreadable, her complexion as smooth as Devonshire cream. "Your cousin's steps took him here, and I had a mind to inquire of Lady Farnham as to the health of her daughter."

"How considerate," Cornelia murmured, pouring herself a glass of sherry. "Amazingly so for a man with so many demands upon his time, Lord Bonham."

"And you are aware of the many demands upon my time, Lady Dagenham?" He sounded faintly incredulous. "Such perspicacity . . . I am amazed."

Cornelia smiled. "Forgive me if I jumped to conclusions, viscount. I assumed that a gentleman in your position would have much to occupy you . . . your clubs, balls, rout parties, racing . . ." Her shoulders lifted in a graceful shrug. "I confess I know little of such matters, sir. As I said yesterday, I am a country mouse."

Aurelia stifled a choke. Nigel stared in open astonishment at his cousin. Viscount Bonham merely raised his sherry glass in the semblance of a toast, and said, "Indeed, ma'am. And as I recall we disposed of that particular description yesterday also."

Cornelia sipped her sherry. Her skin was tingling. She thought she could actually feel the sparkle in her eyes, the glow in her skin as a real sensation. Even her scalp was reacting to whatever excitement was being generated. She had to force herself to remember that Nigel and Aurelia were in the room.

"Did Ellie tell you, Nigel, that Stevie lost his first tooth this morning?" she asked, aware of the absurdity of the non sequitur but unable to think of any other way to strip the atmosphere of its charge. A charge she was certain Nigel and Ellie couldn't miss, let alone the viscount.

"Uh . . . yes," Nigel said. "Exciting for him, I expect."

"No, terrifying, actually," Cornelia corrected. "He was convinced for a while that he was losing parts of himself and that eventually he would disappear altogether."

"I remember losing *my* first tooth," Harry stated, wondering as he said it where the memory had come from, and why now. "I felt the same way. I'd been so proud of having it, then it fell out." He laughed softly. "It took a deal of persuasion to convince me that the little white bump in my gum was going to replace it, and I'd be as good as new."

Cornelia glanced across at him as she set down her workbox. That had been a curious intimacy. One that she found endearing, against her better judgment. He was playing some kind of game. Did he still harbor hopes of buying the house, wearing them down by a refusal to accept Liv's decision? This wasn't purely a social call, she was convinced of it.

She remembered that Letitia had said that the viscount had a house on Mount Street. No need to let on that she knew that already, and it would give her an opening. "So, do you have a house in town, Lord Bonham?" she said. "I wonder, since you appear so anxious to possess this one. Perhaps you only have lodgings?" Her tone was casual, her smile showing only a mild curiosity.

"Indeed, ma'am, I have a house on Mount Street," he responded. "I am hoping to purchase a house on a quiet square for my late sister's family. I believe children need space and a garden. My own house is a bachelor establishment, you understand, but I wish to keep the children under my eye. This house and its situation seemed ideal." He gave a careless shrug.

"Oh, how very sad," Aurelia said with ready sympathy. "How many children?"

"Five," he said truthfully enough. Annabel most certainly had five children, and was probably expecting a sixth by now. She was a formidable breeder, a fact that deeply gratified her expansive, genial country squire of a spouse. He became aware of Cornelia's sharply focused gaze and wondered for an instant if she'd somehow detected the one duplicitous word in his explanation.

"Yes, how very sad," Cornelia concurred. "Was she a younger sister?"

He allowed a somber nod to answer the question. Annabel was a good enough sport to enter into the spirit of this lie, but the time had come to close the subject.

"There must be other more suitable properties in town, sir," Cornelia said, still regarding him closely. "In fact this house isn't really in a fit condition for children."

"Indeed," Aurelia said, "the nursery quarters leave much to be desired. Linton hasn't stopped complaining since we arrived."

"Best not let the earl hear that," Nigel put in with a chuckle. "When he discovered you'd all left against his orders, I thought he'd have an apoplexy. He was going to send an armed brigade after you." He got up to refill his glass.

Cornelia shot him a restraining look. She didn't want private matters discussed in front of Lord Bonham. Nigel, however, interpreted the look as applying to his third glass of sherry.

"Oh, don't look so disapproving, coz," he said, waving his glass at her. "I've seen fellows drink a bottle of claret before breakfast."

"I hope they feel the better for it," Cornelia responded. She had no interest in policing her cousin, but at least his assumption had changed the topic.

"So where's Liv?" Nigel asked, as if suddenly aware of the absence of one of the women.

"She's gone to buy a dog," Cornelia informed him succinctly.

"Buy a dog?" Nigel stared at her. "Liv doesn't care for dogs. They scare her. She won't go near the stables when my father's pointers are out."

"I believe she's gone to buy a dog that won't scare her," Aurelia said, laughing as she and Cornelia exchanged glances.

"Yes, but we have to hope it will scare others," Cornelia said, her lip quivering.

Harry sipped his sherry, his relaxed posture and easy smile concealing his intense interest in the turn the conversation had taken.

"Why?" Nigel demanded. "I'd have thought you'd

enough on your hands with this tumbledown mausoleum without livestock."

"Unfortunately, it seems a necessary precaution," Cornelia informed him. "We have some nocturnal visitations. We don't know whether they're human or mere spirits, but they cause Morecombe to discharge his blunderbuss, a fearsome weapon with an even more fearsome sound. It scares the children, you see. And that upsets Linton." She smiled serenely. "A dog seems the lesser of all evils."

"Lord," Nigel said. "Who'd want to break in here? There's nothing to steal."

"You wouldn't think so, would you," Aurelia agreed. "But maybe there's something we haven't found."

"A treasure trove?" Nigel's gray eyes glittered with enthusiasm. "A cache of gems, perhaps. D'you think the old lady hid treasure . . . in the attic . . . or the cellar? Let's take a look." He jumped to his feet. "Come on, a treasure hunt."

"Nigel, you really are just a boy at times," Cornelia said, laughing as she waved him down again. "I've been down in the cellar, and the only treasure I found there was what you're drinking. But Morecombe and the twins don't have any idea about anything being hidden, and believe me, they would know."

"Perhaps they want it for themselves?" Nigel suggested, unwilling to give up the prospect of hidden treasure.

Aurelia shook her head firmly. "No, they're utterly

and absolutely loyal to Aunt Sophia. They'd take nothing that belonged to her that she hadn't gifted to them."

"I noticed a cat on the area steps," Harry said, still smiling his easy smile. "Perhaps he, or is it she, is responsible for the bumps and bangs?"

"She's called Puss," Cornelia told him as she reached behind her for her workbox. "Not very original, I grant you. But she's the reason Morecombe insisted on leaving the kitchen window open at night. However, that doesn't happen anymore." She raised the lid and trawled through the silks looking for a particular shade of pink to trim one of Susannah's bonnets.

"Well, I'm sure you're wise to take precautions," Harry said, getting to his feet. "I must take my leave, ma'am . . . Lady Farnham. I'm so glad the child has no nightmares about drays and cart horses." He bowed over Aurelia's hand before turning to Cornelia.

She closed the lid of the workbox as she rose to give him her hand. "Good morning, Lord Bonham."

"Lady Dagenham." He raised her hand to his lips. But instead of his lips merely brushing the air over her knuckles he kissed her hand firmly, his long fingers warm and tight around her own, in a gesture that was shockingly intimate between mere acquaintances.

Aurelia's eyes widened, then she moved towards the door with a distant smile that implied she had seen nothing out of the ordinary. Nigel, on the other hand, stared in open amazement, until Aurelia, as she passed him, knocked him with her elbow, and he recollected himself.

Cornelia withdrew her hand, and said coolly, "I wish you success in your house hunting, sir."

He bowed again and took up his hat, gloves, and cane from the gatelegged table where he'd laid them on entering the parlor. There was a faintly mocking gleam in his green eyes as he smiled at her. But the mockery was directed at himself as much as at Cornelia. Something was going on between them that he didn't understand enough to acknowledge any more than she did.

"Dagenham, do you accompany me?" he inquired pleasantly as he turned to the door. "Or shall I leave you ensconced in the bosom of your family?"

Nigel was torn. The prospect of walking through the streets in the viscount's company was more than appealing, and it would do him no end of good socially, but he was also inclined to stay for a lively chat with his cousins.

As he hesitated, the viscount said with a light laugh, "Ah, don't fear, Dagenham. I shan't take offense. Any man worth his salt would prefer the company of your cousins." He nodded his farewells and left the parlor.

"I'll see you out, Lord Bonham." Cornelia spoke softly behind him as she stepped into the hall, closing the parlor door gently. "I doubt Morecombe is around to act as doorman." She moved past him to the front door and reached for the bolt. She was intensely aware of him standing behind her, and as she wrestled with the heavy, unoiled bolt he reached around her and laid his hands over hers to pull back the bolt.

It creaked and came loose. He let his hands fall, and Cornelia pulled open the door, letting cold sunlight into the dingy hall. "What's going on here?" she asked, facing him. "Do you want something from me, Lord Bonham?"

He laughed. "Oh, what a fearsomely direct creature you are. Doesn't it occur to you that quite simply I find you a most attractive woman?" He took both her hands again, holding them lightly.

"I've never been susceptible to flattery or empty compliments, sir," she responded.

His eyes darkened as his fingers closed more tightly over hers. "What makes you think they're either, Nell? Believe me, I'm not in the habit of indulging in such meaningless flippancies myself."

She did believe him. This was not a man to waste his time or energy on pointless pursuits. "Are you trying to get your own back for that trick I played on you?" It was all she could think of.

He shook his head. "We've had done with that, Nell, and you know it." He laughed again, a warm laugh strangely at odds with his next words. "Although, I have to say that if I *were* trying to get my own back, you'd be under no illusions as to what was happening."

He took a step back, holding her at arm's length as he smiled at her, then he released her hands and, as he'd done before, lightly brushed her mouth with his fingertip. "No illusions there either," he said softly. He raised a hand in farewell and strolled casually down the steps to the street.

Cornelia stepped back into the cascade of dust motes caught in the ray of sunlight from the open door. She listened as the sound of his steps receded, then she closed the door slowly.

Harry walked briskly, swinging his cane. He couldn't be sure. But he had not mistaken the wink of silver in Cornelia's workbox as she'd closed the lid. It could have come from anything. A pincushion, a silver button that needed sewing onto some garment. Or it could have been a thimble. *His* thimble. Of course she'd have had one already, but supposing Cornelia had found *his* thimble.

He had started his pursuit of Viscountess Dagenham as a means to gain access to the house. Somehow the pursuit itself had taken on a life of its own that had little to do with its original purpose. But that purpose was still paramount, and if what he sought was in her workbox, then the two strands could come together nicely. The more intimate he became with the lady, the closer he would get to her workbox.

"Cornelia, where are you . . . oh, there you are." Aurelia popped her head around the parlor door. "Why are you standing in the hall?"

"No reason," Cornelia said rather slowly as if she wasn't entirely sure whether there was or there wasn't.

Aurelia looked at her a little strangely. "Well, come back to the parlor. Nigel's telling me what happened when the earl found out we'd gone."

That brought Cornelia out of her reverie. "I'm not sure I want to know," she said, as they returned to the parlor. "He hasn't even written to us."

"Oh, he will," Nigel said from the sideboard, where he was refilling his glass. "He was consulting with his lawyers when I left."

Cornelia frowned. "Why? We left quite legitimately. What have lawyers to do with it?"

"I think he was hoping to find some legal reason to summon you back," Nigel stated. "The old man don't care to be defied, you know, coz."

Cornelia shook her head impatiently as she sat down and opened her workbox. "I know that, but he can't do a thing. He'll calm down once he realizes it's truly a fait accompli." She slipped the thimble on her finger and shook out the stocking she was darning. "I think this stocking is past help."

"The old man don't give up easily, Nell." Nigel laid a finger against the side of his nose, squinting at her in an attempt to look wise.

"Nigel, you're under the hatches already, and it's not yet noon," Aurelia accused, reaching to take the glass from him. "Come now, you've had enough."

Nigel straightened the lapels of his wasp-waisted crimson-and-silver coat. "Nonsense, m'dear. I'm more than capable of holding my drink."

"You'll need to be, love, if you're going to play as high as you say you are," Cornelia said, forgetting her own troublesome thoughts in the realization that her young cousin was as green as a new-chopped oak when it came to life on the town. She didn't want to insult his dignity by appearing in the least maternal, but she couldn't help feeling some responsibility for him.

"You have a handsome allowance, Nigel." Aurelia said as she picked up her tambour frame and frowned down at the intricate design.

Nigel coughed into his fist. "Oh, well enough," he said carelessly. "And there's many ways a fellow can improve his situation."

"Newmarket?" Cornelia inquired, without looking up from her darning.

Nigel frowned and stood up abruptly. "The horses are all well and good, coz, but skill at the tables is what counts." He swept up his hat. "Must be going now. Let me know if you find Aunt Sophia's treasure."

"Come again soon, Nigel." Aurelia went over to kiss him warmly.

"Yes, if you need a little hearth and home, we're here," Cornelia said, embracing him in turn.

"Oh, as to that, coz, I doubt I'll be looking for slippers by the fire," he said, drawing on his gloves. "But I'll come by and visit again . . . see how you're getting along," he added kindly. "And if you've a mind to enter society, you'll need to do something about those clothes. Regular dowds you look, if you don't mind my saying so."

"Not at all," Cornelia said cordially. "And we'll look forward to seeing you, when you think a moment spent with your dowdy relatives won't damage your reputation irreparably. I'll see you out." She escorted him to the front door and wrestled once more with the bolt. On this occasion without assistance.

As her cousin stepped out onto the top step, she took one of his hands between both of hers and squeezed it lightly. "Do have a care, Nigel."

"You worry too much, coz. I'm up to snuff, believe me."

I'm sure you think you are. But Cornelia left that unsaid. He would make his own mistakes and with luck learn from them. She said only, "Come and see us again, if you can tear yourself away from your grand friends."

Nigel grinned. "Lucky thing that, Franny running into the road in front of a dray. Don't think Bonham would've troubled to make my acquaintance otherwise." He gave a sagacious nod, raised a hand in a wave, and walked down the street.

Yes, lucky that, Cornelia reflected with a shake of her head. She was about to go back inside when she caught sight of Livia turning the corner onto the square.

Livia appeared to be under some impulsion. She was almost running, the feather in her hat lying flat under the wind, her pelisse snapping at her ankles.

Cornelia shaded her eyes, trying to get a closer look. When she saw what was happening she went into a peal of laughter. "Ellie . . . Ellie, come out here." She called over her shoulder into the hall.

"What is it?" Aurelia came hurrying across the hall to stand beside Cornelia. She shivered, drawing her shawl tightly around her against the wind. "What . . . Oh . . . dear Lord, what has she got?"

The two of them ran down to the street as Livia came tumbling towards them tugged by two minute scraps of pink-tinged fur. Two pairs of black eyes gleamed beneath thick fringes, two button black noses glistened in the cold air.

"Stop me," Livia cried from the end of double leash. "Or stop them . . . they won't slow down."

Aurelia and Cornelia stepped into the path of the hurtling pink scraps as Livia hauled back on the leashes. The party of three came to a breathless, panting stop.

Cornelia looked down at the pavement. "Liv, *what* are these?" It was an incredulous inquiry.

"Dogs," Livia said, a little doubtfully, accepting that the description might seem rather strange to her friends, who had only ever dealt with working farm dogs. "The mews Morecombe sent me to had a litter . . . or rather the lady's Lakeland terrier had had a litter, and she didn't want them, and so I . . ." She let the rest of the sentence trail off.

The two pink scraps began to bark. Well, bark was an exaggeration, Cornelia thought. A high-pitched yap was certainly more to the point.

"They make a noise," Livia pointed out.

"Yes," Aurelia agreed faintly, covering her ears.

"And they don't scare me," Livia declared as if delivering the coup de grâce.

"They scare me," Cornelia said. "I don't even know what they are. Certainly not dogs. And what the devil is Puss going to make of them? They're half her size. She'll eat them for breakfast."

"They're perfect guard dogs," Livia said stoutly, dragging the animals after her up the steps into the house.

"Perhaps she's right," Cornelia said with a grin, watching their uneven progress. "I suspect that any ruffian intent on thievery or vandalism will burst into laughter at first sound and sight of those ridiculous creatures and waken the entire household."

"Anything, my dear, anything will be better than Morecombe's blunderbuss," Aurelia said with feeling.

"How right you are." Cornelia linked arms with her sister-in-law, and they followed the sounds of yapping into the house.

Chapter 10

CORNELIA EDGED AROUND A STEPLADDER in the middle of the hall. The man on top teetered precariously as he took a soapy cloth to the crystal facets of the chandelier. "Watch yer step, m'lady," he called down. "'Tis the devil's own job this, beggin' yer pardon. Getting' a right crick in my neck."

Cornelia moved sideways and squinted up at him. "I can imagine." He was a small, agile-looking man who reminded her of a jockey and she didn't think she'd seen him around the house before. "It's really making a difference though," she said. The diamond drops were glistening in the sunlight that now came through the freshly washed long windows on either side of the front door.

"I don't think I know your name," she queried. "Have you been here before?"

"Started yesterday, m'lady," he responded. "Lester's the name, ma'am."

"Ah, well you're doing a wonderful job, Lester." She smiled and stepped away from the ladder.

The smell of fresh paint and beeswax filled the air as a small army of workmen plied brushes to the decorative moldings of the hall and two scullery maids on hands and knees rubbed wax into the parquet.

Cornelia paused at the open door to the salon, a scene of similar bustle, this time supervised by a dour Morecombe, who after initial disapproval of this refurbishment had eventually decided to run the proceedings. One of the twins, our Ada, Cornelia guessed, hurried past her with her arms full of heavy velvet curtains while behind her Mavis was demonstrating the art of carpet beating to a pale waif, who looked to Cornelia to be little more than twelve. Where the apparently reclusive Morecombe had found all these hands was a mystery, but not one to be probed. The more hands, the sooner the job would be finished and they could open their doors to visitors. Another week should do it, she reckoned.

Livia emerged from the parlor, the two pink dogs skittering on the waxed parquet as they bounded ahead of her. "I have to do something with them, Nell," Livia said, flinging up her hands in despair. "They're into everything, and they're getting under everyone's feet. I can't concentrate on my accounts."

Cornelia regarded the creatures, grandly christened Tristan and Isolde, with a degree of exasperated amusement. Much to her surprise she found them rather endearing, although they were undeniably a nuisance, mostly because of their size, which enabled them to get into any nook or cranny they wished. They could also disappear into the shadowy reaches of the house without anyone being any the wiser. Proper dogs knew their place in the scheme of things; these absurd little animals had absolutely no idea that they had a place. The world was their oyster.

"I'll take them for a walk," she offered. "I could do with some fresh air myself, the smell of paint gives me a headache."

"I own I'd be glad to see the back of them for a while," Livia said with a sigh. "They don't scare me, but they're still dogs, and they're all over the place."

Cornelia laughed. "I'll fetch my pelisse." She hurried to the stairs, dodging mops and buckets. The dogs had not had to prove themselves as guards since their arrival a week earlier. For some reason the nocturnal alarums had ceased. As had visits by Viscount Bonham.

She paused in front of her dresser mirror to tie the ribbons of her gypsy bonnet. Obviously his protestations about furthering their acquaintance had been mere flummery. For which she was not at all sorry. She had enough to do with the house and the children, without worrying about the impertinent Viscount Bonham's next move.

She went back to the hall where Livia waited with the dogs, who were straining at their leashes, yapping eagerly at the front door. "Come on then, you noisy pair,"

Cornelia said, taking their leads. "Is there anything you need, Liv?"

"Not unless you're going past Hatchard's. I'd like a copy of *The Lay of the Last Minstrel*. I left mine at home, and I hadn't finished it."

"I'm sure my steps can take me to Piccadilly," Cornelia said cheerfully. "Although whether Hatchard's allows dogs inside, I don't know." She left with a farewell wave and took a deep revivifying breath of the cold fresh air in Cavendish Square as the ache behind her temples receded.

She set off following the prancing dogs, who seemed to have their own direction in mind, but at the end of the square she hauled them around towards Hanover Square and Piccadilly. A brisk ten-minute walk brought her to Piccadilly, and she paused for a moment to enjoy the bustle, feeling her spirits lift at the sense of being part of this hectic scene. There was more activity going on in this stretch of street than she saw in ten years in sleepy Ringwood. Carriages and street vendors jostled for space, footmen carrying bandboxes were walking behind ladies dressed with such elegance that Cornelia felt impossibly dowdy.

The noise and the crowd had a salutary effect on Tristan and Isolde, who shrank back against her skirts at the seemingly endless parade of booted feet at eye level. She gave an encouraging tug on their leashes as she set off again towards the bow windows of Hatchard's displaying a mouthwatering display of publications.

Ringwood was seriously deficient in bookshops, she reflected as she pushed open the door. In fact not even the busy town of Southampton boasted a respectable bookstore or lending library. Here there was treasure indeed. The dogs made it impossible to stay long, however, and she quickly made her purchase and went back into the thronged street, determined to return for an extended period without the dogs as soon as possible.

Thin sunlight shone from a clear blue sky, and although the air was cold, it was invigorating. City smells of horseflesh, leather, steaming piles of manure were overlaid by perfume wafting from the stylish people hurrying around her, and she was reluctant to return too quickly to the paint-laden atmosphere of Cavendish Square. She set off rather aimlessly, letting the dogs set the pace, and soon found herself in Grosvenor Square. She strolled down South Audley Street and stopped on the corner of Mount Street.

Now how had she arrived here? All unwitting? Or had her unconscious mind directed her feet to this corner? Viscount Bonham lived on Mount Street. She'd barely glanced at his visiting card and couldn't remember the number of his house. She hesitated, the last thing she wanted was to be discovered by the viscount walking down his street, but curiosity, aided by the tugging of the dogs, got the better of her, and she strolled casually along the pavement, scanning the tall gracious houses with their white-honed steps bracketed with intricately decorated iron railings leading up to double front doors.

A tilbury bowled around the far corner, the horse high-stepping between the traces, and the dogs leaped forward, barking excitedly. Cornelia tripped against a raised curbstone and grabbed a railing to save herself from falling to her knees, just managing to hang on to the dogs' leads. She yanked the dogs back with a muttered curse, then realized as she took a step forward that the heel on one of her high-buttoned boots had broken.

She grabbed the railing again to balance herself. How on earth was she to hobble back to Cavendish Square with a broken heel?

Leaning against the railing, she lifted her foot and examined the damage. The heel hung by a thread of leather, she'd have to limp along like Pegleg Pete.

"Hell and the devil!" She swore rather less softly this time and ripped the useless heel from the sole of the boot.

"Why, Lady Dagenham, I can't believe my good fortune. Are you come to call upon me?" She recognized the light voice immediately and felt her color rise at the familiar tinge of mockery lurking behind the words. Of all the pieces of ill luck. Was she actually leaning against the viscount's own railings?

"Viscount Bonham," she said stiffly, putting her foot to the ground, then realizing how absurd she must look with one leg shorter than the other. "My heel broke," she said in somewhat unnecessary explanation, finally raising her eyes to face him.

"So I see," he said. His smile seemed friendly enough, but Cornelia found herself looking suspiciously for a sardonic glint in the green eyes. "How very unfortunate." He glanced around rather pointedly. "I assume your escort has gone for a hackney."

"I don't have an escort," she said, hearing the slight defensive note in her voice. "I was merely walking the dogs."

"Ah." His mouth curved in a slightly quizzical smile. He was dressed for riding in a caped greatcoat and top boots, his beaver hat in one hand, his whip in the other. She noticed for the first time how the sun brought out chestnut highlights in his brown hair. His eyebrows rose incredulously as he saw Tristan and Isolde. "Those are dogs?"

"A good question," she replied with a snap. "And if it hadn't been for them, I wouldn't be in this predicament now."

"An awkward one, I grant you," he said, his mouth still curved. He tapped his boot with the tip of his whip. "We must do something about it. You'd better come inside while I send for my carriage, and I'll convey you home."

"There's no need, thank you," she responded. She had no desire to be beholden to Lord Bonham.

"My dear girl, you cannot possibly stagger all the way back to Cavendish Square with only one shoe," he pointed out.

"Why must you use that patronizing tone?" she demanded crossly. "I realize I'm at a disadvantage, but it's most unchivalrous of you to exploit it."

"Forgive me," he said with a bow, and now his eyes were full of laughter. "I meant only to be helpful. Will you do me the honor of entering my house, ma'am, and if you'd prefer, I'll send a footman to summon a hackney." He offered his arm.

Cornelia glanced up the street hoping to see a fortuitous hackney coming around the far corner. As ill luck would have it, the street was deserted. He was right, she couldn't stand here on one foot waiting for salvation.

"Thank you, Lord Bonham." She ignored his proffered arm, however, instead hauled on the dogs' leads as she limped up the steps on her broken boot.

The front door opened as she reached the top step. Harry greeted his butler as he eased Cornelia into the hall with a hand under her elbow. "Ah, Hector, Lady Dagenham has had the misfortune to break her bootheel. See if Eric can fix it temporarily and take these creatures somewhere." He gestured vaguely towards the dogs.

Hector stared at them for an instant then recollected himself. "At once, my lord." He snapped his fingers at a hovering footman. "Take these animals to the scullery, Fred."

Cornelia relinquished the leads with relief. She handed over her boot and its separated heel to the butler, who received both with an impassive bow.

"And bring coffee in the salon," the viscount instructed over his shoulder as he again took his guest's elbow and directed her hobbling step towards the room in question.

She looked around with covert interest. Looking, she realized, for any signs of a female presence. She had had an instinctive conviction that Lord Bonham was a bachelor. Everything about his behavior indicated it, but an appropriate opportunity to confirm that impression had never arisen. However, there were no female touches in the room. It was a gracious apartment, the walls hung with French paper, the Aubusson carpet glowing with rich hues, the furniture all in the first style of elegance. But no sign of a workbox, a tambour frame, or even a vase of flowers. The pictures were all impersonal, no portraits, no intimate scenes.

"Allow me to take your pelisse." His lordship reached with unwarranted familiarity over her shoulders to unfasten the top button. Definitely no wife on the scene, Cornelia decided.

She twisted her body sideways. "Thank you, but I'll keep it on."

"As you please. But at least take off your bonnet." His lordship directed her towards a scroll-ended sofa offering solicitously, "Would you like coffee, or perhaps a glass of sherry after your ordeal?"

Cornelia sat down and arranged herself as gracefully as she could with her one shoe. She untied the ribbons of her bonnet and set the hat on the seat beside her. "A broken heel is hardly an ordeal, Lord Bonham. And coffee would be lovely, thank you." She had recovered her composure now and with it her mettle. Her host was playing his usual game again and she was more than ready to enter the lists. She removed her gloves finger by finger, set them beside her hat, and folded her hands in her lap, regarding him in cool silence.

Harry returned her regard in the same silence. He had kept away from Cavendish Square in the last few days, while Lester established a foothold there and did some discreet reconnaissance. The opportunity for Lester to join the workforce putting the house in order had been heaven-sent. There was now always the possibility that, with the run of the house, he would find a way to retrieve the thimble with no one any the wiser.

But if that didn't happen, then Harry himself would have to step into his own role in the search and retrieval. For that he needed an intimate connection with Cornelia Dagenham. He was sure he had already managed to arouse the lady's interest, and a strategic absence could only sharpen it. Her sudden appearance on his doorstep seemed to prove him right, unless it was purely fortuitous, but that seemed like too much of a coincidence.

He caught himself reflecting that whatever the reason for her appearance, it pleased him deeply, and his pleasure had little to do with the prospect of retrieving the thimble. Everything about her fascinated him. She was a challenge, serene, composed, despite her present disadvantage, and radiating a most powerful sensuality. A sensuality all the more arousing because he wasn't convinced she was aware of it.

What kind of marriage had she had? One that had unlocked the door to that sensuality, or merely half turned the key?

His body stirred at a reverie that had become uncomfortably lustful and he welcomed the diversion as a footman entered with coffee. The silence continued until the coffee had been poured, dainty Sèvres cups passed around, and the servant had left the salon.

Harry, a slight frown in his eye, turned the conversation in a direction that would banish lustful thoughts. "Country ways don't always go down too well in town," he said abruptly.

"I beg your pardon?" She sipped her coffee, her spine prickling at the implication of criticism.

He pursed his lips. "Nell, ladies do not roam the streets without any form of escort."

She decided to ignore the familiarity, "Nonsense. I'm a widow way past the age of discretion. My reputation is in no danger, I assure you."

"Well, now there you're wrong," he said, putting down his cup. "In this town, reputation is all and everything, and having it compromised is a very uncomfortable matter."

She looked at him sharply, alerted by something in his voice. Her indignation faded. "You sound as if you know something about that."

He turned away, but not before she'd caught the dark

shadow that crossed his eyes. He stood, hands behind his back, gazing out of one of the long windows overlooking the street. His shoulders moved in the semblance of a shrug, and his tone was careless as he said, "It may be unjust, but it's a much more serious matter for women."

Cornelia frowned. His tone told her to drop the subject, but a perverse instinct pushed her to probe further. She put her cup aside and reached down to unfasten her remaining boot. She was tired of feeling unbalanced, and it also gave her the excuse not to look at him as she said, "Maybe so. But I get the feeling you've been touched by the injustice yourself. Some member of your family perhaps?"

Anne's body at the foot of the stairs, limbs asprawl, the strange angle of her neck.

"Not at all," he stated with sudden brusqueness. "I was merely issuing a friendly word to the wise." He spun around from the window and went to the sideboard, where he poured himself a glass of sherry. "If you and your friends intend to enter society, then roaming the streets with only a pair of imitation dogs as escort will do you no good."

Cornelia stretched her stockinged feet thoughtfully, flexing her toes. "I'm grateful for the advice." Her smile was dulcet but didn't deceive him for a moment. "It's kind of you to have such a care for my reputation, even though such care loses a little of its sincerity in present circumstances. I am, when all's said and done, alone

with an unmarried man in his house at his invitation."
She waited to see if he would correct her statement, but
he didn't.

He caught himself gazing at her feet. They were
very long, with very high arches, and there was something undeniably erotic about them. His eyes traveled
upwards. The erect posture, straight back, slim shoulders, the long neck. The direct challenge in the blue
eyes. She was playing with fire and enjoying every
minute of it.

"You are a very dangerous woman, Lady Dagenham," he said softly.

The air crackled and it wasn't just the sudden hiss and
spit of a log in the grate. He stepped towards her, reaching for her hands, drawing her to her feet. Even when
she was shoeless, her eyes were almost on a level with his
own. "You give no quarter, do you?" he murmured, running the palm of his hand against her cheek.

Cornelia wanted to move but couldn't. The pulse in
her throat was beating so fast she could barely swallow,
and her cheek was alive beneath the smooth palm. She
had never considered herself in the least dangerous, in
the least ruthless, and yet as he spoke the words she
knew they were true. Something inside her was coming
to life beneath the glint of the green eyes, the light caress
of his hands, the low sensuality of his voice. The woman
she believed she was was not all that she was. The widow,
the respectable mother of two, was also capable of seduction.

And with that conviction came its pair. *This man was dangerous, the most dangerous man she had ever encountered, but she could meet and match him.*

A heady sense of excitement flooded her, jolting the pit of her belly, tightening her loins. When he kissed her, she felt only jubilation, a deep and mysterious sense of triumph. His lips were hard against her mouth, his tongue insistent, his hands palming her face. She opened her mouth for his tongue and welcomed the press of his loins against hers, the hard nudge of his penis and her own moist warmth.

And then reality broke into the tight dark world of pure sensation. She pulled free of his hold at the same moment as he lifted his mouth from hers. They both stepped back. Cornelia averted her head, her fingers inadvertently brushing her mouth.

"So much for reputation," she murmured.

"So much for country mice," he returned with a smile. He touched her shoulder. "Nell?"

She turned back to him, her gaze both straightforward and a little bemused. "I don't know what's happening? I . . . I haven't felt anything like this since Stephen . . ." She looked away again, trying to marshal her thoughts and the words to go with them.

"Your husband?"

"Yes." Her shoulders lifted a little as she sighed. "You've never been married, I take it."

"I *was* married," he said evenly. "She died."

"Ah." She turned back to him. "I'm sorry."

He opened his hands in a gesture of resignation. "It was four years ago. An accident."

"Did you love her?" For some reason the answer mattered.

He didn't reply immediately, then said without expression, "I believed I did." He moved towards her again, taking her hands once more. "Nell, that's in the past. This is the present. From the first moment I met you I've been drawn to you. Have you not felt it too?" He lifted her hands to his mouth, brushing her knuckles with his lips.

"No," Cornelia stated with absolute truth, although she didn't move her hands. "I've disliked you immensely from the moment I laid eyes on you. I thought you felt the same way about me."

He laughed and released her hands. "Your honesty is delightful . . . but tell me now, in truth, do you still dislike me?" He walked to the sideboard and poured her a glass of sherry, refilling his own at the same time.

"In truth . . ." She took the glass from him. "In truth, no." She took a long sip, and said with irritation, "Oh, this is so inconvenient."

"Why?"

"I don't have time for dalliance." Cornelia sipped her sherry. "Liv is the one looking for a husband, not me. And if reputations are so vital in this town, then indulging in a liaison is hardly sensible." Her gaze over the lip of the glass was fierce, but the residue of the exultant triumph of that kiss was as legible as the most impeccable script.

"It could be managed," Harry said. "It *is* managed every hour of every day and night in the five square miles of this town inhabited by the upper ten thousand."

Cornelia raised her eyebrows. "Are you proposing an arrangement, sir? I'm flattered, I assure you, but I fear I would be far too expensive and would make a most unrestful mistress." She tapped her forefinger thoughtfully against her lips. "I would require a house, of course, a carriage, box at the opera—"

"Oh, have done, Nell," he said sharply. "I'm in no mood to jest about this." He came towards her, his green eyes narrowed. "We'll not talk of it further now, but I ask that you think about it." He laid a finger on her lips, pressing lightly. "Come now, we're both adults, we know the world. There's no reason why two people who are so attracted to each other should not take their discreet pleasure where they find it. As I said, it's hardly uncommon."

Cornelia wasn't sure whether to laugh or cry foul. She had never received an indecent proposal before, and against all her instincts, she found this one both exciting and complimentary. Marriage was about so much more than passion that passion itself tended to get lost in the tendrils of domesticity. A relationship based on pure lust . . .

Harry was right that plenty of folk had them in the most august echelons of society. The liaisons of the royal princes, and even, it was rumored rather less scandalously, their sisters, were as near public knowledge as if they'd been broadcast in the broadsheets. They certainly provided fodder for the satirists at *Punch*.

Then she remembered the earl of Markby. And excitement drained away.

Her face closed, and her voice was expressionless as she said, "My situation is a little different from most, sir." She bent to pick up her discarded boot. "I need to go back to Cavendish Square." She raised the boot in an eloquent gesture.

Harry had always been blessed with the knowledge of when to step back. He had no idea what had wiped the last traces of arousal from her countenance, but it was time to leave well enough alone. He inclined his head and reached for the bell. Hector appeared almost immediately.

"Send to the mews for the curricle, Hector. I am escorting Lady Dagenham home."

Hector said solemnly, "Yes, m'lord, right away. Eric was able to perform a temporary repair on her ladyship's boot. I'll fetch it directly." He turned back to the door, pausing with his hand on the latch to inquire, "Should I have the dogs installed in the curricle, my lady?"

"If you would be so kind, Hector," Cornelia said. "Under the seat for preference."

The tiniest curve of the lip gave Hector away. "I will endeavor to arrange them so that they won't be a nuisance, ma'am."

"I doubt you'll succeed, Hector," she responded.

"No, my lady." He slid from the room.

Cornelia sat down to put on her boot. She was not prepared for assistance, but at the same time not surprised when Harry knelt and took the boot from her. He slid it onto her foot, molding the soft leather over her ankles, and fastened the tiny buttons and laces with a dexterity that astonished her. Men didn't usually have such fine hands. Unless they made jewelry, or were engravers. She'd have expected Viscount Bonham to have light hands with a horse's mouth, and a keen eye and swift move with a fencing sword or a hunting pistol, but his long, slender fingers deftly twisted loops around buttons with all the delicacy of an artist.

"There." He sat back on his heels and his hands remained on her ankle, massaging the sharp bone. "Now all we need is the other one . . . Ah, Hector, exactly on cue." He held out his hand for the boot that the butler brought over to him.

Cornelia was past caring what the butler thought about anything. She submitted her foot to another round of the viscount's intimate attention, then firmly stood up, testing her weight on the repaired boot. "Thank you, Hector, I'm most grateful. This will take me home."

"The curricle is at the door, my lord." Hector opened the door onto the hall and moved in stately fashion to the front door. "The dogs are installed."

"You are very kind." Cornelia gave him a warm farewell smile, aware of a slight wobble in the repaired boot as she walked down the steps to the street, where the curricle awaited at the curb, a pair of handsome grays in the traces, a sharp-faced groom holding the reins. Tristan and Isolde had been tethered firmly on short leads to the driver's seat.

Cornelia closed her eyes at the sharp yapping welcome as Harry handed her up.

"I trust they won't do that all the way to Cavendish Square," he commented, taking his own place. "It'll spook my horses."

"I'll keep them quiet." Cornelia bent and scooped the two onto her lap, settling them comfortably under each arm. It seemed to calm them, and they gazed attentively and with a distinct air of superiority from beneath thick fringes at the scene on the street below them.

"Why isn't my reputation damaged by being driven through the streets beside a man in his curricle?" Cornelia inquired sweetly. She needed to return their relationship to its previous footing. She knew where she was in this lightly combative banter.

"Don't be disingenuous. You know perfectly well," Harry replied. "It's too public to be scandalous. Now, if we were in a closed carriage, creeping around in the dark, there might be cause for concern . . . Eric, keep your eyes and your ears on the road."

"Yes, m'lord," the groom said stolidly from his perch at the back of the carriage. He was finding the conversation most interesting, but unfortunately his master and the lady spent the rest of the journey in silence.

Harry drew up outside the house on Cavendish Square and looked with interest at the open front door, the loaded drays lining the pavement in front, the bustle of workmen moving in and out with ladders, buckets of paint, lengths of wood. "You've been busy," he observed.

"Very," Cornelia agreed, bending to unfasten the dogs' leads. "In a few days we should be finished."

"Quite an undertaking, putting that house in order," he said, handing the reins to Eric, who had jumped down and was holding the horses' heads.

Cornelia didn't tell him that only a fraction of the mansion was being refurbished, or that the refurbishment was only skin-deep. She merely nodded, saying, "It's a beautiful house, it seems a pity it was allowed to go to rack and ruin."

"Quite." His tone was dry. He jumped down and held up his hands. "Give me the dogs."

"Take Isolde. If Tristan goes first, she'll fling herself after him." She held out the female of the pair. Harry took the other terrier and set them both on the pavement, holding both leads in one hand. He reached up his free hand to assist Cornelia from the curricle. "I'm not sure how secure that heel is, so be careful."

She had been about to disdain the helping hand but thought better of it. A fortunate precaution, as the heel buckled almost immediately as she put her weight on it, and she found herself hanging on to his hand as she transferred her weight to the other foot.

"I think I had better see you safely inside." Harry

took a firm grip of her elbow. "Eric, walk the horses for ten minutes."

"Please don't trouble, Lord Bonham." Cornelia set her hand on the railing. "I can manage the last few steps into the house with or without a shoe."

"But I insist, Lady Dagenham," he returned as formally.

Cornelia pictured the chaos within, the beating of carpets, the curtainless windows, the overpowering smell of paint, the pails of dirty water, and the army of mops and moppers. "I can't offer you anything in the way of hospitality." She opted for the bald truth.

"I wasn't expecting it," he said cheerfully. "But I own I'm interested to see what progress you've made."

He released the dogs, who were straining against their collars towards the open front door and they raced into the hall with excited yaps. "That's better. They may be small but they certainly know how to make their wishes known. Now, please, allow me." He slid his hand to her waist and half lifted her up the steps into the hall.

Cornelia was no lightweight, and Viscount Bonham, while tall, appeared more lean and lithe than muscular; however, her feet barely skimmed the steps. She found her footing on the parquet of the hall, and found herself to be slightly out of breath despite the lack of exertion that had brought her there.

"Such gallantry, my lord," she murmured.

"What else did you expect, ma'am?"

"From a man who makes salacious proposals to a bare acquaintance, anything, I daresay," she responded.

Harry's response died on his lips as Lady Farnham appeared on the curve of the stairs.

"Nell, is that you? Oh, this is such chaos . . . oh, Lord Bonham, what a surprise." Aurelia collected herself and came down the stairs, a smile on her lips, her hand outstretched in welcome. "I fear we're ill equipped for visitors. Did you meet Lady Dagenham on the street?"

"Not exactly, Lady Farnham." He took the hand and raised it to his lips. "Lady Dagenham had an unfortunate accident and fetched up on my doorstep." He shot Cornelia a wicked smile.

"Oh, what happened, Nell?" Aurelia was all concern, hurrying down the last few steps. "Are you hurt?"

"No, not at all," her sister-in-law reassured. "My heel broke when the dogs started at a horse, and I tripped on a curbstone. Lord Bonham was kind enough to bring me home."

Aurelia shot her a puzzled glance. What on earth could have taken Nell to Mount Street and the doorstep of her nemesis? "How kind of you, viscount," she murmured. "Won't you come into the parlor? The least we can do is offer you a glass of sherry or Madeira." She turned towards the door in question.

"Mischief-maker," Cornelia hissed at Harry.

He gave her a bland smile. "My lips are sealed." He followed Aurelia into the parlor.

Cornelia hesitated. He would not say anything to her friends about what had transpired between them. He may have implied that he was ready to make mischief, but she knew he wouldn't actually do it. She had no idea why she felt he had some kind of honor . . . but he did. It seemed Harry Bonham was a man to be known by instinct not by deduction.

She shrugged and made her unstable way upstairs to find a pair of shoes with intact heels.

When she came down again, Viscount Bonham was taking his leave of Aurelia and Livia. He smiled at Cornelia, and it was not a social smile. It was a smile that held a wealth of understanding and promise.

Cornelia struggled to ignore both. She said easily, "Oh, are you leaving, viscount?"

"Yes, sadly, ma'am. But it's cold, and I can't leave my horses too long." He bowed over her extended hand.

"No, of course not. I must thank you for your assistance . . . And such a kind offer." Her smile, cool and courteous, was a challenge in itself.

"Oh, not kind, ma'am, not in the least. One that benefits us both," he returned. His gaze slid down her body, and she felt her skin quicken in response.

Prudently, Cornelia stepped back from the brink. "Let me see you out, sir." She walked to the open door.

Harry followed, drawing on his driving gloves. He glanced back at the bustle in the hall. Lester was folding up the stepladder, and for an instant, their eyes met. The question in the viscount's was answered by an infinitesimal shake of the other's head. No luck thus far.

It was time Harry went to work in earnest. He stepped outside the front door and turned back to Cornelia. "Tell me, Nell, are you all serious about entering society?" There was no mockery in his voice, nothing sardonic in his tone, and nothing of passion either.

Cornelia took the question at face value. "Yes, Liv needs to find a husband. Ellie and I are her chaperones."

He laughed softly. "Chaperones indeed. I don't know about Lady Farnham, but I suspect, ma'am, that you will prove an inadequate chaperone."

"Then you are mistaken, sir," she stated with composure. "Whatever impression I may have given you this morning means nothing. I may have yielded to a degree of temptation . . . but I am more than capable of withstanding temptation." She gave a short emphatic nod as if to punctuate the statement. "I bid you good morning, Lord Bonham."

He stroked his chin, frowning at her. "I can be of assistance, Nell. For your friend's sake, why not accept what's freely given?"

"Freely given?" She looked at him suspiciously.

"I swear it."

"Then what do you suggest?" She folded her arms, hunching her shoulders, unsure whether it was the ambient temperature that was cold or something inside herself.

"You all need new wardrobes . . . or a semblance of such," he stated flatly. "You look—"

"Positive dowds," she finished for him. "Yes, my cousin has already said so with lamentable lack of delicacy. So how else can you be of assistance, Lord Bonham?"

"I can bring visitors with the right influence to your doorstep," he said mildly. "If you'll take my advice about whom to use to dress you all, when you're ready, I will deliver a patroness of Almack's to your drawing room."

Cornelia considered this. She had little doubt that the viscount could do what he promised, but there was something dangerously intimate about his involvement in the improvement of their wardrobe. But then she reflected there were three of them. There was nothing intimate about one man advising three women in matters of fashion.

"And why would you be so generous with your time, sir?"

He looked at her. "I leave that to your imagination, Nell." He walked down to his waiting carriage, turning to tip his hat. "Do you accept my offer?"

Everything told her to say no. Instead, Cornelia said thank you.

"One condition . . ." He had one foot on the curricle step.

"I thought so."

"My name is *Harry*." He jumped lightly into the curricle and took the reins from Eric. "Use it."

She didn't stay to watch him round the square, but went back inside her mind in a turmoil that didn't begin to match her confused emotions.

Harry took the road to Richmond. He needed the space and privacy that Hyde Park couldn't give him. He might meet acquaintances at Richmond, but it was much less likely than in the city, and he needed to clear his head. He had thought he was playing a light game of flirtation, one that might give him a little personal satisfaction. The woman was too composed, too assured, and he'd had the idea of mixing just a little revenge with the business at hand. He had wanted to break her composure. Oblige her to acknowledge her own sensuality. Maybe he'd succeeded, but he'd certainly ensnared himself in his own web.

Chapter 11

Nigel Dagenham raised his head from his hands and stared for the hundredth time at the sheaf of papers on the small table in front of him. The column of figures on the topmost sheet remained the same. He picked up a quill and moved the candle closer, totting up the sum once more, but this time with no stirring of hope. As he'd known it would, the sum total had not budged by a farthing.

Ten thousand guineas. How in the devil's name had he managed to lose such a sum? Such a monstrous sum. It was as much as his father's annual income from the estate.

He threw down the quill and reached for the brandy bottle, pouring a generous measure into the squat glass at his elbow, then began to shuffle through the papers, setting aside the straightforward bills from creditors. The pile of IOUs remained in front of him. With all the hapless despair of the proverbial drowning man and the straw, he tried once more to add up the creditors' bills in such a way that they would account for at least half of the dreadful sum. But try as he might, he couldn't budge the figure from a mere fifteen hundred guineas.

Eight and half thousand guineas were debts of honor.

And they *must* be paid. In full and without delay.

With a groan he dropped his head into his hands again. To renege on such debts would bring unendurable disgrace, not just to himself, but to his entire family. He would be forced to resign from his clubs and slink back to Ringwood. Oxford would never take him back. His father, on his infrequent visits to London, would be ostracized, even the earl of Markby would be tarnished by his nephew's ruin.

An imperative rap at the door brought his head up with a jerk. "Nigel . . . you in there?"

Nigel cursed under his breath and swept the IOUs into the drawer in the little table. His host's son sounded rather the worse for wear, but he had sharp eyes and a devilishly quick wit nevertheless. "Come in, Mac," he called, rising to his feet as the door opened. He set his back to the table and beckoned his visitor forward.

Mackenzie, earl of Garston, the eldest son of the marquess of Coltrain, stood swaying in the doorway, a bottle of claret in his hand. "Lord, Dagenham, where've you been hidin' yourself?" he demanded thickly. "Looked for you all over town . . . no one's seen you in days." He came in, kicking the door shut behind him. "Claret?" He raised the bottle in invitation.

"No thanks, Mac." Nigel indicated the brandy bottle,

trying to sound as carefree as his visitor. "Feeling a bit under the weather, I'm afraid. Thought I'd stay indoors till I'd thrown it off."

Mackenzie squinted at him in the candle's uncertain light. "Don't look too good," he pronounced, thumping down in a chair beside the table. His experienced eye caught and identified the small sheaf of papers. "What's that you got there? Damn creditors, eh? Ignore 'em, I always do." "Care to come to Newmarket tomorrow? . . . there's a dead cert running in the four o'clock. Weatherbell, she's called. Real dark horse, running at a hundred to one. Had it from a fellow who had it from a fellow who knows the jockey. Absolute certainty. I'm putting five hundred guineas on the nag." He tilted the bottle to his lips and threw back his head, his throat working as the ruby liquid went down.

Nigel's attempt at an easy laugh sounded hollow even to his ears. "Haven't got the ready, Mac," he said. "I'm going to have to appeal to the gov'nor for an advance on next quarter as it is."

The earl peered at him. "Really don't look too good," he observed. "Got a look of the crypt about you, old fellow, if you don't mind my saying so."

"Be my guest," Nigel said, thinking of five hundred guineas at a hundred to one . . . Fifty thousand guineas. *Fifty thousand guineas.*

"Seems a shame to waste a certain tip," Mackenzie said, taking another swig of the bottle. "I'd stand you the wager myself, but 'fraid I'm a bit short this quarter. Got anything to pawn?" He glanced around the well-appointed bedchamber as if expecting to see a cache of gold snuffboxes and diamond signet rings somewhere in the shadows.

Nigel shook his head. Nothing he possessed would fetch five hundred guineas in a pawnbroker's, let alone eight and a half thousand.

"Nothing for it then," the earl stated, getting to his feet. "Havant and Green first thing in the morning . . . they'll give you the ready, and once the nag comes in you can pay 'em off straightaway. Won't even notice the interest that way." He tapped the side of his nose and tried for a wink. "Word to the wise, m'friend. This one can't go wrong." He weaved his way to the door. "We'll set off around noon tomorrow."

Nigel slumped down at the table again and stared at the closed door. He reached for the brandy glass and drained it. Five hundred guineas was a paltry sum. Havant and Green were respectable moneylenders. He knew hundreds of fellows who had had recourse to them when in extremis. And so long as the loan was really short-term, a mere couple of days, then Mac was right, the interest would be negligible. He was of age, legally entitled to borrow money. And with fifty thousand guineas in his pocket, he'd be laughing at his troubles.

There wasn't another way. Fleetingly he wondered if Cornelia or one of the other women would lend him five hundred guineas, then dismissed the thought out of hand. They didn't have money to spare, and even if they did, he was positive neither Nell nor Ellie would countenance staking him to a wager on a horse. Liv possibly, but he couldn't bring himself to ask her. And she'd tell the others anyway, and they'd put a stop to it.

But he could borrow it legitimately as a business deal, and by this time tomorrow all his problems would be solved. Those pesky IOUs would be redeemed and he'd be free as a bird. And he'd be damned careful in future how he played, he decided with a surge of righteousness. He'd learned his lesson. Only fools made the same mistake twice.

Thus buoyed, Nigel sallied forth in search of supper and entertainment. He found both at the Black Cock on Jermyn Street and eventually rolled home to the Coltrain mansion on Park Street just before dawn, befuddled and aware of a faint and inconvenient unease beneath his optimism. He fell into bed and was awoken soon after ten o'clock by the household manservant deputed to wait upon him.

"His lordship said you would be driving out with him at noon, sir," the man stated, setting a tray of coffee on the dressing table. "You'll be wearing riding dress, I understand from his lordship."

Why was he driving out? Nigel pressed a hand to his temples where Thor seemed to have taken up residence with a pair of hammers. Oh, Newmarket. He remembered now, and with the memory came the miserable reminder of why he was going to the races and what he had to do before starting out.

Why had Mac specified riding dress? Did one call upon moneylenders in such informal attire? Wouldn't he look older and more a man about town in the emerald-and-silver-striped waistcoat with the daffodil yellow coat? An outfit that he recalled with a shudder had cost him close to two hundred guineas at Stultz. The bill lay in the pile on the table.

He was rescued from this doleful train of thought by the precipitate entrance of Mackenzie, looking enviably fresh after his own night of debauchery. "Ah, you're up, my good fellow. Good . . . you've a call to pay this morning, remember." He grinned.

"Good God, Mac, how d'you do it?" Nigel grumbled. "You were as drunk as a lord last time I saw you, and about to go off to the bawdyhouse with that wench . . . Lord, she had an arse on her," he added reminiscently. "Magnificent."

"And not just a promise," his friend said with a lascivious chuckle. "She could move like—"

"Oh, enough," Nigel begged with a groan. "I haven't had coffee yet."

"Well, get up and get going. You've a call to make in Holborn before we can head out of town. I'm going to make your fortune today, my friend." Mackenzie poured coffee. "Yes, Brian, lay out Mr. Dagenham's riding dress." He nodded his approval to the footman who was brushing the collar of Nigel's riding coat. "Just the thing for these little meetings."

"I thought the silver-and-emerald waistcoat," Nigel demurred. "More town polish."

"Definitely not, old man." Mackenzie shook his head vigorously. "Riding dress is much more businesslike, and besides you'll have no time to change when you get back. Don't forget we leave at noon, if we're to make the race." He breezed out, leaving Nigel to drag himself from bed.

Nigel managed a cup of coffee but eschewed the breakfast table; his stomach wasn't up to coddled eggs and sirloin.

Since he didn't have his own horse in town, he was obliged to hire a hack from a livery stable whenever he needed to ride. Mackenzie had set up an account for him at a stable in Hyde Park, cheerfully heedless of the expense this involved. Nigel's account was now seriously in arrears, and his heart sank when the owner of the stable emerged from his office as Nigel stood waiting for the horse to be saddled.

"Ah, Mr. Dagenham," Mr. Shelby said, walking across the cobbles towards him. "Riding again are we, today?"

"I can't imagine why else I would be here, Shelby," Nigel said with hauteur. Humility would get him nowhere, arrogance might.

"Quite so, sir." Shelby was a short stout man who barely reached Nigel's shoulder, but he had the shoulders and barrel chest of a prizefighter gone to seed. And he appeared impervious to intimidation. Indeed, had Nigel known it, Shelby dealt with impoverished, blustering young bucks and their overweening sense of entitlement every day and had no difficulty sending them about their business with the requisite flea in the ear.

"There's a little matter of your account, Mr. Dagenham," he said, puffing on a noxious corncob pipe as he rested deceptively mild eyes on the young man's countenance. "When would you be thinking of settling it?"

"For God's sake, man, are you questioning my credit?" Nigel blustered. "I'll take my business elsewhere, I warn you."

"Well, as to that, it's up to you," Shelby said amiably. "But I'd still like to know when I can expect payment for the last two weeks."

"Tomorrow," Nigel stated. A groom was leading the hack out of the stables. "You'll be paid tomorrow, and damn your impudence, Shelby." He swung onto his mount. "And let me tell you, if you don't mend your manners, my good man, you'll lose my custom." He swung the horse towards the gates into the park and kicked the animal into a sudden canter.

"And when have I heard that before, my young sprig?" Shelby muttered to himself, pulling on his pipe. He shook his head and returned to his office.

Nigel, seeking relief from embarrassment in anger, rode the horse hard through the thronged streets until he reached Holborn. The broad thoroughfare ran from St. Paul's to Chancery Lane and was principally the territory of bankers and financiers of all varieties, both respectable and otherwise. He drew rein outside the premises of Havant and Green. Nothing about the building indicated that they were in the business of lending money to desperate individuals at ruinous rates of interest. It was tidy, with well-honed steps and well-washed windows. The nameplate beside the door said merely MESSRS HAVANT AND GREEN, BROKERS.

A grimy urchin ran up as Nigel swung down from his mount. The lad took the bridle without waiting for an invitation. "I'll walk 'im fer you, m'lord," he said, pulling his forelock. "'Tis cold fer 'im to be standin' around."

A row of black iron hitching posts lined the pavement in front of the buildings. Paying an urchin to hold his horse struck Nigel as an unnecessary expense in present circumstances, and particularly on his present errand. He dismissed the boy with a curt word. Ignoring the lad's muttered imprecations, he tethered the hack himself. Then he squared his shoulders and approached the shiny black door, which was opened almost immediately by a black-suited gentleman who bowed him within.

Nigel emerged half an hour later, feeling utterly bemused but triumphant. Messrs. Havant and Green, or their representatives, he was unsure which, had heard him out in sympathetic silence, punctuated only by understanding nods. They had given him papers to sign, rather a lot he thought for five hundred guineas, but the guineas had been counted out on the desk in front of him, and they were now securely tucked into his inside pocket. It had been so easy. Last night he'd been in despair, and this morning he was full of optimism. He had money in his pocket, the sun shone, and an entertaining day of racing in the company of his friends lay ahead.

He mounted his horse and turned the animal's head back towards Chancery Lane and Mayfair.

Viscount Bonham stood in the doorway of a small shop across the street. It was ostensibly a printers and engravers, but behind the shop front was another small room, a workroom that contained those tools of Harry's trade that he found it convenient to keep outside his own house, the torches and crucibles, the intricate implements he used for molding and inscribing gold and silver into the code-carrying weapons of war.

He watched Nigel Dagenham untie his horse from outside Messrs. Havant and Green and ride off. So the young fool had recourse to moneylenders . . . he wouldn't be the first and most definitely not the last. It was a piece of information that might prove useful at some point. How, he didn't know as yet, but Harry dealt in the world of dirty secrets, and he knew their value.

His gaze suddenly sharpened as he saw a figure across the street move out of the shadowed mouth of a narrow alley and slide into the crowd. He was joined almost immediately by a second man, and they moved swiftly after Nigel Dagenham, whose progress was little faster than a pedestrian's, and wouldn't speed up until he reached the crossing with Chancery Lane. In the subdued quarters of the Inns of Court, he would encounter much less traffic.

Harry's eyes followed the two men as they slipped through the throng. He knew what they were. He'd spent many hours eluding such men. Watchers, stalkers, spies—they all had an unmistakable way of moving. Indeed to Harry it seemed they gave off a particular distinctive aura. So who was having Nigel Dagenham watched, and why?

It was a disturbing question, and he didn't like the answer he came up with, not one little bit. He turned back to his workroom, to the charcoal burner and his drills and anvil. He tucked the issue of Nigel Dagenham into a far corner of his mind where it would stay until he was ready to examine it once more. For the moment he needed all his concentration for his work on the tiny snuffbox with its false bottom. The substitute for the lost thimble. It had to be ready for the courier by dawn.

"So, Jean, our young friend has fallen into the hands of the moneylenders." The desiccated man behind the desk in the tall house on Gray's Inn Road turned his head slowly towards his visitor, candlelight throwing the shadow of his sharp nose huge and elongated onto the wall beside him.

"Oui, milord." Jean nodded, hands clasped at his back, his eyes, sunken deep in the hatchet face, fixed intently on his superior. "Yesterday he attempted to recoup his losses on a horse race."

"I see. And how did his fortunes progress, Jean?"

The other man shrugged, spreading his hands wide. *"Hélas,"* he said simply.

A meager smile flickered across milord's ascetic lips. "I see," he repeated. "A ripe peach ready to drop then?"

"Almost, milord. A little more pressure, perhaps."

The hissing of the damp coals in the fireplace was the only sound in the gloomy chamber as milord gazed at the grime-encrusted panes of the mullioned window. A steady rain lashed the glass.

"Then we had better apply it, Jean," he pronounced finally. "Time is running short. We must disable or at the very least create havoc within the British network in France before Napoleon and the Tsar meet. No word of the treaty must be allowed to reach our enemies until it is signed."

"It's understood, milord." Jean bowed and turned to go, then hesitated. It was risky to ask his superior for information that had not been freely given, but sometimes, if milord was in a mellow mood, or what passed for such with him, he would answer a question.

"It is certain then, milord, that the emperor will negotiate with Alexander?"

"After Eylau it is only a matter of time."

Jean waited for a second and then accepted that he

had been given all that was forthcoming. At the beginning of February the French and Russian armies had fought the battle of Eylau to a technical French victory but a practical draw, with massive losses on both sides. It was in the interests of both mighty empires to cease hostilities and join forces against the coalition of Austria, England, and Prussia.

"Alexander needs one final push." Surprisingly, milord spoke again just as Jean laid a hand on the door latch. "Rather in the manner of our ripening peach." Another thin smile flickered over exiguous lips. "You may rest assured, Jean, that Napoleon will administer the push in the spring. One more victory over the Russians, and a treaty will be signed by early summer."

"Yes, milord. Thank you, milord."

"So get on with your own task, Jean. I want that thimble . . . the emperor wants that thimble."

Jean ducked his head in a semblance of a bow and hastily left the chamber. He had no time to waste. Milord gave no second chances, and Jean had no desire to meet the knife on the stair like the unfortunate Victor.

Chapter 12

NIGEL FELT NUMB. Numb except for his head, which screamed with pain. Gin and water, particularly in the quantities he'd been drinking, was sheer poison. He lay down on his bed, closing his eyes in a vain effort to sleep. But all he could think of was that moment when Weatherbell had stumbled within a length of the winning post. Slowly the full horror of what he was facing hit him with all the shattering power of a firing squad. The interest rate on the loan from Havant and Green started at 30 percent, but that hadn't seemed like a problem since he would only carry the debt for twenty-four hours, and with fifty thousand guineas he could easily afford such a sum. But now he had to face the fact that after two days the rate went up to 50 percent, then increased every month after that. Even if he could scrape together the interest, he would never have a prayer of paying off the principal.

He got off the bed and went to the window staring

down at the street below. It was a dreary morning. The night's rain had stopped, but the trees dripped, and the sky was still low and leaden. There were few pedestrians around, and those there were stepped gingerly over the puddle-strewn cobbles.

His head felt as if it would burst, and the walls seemed to be closing in on him. He needed to get out, somewhere soothing.

Half an hour later he was knocking on the door to Livia's house in Cavendish Square. A frigid, damp wind gusted across the garden, and he shrank deeper into his greatcoat. The door opened slowly, and Morecombe peered at him.

"Aye?"

"It's me, you old fool," Nigel said, in no mood for playing the retainer's games. "The Honorable Nigel Dagenham, cousin of Lady Dagenham. Are the ladies at home?"

"Aye." Morecombe didn't budge.

"I'll announce myself." Nigel thrust him aside as he pushed open the door and strode into the hall. "Are they in the parlor?"

"Reckon ye'd best find that out fer yerself," Morecombe said, closing the door firmly. "I've me own work to do." He creaked off towards the kitchen regions, leaving the visitor fulminating in the hall.

Annoyed though he was, Nigel instantly saw the improvements that had been made since his last visit. He could smell fresh paint, dried lavender, and beeswax.

The chandelier had a full complement of candles and threw a brilliant illumination around the hall. For the first time he noticed the few pieces of furniture scattered around the apartment. Choice pieces now that they gleamed with polish and glowed in the golden light, and there was a rather fine rug beneath his feet that he would swear had not been there before.

Curious, he stuck his head around the door to the salon and blinked in amazement. A noble room, no doubt about it now that its lines had been revealed. The furniture was not in the first style, but it had a certain dignity, despite the odd scuff. The curtains and carpet were a little worn, but not in a way that screamed poverty. More a lack of interest in the obvious trappings of wealth. It was empty, but a fire blazed in the grate, and the lamps had been lit, making it warm and welcoming.

It certainly reflected the temperaments of the house's present occupants, he reflected, feeling comforted despite his wretchedness. He went on to the parlor and after a brief knock opened the door.

All three women were in there, seated around the table, heads bent over a pile of magazines while the three children played in front of the fire. Tristan and Isolde hurled themselves at the visitor's boots, yapping frantically.

Nigel grimaced as the sound went straight through his head. "Be quiet." He tried to push them away with his boots, but they bounced right back at him.

"Good God, Nigel, you look appalling," Cornelia said, getting up from her chair. "Are you ill, love?"

"No," he said. "But my head aches. Can't you stop these beasts from making this ghastly racket?"

"Not easily," she said, bending to scoop them up. "Stevie, darling, will you go to the kitchen and ask Morecombe to come and take the dogs away?"

"All right," the child said willingly. "Coming, Franny?" They ran off with squeals of laughter, the door banging shut behind them, making Nigel wince anew. Susannah lurched in their wake, only to be stymied by the closed door. She sat down with a thump and opened her mouth on a cry of protest.

Nigel began to regret his impulse to visit the domestic haven. Cornelia was holding the dogs, who were still offering periodic yaps, gazing at him from beneath absurdly thick fringes that must, he thought, obscure their vision. Susannah's protests were approaching full voice, and in desperation he turned and opened the door for her. She toddled forth, tears instantly dried, calling for her brother.

"That wasn't very clever, Nigel," Cornelia said, thrusting the dogs at him. "She's only three. You have to watch her all the time." She went after her daughter.

Nigel looked helplessly at his burden, which miraculously had ceased yapping. "Where shall I put them?" he asked, before realizing that Livia and Aurelia were rocking with silent laughter.

"Anywhere," Aurelia said, taking pity on him.

"They'll stop yapping now that they've greeted you. Sit down. Nell's right, you look dreadful. Are you sure you're not sickening for something?"

"No, don't fuss, Ellie." He dropped the dogs with an air of relief. "I'm perfectly well, I just came for some peace and quiet."

"That's a little optimistic around here," Cornelia said, laughing as she returned to the parlor, Susannah clasped firmly in her arms. "The children are sick of being cooped up, but they can't go out in this weather, and the same applies to the dogs. The only one content to be inside is Puss. She's curled up on the rug in front of the fire in my room and shows no inclination to move."

"What a menagerie," Nigel muttered, depositing himself in a chair. "But I have to say, coz, you've done wonders with this place in such a short time."

"Yes, it's surprising what five thousand guineas and an army of helpers can achieve," Liv said complacently.

"You spent five thousand guineas?" Nigel sat up abruptly. He was about to say it was a fortune until he remembered that he had gambled away almost twice that. He slumped back in his chair.

"No, of course not," Liv said. "Nowhere near, but enough to make our surroundings outwardly respectable, and now we're concentrating on making ourselves so."

She waved at the magazines. "See, fashion magazines. If we're clever, we think we can manage with one riding dress, one morning gown, one afternoon gown, and one ball gown each. A variety of accessories . . . shawls, ribbons, scarves, different trimmings . . . should make the outfits look different, and Ellie and I are much the same shape, so we think we can wear each other's gowns . . . not Nell, because she's so much taller than us . . . but we can share hats and cloaks and—"

"Wait . . ." Nigel held up a hand, exclaiming in horror, "You're telling me you're going to enter society with just one wardrobe apiece. No one *ever* wears the same gown twice, Liv."

"No one will know," Aurelia said placidly. "We're very clever needlewomen ourselves, and we have a seamstress at our disposal who's a genius. She knows all the latest fashions and has any number of tricks up her sleeve for mixing and matching. Besides, it's only for a couple of months until . . ." She fell silent, glancing at Livia with a guilty grimace.

"Until what?"

"Until I find a husband," Livia declared. "Now I have a dowry of sorts. I shan't be overly particular, I don't need an earl or such like, but I do need my own establishment. And I want children," she added almost in an undertone.

Nigel blushed a little at this confidence. "Well, I'm sure that's very laudable, Liv, and I hope you get exactly want you want."

The sound of the door knocker, briskly applied, set the dogs yapping again, skittering towards the door, noses pressed to the gap between the door and the floor, rear ends wagging violently in anticipation of some new excitement.

The parlor door opened to admit Morecombe who said, "Lord Stevie said you wanted me, ma'am." Behind him the front door knocker sounded again, even more imperatively.

"Yes, please, Morecombe . . . Could you take the dogs to the kitchen?" Cornelia said distractedly. "And see who's . . . no, don't bother, I'll go myself." She scooped up the dogs, dumped them unceremoniously into the retainer's arms, and hastened across the hall to answer the equally unceremonious banging of the knocker.

The bolts were now well oiled, and she caught herself thinking she should thank the new man, Lester. He seemed to find these little irritations and put them right without anyone asking. The door opened without a creak and she found herself eye to eye with Viscount Bonham.

A surge of something unnameable went through her with the power of a lightning bolt, and it took her several seconds to find her voice, and even then it sounded a little strange to her own ears. "My lord, this is a surprise . . . it's such a foul morning I didn't expect anyone to be abroad."

"A little rain never deterred me, Nell," he said, stepping briskly into the hall, shrugging out of his greatcoat as he did so. He shook drops off his beaver hat, tossed it onto the Jacobean bench that stood beside the door, and draped his coat beside it. He had learned not to expect the niceties of a butler's greeting in this household.

"So, how are you amusing yourselves on this miserable day?" he asked, regarding her closely. Her hair was coming loose from the heavy chignon at the nape of her neck, and he had an almost irresistible urge to free the rest of it . . . three pins and he would be able to weigh the thick luxuriant buttery mass in his hand.

She gave him one of her straight looks, a tiny question in the steady blue eyes. He smiled and saw the immediate flash that made her appear much younger, a little less certain, than she really was . . . an involuntary recognition of the sensual current that crackled between them.

And then she had it under control. Her responding smile was that of a hostess. "With those fashion magazines you sent us. We're most grateful for that thought, sir. And for the recommendation of the seamstress. Miss Claire is exactly what we need." She turned to lead him to the parlor, saying pleasantly over her shoulder, "I wonder that you would know someone quite so comfortable with the need to watch the budget."

"So you think me a mere fribble," he remarked, even as he reached out and caught her arm. "Nell, we had an agreement, if you recall."

She turned to face him. "I don't object to calling you Harry in private, *Harry*, but I doubt such informality would be appropriate in public. My friends and I intend to make an entrance, one unsullied by the slightest possibility of talk."

He looked around him with an air of exaggerated interest. "The hall appears to be deserted."

"For the moment," she agreed. "But my friends are unaware of this . . . agreement, as you choose to call it . . . and I would have them remain so. In this house, if you please, we adopt a formal address."

He detected the undercurrent of anxiety in her statement and once again accepted the need to back away. He would find out later what caused it, but for now discretion was the better part of valor. "Of course, ma'am. I am yours to command."

Her lips twitched at the ironic edge to his voice, but she smiled her acceptance and led the way into the parlor.

"Ah, Dagenham, you had the same thought I see," Harry said with a friendly handshake as he greeted Nigel. "Hearth and home provide a pleasant respite from the gaming tables, eh?"

He watched the young man's expression as the handshake was returned. A wan smile greeted the pleasantry, and the man's complexion was more whey than cream. Harry thought of the two men he'd just seen busily clipping the hedge in the square garden opposite. A different pair this time, but gardeners they most certainly were not. They might fool a casual passerby, but they couldn't fool Viscount Bonham. He had smelled them as pungently as he'd caught the aroma off the two in Holborn. Someone had a most unhealthy interest in Nigel Dagenham.

"Yes, indeed, Bonham." Nigel managed a weak laugh and touched his temples. "Too much daffy last night, I've the devil of a head."

"A raw egg beaten in a pint of milk," Livia said with

authority. "I had that from my father's head groom. He swore by it."

Nigel shuddered. "I'll take your word for it, Liv."

"What can I offer you, Lord Bonham?" Aurelia had gone to the sideboard. "I can ring for tea," she said a shade doubtfully, "but I have an excellent burgundy here. Lady Dagenham says it's a first-class vintage."

"Then I'd be delighted to try a glass, thank you." Harry took a chair beside the secretaire. There were no examples of Nell's penmanship on display. But his eye fell upon the workbox on the drum table beside the window. He glanced across at her. She was sitting on the sofa with the little girl in her lap. The child was leaning against her mother's shoulder, lips slightly parted, eyelids heavy as she drifted into sleep. Cornelia had a faraway expression on her face, and he wondered where she was, what she was seeing. It gave him a feeling of exclusion that chilled him without his knowing why. He had no rights to such a feeling.

Aurelia handed him a glass of wine. "We wanted to thank you for your help, sir," she said, indicating the magazines. "We are making good use of these, and Miss Claire is such a sensible woman—"

"Yes, so Lady Dagenham told me," he broke in. "My housekeeper is a fund of knowledge about such matters. She has a wealth of friends and acquaintances eager for work. I am happy to have been of service, Lady Farnham." He sipped his wine. "Do you have a date when you think you'll be ready to receive callers?"

"Any day now, sir," Cornelia said, her focus returning to the room. "Our cards have been engraved. Since both Ellie . . . Lady Farnham . . . and I have been presented at court, we thought we would pay some calls, then, depending on who returns the calls, send out invitations to a small soirée."

She frowned at him, trying to assess his reaction. "Does that seem a sensible way to proceed, my lord?"

"Eminently," he said, crossing one booted leg over the other. "You're right, this is an excellent burgundy . . . I will engage to bring Lady Sefton to call upon you. She's the easiest of the patronesses at Almack's to deal with, and once you have the vouchers, then you may spend as much or as little time as you wish in the social whirl." His tone managed to convey his own lack of interest in such a whirl.

"I take it you have little time for the social dance," Cornelia observed, idly twining a curling lock of her child's hair around her finger.

He shrugged. "It has its amusements." His gaze darted towards Nigel, who had contributed little or nothing to the conversation. "Isn't that so, Dagenham?"

Nigel shook himself. "Yes . . . yes, of course, viscount. Quite so . . . quite so."

Harry was certain the man hadn't heard a word spoken in the last fifteen or twenty minutes. Matters were presumably going from bad to worse as they had a habit of doing. Creditors could be put off, satisfied with a little on account; but if it was gambling debts that he couldn't pay, then he was in serious trouble.

Was it *that* trouble that had attracted the dangerous attention of those men who were following him? If they were after the thimble, then they might see Nigel Dagenham as a possible tool to help them to it. A vulnerable, green youth who found himself in a desperate situation, one that could be exploited. Maybe he'd be open to *persuasion* of some kind or another. They were up to no good, that was for sure.

And they were far too close to these women and their children for his comfort.

His eye darted once more to the drum table. The workbox was closed. He rose leisurely to his feet and began to stroll around the room. He looked through the rain-smeared windows, refilled his glass, kicked a falling log back into the fire. Each step brought him casually closer to the workbox.

The door opened as his careless peregrinations landed him beside the drum table. Stevie and Franny tumbled into the parlor, squealing with delight. "Mama, our Ada showed us how to roll out pastry," Franny gasped. "See my flower." She held an approximation of a flower in unbaked pastry reverently on the palm of her hand.

"An' our Mavis showed me how to make a dog," Stevie crowed, waving his own creation vigorously in the air. It collapsed in on itself and he stared at it in puzzlement as he caught the detritus in the palm of his hand. "It broke."

"Because it hadn't been cooked, sweetie," Cornelia said, laying the sleeping Susannah carefully down on the sofa beside her. "When it's baked it'll be hard, then it won't break."

"I knew that," Franny said, touching her flower with a tiny fingertip. "Mine's not broke."

Stevie visibly gathered himself for battle, but Harry, a veteran of such frays, moved swiftly. He sat down on a low ottoman. "Give it to me, Stevie, and I'll show you something." He held out his hand to receive the lump from a small hot hand. "While the dough's still soft, you can make a soldier," he said. "Better still, a knight." His fingers began to fashion the dough.

Cornelia was rapt as she watched those long, slender fingers, deft and skillful, kneading the rather grubby dough, pinching, shaping the mass into an utterly recognizable shape of a medieval knight complete with sword, shield, and helmet.

"I don't like this flower," Franny cried. "Make me a knight." She thrust her dough at Harry.

He took it, giving the child a quick smile. "Do you really want a knight, Franny? How about a horse, or a swan?"

"I want what Stevie has," Franny declared firmly.

"Then you must have it." He cast a glance up at Cornelia, who was leaning forward watching, and he was rewarded by a frank smile of appreciation. He produced the required knight and got up from the ottoman, every muscle of his body straining towards the workbox on the drum table.

He had to open it, to confirm what he knew in his blood. *His* thimble was in there.

"You know children, Lord Bonham," Aurelia said, as Stevie and Franny raced off to the kitchen to persuade the twins to bake their knights. "You must be close to your sister's children."

Harry remembered with a shock that Annabel had supposedly left him with five nephews and nieces to take care of. "I have several sisters, Lady Farnham," he said with complete truth.

"An extended family must be a great help to your late sister's family," Cornelia remarked with quick sympathy.

"Yes," agreed Harry without too much enthusiasm. The ramifications of his convenient white lie were making him uncomfortable. "What a pretty workbox," he observed, wandering across to the drum table. He ran a finger over the mother-of-pearl inlay. "French?"

"No, Italian," Cornelia said. "It belonged to my mother."

"May I?" He lifted the lid without waiting for permission. The thimble lay neatly in a compartment beside the skeins of colored silks. He could palm it in a second, and this would all be over. But Cornelia had come up behind him and now stood at his shoulder.

She reached over and took the workbox, "I love the painted panel in the lid. Aren't the colors exquisite?"

"Delightful," he agreed. He wasn't going to be able to

liberate his thimble now, but confirmation of its presence was a huge step forward.

Cornelia closed the box and set it back on the table.

Harry took his leave shortly thereafter. Dagenham's shadows were not immediately visible, but he knew they were there somewhere, waiting for their quarry to leave. Would they lose interest in Dagenham once the thimble was safely in English hands? Or did they have a more far-reaching interest in the young man? He wouldn't be the first unlucky creature to have exposed a vulnerability that could be turned to good purpose by enemy agents. He'd need to alert his own side to keep an eye on Nigel. But first things first.

He walked home, his mind thrumming with various strategies for getting hold of the thimble. Lester was well placed for the retrieval, since he seemed to have established a presence in the household. It needed to be done quickly. Particularly with the ominous presence of Nigel Dagenham's watchers hovering so closely.

He reached his own house just as it began to rain again. "Miserable day, my lord," Hector observed as he took the viscount's outer garments. "Will you want the carriage this evening?"

"Am I going somewhere, Hector?" Harry asked in surprise.

"I understood you were dining with Her Grace, sir." Hector smoothed the brim of his master's beaver hat.

"Oh, Lord, I'd forgotten." Harry grimaced with annoyance. The lady in question was his great-aunt who was paying one of her infrequent visits to town. She was a *grande dame* of the old school and never let her relatives forget it. A summons from the duchess of Gracechurch could not be ignored with impunity, although the evening promised to be dull as ditchwater when he wasn't attempting to defend himself from unexpected attacks. But the old woman had stood by him when the scandal broke, as had all his family, and for that he reckoned he owed her his presence at her dinner table however lamentable the fare and irksome the conversation.

"Yes, I'd better take the carriage," he said, heading for the stairs. "What time am I supposed to be there?"

"Her Grace's invitation said six o'clock, my lord."

Harry nodded, unsurprised at the unfashionably early hour. His aunt was set in her ways that themselves were firmly rooted in the mores of a world some two decades earlier. At least it promised an early end to a tortuous evening.

"Is Lester around?"

"I believe he came in half an hour ago, sir."

"Ask him to come up to my office." Harry strode up the stairs.

"I'll have the carriage brought around for five thirty, my lord," Hector said to his retreating back.

Harry raised a hand in acknowledgment and continued up to his attic sanctuary, where a fire crackled merrily in the grate, and the lamps were lit banishing the gloom beyond the windows. A letter with a familiar seal lay on the desk. He poured himself a glass of wine from the decanter on a side table and stood with his back to the fire as he slit the seal with his fingernail. He frowned as he read the letter's contents.

He was still frowning when a brisk knock at the door heralded Lester's appearance. "You sent for me, m'lord?"

"Yes, come in. Wine?" Harry gestured towards the decanter.

"No, thank you, m'lord. A pint of ale is more my tipple," Lester said. He saw the frown. "Something up, sir?"

"I need you to go to Portsmouth this afternoon," Harry said, tapping the letter against the palm of his hand. "Which is a damned nuisance, because I've found the thimble."

Lester whistled softly. "You've got it then, sir?" His gaze darted around the chamber in search of the precious object.

Harry shook his head. "No, not as yet, but I've seen it. It's in Lady Dagenham's workbox, as I suspected."

"Well, it's all right and tight there then."

"Yes, but not nearly as right and tight as it will be back in my possession," Harry said grimly. "And safely destroyed," he added. "There's no time to waste, Lester. It's as near out in the open as it could be."

Lester nodded his comprehension. "And I've got to go to Portsmouth," he stated. "Can't that trip wait a day or two?"

Harry shook his head. "No, it's Ministry orders. There's a fishing boat expected from Le Havre on the dawn tide. It'll have a message from one of our men in Rouen. It needs to be decoded at once."

"What about the man in Portsmouth? Can't he meet the boat and bring it up?"

Harry sighed. "He broke his ankle jumping from a boat to the quay. He can't ride."

"Ah." Lester nodded. "Then I'd best be off, sir. It's close to a hundred miles. I'll be back tomorrow evening. I could get the thimble then."

"I'm not prepared to wait that long. Every moment is dangerous." Harry sipped his wine, his gaze somewhat distracted. "I intend to take it myself tonight and, since it's absence will be noticed, I'll substitute another in its place. I don't want to start a hue and cry in the household." He frowned slightly, his long fingers playing with the stem of his goblet.

"Do you by any chance know where Lady Dagenham keeps her workbox?"

"Well, as to that, sir, it weren't in the ladies' parlor this morning when I went in to fix a loose cupboard door. I'm guessing she took it up to her bedchamber at night."

Harry turned to gaze into the fire, the frown vanished, an amused smile instead playing over his lips. "That would certainly make sense," he said softly. "Do you know where her ladyship's bedchamber is?"

"Oh, yes, sir. It's a big one at the back on the first floor just above the library."

"At the back, eh . . ." Harry turned back slowly. "Secluded then?"

Lester nodded. "Reckon so. There's a bit of a walled garden out back but nothing to speak of."

"Nothing overlooking the back of the house?"

Lester considered. "Not much. The wall's quite high, and there's a few fruit trees in the garden to block a straight sight line. What are you thinking, sir?"

"Just an idea . . . a possibility, Lester. Can you go back to the house on your way to Portsmouth, find some excuse to go upstairs, and do something with Lady Dagenham's bedroom window. Loosen the latch, perhaps?"

Lester nodded, comprehension dawning. "You're going in that way?"

Harry shrugged with apparent insouciance. "It's an avenue. If she keeps the box in there at night . . ."

"I thought we'd done with the breaking and entering, my lord," Lester said with a hint of disapproval.

"In this case I see no alternative," Harry said with a cool smile.

"Whatever you say, my lord."

Lester's expression revealed nothing of his inner thoughts.

Chapter 13

Punctually at six o'clock, Harry stepped down from his carriage in Devonshire Place and mentally braced himself for the upcoming evening as he strode up the steps to the front door of his great-aunt's mansion. In truth he was rather fond of the old lady, but only in the smallest of doses.

The door opened as he reached the top step. "Good evening, Trent." He greeted the elderly man who stood bowing in the doorway.

"Good evening, my lord. It's a pleasure to see you." The butler took Harry's hat and silver-topped cane and waited while he unbuttoned his gloves. "Her Grace is in the blue salon, sir."

Harry raised his eyebrows. The room in question was relatively small compared with the usual receiving rooms in a house that Harry privately thought resembled a mausoleum. "This is to be an intimate evening then?"

"The other guests are not invited until seven o'clock, my lord."

"Oh," Harry said a trifle glumly. His great-aunt obviously intended to corner him about something, and he could guess what.

"I'll bring a bottle of His Grace's '93 Madeira, sir, if that might help," the butler said with a conspiratorial smile.

Harry returned the smile. "It can't hurt, Trent. Thank you." The '93 was a particularly fine vintage. His great-uncle, the duke of Gracechurch, had been a fine judge of wine until the last few years, when his gout had finally forced him to moderate his drinking. Moderation had not sweetened his temper, however, and when he was at his worst, the duchess generally chose to visit town. Presumably an attack lay behind the present visitation.

He followed a footman upstairs to a corner apartment. "Lord Bonham, Your Grace," the footman announced, opening the door.

"Ah, there you are, Bonham. I was wondering what was keeping you." The duchess raised her lorgnette and regarded her great nephew critically.

Harry glanced at the clock on the mantel. "I understand I was summoned for six o'clock, ma'am. Could I have been mistaken?" He came across the salon to bow over her hand.

"How am I supposed to remember what time I said?" the lady demanded, letting her lorgnette drop on its long silver chain. "That's Eliza's business."

Harry relinquished his aunt's hand and turned to bow to the other lady in the room, his great-aunt's companion. A small, middle-aged, brown mouse of a woman dressed in a plain gown of gray muslin, a white cap tied beneath her chin, she rose from her chair and bobbed a curtsy. "Good evening, my lord." She had a pleasant if undistinguished face and a smile of particular sweetness.

"Miss Cox, how are you?" he asked warmly. "Keeping well, I hope."

"Oh, yes . . . yes, indeed, so kind of you to ask, my lord. Too, too kind, I do declare."

"Oh do stop wittering, Eliza," her employer commanded. "Now sit down, Bonham. Where's Trent . . . I told him to bring . . . oh, there you are, man. About time too." She waved imperiously at the butler with her fan. "What's that you've got there?"

"The '93 Madeira, Your Grace," the man said, setting his tray on a console table. "Will you take a glass?" He lifted the decanter.

The duchess sniffed. "Might as well," she said.

Trent poured the wine, and Harry carried a glass over to his aunt. Then he took a second to Miss Cox. "Ratafia, ma'am," he said, setting it on a drum table beside her.

"Oh, thank you, my lord. Just what I like. So kind of you to remember . . . so kind."

"Rot your insides that stuff will . . . nasty sweet muck," the duchess declared, taking a sip from her own glass. "Hmm . . . not bad . . . not bad at all. Gracechurch always was a good judge . . . about some things at least," she added. "Couldn't tell a horse from a donkey though."

Harry refrained from comment. He sat down on a gilt chair opposite his aunt, took an appreciative sip of his Madeira. And waited.

His great-aunt lifted her lorgnette again and examined him.

"Is something amiss, ma'am?" he inquired.

"You look well enough," she conceded. "Whatever else I might say about you, nephew, you always know how to dress."

Harry contented himself with a faint inclination of his head. Knowing his aunt's old-fashioned views on prevailing fashion, he had dressed for the evening in knee britches rather than pantaloons, with the regulation white waistcoat and black tailcoat. His aunt's attire, a hooped gown of lavender silk decorated with dark green velvet bows, was from another era altogether, as was her curled and powdered wig adorned with three ostrich feathers and something resembling a bird in a cage.

"And how is His Grace?" he asked.

"Oh, complaining as usual. It's his own fault . . . won't listen to the leeches. Drank a bottle of port with Hamilton the other afternoon, and he's been laid low ever since," the duchess declared, confirming Harry's earlier suspicions. "But I came up to town to talk to you. When are you going to find yourself another wife, Bonham?"

Harry had known it was coming. "I have no inclination to do so, ma'am." He stood up and went to refill his glass.

"Nonsense . . . you owe it to the family. You need an heir."

Harry turned back, the decanter in hand. "I have two brothers, ma'am. Either one of whom will be more than capable of handling the title and the estates. They both have sons. The family name is in no danger of dying out." He brought the decanter over to her and refilled her glass.

"They don't have a whole brain between 'em," the lady declared scornfully. "You know perfectly well, Bonham, that you can run rings around 'em."

"I disagree, ma'am. Both Edmund and Robert manage their estates, their lives, and their families admirably." A chill note had entered his voice, and his tone was clipped. He returned to his seat and looked at her over the rim of his glass.

The duchess pouted. There was no other way to describe it, he thought, suppressing a chuckle. She knew he would never tolerate criticism of his family and usually she was careful about what she said to him. The Madeira had probably loosened her tongue.

"Well, that's as may be," she stated with a dismissive wave of her fan. "You can believe what you wish. But it's time you had a wife. It's been four years, man. No one pays any attention to the old story anymore."

"His Grace does." He sipped his wine.

"Oh, that old fool." The duchess dismissed her

nephew's father-in-law with a snort of disgust. "The duke's never been able to see what's in front of his nose. He should have known that his daughter—"

"Forgive me, ma'am, but that's enough," Harry said softly but with unmistakable authority. "I don't care to discuss it any further."

It silenced her for a few minutes. Eliza Cox seemed to shrink into her chair and busied herself with her needlework. Harry sat calmly, his face expressionless.

"You'll be taking Primrose Tallant in to dinner," the duchess declared suddenly, as if the previous conversation had never taken place. "She's a plain creature, I grant you, but she's no fool, and there's twenty thousand pounds there."

"I hardly think I need to marry an heiress, ma'am," Harry said with a sigh.

The duchess snorted again. "If you ask me, you don't know what you need."

Harry decided it wasn't worth further discussion. He said casually, "I was hoping to persuade you and Lady Sefton to visit some acquaintances of mine, ma'am. They're but newly arrived in town. I think you might enjoy meeting them."

The duchess's gaze sharpened. "What makes you think so . . . who are they?"

"Viscountess Dagenham, her sister-in-law, Lady Farnham, and a friend of theirs, Lady Livia Lacey."

His great-aunt frowned. "Lacey . . . related to Lady Sophia is she?"

"I believe there is some connection," he said. "Lady Livia inherited Lady Sophia's house in Cavendish Square."

"Hmm." The duchess nodded. "Sophia was quite a woman in her day . . . older than I, of course . . . we moved in different circles." She stroked her chin thoughtfully. "So what's the gal like?"

Harry shrugged. "I don't really know her. She seems pleasant."

"So what's your interest there?" she asked, her eyes fixed intently upon him.

"I have no interest, ma'am," he said patiently. "But I happened to meet the ladies quite by chance. They would benefit from an introduction to society. Lady Dagenham and her sister-in-law are widows." He explained the situation briefly.

The duchess listened, for once without any forceful interjections, and when he'd finished, she said only, "Well, I suppose you may escort me to Cavendish Square. I'll look them over."

"Thank you, ma'am." It was as he'd expected. Her curiosity was aroused. If there was the slightest possibility that her nephew might be showing interest in some woman she didn't know, then she'd review the situation without delay. But whatever her motives, the end result would be the same. Cornelia and her friends would have their social introduction.

And now a long and tedious evening stretched ahead of him until he could get down to the real business of the night. At the thought of that business his blood surged with exhilaration. A few hours of tedium would only enhance the anticipation.

The gods were blessing his enterprise, Harry reflected, looking up at the black sky where not even a hint of starshine or moonlight showed behind lowering clouds. The garden below him as he straddled the wall was dark as the grave, only the faint gnarled shapes of the fruit trees offering contrast. The back of the house rose up against the sky, its windows lightless.

He remained where he was until he could make out the shapes of the various windows and was certain he'd identified Nell's. It wouldn't do to disturb someone else. But it was unmistakable given Lester's explicit directions. The second from the left on the first floor immediately above the library on the ground floor. And a sturdy copper drainpipe was most conveniently situated to its right.

Harry leaned forward to grab the branch of an apple tree that scraped the top of the wall. He launched himself off the wall, dropping soundlessly to the soft ground beneath. He paused, listening. Not a sound, not even the rustle of a vole in the underbrush. He darted at a crouch across the small expanse of open ground until he stood in the shadow of the house, his dark-clad figure blending seamlessly into the background.

He reached for the drainpipe and shook it. As Lester

had promised, it was firmly affixed to the wall. Lester, in his capacity as handyman and general jack of all trades, had effected some repairs on his visit that afternoon.

Harry peered up at the window some fifteen feet above. He couldn't see that the sash was lifted a fraction of an inch above the sill, but Lester had assured him that it was open enough for him to slip his fingers beneath it, and raise it high enough to admit him. A generous dose of oil on the runnels ensured that it would lift without a sound.

He raised his hand above his head and felt the wall alongside the drainpipe. There were enough nicks in the brickwork to give him some toeholds if he needed them. He waited again, straining his ears into the darkness, listening for anything untoward. There was nothing except the iron wheels of a carriage on the street in front, taking home some late-night reveler. The inhabitants of this part of London were for the most apart asleep at three o'clock on a winter morning. In a couple of hours the servants would awake, but for now all was quiet.

He reached for the drainpipe and leaped up, his soft leather shoes getting purchase on the wall, his toes curling into well-placed crannies. He climbed upwards, hand over hand, his feet on either side of the drainpipe to take some of the weight off the narrow copper tube.

He reached the window and leaned sideways carefully, clinging to the drainpipe with one hand, feeling with his other for the gap between window and sill. It was there. Not that he'd doubted Lester for one minute;

nevertheless, he was relieved. He leaned farther, turning his hand around so that he could get a grip on the window, and pushed it up inch by inch. It made not a sound as it crept upwards. He prayed silently that the sleeping woman wouldn't become aware of the sudden draft as the cold night air entered her chamber.

When he judged it open sufficiently to allow him to wriggle through, Harry climbed a little higher on the drainpipe until he could stretch one leg sideways to the window ledge. There was a moment when he seemed to hang in space, then with an agile twist he got himself astride the window ledge, his body hunched over in the narrow aperture. In an instant he had dropped to the floor and remained unmoving on his haunches barely breathing. At first he could hear no sound, then he heard the deep rhythmic breathing of a sound sleeper.

The embers of the fire still glowed in the grate, offering a little light, sufficient to make out the hulking shapes of the furniture. He straightened carefully, listening for any change in the sound coming from the big canopied bed. The curtains were drawn back, revealing the glimmer of white sheeting, the slight mound beneath the coverlet.

A smile touched his lips, and his fingers closed over the little silver object in his pocket. First the thimble exhange, but then . . .

He looked around for the workbox, peering into the shadowy dimness. It would be on a surface somewhere.

Unless, as luck would have it, Nell had not brought it upstairs with her. If he didn't find it here, he'd have to venture downstairs. Not a happy prospect when he recollected those yapping terriers.

And then he saw it. The box was on a table with a lamp beside an armchair on the far side of the fireplace. A length of material was draped over a stool beside it. Presumably the lady had been sewing before she went to bed. He stepped soundlessly towards his holy grail and his foot caught something soft.

Something flew up at him out of the shadows with an unearthly squall. Eyes glaring, fur on end, tail bushed wildly, the cat at bay hissed and spat.

Cornelia sat up in bed. "What the devil . . ." She stared at him incredulously as the cat continued its uproar. *"Harry?"* Her mouth opened slightly, and her eyes, blue even in the shadows, widened like saucers. *"You?* What in the name of all that's good are you doing in here?"

She pushed aside the coverlet and got up in one smooth movement. The white folds of her nightgown settled around her as she continued to stare at him.

"Get this cat away from me," he said. He had only one card left, and he had to play it to win. "Before it wakes the entire house."

Cornelia bent down and clicked her fingers at the animal, who had fallen silent but was still at bay. "It's probably too late for that." She wasn't sure what dream world she was inhabiting. Harry was standing calmly as you please in the middle of her bedchamber in the middle of the night, and he sounded as if it was the most obvious place for him to be.

The sound of heavy feet came from the corridor outside. "Too late," she confirmed, recognizing Morecombe's stolid step.

Harry glanced around, then darted to the far side of the bed, concealing himself somewhat inadequately behind a fold of the bed curtains.

"My lady . . . my lady . . ." Morecombe banged on the door. "Is everything all right in there?"

"Oh, God," said Cornelia. "He'll have the blunderbuss out in a minute." She ran to the door, opening it carefully. "Yes, everything's fine, Morecombe. It was just the cat, she—"

The rest of the sentence was drowned as Tristan and Isolde, yapping excitedly, raced between Morecombe's legs and into the room. They rushed at the cat, who, already agitated, reared up and hurled herself at them, hissing, spitting, and clawing. The dogs squealed in terror and turned tail, the cat on their heels.

The threesome disappeared into the darkness of the corridor, squalling and yapping, claws skittering on the polished wooden floor.

Morecombe flourished his blunderbuss and peered around Cornelia. "You sure there's nothing wrong, m'lady?"

"Yes, quite sure, thank you." Cornelia was afraid she was about to burst into hysterical laughter. Thank God the dogs hadn't had time to flush out Harry. He was barely concealed by the curtain as it was.

"Your window's open," the butler stated suspiciously. "'Tis the middle of winter."

"Oh, yes . . . so it is. I like fresh air, Morecombe. I find it helps me sleep."

"Newfangled nonsense," he said. "Catch your death, you will." He took one more look around, sniffed disapprovingly, and retreated. "I'll leave you to it, then."

The door closed behind him, and Cornelia waited for what she was knew was coming next. "Nell . . . Nell . . . what's going on?"

Cornelia opened the door and stood in the doorway holding the door half-closed at her back. She spoke in a rushed whisper, trying to sound sleepy and bemused, but also careless as if her entire body wasn't prickling with awareness of the man in the room behind her. She could almost hear his breathing and wondered how Ellie couldn't hear it too.

"It's nothing, Ellie. I'm sorry to have woken you. I got up in the night and trod on the cat, and she went berserk, and that brought up Morecombe and the pink things and they attacked Puss, or she attacked them, I'm not sure which, and all hell broke loose. It hasn't woken the children has it?"

Aurelia blinked sleepily. "No, I don't hear anything," she said. "But it scared the life out of me. Such a racket."

"I'm sorry," Cornelia said with a self-deprecating shrug.

Aurelia shivered. "There's a howling gale, Nell. Is the window open or something?"

What madwoman opened her bedroom window wide in the middle of winter? "I had a headache when I went to bed," Cornelia improvised. "I thought a little air might help."

"Well, for heaven's sake shut it now," Aurelia said, yawning and shivering at the same time. "I'm going back to bed. I'm astonished that racket didn't wake Liv."

"She sleeps through almost anything," Cornelia said, stepping back into her room. "Good night, Ellie. Sorry to have woken you." She closed the door and very quietly turned the key.

❧

Cornelia stood with her back to the closed door, saying nothing. She was at a loss for words after the last quarter of an hour of intense improvisation.

Harry moved out from behind the curtains and went to close the window. If he hadn't been so intent on the workbox he would have thought to close it immediately after he'd entered the chamber. But then he'd been distracted too by the shape in the bed, and the luscious prospect of awakening the sleeper once the thimbles were safely exchanged.

Neither prospect was a reality now. One thimble remained in the workbox, the other in his pocket, and Nell was very wide-awake. Those penetrating blue eyes were regarding him with mingled unease and anger, but there was also a glimmer of anticipation. Her hair tumbled in a thick luxuriant mass around her shoulders, framing her face where color bloomed on her high cheekbones.

Still silent, she moved to the fireplace. She took a long taper from a jar on the mantel and bent to light it in the embers. When it glowed, she lit the lamp on the side table.

Harry could see the outline of her body beneath the thin shift as the light flared. She straightened and turned to face him. And he could see the dark points of her nipples.

"What are you doing here?" Her voice was quiet.

He smiled slowly. "I came to make good on a promise, Nell."

"You made me no promises," she said, resting her hands behind her on the table, her eyes not moving from his face.

"Didn't I?" he said. "How remiss of me. I certainly made one to myself." He took a step forward, and she stiffened. He changed direction and turned instead to the fire. Kneeling, he piled kindling on top of the embers and waited for them to catch before adding coals from the copper scuttle.

"That's better." He stood up again, brushing off his hands. "I'm sorry about the window. I should have closed it immediately. But I was distracted."

"By what?" The tip of her tongue touched her lips in an involuntary movement.

"Can't you guess?" He had caught the movement, sensed the stiffness leave her, saw the anticipation in her gaze take precedence over the anger and unease. "I can't stop thinking about you, Nell. You've inhabited my mind every minute of every day and every night since I first laid eyes on you."

Cornelia's eyes narrowed. "Now that is pushing belief," she said. "You thought me an ill-mannered servant."

"Oh, I don't deny it," he said. "Any more than I'll deny that I disliked you intensely on our second meeting, and could have wrung your neck at the first opportunity." He took a step towards her. "But that didn't alter anything, Nell. I have wanted you with a passion whether you were driving me to fury or to desire." He reached for her hands, drawing her closer.

She made no attempt to pull away, but neither did she lean into him. She simply stood very still, as if holding herself in readiness for something.

He ran his hands up and under the cascade of her hair, trawling his fingers through the buttery mass as he'd longed to do. He took a thick swatch of her hair in one hand and held it aside as he pressed his lips into the hollow of her shoulder. And then he felt the shudder run through her and knew he'd been right. She had a passion to match his own.

He took her chin between thumb and forefinger and lifted her face so that her gaze met his, and she could see the brilliant sensual sheen in his green eyes, could sense his vibrant longing.

And she was lost in that gaze, her body losing its shape and identity in some way as she felt herself slipping into a half world, where the physical objects around her seemed to lose their solidity. She was aware now only of herself and of this man whose heat she could feel, whose scent filled her nostrils with a musky male odor of arousal.

Greedily she took his mouth with her own, tasting wine and cloves as her tongue danced against his. His arms were around her, holding her tightly against him, as if he would imprint her upon his body. He felt her nipples press hard against his shirt, the sharp bones of her hips pushing against him, and his penis rose strongly against her belly. She gasped a little and slid her hand down between them to rub the jutting flesh. And he groaned, sucking on her lower lip, sliding his own hands around her body to grasp her bottom, his fingers squeezing and kneading the firm round curves that clenched tightly against his hands.

He drew his head back, looked at her, at her swollen, kiss-reddened lips, her flushed cheeks, and the passion-filled eyes. "Take this off," he said, and although his voice was barely above a whisper, the demand was harshly urgent. He fumbled with the buttons of her nightgown, and she drew away, pulling the garment over her head and tossing it to the floor.

Naked she stood in front of him, her eyes hooded, her breasts moving swiftly with her rapid breath. And her smile held the familiar challenge mixed now with a deep lustful self-awareness. She passed her hands over her own body, as if offering herself to him.

He reached for her, cupping her breasts in his palms. He bent his head to kiss the full curves, running his tongue over the sweet flesh. He hadn't expected such fullness. Her height had masked the rich swell. His tongue detected tiny ridges in the smooth skin, the little silver marks left by the children she had carried. An unexpected tenderness flowed through him, for a moment dampening the urgency of ardor. He ran his tongue into the deep cleft, lightly touched the nipples in a moist caress, moved his tongue up to the hollow of her throat even as he cupped her breasts in his hands.

Her head fell back, offering him the white column, and he licked upwards under her chin and was rewarded with a tiny laugh of protest at the tickling sensation. He lifted his head and smiled into her face. "You are exquisite," he said.

The simple declaration gave her immense pleasure. "Take off your clothes," she said. "I would see you too."

He nodded, kicking off his shoes. He shrugged out of his black coat before beginning to unbutton his dark shirt.

Cornelia watched, gazing avidly as his body was revealed. It was an athlete's body, but that she had expected. Slim and wiry, the muscles in arms and shoulders defined but not obvious. Her fingers itched to help him with the buttons of his britches, but she held herself still, her hands lightly clenched against her bare thighs, as he pushed the garment off his hips.

A concave belly, slim hips, long lean thighs. Once again her tongue touched her lips as she took in the upstanding promise of his penis. She reached for it, enclosing the shaft in her hand, feeling the blood pulsing in the ridged veins. Her eyes lifted to his with a distinct hint of lascivious mischief in them.

"Does it please you, madam?" he asked lightly, responding to this change.

"I believe it does, sir, but I'd like to be sure," she returned with a demure smile. "Perhaps it's time for a demonstration."

He laughed softly. "Oh, have a care what you wish for, my lady." With a swift dip, he swept her up into his arms and carried her to the bed, dumping her unceremoniously in the middle. He stood over her, still laughing, and she reached up for him.

"Let me take my stockings off," he protested, stepping back. "There's something distinctly unromantic about making love in one's stockings."

He turned his back, bending to pull off his stockings, and Cornelia gazed at the curve of his spine, the column of dark hair running down between his taut buttocks, at the heavy hang of his balls.

She rolled onto her side and stretched out a hand to touch his backside. He straightened up a little but otherwise didn't move, letting her explore at will. She slipped her hand between his thighs to cup his balls, pressing her finger against the shaft of his penis where it sprang from his body.

He inhaled sharply. "Enough now." He turned around and came down on the bed beside her. He stroked a lock of hair from her forehead, murmuring, "I want this to last, Nell."

She smiled, a slow, languorous smile, and reached for him again. "We have all night. I want you *now*." Even as she spoke them, the words astonished her. Before this night she could never have imagined herself making such a direct and uninhibited statement of desire.

Harry swung himself over her. He was at the very edge of his own control now; her scent enveloped him in a heady mix of lust and cleanliness, arousal, rosewater, and soap. He slid his hands beneath her bottom, lifting her to meet him as she raised her hips and pressed forward with her own urgency. He thrust deep within her, felt her close around him, her body tight, warm, and welcoming.

Cornelia closed her eyes, realizing how much she had missed this simple sensation of holding her man inside her, then her eyes shot open as the sensation changed, became something she had not missed because she had not experienced it before. She felt his penis pressing hard against her womb, her inner muscles contracted, her body was slippery and her belly was tight, a spiral of tension that locked her thighs and buttocks, sent waves of sensation through her. She stared up at him as the tension built, the spiral tightened, then it burst, and she opened her mouth.

Harry silenced her cry with his mouth, holding himself still as her climax wracked her, and then while the convulsive movements of her inner muscles continued, he moved within her, increasing his rhythm until he felt her rocked again with sensation. He kept his mouth on hers and let himself go. The wave rocked him as it crashed over Cornelia, and at last he fell forward, beached upon her, as the wave receded.

It seemed many minutes before she moved. Her hand stroked down his back, and she shifted her body in gentle protest at the weight of him. He groaned softly and rolled sideways to lie beside her. He touched the curve of her cheek.

"You have unmanned me, sweetheart," he murmured, kissing her ear. "I had expected to enjoy myself, but not to be so transported."

Cornelia smiled and turned her head on the pillow to look at him. She didn't say that she had never experienced anything quite so wonderful as the last few minutes, but her smile told him all he needed to know. Her eyes glowed with fulfillment and the residue of passion, her body gleamed with a faint sheen of sweat, her complexion was translucently radiant.

"So, you come a thief in the night," she mused in a bare whisper. "A Casanova through the window. Are you ordinarily given to such dramas, my lord?"

He laughed softly. "No, not in general, but I had the sense that an unusual approach was necessary with you, my lady." He kissed her mouth. "You are so entrenched in your life, so surrounded by the trappings of domesticity, a simple siege seemed unlikely to carry the day."

So entrenched in her life. The words banished Cornelia's sensual lethargy. Her life was circumscribed by domesticity, ruled by the long shadow of the earl of Markby. If the earl could see her now . . .

The image was so absurd that she nearly laughed aloud. Or would have done so if it had not also been horrendous. The merest breath of scandal would be enough for him. The idea of his grandson's mother lying shamelessly in the arms of a near stranger, a man of whom she knew almost nothing, except what he chose to present. A wealthy viscount, a widower, a man about town. *What else was he?*

Harry felt her sudden withdrawal. "What is it?" He propped himself on one elbow and smiled down at her with a hint of puzzlement.

"Nothing really," she said with a quick shake of her head. "An inconvenient reminder, that's all."

"Ah." He touched the tip of her nose. "How inconvenient?"

She shook her head again with a smile. "Irrelevantly so."

He nodded in acceptance and moved his hand down the side of her body from her shoulder to the indentation of her waist in a long smooth caress. "Such richness," he murmured, burying his lips in the hollow of her throat where the pulse began to beat fast.

Cornelia dismissed her questions and with them the

faint unease that had prompted them. For the moment she needed to know nothing more about him than this. She stretched languidly beneath his hands as he began to explore her body anew, bringing her skin to tingling sensitivity. This was just a dream, a lustful and lusty dream. No one was watching, no one would ever guess how Lady Dagenham had once spent the long reaches of a dark winter night.

It was a quieter loving this time, each taking the time to savor the other. Harry moved slowly within her, drawing himself back to the very edge of her body, holding himself there, watching her face as she gazed wide-eyed into his face hanging above her. The lines of his face were softened, his mouth full and sensual, lips slightly parted as he gauged her reactions. When he sheathed himself inch by inch within her, she drew in her breath, caught her lip between her teeth, pressed her heels into the taut muscular buttocks. He resisted her urgency, kissed the corner of her mouth, drew back once more, teasing her.

Her back arched as her buttocks and thighs tightened, and her inner muscles gripped him, holding him deep within her. He moved a hand down between their bodies and touched her where they were joined and her body leaped beneath him. She flung her arms above her head, moving her raised hips around the shaft of flesh buried within her, moved upwards to the caressing finger, unsure now which part of him was causing this exquisite sensation but sure that she wanted it never to stop.

And when it did, it was in a rushing torrent of delight

that brought tears to her eyes and the taste of blood in her mouth where she bit her lip to keep from shouting her joy to the night wind.

Harry slid his arms around her, pressed her against him as if he would join every inch of their bodies, their sweat-slick skins, and buried his mouth in her hair to silent his own cries.

He fell to the bed beside her, rolling her sideways against him, and closed his eyes, his heart pounding, a red mist behind his eyelids. He felt her fall into sleep, her body limp, one leg sprawled across his thighs, her head heavy on his chest.

But he had to leave her. He could discern the faint graying of the dark beyond the window. But how long *had* he been here, dallying with the widow? He raised his head, trying not to disturb Nell, and peered at the clock above the mantel. *Five o'clock.* The servants would be up any minute.

Nell seemed dead to the world. He lifted her leg from over his thighs and cradled her head as he slid out from beside her, laying it gently on the pillow. She didn't move, her long white body gleaming in the darkness.

His eyes darted to the workbox. Now, while she slept, was his opportunity.

"Harry?" She raised her head from the pillow. "Where are you going?"

"It's nearly dawn, sweetheart." He bent to kiss her. "If I don't leave now, your maid will find me here when she brings your chocolate."

Cornelia struggled up against the pillows and chuckled weakly. "What maid? We don't run to abigails in this house."

"Nevertheless, I must go." He bent to his discarded clothes and scrambled into them. Then he went to the window, pushing it up. He swung a leg over the ledge and looked back at her, now sitting bolt upright in the bed.

"Until the next time, sweetheart," he promised softly. He reached for the drainpipe, hung for a second, then swung sideways and was gone.

Cornelia jumped from bed and ran to the window. She leaned out watching his agile descent and the neat drop into the soft earth of the flower bed below. "How are you going to get over the wall?" she whispered. But if he heard her he chose not to respond. She watched as he darted across the garden, the light growing stronger by the minute. He leaped for a low branch of an apple tree and shinnied up it, then straddled the wall and a second later was gone.

Cornelia closed the window softly. Her body was still singing, and she stood for a minute running her hands over herself, remembering the touches that had brought her alive after so long. And even with Stephen . . . but she quashed the thought. Such a comparison would be disloyal. Her husband had been a gentle lover, but she guessed fairly inexperienced. He had not known how to arouse his partner, and she had not known what to expect, so they had been contented with what they had shared. And it brought them children . . . *her* children, now only hers. She could not lose them.

Panic rose for an instant in her throat. She swallowed it, breathing deeply. Her pleasure in the night faded. From beyond her door came the unmistakable sounds of the house waking. A child's cry from the nursery, the excitable yap of a dog, the sound of the front door.

Her eye fell on the puddle of white . . . her nightgown on the floor in front of the fire. She picked it up, shook it out, and for a moment felt again the glory of the night, aware of the stickiness on her inner thighs, the slight soreness between her legs, the glorious sense of a well-used body.

She dropped the garment over her head and went to the armoire for her robe. It was time to put on the day.

Chapter 14

So what do you think, Nell? Will this do?" Livia, careful not to disturb the pins that held her into the gown, turned in front of the long mirror in the spare bedchamber that had become the seamstress's workroom. "It's very fine, I think." She stroked the silver-striped cream taffeta skirt of the ball gown. "It is, isn't it?"

"It's lovely," Cornelia said, reaching over Livia's shoulders to adjust the neck of the gown. "But this needs to be lower . . . don't you agree, Claire?"

"Yes, indeed, m'lady," the seamstress agreed, stepping forward to make her own adjustments. "And if Lady Livia feels a little exposed, then a fichu . . . ?" She let the question die of its own accord.

"Certainly not," Cornelia declared with a quick conspiratorial smile at the seamstress. "You have lovely breasts, Liv, and they need to be seen."

"Quite right," the seamstress declared with the familiarity of many fittings.

"My father . . . ?"Liv protested without conviction.

"The vicar will not see you to object." Aurelia pointed out, entering the fray. She'd been standing to one side, making her own observations. "It's a gorgeous gown, Liv. You'll wear it to your first Almack's assembly ball, and the bucks will be at your feet."

Livia laughed. "That I doubt, but I appreciate the reassurance, Ellie. Now it's your turn." She gestured towards the dove gray silk that lay over the chaise longue.

"One minute, Lady Livia," Claire said. She unpinned the creation from her body, and Livia stepped back with a shake of her shift and a twitch of her shoulders.

"Now, Lady Farnham." Claire picked up the dove gray silk with a degree of reverence. "If you would stand in front of the mirror?"

Aurelia stood for her fitting, watching her reflection. The gown was, as she'd specified, quite demure, even matronly, she thought with a little flicker of dislike. But she had made the decision for herself. She was a chaperone. A widowed mother. The gown was unpinned, and she sat on a low stool to watch Cornelia's fitting.

Cornelia's ball gown was an azure blue silk, very similar in style to Aurelia's own. A decorous décolletage, a dainty froth of lace over the shoulders. The color, however, beautifully complemented Nell's eyes, and the shape made the most of her long waist. It ended in an embroidered hem that fell just above her ankles. Aurelia had always envied those nicely turned ankles.

"It's very pretty, Nell," she said.

Her friend surprised her. "Yes." Cornelia frowned at her image. "Too pretty. I don't like pretty." She plucked at the neckline. "Claire, could you lower this?"

"Yes, easily, Lady Dagenham." Claire was there with her pincushion.

"And do something more interesting with this lace." Cornelia plucked at the discreet lace on her upper arms.

"A little puff sleeve, m'lady," Claire suggested, wielding pins. "Very fashionable."

"Good," Cornelia said. "Then do that."

"But you liked the gown perfectly well two days ago," Aurelia pointed out.

"Yes, but I've changed my mind," Cornelia stated, aware of her sister-in-law's puzzlement but unable to explain it away. The only way she could explain it to herself was that something had opened or awoken within her, the recognition that she was a sexual being, something more than a loving mother and a dutiful widow. And she wanted to glory in that side of herself, not hide it away behind demure and matronly widow's weeds.

Aurelia regarded Cornelia quizzically. "I hadn't realized that you intended to burst upon the ton in full glory, Nell."

"I don't really, Ellie. But we might as well look our best," Cornelia said carelessly. "You should alter your gown too. We're chaperones for Liv, but we don't have to look like matronly dowds."

The seamstress coughed. "I beg your pardon, ma'am, but I would not send you into society looking like dowds."

Cornelia was instantly apologetic. "No, Claire, I didn't mean that at all. I meant only that Ellie and I haven't seen much of the outside world since we were widowed. But I don't think we should dress as if we're only fit for sitting against the wall watching our protégée dance."

She looked at Aurelia. "Come on, Ellie, you're twenty-nine. You don't have to put yourself on the market, but you could feel that you were in contention and play the game."

Aurelia looked at her friends. Looked at herself in the mirror over Nell's shoulder and made up her mind. "Very well, if you're going to play the game, Nell, then so will I."

Claire nodded with satisfaction. "Three such beautiful ladies. It will be a real pleasure to dress you." She gathered up the unfinished gowns and arranged them reverently on the dressmaker's dummies.

"We'll leave you to it then," Aurelia said, moving to the door, Livia following her. She glanced back at Cornelia, who was still sitting on the edge of the threadbare chaise beneath the window. Her friend wore a distracted air that was most unlike her. Ordinarily, Nell was utterly focused on whatever she was doing, but for the last two or three days it seemed as if she was only half-there. She would sometimes start a sentence and let it fade away uncompleted. Either that or she would stare into the middle distance for minutes at a time, just as she was doing now.

"Penny for them, Nell," she said lightly.

Cornelia looked startled. "What? Oh, sorry, I was miles away."

"Yes, so I noticed," Aurelia said. "Are you coming?"

"Oh, yes, of course." Cornelia seemed almost visibly to shake herself as she stood up and followed them out of the room.

Aurelia said with a laugh, "What's the matter with you, Nell?"

Cornelia shook her head. "I'm not sleeping very well," she offered, and hurried away in the direction of the nursery stairs.

"Just what's going on with her?" Aurelia demanded of Livia. "You've noticed how strangely she's behaving, surely?"

"She does seem a bit distracted," Livia said. "But if she's tired . . ."

"Stuff," Aurelia scoffed. "Nell could be dead on her feet, and she would still be focused. She's just not here most of the time."

"No, I suppose you're right. Now you mention it." Livia frowned. "And why this sudden urge to be fashionable? Nell doesn't give a fig about clothes."

"That's not entirely true," Aurelia said. "But her style has never been . . . what's the word I want . . . *daring,* that's it. It makes sense I suppose to make our new clothes as modish as possible but such a pronounced décolletage?" She shrugged in puzzlement.

"Well, I think she's right, for what it's worth," Livia

stated. "We don't want to look like country bumpkins. Just think of that gown Letitia was wearing when she came to call yesterday. It was practically transparent. I don't know why she didn't freeze to death. The materials are all so thin, and the necklines are so low . . . and if that's for daytime wear, the devil only knows what they'll wear at night."

"Well, Letitia certainly managed to get in a few disparaging comments on our own dress," Aurelia said with a grimace.

"Nell put her in her place, though." Livia chuckled. "You remember, when Letitia made that comment about how plain your gown was and how horizontal stripes were all the fashion now, and Nell said she always thought that stripes increased one's girth, but that you, at least, would be able to get away with it, seeing as how slender you are. And then she looked at Letitia and suggested that perhaps a vertical stripe might lessen the impression of a certain thickness."

Aurelia smiled, but a trifle guiltily. "We shouldn't be unkind, but Letitia did deserve to be taken down a peg."

"Well, next time she sees us, she won't have any call to make disparaging comments," Livia stated.

Cornelia forced herself to concentrate on Stevie's convoluted description of his morning's visit to Hyde Park with Daisy. Franny's frequent interruptions didn't make the narrative flow any faster, and the temptation to let her mind follow its own path was almost irresistible, but she knew that Stevie would sense the first moment her concentration wavered, and his hurt recriminations would only make her feel horribly guilty.

For once she welcomed Linton's firm declaration that it was time for the children's afternoon nap and left the nursery, making her way to her own bedchamber. She needed solitude and knew that her present mood was already attracting her friends' curiosity. And she had no way of satisfying that curiosity.

She sat beside the fire and took up her workbox, preparing to finish sewing the braided trim on a sleeveless velvet jacket designed to accompany the new walking dress Claire had made for her. The addition of the jacket would transform the outfit sufficiently to make it seem like another one altogether.

Absently she turned the thimble around on her finger, trying as she so often did to decipher the engraving. It seemed just a series of hieroglyphics, almost Egyptian in origin she thought. Whatever they were, whatever they meant, it was a lovely object in its own right.

Then her hands fell into her lap and her eyes rested on the fire. It had been two days since that night with Harry, and he hadn't come knocking, either on the front door or via her bedchamber window. She told herself that it was all to the good if she'd seen the last of him. No one knew about that one extraordinary night of bliss, and they never would. But it couldn't happen again . . . *mustn't* happen again.

But she knew she hadn't seen the last of Harry Bonham. He would be back. And what she would do then she had no idea. She knew what she *should* do, but Cornelia had enough self-knowledge to know that in this case that might not be what she *would* do.

A knock at the door brought her back to the room. "Nell?" The door opened, and Aurelia put her head around. "Oh, there you are. We were wondering where you'd got to. You weren't in the nursery."

She came fully into the room. "A messenger just brought this." She held out a letter, quite a thick one. "I think it's from the viscount. It looks like his crest."

Cornelia took the letter with a word of thanks. Her heart jumped against her ribs as her fingers closed over the paper, just as if she were some love-struck girl, she thought with a mixture of amusement and disgust.

"I wonder why he's taken to writing to us," she observed lightly. She turned the packet over and slit the wafer with a fingernail. She opened the folded sheets and looked in surprise at the list of names inscribed on both sides of the two sheets. "What on earth . . . ? Oh, it's a list of the people he says we should leave cards with."

"Do we know any of them?" Aurelia leaned over her shoulder to read the list. "Oh, yes, I recognize some of them. Lady Bellingham was a friend of my mother's. And . . . oh, and he's suggesting we call upon Letitia. Of course he doesn't know we've already done that, perforce."

"We'll have to return her call of yesterday anyway," said Cornelia somewhat dourly.

"May I see the list?" Aurelia took the paper from her sister-in-law and read the list again. "There must be about thirty names here. That'll keep us busy for a few afternoons."

"We need a carriage to make calls," Cornelia pointed out. "We'll have to hire one from a livery stable."

Aurelia frowned. "It'll make us look a bit shabby, won't it?"

Her sister-in-law shrugged. "It can't be helped, Ellie. We can't afford to set up our own stable. Maybe Nigel will be able to help."

"He's staying with the marquess of Coltrain, I'll send him a note." Aurelia handed her back the sheet and went to the door. "Are you coming down?"

"Later. I want to finish sewing this braid."

"You could do that in the parlor," Aurelia pointed out, watching Cornelia closely.

"Yes, I could," Cornelia agreed, recognizing that insistence on solitude would actually stimulate the questions she was trying to avoid. "I'll come down." She slipped the thimble from her finger and dropped it into the workbox before gathering up the jacket and braid and following Aurelia downstairs.

Harry glanced impatiently at the clock on the broad mantel in the paneled chamber at the War Office. The discussion had been going on interminably and as far as Harry was concerned to no good purpose.

"If I might make a suggestion, sir," he said politely, breaking into the minister's monologue.

The minister for war pulled on his bushy white moustaches. "What is it, Bonham?"

"Before we continue this discussion as to the importance of the information contained in the dispatches . . ." Harry indicated the documents in front of him on the table. "I think we should consider the possibility that the information itself is compromised."

The six other men around the table looked down at their own piles of papers as if the documents themselves might suddenly break into speech.

"Compromised? How so?" The minister frowned, his beetle brows meeting above the bridge of his nose. "This is the most comprehensive description of the plans for a meeting between Alexander and Bonaparte ever to fall into our hands. How should it be compromised?"

Harry sighed a little. "As you say, sir, the most comprehensive description ever to fall into our hands. A gift horse you might say?" He raised an eyebrow. "I think we should consider the possibility of a *Trojan* horse."

There was a short silence. "You're saying this may be misinformation, Harry?" The prime minister sounded incredulous and not for the first time Harry wished he still worked for the formidable brain of William Pitt. But Pitt had died the previous year. The duke of Portland had succeeded him, and in Harry's opinion very much to the detriment of the country.

"I'm almost certain of it, sir," he said calmly, concealing his irritation.

"But how could that be?" His Grace continued to sound incredulous. "It was brought to us by one of our most credible agents."

"Even credible agents can be fooled, sir." Harry picked up the documents and looked around the table. "Gentlemen, I cracked this code in approximately thirty minutes. Now I'm willing to concede that I am rather good at my job, but for a document of this importance to be encrypted in a code I can crack in half an hour defies belief. I suggest that they wanted us to crack it, and crack it quickly. And why would they want that?"

He smiled amiably around the table and let them answer the question themselves.

"To mislead us?" the prime minister said.

"Precisely, sir." Harry gave him the nod of a schoolmaster congratulating an apt pupil. He glanced again at the clock. It was four in the afternoon, and he hadn't been home in two days. An urgent summons to the War Office to deal with a courier's delivery of encrypted documents had kept him chained to his desk. They had not all been as simple to break as the one presently under discussion.

Now he had better things to do with his time.

"If that's so, what do you suggest we do, Bonham?" one of the other men asked.

"Provide them with some misinformation of our own," Harry said, as if the answer was obvious, as to him it was. "They're playing games, so we play them too. I'll craft an encoded document describing how we're going to respond to this information." He tapped the papers in front of him.

"I'll ensure that they can break my code relatively quickly, not quite as fast as I did theirs, however." His mouth twisted in an ironic grin. "I obviously have more respect for their encrypters than they have for ours." He flicked disdainfully at the papers. "This was an insult."

"And they'll believe we took this information at face value?" His Grace was still uncertain.

"Some of them will, sir," Harry said. "But there'll be someone somewhere who'll see the joke. There always is. At best it'll tie them up for a while, at worst they'll be hopping mad that we saw through them."

"But what if this information *is* correct?" The prime minister peered at him through his lorgnette. "I don't see how we can afford to take the risk that it isn't."

"That, sir, is a matter for the War Office," Harry said, beginning to put his papers together. "If you think it wise to make contingency plans, then it's not my business to stop you. But I do think it would be wise in addition to let me fashion some misinformation of our own."

"Indeed, Prime Minister, Viscount Bonham's advice

has been proved right on many occasions," the minister said.

The prime minister grimaced at the tabletop, then said decisively, "Very well, Bonham. Make your document, and we'll send it through the usual channels."

Harry rose to his feet and bowed. "It will be my pleasure, sir. You'll have it in the morning. Gentlemen, I wish you good afternoon."

He strode to the door and attained the relative peace of the corridor with a sigh of relief. A passing ensign saluted him. Harry made a halfhearted gesture in response and hurried to his own office. The task would take him about two hours using a code that he'd used before, with a few minor changes that might puzzle the French decoders for a short while. But nothing arduous . . . then he would be free.

Free to plan his next meeting with Nell.

For the first time that he could remember, his utter concentration on his work had been invaded by errant memories. Her scent, the feel of her hair, the softness of her skin, the luscious moist warmth of her sex. The folds of flesh that had opened to his touch, the urgent press of her loins as her climax had neared. The way her eyes took on the depth and glow of sapphires as she held his gaze, drawing his self into hers as she drew his body within her.

He had made love to many women, but he'd never experienced anything like those two hours with Nell.

Anne. No, there had been only duty there. She had

not enjoyed their lovemaking, and so he had not either. Of course he hadn't known about Jeffrey Vibart. Had he known, he might have felt less responsible for his wife's clear lack of enthusiasm for the act of love.

He slammed the door to his office behind him as he went in. It was a cramped space befitting a man whose work was basically unacknowledged. It was war work that carried no honor, no grandeur, no martyrdom, and as such was regarded as a dirty necessity, one that didn't have to be openly designated.

He sat at his scratched desk, sharpened a quill, and began work.

It was dark when he'd finished. He folded the parchment and opened the door to the corridor. "Stewart?"

"Yes, Lord Bonham." A young man appeared instantly from a door opposite, his hair tousled, his myopic eyes blinking behind spectacles, his black coat seemingly coated with a fine layer of dust. "Is it finished, sir?"

"Finished," Harry affirmed, handing him the document. "Check it through thoroughly in case I've made a mistake."

"You never make mistakes, sir," the young man said with a degree of reverence.

Harry smiled wearily. "There's always a first time, Stewart. You know the code, make sure there are no slips, and then send it down the usual channels."

"At once, my lord. You'll be at home if I need to check anything with you?"

"I'll be asleep, Stewart, so be absolutely certain your questions are necessary before you wake me," Harry warned. He was smiling, but his assistant was in no doubt as to the seriousness of the warning.

"Yes, sir." He disappeared into his own cubbyhole.

Harry stretched, hearing his shoulders crack. He needed fresh air and exercise before he could sleep. And he needed sleep before he could see Nell.

Nigel stared down at his hand of cards, trying to remember what card the banker had laid down last. His head seemed full of fluff. He couldn't think straight. He was aware of the soft voices of the groom porters calling the odds, the sibilant swish of cards being dealt, the brilliant illumination of the candelabra throwing light across the baize tables, the slightly raised voices as players gestured with an empty glass to a servant hovering with a decanter.

He had never played in a gaming hell before. Mac had told him that Pickering Place was the most exclusive hell. Everyone who was anyone played here. But Nigel had not seen at the tables Viscount Bonham, or any of the gentlemen who seemed the viscount's especial friends.

His head ached. He laid down the queen of hearts and watched the banker cover it with the king. He had no idea how much he'd lost as he scrawled yet another IOU. He felt a hand on his shoulder and looked up into the face of a man he hadn't seen before.

"A word with you, Mr. Dagenham," the man said courteously, but the hand was tight on his shoulder, and Nigel saw that he was flanked by two other dark-clad gentlemen.

Nigel was aware his smile was feeble as he said with an appearance of composure, "Of course. What can I do for you?" He rose from the table, twitching the hand from his shoulder, and taking out his snuffbox.

"Perhaps we could talk in private," the man said, waiting while Nigel took a pinch of snuff that he didn't want. "If you'd be so kind as to follow me." He gestured to a door at the side of the room.

Nigel followed him, numbed by the sense of inevitability. He followed the three men into a small inner chamber, and the man who had spoken to him said pleasantly, "May I offer you a glass of cognac, Mr. Dagenham?"

"Thank you," Nigel said, hearing his voice as if it came from somewhere outside himself. He took the glass offered to him and declined the seat also offered.

His interlocutor smiled, but it was not the nicest smile. "We seem to have a little problem, Mr. Dagenham. These, I believe, are all yours."

Nigel saw with a shock that the man held a stack of IOUs. "Not tonight," he stammered. "It's not possible I ran those up tonight."

"No, of course not," the other said in soothing tones as he riffled the papers as if they were a pack of cards. "Not tonight, no. But . . . uh . . . over the last few weeks, shall we say?"

Nigel swallowed, his mind trying to grasp the fact that this man appeared to be holding all his IOUs garnered at the tables in every gaming club in Mayfair. "How . . . how did you get those?" he managed at last.

The man smiled and laid them down on the desk. "Don't worry about that, Mr. Dagenham. Let's concern ourselves more with how you intend to pay them."

Nigel glanced around the room. There seemed to be no way out apart from the door behind him, and the two other men stood on either side of that door. There were no windows, and the lamp on the desk threw an uncertain light.

"What business is it of yours?" he demanded, finding strength in desperation. "I understand that my debts in this place might be of interest to you, but those . . ." He flung a hand in a gesture that he hoped was carelessly dismissive. "Those can have nothing to do with you."

The man looked a little sorrowful. "Ah, well I have to inform you, Mr. Dagenham, that you are unfortunately mistaken. I acquired these debts of honor." He raised the papers and waved them in a gesture rather similar to Nigel's own. "And I am now your creditor." His eyes narrowed suddenly. "And I ask you, again, how you intend to settle your debts, sir."

Nigel licked his lips. Nothing here made any sense. He had gambled in all the clubs of the ton. In White's and Watier's and Brookes's. The most elite members of society held his notes. So how had those notes ended up in a hell on Pickering Place in the hands of a man who was not, most definitely *not,* a gentleman?

"I don't understand," he said. "Give me my notes!"

The man tucked them away in a drawer in the desk. "I can't do that, sir. These belong to me." He gave Nigel a flickering smile. "You should be grateful, sir. Your debts of honor are all paid, as, indeed, is your debt to Havant and Green. Your credit is good . . . except here."

Nigel struggled to grasp the fact that all his debts had been cleared. It explained why when he'd ventured into White's the previous day he had not been ostracized, something he'd been terrified of. "Why?" he demanded. "Why would you settle my debts?"

"Ah, well someone else can explain that to you, sir." The man smiled his flickering smile and turned a key in the drawer where he'd placed Nigel's IOUs. "If you'd wait here, sir, he'll join you immediately."

Chapter 15

HARRY DISMOUNTED AND HANDED the reins of his horse to Eric. "Take him home, I'll walk back," he instructed before ascending the stairs to the front door of the house on Cavendish Square. He raised the knocker and let it fall, then stepped back, waiting. It was always interesting to see who would open this door. One of the women, or the taciturn and disapproving Morecombe.

He was kept waiting for long enough to know that it would be the retainer, eventually. Nell and her friends tended to be much swifter in their responses. The door creaked open, and, as he'd expected, Morecombe peered at him through the narrow aperture.

"Aye?" he demanded.

"Is Lady Dagenham within, Morecombe?" Harry asked, pushing the door wide and stepping inside past the retainer. He took off his hat and tossed it onto the bench.

"She could be," Morecombe said. "Haven't seen her go out."

"Then perhaps you'd announce me." Harry offered a genial smile as he shrugged out of his greatcoat. "Viscount Bonham, Morecombe," he reminded gently when the man stood seemingly irresolute, gazing blankly at him.

"Oh, aye." Morecombe nodded. "The ladies are in the kitchen." He shuffled off to the nether regions of the house, leaving Harry standing in the hall.

Harry shook his head in resignation and looked around, noting the polish and the wax and the luster of the chandelier. Matters had improved considerably on Cavendish Square. He took a look in the salon and nodded his approval. He was about to investigate the dining room on the far side of the hall when he heard the step he'd been waiting for.

Cornelia emerged from the gloom of the corridor behind the stairs that led to the kitchen. She paused for an instant before stepping into the full light of the hall, gathering herself. Then she came forward, hand outstretched.

"Lord Bonham, we've missed you the last few days." Her voice was socially polite, her smile the same, but her eyes told a different story.

"Ma'am." He took her hand and kissed it, his gaze holding hers for an instant. "If it had been possible, I would not have been absent so long."

"Ah?" She tilted her head to one side and regarded him with a quizzical smile. He was as always a vision of understated elegance in fawn buckskin riding britches and a dark green coat. "Business, sir?"

"Unfortunately," he agreed, still holding her hand. He could feel the tremor in her fingers, and his own closed more tightly over hers. "A nuisance, but unavoidable."

"I see. How unusual, my lord. Most gentlemen about town manage to avoid unavoidable business."

A smile licked his lips. "And what makes you think, my lady, that I fall into that idle category?"

"A foolish error, forgive me," she returned, a tinge of color blossoming on her high cheekbones. "Experience should have taught me better."

"I would think so," he said solemnly. "Did you receive the list of names I sent you?"

"Yes, and we're most grateful," she said, finally taking back her hand. "Come into the parlor. May I offer you a glass of sherry?"

"Thank you." He followed her into the shabby informality of the parlor. The tension in the air was a palpable force, a wicked energy that flowed between them, made all the more exciting by this game of ignorance. "Where are Lady Farnham and Lady Livia?"

"Liv is walking the dogs, and Ellie is making junket for Franny," Cornelia said, pouring two glasses of sherry. The mundane statement brought them both down to earth, but even so did little to dissipate the tension. She handed him a glass and raised her own to her lips.

"How is the dressmaking going?" Harry inquired. Cornelia was wearing one of her usual plain round gowns, her hair twisted into a heavy chignon on her nape, nothing about her indicating a smidgen of interest in fashion.

She was abruptly aware of her unmodish appearance. "Oh, rather well," she said airily. "You wouldn't believe it to see us now, but we all three have magnificent outfits. We simply await the opportunity to burst upon the town in all our finery."

He laughed a little. He wanted to reach for her, pull her to him, run his hands over her body, reminding himself of its indentations and curves. He could catch her scent, lavender and rosewater, and beneath just the hint of female arousal.

"Nell," he said softly, his eyes narrowed. "Nell?"

"No." She put out her hands as if to ward him off. "Don't speak in that tone, Harry. It's hard enough to hold myself together without that. And anyone could walk in."

He bowed his head in acknowledgment. "I will come to you tonight."

"No," she said, but without conviction.

Before he could question her denial, the door opened. Aurelia came in holding a jelly mold. "Nell, would you believe . . . oh, Lord Bonham. We were wondering where you'd been hiding."

"Nowhere, Lady Farnham," he said, raising her free hand to his lips. He glanced interrogatively at what she held in her other hand.

"It's a jelly mold," Aurelia said. "I thought it was in the shape of a rabbit, but—" She began to laugh. "It's too absurd, but what on earth was Aunt Sophia doing with *this* in her kitchen?" She held up the mold.

Cornelia peered at it, then took it from her. "Dear God," she murmured. "Is that what I think it is?"

Aurelia nodded, her laughter getting the better of her.

Harry took the object from Cornelia and held it up. "Hell and the devil," he said with some awe. "This was in the house of a reclusive old lady?"

"Apparently," Aurelia said through her laughter. "Morecombe became very dignified and reticent when I asked him about it, but I think Aunt Sophia lived a rather daring existence at some point."

"Did you make the junket?" Cornelia asked, taking back the mold and examining it closely. It was in the shape of a naked woman, a very uninhibitedly naked woman.

"I thought it was a rabbit, until I unmolded it," Aurelia protested, then collapsed on the chaise with a renewed surge of laughter. "I had to throw it in the sink before Franny realized what it was."

Cornelia dropped into a chair with a shout of laughter, and Harry watched them both for a moment or two, enjoying their amusement. They might give the superficial impression of country mice, but these women had the most deliciously mature and unconventional senses of humor. Apart from the fact that he didn't know any woman of their class who would spend an afternoon in the kitchen making junket for a child, he certainly didn't know any women who would find the risqué mold as hilarious as these two did.

He felt as if he was bathing in a refreshing stream. No artifice, no simpering, no display of maidenly dismay. Just straightforward reactions.

Aurelia wiped her eyes with the back of her hand. "So what brings you to our door, Lord Bonham?"

"A social call," he replied. "But with an underlying purpose. I was wondering if you were ready to receive visitors as yet?"

"We already receive *you*," Cornelia pointed out, bringing the decanter over to his glass.

"Oddly, I don't consider myself a mere social visitor, Lady Dagenham," he responded aridly. "It cuts me to the quick that you should."

"We don't," Aurelia protested. "Nell's just teasing."

He glanced at Cornelia, raising his eyebrows in a question that was only half-amused. She raised one hand a little, inclining her head as if in acknowledgment of a hit. "Maybe I don't," she said. "But to answer your question, I believe we are ready. What do you think, Ellie?"

"Certainly," her sister-in-law affirmed. "We intend to start paying calls ourselves as soon as we've sorted something out about a carriage. We were hoping to employ Nigel on the task, but we haven't seen him either in days. We were about to send him a message at the marquess of Coltrain's house, where he's staying."

"Or *was* staying," Cornelia interjected. "Maybe he's found lodgings of his own." She shrugged. "He'll turn up, he always does."

"Well, in his absence, perhaps I can be of assistance," Harry offered. "As it happens I acquired a second coachman some weeks ago, and I really don't have enough work for him. I'd be happy to lend him to you whenever you need. As for the carriage, I have a barouche that I almost never use . . . I keep it for my sisters and their children when they visit. I'd be happy to put it at your disposal."

"We couldn't possibly accept such generosity, my lord," Cornelia said instantly and with a vehemence that was almost impolite. "It's very kind of you, but indeed we will manage for ourselves."

His offer would have been unimpeachable coming from a relative, or even a very old and close family friend, but from a mere acquaintance it was surely quite inappropriate. It made her think of mistresses and kept women, and she wouldn't be the only person to catch a whiff of impropriety in the offer, however innocent it might be. The earl could well see in it an opportunity to bring their London sojourn to an end should it come to his ears.

Harry frowned a little at her vehemence, but he bowed his acquiescence. "If you insist, ma'am. But the offer remains should you change your mind."

"We won't," she said firmly.

"But we're very grateful for the offer, sir," Aurelia said, trying with a warm smile to make up for Cornelia's trenchant refusal.

"Well, I trust you won't refuse my next offer," he said,

leaning back in his chair, crossing booted ankles with an air of relaxation. "If you have no objection, I would like to bring my great-aunt, the duchess of Gracechurch, to visit you. She's in town for a few days, and she knows everyone." He paused, choosing his words carefully, reluctant to sound in the least patronizing to these fiercely independent ladies. "Her approval will guarantee all the social openings you might wish for."

"Then that is an offer we'll accept with the utmost pleasure," Cornelia said swiftly. "When will you bring her?"

"Tomorrow, if that's not too soon."

Aurelia shook her head. "Not in the least. The drawing room is finished, and our afternoon gowns are ready."

"Then I'll see you tomorrow afternoon." He rose to take his leave. "If I run into your cousin, Lady Dagenham, I'll tell him you'd like to see him." He extended his hand first to Aurelia. "Good day, Lady Farnham."

"Lord Bonham." She shook his hand warmly. "You've been very kind."

He smiled and brushed his lips across her knuckles. "My pleasure entirely, ma'am." He released her hand and turned to Cornelia. "See me out, Lady Dagenham."

Cornelia heard an unmistakable proprietorial note in the demand. It was accompanied by a smile that, while it took the peremptory edge off it, somehow seemed to imply an even greater intimacy.

She stiffened, wondering if Aurelia had heard it. It

was certainly a peculiar tone to use among mere acquaintances. She preceded him to the door coolly enough however, remarking with a light laugh, "You have the measure of our household, Viscount. As you so rightly assume, Morecombe is bound to be otherwise engaged."

Harry followed her into the hall. She opened the door, and the afternoon sunlight, pale and cool, sent a delicate stream of light across the parquet. "You've done wonders in such a short time," he said, looking up at the sparkling chandelier.

"Thank you." Cornelia offered him a social smile that masked the surge of desire curling her toes in her silk-slippered feet.

There was nothing social about his response. His green eyes were narrowed, and his pupils were small and black as chips of agate as he looked at her unsmiling. "Leave your window open," he instructed in an undertone. "And for God's sake make sure that damned cat is elsewhere."

Then he stepped through the door, pausing on the top step to say over his shoulder, "And those ridiculous dogs too." Without waiting for a reply, he strode down to the street and walked away without a backward glance.

"*Arrogant so-and-so,*" Cornelia muttered to herself, aware of her own most powerful arousal. It would serve him right if she locked and bolted her window and slept with the cat and both dogs on her feet.

Except of course that she wouldn't. And the damned man knew it.

"Why are you standing there with the door open, Nell?"

Cornelia hastily closed the door at Aurelia's voice behind her. "Just enjoying the sunshine," she said casually.

"That was a very kind offer the viscount made," Aurelia said, looking thoughtfully at her sister-in-law, who still stood unmoving by the door. "Couldn't we have accepted it?"

"Of course we couldn't, Ellie." Cornelia sounded almost angry. "The man's a stranger . . . or, at least, only a bare acquaintance. What would it look like, to accept such a gift?"

Aurelia shrugged. "I think of him rather as a friend these days." She turned back to the parlor. "He certainly doesn't stand on ceremony with us."

She cast a quick glance at her sister-in-law as she said this, but Cornelia appeared not to have heard her. Aurelia went on, "But I don't see why anyone should know that we're driving around in his second-best carriage anyway."

Cornelia followed her into the parlor. "Can you imagine the construction Markby would put upon it if it came to his ears?"

Aurelia looked at her in puzzled astonishment. "What possible construction could there be, Nell? It was an offer made to benefit all three of us."

And Cornelia realized that *her* knowledge of the truly

scandalous liaison between herself and Lord Bonham was coloring all her interpretations. Without that knowledge, there was really nothing objectionable in the offer. Ellie was as clearheaded as anyone about such issues, and if she saw nothing wrong with it, then probably there was nothing wrong. But then Ellie didn't know the truth. The truth changed everything.

She said with a feigned carelessness, "Maybe I'm being overcautious, but you know as well as I do how little it would take for the earl to find an excuse to drag us back."

Aurelia laughed. "You think he'll decide that we're Viscount Bonham's harem? Really, Nell, that's absurd." Her laughter deepened. "Lord Bonham's three kept women on Cavendish Square."

Cornelia managed a tight smile. "You're right, Ellie, it is absurd, but I still think we should endeavor to manage this carriage business for ourselves."

Aurelia threw up her hands in defeat. "As you wish, Nell. Let's send a note to Nigel. Funny that he hasn't been around lately," she said, going to the secretaire. She answered her own question. "I imagine he's amusing himself too much to worry about his dowdy cousins."

∽∾

Harry had reached the corner of Wimpole Street when he heard the sound of rapid footsteps behind him. He slowed, recognizing them, but didn't pause until he turned the corner, and they were out of sight of the house.

"Lester," he greeted briefly.

"Aye, sir," the man said, coming abreast of his master. "I think I can make the exchange with the thimbles, sir. That nurse, Linton, was grumbling that the ladies were going out with the children to see the lions at the Exchange this afternoon." He managed a fair imitation of the nurse's voice as he said, "And who's going to have to deal with them when they come back exhausted, poor little mites. As if I don't have enough to do . . . and Lady Susannah has the beginning of a head cold . . ."

Harry smiled, but he hesitated a little before agreeing. If Lester was caught, they'd have the devil's own job keeping him out of the hands of the Watch. But then again, Lester was experienced, and if the women were safely out of the house . . .

He reached into his pocket for the thimble. "If you think you can do it safely, Lester, I own I'll be glad to have this over and done with."

Lester took the small object and held it up. "Looks just the same, sir," he observed with something like awe.

"It's not," Harry said a touch morosely. He didn't like cutting corners, and the engraving on this thimble came nowhere close to his standards. "I was in a hurry, the engraving's clumsy. But it should pass muster with Lady Dagenham. If our French or Russian friends do get their hands on it, they'll realize soon enough that it's a fake."

He frowned with irritation. The original thimble represented hours of wasted work, and when he did get hold of it again he would have to melt it down to destroy the codes engraved upon it. Even though the snuffbox substitute was already on its way by courier, everything about the original thimble would shriek authenticity to British agents, and it could not be left intact. In the wrong hands it would be a powerful weapon for the dissemination of misinformation, not to mention the identification of English agents and double agents all across the Continent.

The sooner it was a puddle of molten silver, the better, but the enemy wouldn't know that, and he had to assume they were still planning its retrieval. One reason why Lester would remain on guard in the house on Cavendish Square. Harry had more faith in Lester's little finger than in the combined force of Morecombe's blunderbuss and those noisy little pink creatures.

And that brought him to Nigel Dagenham. The apparently missing cousin. Where was he?

Harry had intended to alert the Ministry to the possibility of Nigel Dagenham's recruitment by a French agent, but then he'd been closeted in his grimy space at the War Office, and the whole business had gone out of his head. He hadn't thought it particularly urgent, it took time and careful planning to effect such a recruitment but if the cub had disappeared, it was high time they ran him to ground.

He glanced at his fob watch. Four o'clock. Too early for the evening's gaming and too late even for those diehards who gambled all night and well into the next day. Those would be sound asleep at this hour readying themselves for the tables later that night. Most of his own friends would either be riding or driving in Hyde Park, or frequenting fencing studios or boxing clubs. Somehow he didn't think Nigel Dagenham would be among them. He was too much of a dissolute for the sweaty Corinthian pleasures. No, Dagenham would be sleeping off the effects of a heavy night.

He turned his steps towards Albermarle Street. A little hard exercise would clear his own head, and maybe he'd run into someone who had seen young Dagenham in the last few days. "Just keep an eye on the workbox, Lester. As long as you're in the house, I know no one else can get close to it."

"Aye, sir." Lester half turned back the way he'd come as he continued, "Will you want me to stay in the house tonight?"

A slight smile flickered across his master's cool green eyes. "No, Lester, I'll take care of it tonight."

Lester said nothing, his expression giving nothing away. The ladies in Cavendish Square had nothing in common with the viscount's customary amours, and nothing that he could see with the late Lady Bonham. But then he wouldn't expect Lord Bonham to be tempted to dalliance with a woman remotely resembling his dead wife.

Harry turned onto Albermarle Street and went up the steps to number seven. A discreet plate by the door said simply, MAÎTRE ALBERT. The master swordsman was slowing a little now, but he was still the most skilled fencing master in town.

The door was not locked and yielded to a turn of the handle. Harry ran lightly up the narrow flight of stairs at the end of the narrow hall and opened the double doors at the head of the staircase. The long mirrored *salle* was quiet, the only sounds the touch of steel on steel and the soft thud of stockinged feet on the wooden boards. The air smelled of fresh sweat, and the long windows at the far end were opened, letting in the chilly afternoon air. The sky was beginning to darken as the early dusk drew in but the long room was lit by a line of tapers in sconces along both sidewalls.

A man watching the several pairs of fencers on the floor moved towards Harry as soon as he entered. "Lord Bonham, I haven't seen you in a while." He greeted the viscount with a bow that was neither subservient nor one between equals. "Do you care to try some hits?"

"If you please, Maître." Harry shrugged out of his coat.

"Epée or saber?" Maitre Albert walked to the far wall and the neatly racked pairs of swords. He glanced back at Harry and answered his own question. "Epée, I think."

"Whatever you say, Maître." Harry sat on the long low bench that ran along the wall and removed his boots. He pulled off his cravat, shaking out the folds with a carelessness that would have horrified his valet, and rolled up his ruffled shirtsleeves.

"Have a little mercy," he requested with a grin as he took the proffered hilt of the épée. "It has been at least two weeks."

Maître Albert shook his head. "Two weeks won't slow *you* down, my lord."

They took their places on the floor, saluted with their swords, and began. Harry as always forgot everything but the matter in hand. He saw only the flashing blades, felt only the tingle in his wrist as the blades made contact. He lunged, feinted, engaged in the wonderful mental exercise of outwitting the master, even as his body stretched and the tension of hours hunched over a desk left his shoulders and his neck, and he felt the muscles elongate and spring back.

He slipped beneath the master's guard in sixte, touched his breast with the foiled tip of his sword, and Maître Albert fell back, acknowledging the hit with the fencer's upthrown hand. "*Touché.* As I said, my lord, two weeks wouldn't slow you."

"Bravo, Harry," Sir Nicholas Petersham, who had just finished his own bout, dropped his saber point to the floor. He bowed to his opponent, who returned the courtesy. "I still haven't managed a hit with an épée in a bout with Albert. Have you, Forster?"

Lord Forster, a tall, willowy gentleman with pale eyes and a rather lackluster manner that belied a fierce competitiveness, sighed and wiped his brow with his handkerchief. "Alas, no, Nick. But none of us is a match for Harry."

Harry laughed. "And you, David, have pinked me at least twice with the épée. So let's have none of that false modesty."

Lord Forster gracefully shrugged slender shoulders. "Mere luck, dear fellow, mere luck."

"Then let us try luck again," Harry offered, his own competitive streak flaring. He raised his épée in a salute. "Unless you're fatigued after your bout with Nick."

It was all the spur needed. David exchanged his saber for the épée handed him by Maître Albert and responded to Harry's salute. They took to the floor, Maître Albert retreating with a knowing smile. He stood beside Nick, watching the two very evenly matched fencers. But Harry had the mental edge, and they both knew it. He was physically no better a duelist than his opponent, but he had the devious mind of a chess player and could see more than the usual several moves ahead to plan his strategy.

The blades engaged, retired, advanced in a steady dance, the two duelists perspiring freely as the tempo increased. There came a moment when a slight stumble in his footwork left David's left side unprotected. Harry disengaged his blade, his foiled point dipped beneath his opponent's sword, and made contact with the other man's chest.

Harry retired his blade, laughing as he danced backwards, ready to engage in quarte. But David dropped his point with a gesture of defeat. "Enough," he said, wiping his brow with the sleeve of his forearm. "I'll yield to you this time, Harry, but we'll have a return match, then you'll see who's master."

Harry laughed and extended his hand. "I'm sure I shall, David. I'm sure I shall," he agreed as he mopped his own brow.

The other man laughed with him and clapped an arm around his shoulders. "That feint in sixte was a neat trick."

"Albert taught it to me the last time we fenced," Harry said, acknowledging the master with a bow of his head. "I'm parched. Let's find a tavern and a pint of ale. How about you, Nick?"

"Oh, yes, anytime," the other agreed amiably, picking up his discarded coat.

They made their farewells to Maître Albert and went out into the gathering dusk. The new gas lamps had been lit, and their strange yellow light cast an unearthly sulfurous glow through the gloom. It was chilly, and the sweat dried rapidly as the three men made their way towards Piccadilly and the lights of a tavern.

"So, family matters been keeping you out of circulation, Harry?" Nick asked, as he raised his foaming tankard to his lips.

"You guessed it," Harry responded lightly, swiping foam from his upper lip with a finger.

"Thought as much." Nick nodded, but his eyes were shrewd as he regarded his friend across the scratched and stained deal table in the window of the Red Fox. "They really keep you busy."

Harry had the idea that Nick had guessed there was more to his absences than his regular excuse of family business, but he didn't think Nick would press him on it. For one it would be a grave discourtesy to imply that he didn't believe Harry's excuse and, for another, he was sure that Nick had some inkling that government business was involved. And if so, he knew to hold his tongue.

He changed the subject. "I have some business with young Dagenham," he said. "I can't seem to find him anywhere. Have you seen him, Nick . . . David?"

"Don't know the man," Lord Foster said, raising a hand to a tavern wench passing with a full jug of ale. "We need refills over here."

"Right away, sir." The girl curtsied and leaned over to fill their tankards, her low-cut bodice giving them all the view they could wish for.

"Bonny lass," David observed, swiveling to follow her hip-swinging progress between the tables.

"You always did have a taste for the low life, Forster," Nick observed genially. "And to answer your question, Harry, the last time I saw young Dagenham he was playing at Pickering Place . . . damned young fool," he added, burying his nose in his tankard again.

Harry grimaced, silently concurring with the judgment. "How long ago was that?"

Nick frowned. "Oh, three, maybe four days ago . . . can't remember exactly. You know how it is, one evening just runs into another."

"Reprobate," Harry accused with a mocking smile.

Nick just laughed. "Why the interest in Dagenham, Harry? It's not like you to take up a cub."

"No," Harry agreed. "But I happened to meet a cousin of his a couple of weeks ago."

"Female?" hazarded David.

"A widow," Harry said calmly. "She and her sister-in-law and a friend have set up house in Cavendish Square."

"Haven't seen them about." David blinked in the dim light.

"No, they've been keeping to themselves up until now. But, rest assured, you'll see them in due course." Harry set his tankard on the table and pushed back his seat.

"Just a minute, Harry." Nick laid a restraining hand on his sleeve. "Enough of your riddles. Are they going to interest us?"

"Yes, is there money?" David, perennially under-funded, asked quickly.

Harry shrugged. "Not at all sure," he said easily, although he knew perfectly well there was little enough. "But a house in Cavendish Square doesn't come cheap."

"Indeed not." David gave a sagacious nod. "Best pay a call on . . . On whom?"

"Lady Dagenham, Lady Farnham, and Lady Livia Lacey," Harry said as he drew on his gloves. "Two widows and one spinster."

"So they're all on the market?" Nick mused, regarding

his friend through narrowed eyes. "You have an interest there, Harry? Best say before David here puts an oar in."

Harry shook his head. "You know me, Nick." He raised a hand in farewell and weaved his way through the crowd to the door.

"Aye, we know you, Harry," Nick said softly. "Once bitten twice shy."

"Can't blame the man," David said. "That was a bad business with his wife."

"The worst," Nick agreed. "I never understood why he married her in the first place."

"The daughter of a duke," David reminded him, calling for more ale.

"Yes, but Harry wouldn't give a fig for that." Nick shook his head. "No, fact is he liked her. I always thought there was something fishy about her, though."

"Mustn't speak ill of the dead," David said, but without conviction. "Dreadful way to die."

Nick drummed his fingers on the table. "If only Harry hadn't been in the house at the time."

David looked at him sharply. "You don't think . . ."

"No, not for one minute," Nick denied. "But it looked bad, particularly once the whole business with Vibart came out."

"Can't understand why the duke forced the issue, though. You'd think he'd want to protect his daughter's reputation. By insisting on criminal charges he exposed her for what she was. Little better than a whore."

"Now who's speaking ill of the dead?" Nick said with

a short and humorless laugh. "But Harry was exonerated and the duke just looks a fool by refusing to let it go."

David shook his head gloomily. "Harry'll never live it down though. There'll always be a taint, a hint of doubt. If he marries again, it won't be into the ton, I'll wager anything you like on that."

"I wouldn't take your wager," Nick stated. "Harry wouldn't marry again if you paid him Midas's gold." He pushed back his chair. "I must be going. You going home? I'll walk with you as far as Portman Square."

Chapter 16

HARRY MADE THE ROUNDS of the clubs, but none of the doormen or the flunkeys remembered seeing Mr. Dagenham in the last few days, although they all remembered the man, and for the same reason. His IOUs. It seemed the young man had built up substantial debt among the members.

"There was some mention of blackballing, my lord," the dignified and very experienced butler at White's offered in a discreet undertone. "But I gather Mr. Dagenham settled his debts in the end, and nothing more was said. Hasn't been around in a while though. Rusticating in the country probably. It's hard for youngsters to get burned like that. Always feel they daren't show their faces in society again. But it passes. We'll be seeing him again in a year or two, mark my words, my lord. When he's not so green."

"I'm sure you're right, Naseby." Harry slid a guinea

into the man's gloved palm. "You've seen enough of them come and go in your time."

"That I have, my lord, that I have." The steward bowed as his knowing fingers identified the coin in his hand. "And thank you, my lord."

"Thank you, Naseby." Harry went back down to the street. Now where? It was still too early for the gaming hells to be functioning, and he had plans for the night that did not include chasing after some youngster who'd managed to get himself into trouble. Into it, but also out of it, it would seem. Just where had the money come from to pay his debts?

He decided to walk home to Mount Street and his dinner but stopped when the marquess of Coltrain's carriage wheeled to a halt outside White's. He turned back to the club, waiting politely as the footman let down the step, and the marquis himself stepped down to the pavement.

"Good evening, Coltrain." He bowed to the marquis.

His lordship was a small, dapper gentleman with the raddled complexion of a man who had long enjoyed a love affair with the bottle. He looked up at his much taller interlocutor. "Ah, Bonham, good evening. You going into the club?"

"Not this evening, but I was hoping to run into you."

Lord Coltrain looked astonished. They were barely acquainted, and for all practical purposes, different generations. "Ah, well . . . what can I do for you?"

"I was looking for your guest . . . Nigel Dagenham. I

haven't been able to find him for a few days. I trust he's not unwell."

"Good God, I wouldn't know," the marquess said. "He's Garston's guest, not mine. But now you mention it, I haven't seen him in the house either." He shook his head. "Not that I'd expect to, the hours these young pups keep. Don't get to bed afore noon, and they get up at midnight to fritter away their time and money at the tables."

"I daresay you did the same at their age, sir," Harry said, thinking that Coltrain, for all his protestations, was still an inveterate gambler. It was said he'd run through two fortunes before he'd reached thirty. Only the seemingly limitless fortune left him by a distant relative who owned coal mines in Northumberland had saved him from ruin.

The marquess chuckled a little. "Oh, perhaps so. Mustn't begrudge the youngsters their youth now. Recommend you find Mac, Bonham. He'll know where Dagenham is." With that he tottered a little unsteadily up to the door of White's.

Harry was not going to find Mackenzie, the earl of Garston, anywhere at this hour. It would have to wait until tomorrow. But he couldn't shake off a sense of unease as he continued on his way home, and with a sigh of irritation turned his steps instead to Horseguards.

The man he sought was fortunately easy to find. The head of the British secret service was as unassuming as his need for discretion dictated. He operated from a suite of offices running off a long, dim corridor that reeked of dust and mice, and when Harry tapped at his open door, was engaged in moving pins around a map of the French coastline spread out on a table.

He looked up and greeted his visitor with genuine warmth. "Harry, what brings you here at this time of day. Can't get enough of the place, eh?"

"I've had more than enough of it in the last weeks, Simon," Harry said with a dry smile. "But something's bothering me and I think we should look into it." He perched on a corner of the table and looked at the map. "Networks?"

"Aye." The other man looked grim as he removed a pin. "They've taken out the outpost at Rochelle. God knows where they got their information."

"All gone?" Harry whistled his own dismay.

"We think so. Nothing from anyone so far, at least. If anyone survived, they'll make contact within the next twenty-four hours." Simon Grant shrugged and exhaled noisily. "So, take my mind off this, Harry, and give me something else to worry about."

His face, drawn and deeply lined, and his tired, sunken eyes gave credence to his words. He was a man who rarely slept, who felt that he held the lives of every agent in the far-flung field in the palm of his hand. And Harry had long believed that the responsibility was slowly killing him.

He regarded him now with sympathy and a flicker of guilt that he was going to add to his tribulations, but it had to be done. Only Simon Grant could order what had to be ordered.

The spymaster read his expression, and a weary smile flickered over his lips. "Let's have a glass of claret," he suggested, waving to the desk. "I'm parched. Sit down, Harry."

Harry took the seat across from the desk, accepted a rather dusty glass of claret, and told Simon about his fears for Nigel Dagenham.

"You think this is connected in some way to the thimble?" Simon ran a finger around the rim of his glass setting it ringing in the quiet room.

"I don't know for a fact, but it seems too much of a coincidence. I think we have to find him anyway. If they haven't netted him yet, they might just be waiting for the perfect opportunity."

Simon nodded, sipped his wine, set down the glass, and reached for a sheet of parchment. "I can't really spare anyone, but if you think it's urgent then so be it. I'll put Coles and Addison onto it. If he's out there somewhere, they'll find him." He dipped the quill into the ink pot. "What do you want them to do with him once they find him?"

"Nothing," Harry said firmly. "Just lead me to him, that's all. I'll do the rest."

Simon Grant looked up curiously. "You have an interest in him, Harry?"

"Let's just say, in the family," Harry returned, setting

down his glass and getting to his feet. "Sorry to have added to your burdens, Simon."

The other man waved this away. "You relieve me of them often enough. Anyway, forewarned is forearmed. As long as we can contain this situation, we might even be able to use him ourselves. If the French, or even the Russians, are trying to net him, maybe we should just let that happen, then turn him ourselves."

Harry made no response to this, it was the way Simon's mind worked. If it came down to it, then Harry would intervene. He didn't think Nigel Dagenham would make a reliable double agent.

He made his farewells and left the Ministry. His only real interest in Nigel Dagenham lay in his dangerous proximity to the women and children in Cavendish Square. The enemy wouldn't give a tinker's damn about collateral damage. If Nigel was to be their path to the thimble, then the women and their children were in danger. Removing the thimble was no longer sufficient. He had to find Dagenham and take him out of the picture. And Simon's men were the quickest way to do that.

"So what time should we be ready to receive the duchess of Gracechurch tomorrow, do you think?" Livia inquired, taking a slice of partridge from the serving dish one of the twins had placed on the dining table. A covered dish of brussel sprouts was set down beside it.

"By three o'clock," Aurelia said, helping herself to roast potatoes. "That's the usual time."

She looked up with a smile as one of the twins put a gravy boat beside her. "Thank you, Ada." She addressed the woman with confidence, having noticed some days earlier that Ada had the tiniest mole just above her left eyebrow. This twin bore the blemish.

"We should have tea, of course," Livia said, her mind running happily along these tracks. "Ada, do you think you could make some of those exquisite little sponge cakes?"

"That's our Mavis what makes them," Ada said stolidly.

"Oh . . . well, do you think she would make them for us?" Livia offered a winning smile.

"You'd have to ask her that, mum," Ada stated. "She'll be bringin' in the neeps in a minute." With which she exited the dining room.

"Neeps?" Aurelia looked at her companions.

"Turnips, I think," Cornelia said. "It's what they call them up north . . . oh, and in Scotland too."

"How on earth did you know that?"

"I'm not sure . . . oh, yes, now I remember. When Stevie was born, we had a nursery maid who came from somewhere north of Durham. I heard her talking about neeps once. Linton complained that she couldn't understand a word the girl said, so, she had to go." This conclusion was stated as a self-evident truth, and Aurelia understood it as such.

"It's so hard to communicate with the twins," Livia lamented. "But they're such wonderful cooks. This partridge is delicious . . . oh, and the sprouts have chestnuts mixed in with them. We never eat this well at home." She gave an exaggerated sigh. Her father, the Reverend Lacey, did not approve of fancy cooking. Plain fare was good enough for his table, as he said almost every dinnertime after grace was said. Plain food and one or at most two glasses of wine for health's sake.

Mavis entered with the turnips, and Livia quickly asked about the sponge cakes. The twin seemed to give the request grave consideration. "Would those be the ones with the dried cherries, mum? Or the ones with the currants?"

"Both?" Livia suggested somewhat tentatively. "They're both delicious, Mavis."

Mavis merely ducked her head in acknowledgment and marched out of the dining room.

"Was that a yes?" Livia asked.

"I think so," Aurelia said. "They're actually very obliging, just rather taciturn." She poured gravy over her partridge and passed the boat across to Cornelia sitting opposite. "Gravy, Nell?"

"Oh, yes, thank you." Cornelia helped herself, absently watching the stream of rich, vinous sauce coat the thin slices of partridge breast on her plate.

Livia exchanged a look with Aurelia. "You'll drown it in a minute, Nell," she observed. She bent to give the dogs sitting on her feet beneath the table a piece of meat each.

Cornelia shook herself back to the room and set the boat down in its saucer. "It smells so wonderful," she offered as excuse. "Could I try the neeps, Ellie?"

Aurelia pushed the tureen towards her. "We seem to have come a long way since our first meal in this house," she said. "Do you remember bread and cheese and potato soup in the parlor that first night? It was so cold and miserable."

"And now look at it." Livia waved her fork at their surroundings. "We could have a dinner party now that this room is so respectable."

Cornelia forced herself to enter the conversation with a fully focused mind. "I didn't think the dining salon would come up as well as it has," she said. "But the cream and gold paint has done wonders; it really brings out the moldings."

"And the fresco on the ceiling," Aurelia said, craning her neck to look above her. "But you know something, I don't think that fresco is all that it purports to be. The painter had a very odd gleam in his eye when he came down the ladder after touching it up, and he almost blushed when I asked him if he liked the design."

"Well, maybe it has hidden treasures, like the jelly mold," Cornelia said, finally fully engaged in this subject.

"The cherubs are certainly very cherubic." Livia gazed up at it herself. "I suspect that to get the full imagery, you would have to be up close."

"Then we should get a stepladder and go up for a

closer look," Cornelia stated. "There's so much in this house that we haven't properly explored yet."

"Like the attics." Livia speared another slice of partridge. "I had a quick look, but it was so filthy I came back down in a hurry. But there are all sorts of boxes and chests up there."

"I think Aunt Sophia's life is probably worth exploring," Cornelia said. "When we've done what we came here to do."

"Which is to burst in full fig upon an unsuspecting London society," Aurelia declared. "And we start tomorrow."

"Viscount Bonham has been so kind," Livia said. "And after such a dreadful start." She laughed. "We insulted him, deceived him, made fun of him, and he repays us with kindness. Isn't that amazing?"

"Utterly," Cornelia concurred dryly.

"Oh, you're so suspicious, Nell," Livia accused. "You sound as if he must have some ulterior motive; but he knows he can't have the house, so what else could he want?"

"I can't imagine," Aurelia said, keeping her eyes on her plate. "I daresay he enjoys our company."

Or yours Nell. She didn't think Livia had picked up on the strange tension that swirled in any room that contained Nell and Harry Bonham. And she didn't think Liv saw as much into Nell's distraction as she did. But she'd keep her own counsel for the present.

"Maybe," Cornelia said, because it seemed a response

was required. She wasn't sure how long she could keep this secret from her friends. It wasn't that she was afraid they would not keep her confidence, or even that they would disapprove of this crazy liaison, but she was afraid that if she made it public, put it into words, then it would become a reality that she would have to deal with. As it was, she could pretend it was taking place in some other universe, to someone who was not her flesh-and-blood self. And if she could keep it on that dreamlike level, then it threatened nothing.

But she knew that what had happened between herself and Harry Bonham, and what was going to happen again tonight, most definitely involved her own flesh-and-blood self. The very core of her self.

And she was drifting again, and Ellie was talking to her, and she had to bring herself back.

Somehow she managed to get through the rest of the evening without losing herself again, and when she parted with Liv and Ellie at her bedroom door, she didn't think either of them looked at her strangely.

The fire in her bedchamber was lit, the coverlet on the bed turned back. She set her carrying candle on the bedside table and took a taper to the fire to light the candles on the table beside the chair and the two on the mantel. Then she undressed in front of the fire, carefully hanging her clothes in the armoire, each movement very deliberate. She dropped her nightgown over her head and fastened the tiny buttons at the neck. She wrapped herself in a thick robe, then went to the window.

She gazed out into the darkness, making out the twisted shapes of the apple trees and the outline of the garden wall. A quarter moon was revealed every now and again between scudding clouds. She raised the window and took a breath of the chill air. It smelled like rain. Hastily, she lowered the window to just an inch above the sill. But even so a sharp needle of cold air entered the chamber. The cat, who'd been asleep before the fire, made a mew of protest.

"Forgive me, Puss, but tonight you have to find somewhere else to sleep," she said, bending to pick up the cat. She put her outside the door, closed it, and turned the lock. She heard her scratch at the door in a fast and furious rhythm that if Cornelia hadn't known her she would have interpreted as desperation. She ignored it and finally the cat sloped off in search of another warm spot. The dogs were with Livia.

All Cornelia had to do now was await her Casanova.

She was drifting in a strange dreamlike state in the fireside chair when she heard the first scraping sound beyond the window. She remained in her chair, eyes half-closed, watching the black space of the window. Watching as a hand slid between window and sill and pushed up the window far enough to let him in. Her heart was beating fast against her ribs, and yet she felt oddly paralyzed, only her eyes moving as she watched him edge over the sill and enter the chamber.

Harry closed the window before slowly turning back to her. He was dressed all in black, as he had been on that other night visitation, his black coat buttoned to his throat, a black muffler twisted around his neck. Even his gloves were black. Only his eyes offered color, a deep emerald green as they gazed upon her, seeming to encompass her very self, to take her into himself, to become a part of him despite the distance that lay between them as he stood by the window, and she sat in her chair by the fire.

He smiled suddenly, and the moment of paralysis that had seemed to hold them both dissipated. He stepped quickly across the rug towards her. He put his hands on the arms of the chair where she sat and bent over to kiss her mouth. Her head fell back against the seat back, and the tip of her tongue touched his. She reached up both hands to take his face between her palms. His cheeks were cold against her palms, but his mouth on hers was warm and moist and pliable.

At last he straightened, raising his head slowly, reluctantly. Her lips burned from the demanding pressure of that kiss, and she touched them with a fingertip, looking up at him as he stood above her. They had said nothing to each other since he'd come through the window, and the silence seemed right. This conversation was one of pure bodily sensation, nothing of the mind, of reason, of rationality in it.

He reached down and took her hands, drawing her to her feet. He ran his hands through the heavy buttery mass of her hair as it clustered around her face and over her shoulders. And he kissed her eyelids, a flickering dart of his tongue that made her smile.

She untwisted the muffler from around his neck, casting it aside, then began to unbutton his coat, her fingers deft. Harry stood still and let her work, while his own hands played in her hair, twisting the loose curls around his fingers.

He moved his shoulders in a helpful shrug as she pushed off his snugly fitting coat. It fell to the floor, and he let it lie. Cornelia turned her attention to his shirt, the buttons flying open now as her breath speeded. She pushed the shirt away from his body and ran her hands over his chest, teasing the small hard nipples with a fingertip. She bent her head and licked his nipples and chuckled softly as they hardened in response. She hadn't realized that a man's nipples could be as sensitive as a woman's.

Her tongue moved across his chest, and her fingers worked at the buttons of his britches, her hands roughly pushing the loosened trousers over his hips. A fingernail caught his skin but neither of them noticed the thin red scratch. She dropped to her knees as her tongue painted a moist path down his belly, lingering on the deep indentation of his navel. Her hands gripped his buttocks as she stroked her tongue along the thick, rigid shaft of his penis springing up from its nest of dark curls. She licked the salt from its tip, and her hand slid around between his thighs, cupping his balls, a finger sliding wickedly, knowingly, upwards into the cleft of his buttocks.

His sharp intake of breath made her smile even

through the mist of lust that engulfed her. She had never played with a man's body before, would never have believed that she would know how to bring this depth of pleasure to them both, but she knew, her body knew. It was a deep, atavistic knowledge.

Harry played with her hair, gazing intently down at the bent head, as she brought him closer and closer to climax. When he was on the edge, but still in control, he lifted her head, looked down into her eyes that were like drowned sapphires, their piercing blue light wavery as if seen through a mist. Her lips were parted, and her tongue darted across them catching the salt taste of him.

"Stand up now," he whispered, his voice husky and strange to him. He bent and lifted her to her feet. He palmed her face and kissed her mouth, his tongue moving deeply within. He unfastened the girdle of her robe and pushed the thick covering away from her shoulders. He ran his hands down her body, pressing the nightgown to her shape, outlining the curve of her generous breasts, the swell of her hips, the small roundness of her belly. The muslin was thin, and her skin was an ivory shadow beneath, apart from the rose crowns of her nipples.

He moved a hand to the apex of her thighs, cupping the soft mound of her sex beneath the muslin, feeling her heat, the rough tangle of pubic hair enticing beneath his fingers. There was something intensely erotic about touching her in this way over her nightgown that concealed even as it revealed. He explored her body's intimacies, but he explored them through a veil.

And still only those three little words had been spoken. The only sounds were the hiss of the fire, their soft sibilant breath as they stood, touching each other, their eyes fused as they looked within the other for the questions, the physical responses that would answer those questions.

Finally, the intensity broke as it had to. Cornelia took a small step backwards, unbuttoning her nightgown, her eyes, however, never leaving Harry's. She dragged the garment over her head and tossed it aside.

Harry ran his eyes in a lingering caress down the body bared to his gaze. He smiled, and said, "There you stand, sweetheart, glorious in your nakedness, and I'm hobbled by the britches around my ankles."

Cornelia laughed, a deep, sensual laugh of delight at the absurdity of it all, and the delicious promise of it all. "Come to me." She held out her arms, then fell with wonderful dramatic effect onto the bed behind her, her body sprawled in wanton invitation, her eyes filled with sensual mischief as she watched him kick off his boots and britches.

He put one knee on the bed beside her and stroked down her body once more, this time loving the feel of her skin against his fingers. He stroked as if he was sculpting her, and his eyes followed his fingers as if he would commit every inch of her to memory.

And Cornelia lay still for this exploration of eyes and hands, her arms flung wide, her legs parted, her breasts flattened across her rib cage. When he brought his other knee to the bed and swung astride her, she watched him with narrowed eyes, running her own palms across his concave belly, the hard points of his hipbones. He slid a hand between her thighs, unerringly found all the essential parts of her, and her hips arced on a wave of sensation.

As the wave receded, she looked up into his smiling eyes, and said, "I wanted to give you that, but you stopped me."

"Ah, sweetheart, Mother Nature gives her gifts with a prejudice," he murmured, chuckling. "Women are blessed with the ability to manage the peaks many times in succession. The poor male of the species, alas, has but one chance at glory before he's spent."

Cornelia's smothered laughter brought tears to her eyes. He looked and sounded so comically dismayed, and it was so absolutely at odds with the man she knew. The suave, elegant, controlled aristocrat.

But as she'd always known, there was a lot more to Harry Bonham than that.

The fleeting thought was gone before it was barely formed. He was leaning over her now, his eyes no longer laughing but filled with an urgency of passion that rekindled her own. He ran his hands beneath her thighs, then lifted her legs onto his shoulders. He held her bottom on the shelf of his palms and drove deep into her raised body. So deep she felt him become a part of her, no longer an invading presence but an essential part of her core.

She lifted her hips high off the bed trying to take him

farther into herself, her inner muscles tightening around him, possessing him, making him hers. He withdrew from her body an instant before the end, as he had done before, and she felt a second of loss that was engulfed in her own orgasmic convulsion. And when it was over and her legs fell from his shoulders and he dropped heavily onto her, she clasped him tightly, their sweat mingling, their loins no longer joined but pulsing in unison, and for a moment there was only the exhausted sweaty exultation of utter fulfillment.

Then, as always, came reality. Cornelia moved first, her hand lightly brushing Harry's back, and with instant courtesy, he rolled to the bed beside her. He laid a hand on her belly, his breathing heavy.

She laid her own hand over his, feeling the rise and fall of her belly. The fire was low and the candles were guttering. In the half dark nothing seemed as it had been. These dreamlike midnight trysts were insane. She was insane to risk everything for a few brilliant incandescent moments of sensual heaven.

"What is it?" Harry spoke in his ordinary voice, sliding his hand out from beneath hers. He sat up, swinging his legs over the side of the bed, twisting to look at her. "What is it, Nell?"

"Nothing," she said, aware of how inadequate that was. She struggled to sit up, pulling the pillows behind her. "Just one of those odd moments of uncertainty. You know how it is." Her light laugh wouldn't have convinced an earthworm.

"What uncertainty?" He regarded her gravely. "One minute you're transported, and the next you're rigid with some doubt, unhappiness . . . I don't know. Tell me."

It was not a demand Cornelia knew how to deal with. In her experience men didn't feel these undercurrents, they were the rivers that only other women understood. Men, if they sensed trouble, could be easily put off with a laugh, an affectionate murmur, a mild reference to domestic issues. Not Harry Bonham, apparently.

"I can't do this," she said.

Harry stood up. He leaned over her for a second, lifted her slightly to release the coverlet beneath her, and deftly inserted her between mattress and cover. "You'll get cold," he said prosaically.

"So will you." It seemed the only adequate response. Cornelia drew the coverlet up to her chin as she hitched herself higher on the pillows. She wanted to turn back the cover and invite him into the warmth, to feel his skin against hers, but it couldn't be done.

Harry pulled on his britches, then bent to throw more coal on the fire. He straightened and turned to her, his back to the fire. "So, why not, Nell?"

The quiet question hung in the air for a long time, it seemed. Cornelia closed her eyes, trying to find the right words. Harry didn't move from his position in front of the fire. He stood, his hands loosely at his sides, his green gaze intent upon her face.

"It's hard to explain," she said finally.

"But you must try," he returned in the same quiet voice as before.

"Very well." She raised her eyes and looked at him. "I don't like secrets. I don't like anything underhand. It makes me uncomfortable."

His eyes narrowed as he watched her expression. "I can understand that, but I don't think that's all that's troubling you."

Cornelia's restless fingers pleated the hem of the sheet. "I have children."

"I am aware of that," he said dryly. "But what have they to do with this?"

"What have they to do with this?" she demanded in exasperation. "Why, everything, of course. I can't do anything that would have an adverse effect on them, surely you see that?"

"Yes, of course I do," he responded, sounding exasperated in his turn. "But I fail to see how snatching a few clandestine hours of lovemaking can have any effect on them at all."

"Firstly, as I just said, I don't like clandestine." The edge of anger in the room was helping her now. "And secondly, even if I was willing, do you really think we could keep this a secret for very long?"

When Harry thought of all the secrets he held and had held over the years he almost laughed. "*I* certainly could," he said. "I'm a master at keeping secrets."

He came over to the bed and, leaning down, took her hands between his. "Nell, my dearest girl, I can safely promise you that no one will ever know of this unless you tell them yourself."

She shook her head. "That's not good enough, Harry. I have too much to lose if even a breath of scandal comes anywhere near me. I can't take any risks."

He released her hands and straightened. He frowned. "So just what is at stake?"

"My children," she said simply. She met his frowning gaze and shook her head. "My son is the heir to the earl of Markby, his grandfather. Before Stephen went off to war he agreed that in the event of his death, I should have full and sole custody of our children. His father, as you might imagine, is furious and will do anything he can to challenge that custody. If I give him the slightest opening, he'll take the children from me. And there isn't a court in the land who wouldn't support him if the mother of his grandson and heir is touched by scandal."

Harry pulled thoughtfully at his earlobe. "I see your concern, but no one's going to find out, Nell. Unless, as I said, you tell them yourself."

"That's easy for you to say." She couldn't disguise the bitterness in her voice. "But you risk nothing, Harry. I risk everything."

He said nothing, merely stood looking at her, a deep frown drawing his arched eyebrows together, then he turned away and picked up his shirt from the floor. He dressed rapidly, sitting on the edge of the bed beside her to pull on his boots. Then he leaned sideways and kissed her, a light, unlover-like, farewell salute.

"We'll discuss this another time." He brushed her cheek with the side of his forefinger and stood up. "I'll see you this afternoon . . . in a rather different situation." A smile glimmered, then he pushed up the window and was gone.

Cornelia got out of bed and went to the window. She looked out into the graying dark but the black-clad figure blended so seamlessly with the shadows that she couldn't make him out although she knew he must still be in the garden.

She stood hugging herself with crossed arms, wondering why she was so intent on bringing this extraordinary dream idyll to a close. Harry was probably right. No one would ever know. She was certain that he would keep the secret. It was impossible to imagine him breaking his word just as she knew instinctively that he hadn't been joking when he'd called himself a master of secrets.

What exactly did she know about this man beyond the surface he had shown her? He had siblings, a family he was clearly close to. He'd been married. His wife had died in an accident. He said he had loved his wife . . . no, wait a minute . . . that wasn't what he'd said. She heard his voice again. *I believed that I did.* That was exactly what he'd said. Not a simple affirmative . . . no, not at all.

So what did that mean? And anyway, was it relevant to this little adventure they were having? No, she decided, not really. A past marriage of convenience had absolutely nothing to do with the present. So what was behind her perverse determination to end this before it had really begun? It was true she hated secrets, anything underhand. It had always been so, even as a child she'd been incapable of lying. Her face always gave her away, that and the lack of conviction in her voice. But she was an adult in a grown-up world, and this was a grown-up situation. It would harm no one, and if the last two occasions were anything to go by would bring her only unalloyed delight.

But she didn't want an irregular liaison. It seemed to be as simple as that. Even though there was nothing adulterous in such an affair. No one was being betrayed or hurt in any way. Nevertheless, it didn't feel right. It was as if there was something shameful in it. Hole in the corner, hiding in the shadows . . .

"Damned inconvenient scruples," she muttered, slamming the window shut with a near bang. She could hardly expect a proposal of marriage after two idyllic interludes between the sheets. Even if she wanted one, or would even be prepared to entertain one.

Chapter 17

CORNELIA EXAMINED HER REFLECTION critically in the cheval glass in her bedchamber. Her afternoon gown of jonquil crepe was a far cry from her usual plain round gowns. The neckline was a deep vee that met a dark green velvet sash caught beneath her breasts. The shape of her breasts and the cleft between them was accentuated in a most flattering fashion, she decided, fastening an amethyst pendant around her neck. Little puff sleeves offered minimum coverage, but her bare arms had a rather nice roundness to them. All in all, the effect was pleasing, even if the reality was somewhat chilly. But she had a cashmere shawl with a dark green fringe that would complement the gown beautifully and at least keep unsightly goose pimples at bay.

For this afternoon's social call she had drawn her thick hair into a Greek chignon banded with dark green velvet to match the sash of her gown and her flat silk slippers. The whole effect was very harmonious, she thought.

Would Harry find it so? She pushed the thought from her. Viscount Bonham's opinion was irrelevant. Or *should* be. Innate honesty forced the addendum.

"Nell, are you ready?" Livia called from the corridor, tapping lightly on the door as she spoke. "Ellie and I are so elegant, you wouldn't believe." She opened the door and popped her head brightly around it. "Oh, you look magnificent. Almost regal."

"Let me look at you two," Cornelia demanded with a laugh, more than happy to have her thoughts diverted. "Oh, yes, most elegant." Her friends stood side by side in the doorway, Aurelia in a gown of rose silk that brought out her pale blond hair and deep brown eyes, and Livia in cream muslin, her blue-black hair falling in artful ringlets around her ears.

"Her Grace should find nothing of the country mouse about her hostesses this afternoon," Cornelia commented, draping her shawl around her shoulders. "I just hope Morecombe built up a really a good fire in the salon. Chattering teeth and gooseflesh are not exactly attractive or sophisticated."

They laughed and with one final twitch at her skirt, she followed them downstairs just as the longcase clock in the hall struck three. She was aware of an unusual nervousness. Social occasions had ceased to alarm her many years ago, and there was nothing about an afternoon visitor that should make her nervous. Ellie and Liv seemed perfectly relaxed, a little excited even. All Cornelia felt was uncertainty.

But she knew why. *Harry.* Harry would be there and the memory of all that they had shared the previous night, and how they had parted, would be in the room with them like the proverbial elephant in the corner. And somehow she had to behave as if she didn't know it was there.

The salon was reassuringly welcoming, its old world elegance clear despite the slight shabbiness of the furnishings. Livia looked around her domain with pleasure. "I'm glad we didn't try to replace any of the furniture or the curtains," she said. "There's a coherence to the room, as if it's supposed to be exactly as it is."

"I think that's true of the house in general," Aurelia observed, adjusting the position of a cushion on the chaise. "It has a definite personality."

"Maybe that's why Aunt Sophia didn't want me to sell it," Livia mused, going to the long windows that overlooked the street. "Oh, here's Lord Bonham, riding beside a barouche. Oh, and there are *two* ladies in the carriage."

"I thought he was just bringing his great-aunt." Aurelia hurried over to stand beside Livia. "Ah, the other one is Lady Sefton."

"He certainly keeps his promises," Cornelia said, raising her eyebrows a little. "He promised to bring us one of the patronesses of Almack's. But do come away from the window, both of you. If they look up, they'll see you gawking."

Aurelia and Livia jumped back hastily and deposited

themselves in graceful poses on the sofa. Cornelia chose
to stand by the fireplace, the calmness of her expression
belied by the agitated pace of her pulse.

Morecombe opened the door and put his head
around it. "Some ladies, ma'am, and that Lord Bonham," he declared.

"Thank you, Morecombe," Harry said, opening the
door wide for his companions.

Cornelia stepped forward quickly, a smile on her face
and her hand outstretched. "You must excuse Morecombe. He has some eccentric ways, but he was a fa-
vored servant of Lady Sophia Lacey's, and it was her
expressed wish in her will that Lady Livia keep him on.
Do come by the fire, Your Grace. Lady Sefton how kind
of you to call."

Harry's great-aunt was an elderly lady wrapped in a
voluminous fur-trimmed pelisse and wearing an amazing fur bonnet that remarkably resembled a fox's head.
She raised her lorgnette even as she took Cornelia's outstretched hand. "Glad to know you, Lady Dagenham."
Disconcertingly she looked over her shoulder at her
great-nephew and confided, "Not a bad lookin' gal . . .
for her age."

"I'm sure Lady Dagenham is gratified to hear it,
ma'am," Harry said smoothly, bowing to Cornelia. His
eyes twinkled. "Your servant, Lady Dagenham. You
must forgive my aunt's outspokenness."

"Indeed, Her Grace is too kind, sir," Cornelia murmured, struggling to keep a straight face.

"Pshaw," expostulated the lady. "I've no time for namby-pamby nonsense. Say what you mean. That's what I always say."

"You are always the soul of tact, ma'am," Harry murmured.

Cornelia turned swiftly to their third guest. "Lady Sefton, I know you're acquainted with Lady Farnham. May I introduce Lady Livia Lacey."

"I knew your mother, I believe," Lady Sefton said, taking the seat that Livia offered her, arranging her diaphanous muslin skirts gracefully around her. "Quite the beauty she was before she married. You resemble her, my dear." She was clearly disposed to be gracious.

The duchess, however, refused a seat and stared rudely around the salon through her lorgnette as if appraising its furnishings. "Not a bad Turner," she observed almost sotto voce, then peered at the painting above the mantel. "Hmm. Morland. Overrated."

"Ma'am, will you take tea?" Livia asked, after casting a helpless glance at Cornelia, who appeared to be enjoying herself hugely.

Her Grace waved a dismissive hand. "Can't stand the stuff, maudles your insides. I'll take sherry."

"Of course," Cornelia said, going to the sideboard. All her nervousness had vanished, and the elephant in the corner had miraculously failed to appear. Harry seemed his usual self, slightly amused, with a crinkling conspiratorial smile in his eyes whenever their gaze met. It was as if he'd completely forgotten how they'd parted.

"Would you perhaps care to take off your pelisse and . . . and hat, ma'am?" she asked solemnly. *If that monstrosity can be called a hat.*

"No, I don't care to," the lady said, finally depositing herself on a tiny gilt chair that trembled beneath her. "Can't risk catching cold." She took the glass that Cornelia handed her and sipped. "Not bad," she pronounced. "Well, sit down, Bonham, don't stand there like an overgrown weed."

"Yes, ma'am," Harry murmured, sitting obediently on the edge of a chaise. Resolutely, he kept from looking again anywhere in Cornelia's vicinity. He should have warned her about his aunt's eccentricities, but somehow it had slipped his mind, and while he was so accustomed to them that they washed over him, he could well understand how someone would react on a first meeting. Particularly someone with Cornelia's lively sense of the ridiculous.

Their visitors stayed for twenty minutes and when they rose to leave, Lady Sefton said, "Vouchers, of course. You'll be needing vouchers for Almack's, I daresay."

"That would be most gracious, Lady Sefton," Cornelia responded. "Of course we had them in our first season, but since then . . ." She offered a self-deprecating smile. "We've been minding hearth and home."

"Oh, waste of time," the duchess pronounced. "You've children I daresay."

"Yes, ma'am," Cornelia agreed.

"Ruin your figure," the lady declared, then raised her lorgnette again to peer at Cornelia. "Though I must say, yours isn't too bad." She turned aside to her great-nephew. "Not too bad at all, Bonham. Now take me to the carriage." She laid an imperious hand on his arm.

Harry bowed to his hostesses before offering Lady Sefton his free arm. "Good afternoon, ladies."

"Good afternoon, Lord Bonham. Duchess . . . Lady Sefton." It was almost a chorus as they bowed their guests from the room.

"Allow me to see you out." Cornelia moved swiftly after them. There was no point summoning More-combe.

"You tend your own door?" the duchess demanded, as Cornelia opened it. "How very odd."

"We too have our eccentricities, ma'am," Cornelia responded sweetly.

Her Grace looked at her sharply, without the aid of the lorgnette this time. "Is that so?" she said. "Well, come along, Bonham."

Harry glanced over his shoulder and grinned at Cornelia. It was such a complicit grin, so full of shared amusement and shared joy, that it took her breath away. She stepped back and closed the door swiftly. She was not going to be able to hold to her resolution. Why had she ever thought she could?

"What a dragon!" Livia exclaimed, as Cornelia returned to the salon. "She seemed to like you though, Nell."

"She has a funny way of showing it," Cornelia said. "I'm not bad-looking for my age, and somehow my figure has withstood the effects of procreation." She went restlessly to the window, watching the barouche bowl off down the street, Harry riding in solemn escort beside it. She watched him out of sight before saying cheerfully, "Still, we have our social opening now."

"We had better return the call," Aurelia said, pouring more tea. "And to Lady Sefton too. When shall we do it?"

"We still haven't solved the problem of a carriage," Cornelia reminded them. "Where *is* Nigel? Could he have gone back to Ringwood do you think?"

"Not without telling us," Livia stated. "He would have sent a note at the very least."

"I suppose so. But if he's not still staying at Lord Coltrain's, why did the butler take the note we sent around? Surely he would have said Nigel had left, if he *has* left."

"He's probably gone to Newmarket or somewhere . . . maybe to a hunting box with some of his new friends," Aurelia suggested. "He wouldn't think to let us know if he was just going out of town for a week or so."

"I suppose you're right." Cornelia bent to pile teacups onto the tray. "I'll take these back to the kitchen."

"No, ring for Hester, the new scullery maid, Nell. You shouldn't carry dirty dishes in that gown," Aurelia protested, pulling vigorously on the frayed bellpull beside the fireplace.

Cornelia shrugged and acquiesced. Ellie had a point. She sat down again, picking up her workbox. A button needed sewing on one of Susannah's pinafores.

Instead of Hester, however, the bell was answered by the new handyman. "Oh, Lester, I didn't think you did drawing room duty," she said in surprise, slipping her thimble on her finger. A slightly puzzled frown crossed her eyes, and she looked down at her finger.

"Oh, I help out wherever it's needed, my lady," Lester said swiftly, catching the frown. His gaze flicked over the thimble. It looked just the same to him. He picked up the tray and went to the door.

"I'll bring the dogs back, Lady Livia," he said. "Now that the visitors have gone. They're upsetting the kitchen something chronic, all that yapping and scrabbling to get out."

"Oh, dear, yes, you'd better bring them at once, thank you, Lester."

The door closed behind Lester and Cornelia once again looked down at her finger. She twisted the thimble experimentally. "This is funny."

"What is?" Aurelia asked.

"The thimble feels different."

"How could a thimble feel different, Nell?"

"Well, it used to fit perfectly. It felt really comfortable, but now it's rather loose." She turned it again. "See how easily it moves."

"Maybe your finger's thinner," Livia suggested.

Cornelia frowned at this. She removed the thimble

and examined it. "It's the same, and yet it's not," she insisted. "I'm sure there was a mark like an epsilon just above this little figure here, but it's gone."

"You're imagining things, Nell," Aurelia said. "There's so much engraved in such a tiny space, you couldn't possibly remember every detail."

Cornelia gave up the puzzle. "Maybe you're right."

Morecombe brought the dogs back, his long-suffering expression eloquent of his disapproval.

Cornelia finished sewing on the button, and as she bit off the thread, said on impulse, "Morecombe, do you know where we could hire a carriage cheaply? Just to drive around town."

"Why'd you want to hire one?" he asked, releasing the dogs. "What's wrong with Lady Sophia's?"

The three women stared at him. "Aunt Sophia kept a carriage?" Livia asked, struggling to fend off the dogs, who wanted to climb up onto her elegant lap.

"O'course she did," Morecombe said, sounding indignant at the question. "Lady Sophia knew what was what for a lady of her standing."

"Yes, I'm sure she did," Aurelia said soothingly. "But we understood that she didn't get out much in the last few years."

"Well, neither she did," the man declared. "But that don't mean she couldn't if she wanted to."

"So there's a carriage." Cornelia returned the thimble to her workbox. "Where is it kept, Morecombe?"

"In t'mews," he said as if it was self-evident.

Cornelia bit her lip. "And where would we find the mews?"

"T'other side of the square."

"And horses?"

He shook his head. "No, Lady Sophia got rid of the horses, said they were eatin' their heads off."

"A horseless carriage isn't going to be much good to us," Livia said with a sigh.

"You want a horse, ma'am, why don't you say so? I could get you one if'n you want one. But reckon as how that carriage'll need a pair, it being as big as it is."

"How big?" Cornelia said with foreboding.

Morecombe shrugged. "Big enough for Lady Sophia at any rate. Her ladyship knew what was due her consequence."

"I think we should go and see it," Cornelia announced, getting to her feet. "Will you direct us, Morecombe?"

"Oh, aye," he said, going to the window and pointing. "'Tis behind number sixteen across the garden. Don't think nobody's been near it in nigh on ten years."

"Perhaps you'd accompany us," Livia suggested.

"You'll need the key." He went off, leaving them wondering if he'd agreed to go with them or not.

However, he reappeared five minutes later brandishing a large brass key and wrapped in a thick greatcoat, a long scarf twined several times around his neck, and a high-crowned beaver hat pulled down low over his ears. He looked equipped for the Arctic, Cornelia thought suppressing a chuckle.

"Thisaway." He preceded them to the front door, then paused. "Catch your deaths you will in them flimsy gowns. Don't know what the world's comin' too."

"Give me a minute, Morecombe," Livia said, turning to the stairs, the dogs crowding her ankles. "I'll fetch shawls for us." She ran upstairs, the dogs prancing ahead of her and was back in a few minutes with an armful of pelisses and shawls. "I shut the dogs up in my bedchamber," she said. "They'd only be in the way."

Morecombe sniffed and opened the door, peering out suspiciously as if he expected some kind of monstrosity to be lying in wait for him. Judging the coast to be clear, he stepped outside.

The women followed him around the square and down a narrow alley that ran alongside number sixteen on the far side. The alley led into a mews courtyard, lined with stables and carriage houses. For the most part they appeared well cared for, the paintwork fresh, the cobbles swept. Except for one at the far end. The double doors sagged on their hinges, and the paint was scraped almost clean.

The women exchanged glances, and Cornelia murmured, "What are the odds those doors haven't been opened in ten years?"

The trouble Morecombe had with the key seemed to prove her right, but eventually it turned in the lock, and he put his shoulder to the doors, pushing, but with little success. The doors refused to budge.

"Perhaps I can help," a cool voice said from behind the

women. They all turned as one. "Lord Bonham," Livia exclaimed in surprise. "Where did you spring from?"

"My aunt decided to drive in the park without my escort," he explained. "So I left her at the Stanhope Gate and came back to see if there was any way I could be of further service to you." He offered a little mock bow. "What exactly do you expect to find in here?" He moved to the double doors.

"A carriage," Cornelia told him, watching as he put one shoulder, elegant in dark blue superfine, to the doors and pushed. They gave slowly and with much creaking but finally stood open.

Harry brushed off his shoulder and stepped inside. "Good God."

"What is it?" The women crowded behind him.

"Apart from cobwebs?" he said lightly. "It looks like a Berlin. At least twenty years old I would hazard."

"Oh, aye, it's all of that right enough," Morecombe confirmed with gloomy satisfaction. "Very fine in its day it was."

"It must have been," Cornelia agreed faintly, as she stepped up beside Harry to examine the huge round body of the carriage. "It's like a gigantic teacup."

"It's lined with crimson silk," Livia said in awe, standing on tiptoe to peer through the dirt-encrusted window. She pulled open the carriage door and sneezed at the cloud of dust. "It's sadly moth-eaten though."

"Well, there's no way we can pay calls in that," Aurelia pronounced.

" 'Twas good enough for Lady Sophia," Morecombe stated.

Harry felt Cornelia shaking with laughter beside him. He glanced at her, and she put her hand to her mouth, her eyes brimful of mischief. "Oh, I don't know," he said gravely, his own eyes dancing. "Perhaps it can be made serviceable again. Think what an impression you'll make on the town."

"It doesn't bear thinking about," Livia said.

"I think we could make quite a stir," Cornelia announced, suddenly taken by the absurd possibilities. "Why shouldn't we be a little eccentric? The ladies of Cavendish Square driving around in such crimson-squabbed magnificence, even if it is a little moth-eaten. No one will be able to ignore us."

"That is certainly true," Harry agreed. His suggestion had not been intended as serious, but now, like Cornelia, he could see through the absurdity to the possibility.

"Let's face it," Cornelia said briskly. "We are three unremarkable women. We're not debutantes, we have neither wealth, great lineage, nor outstanding beauty. We need to be eccentric if we want to be noticed."

"I think you do yourselves some injustice," Harry said. "Nevertheless . . ."

"Nevertheless, Nell is right." Aurelia chuckled. "We shall be known as the ladies in the teacup."

They all three burst into laughter and Harry once again thought that he had never encountered three such unusual women. Cornelia entranced him, but they all entertained him.

"If you will permit me, I'll send a coachmaker to see what needs to be done to put this . . . this teacup . . . on the streets again." He closed the carriage door carefully. "You will need at least a pair of horses."

"Morecombe says he can arrange for that," Cornelia said swiftly before any more generous offers were forthcoming. She could see nothing wrong with allowing him to send a coachmaker to effect repairs, and they would pay for them themselves, but horses were another matter.

Harry shrugged. "If you say so."

Morecombe was walking around the carriage with an air of reverence. "Oh, quite magnificent this was, when Lady Sophia went out of an evening. Her hoops were so wide she had to step in sideways. And her coiffure was powdered an' dressed so high it brushed the top of the carriage."

The women stared at him, astonished at this extraordinary eloquence from the taciturn retainer. Suddenly self-conscious, Morecombe coughed and stalked to the doors of the carriage house. "I'll be locking her up now."

They followed him out, and Harry pulled the heavy doors to. Morecombe insisted on wrestling with the key himself, and Cornelia murmured, "Does he really imagine someone's going to come in and steal it away?"

"It's a museum piece," Harry said, offering her his arm. "Will you walk a little with me in the garden, Lady

Dagenham?" His eyes were no longer amused; instead, they rested on her face with a powerful intensity that made Cornelia's skin prickle. She could almost feel the heat of his body so close to hers. She seemed to be leaning towards him, as if pulled by invisible threads as she put her hand on his arm.

Then she became aware of Aurelia and Livia looking at them. She let her hand drop, and said casually, "Oh, a little stroll will do us all good, don't you think, Ellie . . . Liv."

Livia was about to agree when Aurelia stepped heavily on her toe, and said, "No, I promised to read to Franny, but you go, Nell."

Livia recovered swiftly. "I have a touch of the headache, Nell. I think I'll lie down for half an hour."

"Then, Lady Dagenham, will *you* do me the honor?" Harry's voice had a touch of mockery, a hint of challenge, as if he guessed she was about to refuse.

She wanted to go with him, be with him more than anything, and yet she didn't . . . couldn't . . . not in this hard, practical daylight. It destroyed the illusion of their nights. And she knew he was going to force a conversation that she was not ready to have.

It was an effort but she managed to find a light, careless tone as she said, "I must ask you to forgive me, Lord Bonham. I have things to do in the house too. Perhaps another time."

He bowed, his green gaze unreadable. He gave her a fractional shake of his head as if he had read her mind and disapproved of what he read. "As you wish, ma'am." He turned and walked away out of the mews.

Cornelia became aware of her friends' puzzled looks. "What?" she demanded.

If Nell wasn't prepared to confide in them, then they had to honor her reticence. Ellie said easily, "Why, nothing. Let's go home, it grows chilly."

Chapter 18

Harry dismounted in the filthy alley outside the George and Dragon. His nose wrinkled in disgust at the stench and the fetid pool into which he'd just placed one immaculately polished top boot. His informants had traced Nigel Dagenham to this hellhole in London's East End and despite his irritation with the young man, Harry couldn't help a flash of sympathy.

He handed the reins of his chestnut to Eric, who was staring straight ahead as if trying to ignore his surroundings. "Should I walk 'em, m'lord? It won't do 'em much good standing around 'ere." The question was muffled, coming as it did through a handkerchief he held over his mouth and nose.

"I rather think you mean it won't do you much good," Harry corrected wryly.

"Well, as to that, m'lord, there's disease all over in these alleys," Eric said. "Typhoid an' scarlet fever, and the Lord only knows what else." His sigh was filled with reproach.

"I'll not be above ten minutes," Harry promised, and entered the reeking confines of the inn. He found himself in a dark and seemingly deserted taproom, the air redolent of stale beer and the outhouse. The sawdust beneath his boots was clotted and sticky.

He banged his whip on the stained deal counter, and shouted, *"House."*

A man with the broken nose and flabby physique of a prizefighter gone to seed shuffled out of the back regions, eating a gigantic pickled onion. He peered in disbelief at his elegant visitor and seemed disinclined to say anything, merely continued to eat his vinegar-soaked vegetable, staring at the newcomer.

"You have a gentleman putting up here I believe," Harry said impatiently, when it seemed the silence would continue. He waved a hand in front of his face in an effort to dissipate the fumes of the pickled onion.

"Not no more," the man said. He wiped his mouth with the back of his hand and spat disgustedly into the sawdust at his feet. "Did a runner 'e did. Took off in the middle o' the night, wi'out payin' 'is shot. Not a farthing. I should 'ave got the Watch on him."

"No doubt," Harry said. "Although I doubt you see much of the Watch in this neighborhood, my friend." He tapped the counter with his whip in an increasingly impatient rhythm. If Dagenham had run, there had to be a reason for it. One that went beyond his inability to pay his shot in this filthy hovel.

"Show me his lodging."

"Up them stairs." The man gestured with what was left of his onion, sending a shower of vinegar over the counter. "Can't miss it . . . door's at the top."

Harry climbed the rickety staircase. A door, sagging in its frame, stood at the top. He opened it and entered the desolate chamber. "Poor fool," he muttered as he looked around. He kicked at an empty brandy bottle and grimaced. If the lad had been drinking that stuff, he'd be burned to a socket. He'd be lucky to have a gut left.

He examined the few sticks of furniture, pulled the ragged quilt back from the bed and turned the mattress. His movements were both fastidious and efficient, and when he'd examined every corner of the chamber and found nothing more interesting than a mousehole he slapped his gloved hands together and cursed softly. There were no clues here as to where Dagenham had run to next. And no clues as to why.

Harry returned to the taproom, which, once again was deserted. He played his tune on the counter again, and the man reappeared, minus the onion this time, much to Harry's relief.

"Did anyone visit your lodger while he was here?"

"Mebbe, an' mebbe not," the barkeep said, his eyes suddenly shrewd. He blew his nose on his sleeve.

Harry laid a sovereign on the counter. He let the man see the coin, then laid a hand over it. "Why don't we discuss the maybe?"

The man's eyes darted sideways into the gloomy corners of the still-deserted taproom, then fixed upon the gloved hand covering the coin. "Yesterday. A man come lookin' fer 'im. Another one come as well." He shrugged. "I ain't got a real close look, m'lord. They was gone in five minutes."

"And your lodger didn't go with them?"

The man shook his head. "Not what I saw, m'lord. I 'eard 'im movin' about up there fer a bit. This mornin' he done a runner." He spat again.

"Did you notice anything unusual about these visitors?"

"Spoke funny," the man said with a shrug.

It was all he was going to get. Harry raised his hand from the coin and spun on his heel out into the alley. Eric sighed with relief as he handed over the reins. "We'll be out of here now, m'lord?"

Harry gave a curt nod and swung onto Perseus. His informants had found Dagenham yesterday evening. Not that the young fool would have been aware of them. Presumably he'd had his visitors, foreign visitors if the barkeep was to be believed, earlier that day. Visitors who'd either spooked him sufficiently to run away or terrified him into doing what they wanted of him.

Which was what?

Well, they were back to square one. Harry was no longer really concerned for the safety of the women in Cavendish Square. The enemy watchers had disappeared some days ago and even though the Ministry, now that the thimble had been retrieved, had withdrawn its own men from observation, Lester was there, and if the only person they needed to worry about was Nigel Dagenham, then Lester would be more than a match. As indeed would he himself. And Harry intended to be around whenever he could.

Like tonight.

Yesterday, after Cornelia had brushed him off in the mews, so clearly against her own inclinations, he had been too aggravated to pursue her, telling himself that maybe a night of quiet reflection would change her mind. He recognized that it was just pique that made him hope she would spend the night in frustrated passion because he wasn't there to slake it. In truth, he'd spent the night in a state of pent-up frustration himself. To such an extent that he'd contemplated visiting the discreet house on Half Moon Street where he was accustomed to taking his pleasure when the need became imperative.

He hadn't gone however. The prospect had for once seemed tawdry. But tonight he was going to have it out with the Viscountess Dagenham. She was cutting off her nose and spiting both their faces. But first he had to set the dogs on her cousin once more.

Cornelia retired to bed early, pleading a headache. It was not entirely untrue, but it was more a sensation of aggravation in her temples than actual pain. She was restless, sleepless, could settle to nothing. And she well knew why.

She tried reading, but Madame de Staël's, *Delphine,* a novel she had long promised herself she would read, failed to hold her attention. Ordinarily she read French easily, but the words seemed meaningless tonight. She had expected to be excited by the author's portrayal of an independent and artistic woman, but her intellectual interest was as dormant as her linguistic ability.

When she heard the faint tap at the window, she was not startled. It seemed inevitable. She had not opened the window, but she had not drawn the curtains across either. Her actions had been as contradictory as her emotions. She pushed aside the coverlet and rose slowly from the bed. Her body told her to run to the window, her mind to procrastinate.

The tap came again, a little more urgent this time, and she had a mental image of Harry, hanging precariously from the drainpipe. She moved quickly to the window and pushed it up, then turned away, picking up her discarded nightrobe and throwing it around her shoulders.

Harry swung himself over the sill and softly closed the window. He stood looking at her averted figure wrapped in the thick robe.

"Thank you for letting me in, ma'am."

"I could hardly leave you hanging by your fingernails from the drainpipe," she replied.

"It would have been a little unfriendly," he agreed lightly. He crossed the faded carpet in three quick steps, caught her loose hair in one hand and pressed his lips to her nape. He felt her shiver as his tongue licked up the little groove into her scalp, then he released her hair and turned to the fire, bending to throw more coal on the glowing embers.

Cornelia sat on the chest at the foot of the bed and watched his swift economical movements. He was hatless and, as always on these nocturnal visits, dressed completely in black. "I might have been asleep," she said.

"A risk I was willing to take." He straightened and turned to face her, his green eyes brilliant in his pale face. "We have unfinished business, you and I." He drew off his gloves and tossed them onto the chair by the fire. His muffler and coat followed. "A glass of cognac would not come amiss."

"I'll fetch the decanter." She rose and took her carrying candle, now extinguished, from the dresser. She held the wick to the flame of the reading candle beside her bed until the small flame took, then she went to the door, opening it quietly. There was complete silence in the house. She stepped into the corridor and a swish of fur brushed her ankles as Puss darted into the bedroom before she could close the door behind her.

She hesitated, then shrugged. The cat wouldn't raise the alarm as long as Harry didn't step on her tail again. She flitted barefooted down the wide staircase, almost holding her breath lest the terriers sense unusual movement in the house. While she had every right to be fetching the decanter of cognac to her own chamber to help her sleep, she would still prefer not to have to explain herself.

But she retrieved the decanter and two glasses and returned to her bedchamber without disturbance of any kind. Harry still stood with his back to the fire, and he'd drawn the curtains across the window. Puss lay curled in front of the fire, clearly unperturbed by the presence of a comparative stranger in her favorite's bedroom.

Cornelia poured cognac for them both, then resumed her seat on the chest. She regarded him in interrogative silence.

Harry sipped his cognac and raised his eyebrows. "Very well, *I'll* begin. As I recall you said you risked everything, and I risked nothing. It's become very clear to me in the last few days how much I am risking, Nell."

"What?"

He gave a half laugh. "Things I have always believed vital to me . . . to my self-esteem, the person I believe myself to be. Control over events for one." He regarded her over the lip of his goblet. "You are becoming an obsession with me, Nell. I am entranced by you, I want to be with you, I can't get your scent, the feel of your skin, the richness of your hair out of my mind. I have never felt this way about a woman before. It's as if your body is imprinted upon mine."

Cornelia felt herself grow warm at his words. She had never been so complimented before, and she knew he was not making empty speeches. It was not his way, and besides, his eyes told the truth, those deep green eyes that glowed with light. But physical passion was one thing, and she now understood it as she had never understood it before. But it wasn't enough.

"I don't know enough about you." She set her goblet down on the chest beside her. "I know your body, as you know mine, but who are *you*, Harry? Oh, I don't mean the facts. You've mentioned your family, your marriage . . . but that's not enough. It doesn't show me who you *are*. I realize that I haven't yet seen you in your own world. And I suppose that will happen soon now that we're ready to join that public world ourselves, but there's something else about you . . . you hint at business affairs that take you out of town, or somewhere for days at a time. You seem on the surface to be an ordinary person, but I know you're not."

Her voice was very low now but ringing with conviction. "I'm not a fool . . . some ingénue to be easily tempted by the sophisticated man-about-town. I am a widow, a mother, with duties, responsibilities. I cannot blithely ignore those obligations simply because a man makes my body sing."

She took a shuddery breath, overpoweringly aware of how close his body was to hers, of the intensity of his gaze, of the electric crackle of sexual anticipation between them. And she wondered why she was bothering with such futile protestations. Her mind had no say in this . . . no say at all.

Harry made no move. He stared down into his goblet, swirling the tawny liquid. And for the first time he hated his dead wife. Anne had ruined him for all but the lightest and most impermanent of relationships with women. However much he cried out for a relationship that could grow and deepen beyond the ephemeral glories of passion, he could never have it. He could not say to the woman sitting so still on the chest in front of him, a woman so straight and true, that he wanted to be with her always, that there was no need for these clandestine nights together. He could not say that one day they could live together openly, that he could be a father to her children.

Maybe his great-aunt was right, and somewhere there was a woman who could brave the scandal of marriage to Harry Bonham, but from what Cornelia had told him, *she* was not that woman. The old scandal would ruin her. She would lose her children. And so he had nothing to offer her but these nights, and the promise of absolute secrecy. And, as she'd said, secrecy did not sit well with her.

He set down his goblet, and said heavily, "I'm sorry. I can't give you what you want, sweetheart." He opened his hands palms up in a gesture of helplessness, his expression drawn, his eyes lightless.

"Why can't you?" she demanded. She wanted to shout the question but it emerged as a fierce whisper. "Tell me, Harry? *Why can't you?"* But even as she asked the question, she knew it to be futile. He would not tell her for the same reason he couldn't give her what she wanted.

He shook his head slowly. "I'll leave you now."

But she couldn't let him go. Her mind held no sway here, only the imperatives of her heart and her body. She couldn't let him go . . . and the consequences be damned.

She put out an arresting hand. *"No."* Her voice was strong and decisive. She stood slowly and went into his arms.

Nigel didn't think he'd stopped shaking since he'd run from the George and Dragon. His present lodgings were, if anything, even worse than the last, and to make matters yet more desperate, he knew he had to wean himself from the brandy that had enabled him to forget reality.

He didn't understand why they wanted something so absurdly ordinary as a thimble. It made no rational sense at all, and to his muddled brain the getting of it seemed impossible to execute. He had seen it on Cornelia's finger, had actually touched it when she'd taken his hand between hers, but how on earth was he to get it now?

But the consequences of failure had been laid out to him in gruesome detail. Running from his tormentors had proved a lamentable failure, so somehow he had to do what he was told.

But how? He could hardly go back to the Coltrain mansion. He'd left without so much as a scrawled note of explanation. He had no funds for a decent town lodging; anything of value, including clothes, had all been

pawned. He was debt-free, true enough, but he was in
no fit state to show himself to society. He no longer possessed even one decent suit of clothes. He couldn't possibly turn up on his cousin's doorstep in his present
condition. They wouldn't turn him away, but if his family ever found out the trouble he was in, they would dis-
own him. And he wouldn't blame them either.

On a desperate impulse he left the dingy squalor of
his room in the equally squalid lodging house in
Billingsgate and set off to walk to Gray's Inn. There he
would find the Greyhound Tavern. His instructions had
been crystal clear. When he had accomplished his task,
he was to leave the small piece of sealing wax they had
given him in the flowerpot on the window, and return
after three hours precisely. It all sounded so far-fetched
sometimes he could almost believe he was dreaming, but
the grimness of his surroundings was all he needed to remind him that this nightmare was indeed reality.

He didn't know why he was going to the rendezvous
now, but somehow he had the idea that if he looked at
the place, thought about how, once the sealing wax was
in the flowerpot, he would wake up again to a sane
world, then an idea would come to him.

He stood for a long time in a fetid alleyway on the
other side of the Gray's Inn Road, staring at the inn, at
the cracked flowerpot on the sagging windowsill. He
watched the customers stagger in and out of the tavern,
ill-kempt drovers, carters, barrow boys for the most part.
In his present guise he would fit right in, he thought

sourly. He had a handful of coins, enough for a pint of gin. Maybe one kind of spirit would move the other to inspiration.

When he emerged from the tavern an hour later, drunk enough to feel no pain, he had the beginnings of an idea.

"So, are you enjoying yourself, ma'am?"

Cornelia turned her head slowly, a smile hovering on her lips, as Harry stepped up beside her in the window embrasure. Behind them in the ballroom at Almack's the orchestra was playing a cotillion. "Not particularly," she said, but her smile widened as she looked at him. "Perhaps that will change now." Evening dress suited him, but then so did everything, including his birthday suit, she thought, feeling that telltale jolt of unbidden arousal in her loins.

His eyes gleamed as if he'd heard the thought, felt the jolt himself. "I'll do my best to alter things," he said, sliding a wicked hand down her hip. "Any better?"

"Hush," she said, biting her lip to suppress her laughter. "Don't stand so close."

"But this embrasure is so small," he murmured. "I don't appear to have much choice." His fingers did a little dance against the blue silk of her gown, pressing into the warm flesh beneath.

Cornelia hastily stepped backwards out of the embrasure, and he turned, laughing, to stand with his back to the window, facing her. "I expected to find you with a full dance card," he remarked, accepting the end of that little play.

"I've been dancing for two hours," she responded in a tone remarkable for its lack of enthusiasm.

"You don't care to dance?" He sounded surprised. She was such a graceful creature, he couldn't imagine she was anything but a delight on the dance floor.

Cornelia shook her head with a moue of distaste. "In truth, I find this kind of dancing utterly insipid. Or perhaps," she added, "it's my partners I find insipid. Does no one in London have any sensible conversation at all?"

He inclined his head consideringly. "The weather is a popular topic . . . and last night's rout ball at Lady Bartram's . . . oh, and I've heard much discussion on Miss Gossington's marital prospects. It seems she'll catch Lord de Vere after all."

Cornelia laughed. "Oh, you are absurd, but that is about the size of it." She turned to look around the ballroom. "Liv is enjoying herself though. That's the second time she's danced with that gentleman . . . I don't recall his name."

Harry followed her gaze. "Ah, Strachan . . . I hope she's not setting her cap at him. He hasn't two pennies to rub together."

Cornelia turned back to him, regarding him for a second in haughty silence, before declaring, "Liv would never be so vulgar as to *set her cap* at anyone, my lord."

He returned smartly, "Forgive me, ma'am. I didn't mean to imply that Lady Livia was no different from the rest of the aspiring females in this room. Her sensibilities are of course far superior."

Cornelia couldn't hold on to her indignation. His eyes were too full of laughter. "Sometimes I dislike you intensely," she said without any conviction. "If you're not minded to be pleasant, my lord, I suggest you find someone else to talk to."

"Come, let's dance," he said suddenly, reaching for her hand. "I can promise I won't be an insipid partner."

Cornelia allowed herself to be led onto the dance floor, and they took their places in the set. It was a country dance, and there was little opportunity for much conversation, insipid or otherwise, but whenever they came together, Harry contrived some small gesture, a hand squeeze, a conspiratorial wink, that kept her smiling.

As they walked off the floor at the end of the dance, he said rather gravely, "I didn't mean to insult Livia, earlier, it was just a word of warning. One that I'm delighted she has no need of."

Cornelia frowned and said with a little sigh, "I suppose it's what everyone will be saying. I do so loathe this business. It's so superficial."

"It is if you believe, as these women do, that the pinnacle of female ambition must be a husband," he pointed out. "And how else is she to catch one, except on the marriage mart?" He gestured at the salon thronged with eager-eyed young women, fluttering fans, gazing worshipfully up at whatever man was paying them attention. Their chaperones sat along the wall, gossiping, tittering, even as their own eyes never left the activity on the dance floor, watching for the moment when a maternal intervention would be required.

Cornelia looked at him sharply, seeing the slight derisive curl of his lip. "You think so little of my sex?" she questioned.

"Ah, Nell, you know better than that," he protested, his voice once more an undertone. "You of all women should know that's not true."

She flushed a little, the undercurrent in his voice sending prickles of lustful anticipation along her spine.

"Besides," he went on, watching her with the smile once more in his eyes, "I was merely agreeing with you. I like this social dance no more than you do."

"Then why take part in it?"

"I don't, as a rule," he replied. "But I couldn't resist the opportunity to spend the evening in your company."

"Permit me to inform you, sir, that I consider that a shameless piece of flummery," she declared, trying not to laugh.

"Indeed it is not," he protested, lifting her hand to his lips. His eyes glowed, his voice dropped to a whisper, "I'll prove it later tonight."

Cornelia's tongue touched her lips. He was playing with fire. He might not have a reputation to preserve, but she most certainly did. The middle of Almack's assembly rooms was no place for dangerous flirtation. She withdrew her hand from his and said loudly to be heard by those around them, "Excuse me, Lord Bonham, my sister-in-law is beckoning me." She walked quickly away from him.

Harry watched her, a smile lingering on his lips. Her ball gown of azure blue silk suited her coloring to perfection. A short train fell straight from her shoulders accentuating her erect posture. Her hair was dressed in her favorite Greek chignon, banded tonight with black velvet sewn with seed pearls. The pearls at her throat were particularly fine, too, he noted. A family heirloom, he guessed.

All three women drew the eye on this their first major venture into society. They were unusual, as much because they appeared so naturally confident, so blithely indifferent to the sometimes rude stares, the behind-the-hand speculation, that always accompanied the arrival of a newcomer on London's social scene.

They had drawn up in the teacup, which, as they had all predicted, created an instant stir. Had they appeared at all self-conscious about this extraordinarily old-fashioned method of transport, they would have been laughed out of court, branded as country simpletons, and they would have languished in Cavendish Square until, crushed, they decided to return whence they came.

But that had not happened. They were being talked about in every corner of the salon. Everyone knew who they were, their lineages were impeccable if not of the truly upper echelons of the aristocracy. Their mothers were known to have made reasonable if not spectacular alliances. Lady Sefton and the duchess of Gracechurch had vouched for them, so society was disposed to be kind, unless given reason to be otherwise.

And the women were far too astute, far too clever to make a mistake. They were here for Livia, and neither Cornelia nor Aurelia would queer that pitch.

He saw that Livia was leaving the dance floor with her partner, who escorted her to a little gilt chair in a window embrasure and went to the refreshment room. She sat fanning herself, her cheeks a little flushed from exertion in the overheated room.

Harry made his way towards her. "Good evening, Lady Livia. May I procure you a glass of lemonade?"

She looked up with a ready smile. "Oh, no thank you, Lord Bonham. Lord Strachan has gone to fetch me one." She patted the seat beside her. "Won't you sit down?"

Harry did so, gracefully settling his long figure in black silk knee britches onto the fragile chair. "Are you enjoying yourself?"

She gave him a quick up from under smile. "Truth, sir?"

"Truth, ma'am."

"It's all so insipid," she stated. "No one has anything to talk about, and no one listens to a word one says.

They're always looking over your shoulder for someone more interesting."

"Not so much someone more interesting," he said, smiling. "More to see if there's anything worth gossiping about. One must always be in the forefront of gossip, m'dear."

Livia chuckled. "I'm sure that's so, but it's still mortifying to be in the middle of a sentence and realize that your partner hasn't heard a word you've said."

"So what did you think of Strachan?"

"Mildly amusing. When he ceases to be so, I shall tell him I haven't a penny and I'm certain he'll take his congé immediately."

Harry laughed. "Nell said as much."

Livia's black eyes were suddenly shrewd. She closed her fan, tapping it lightly into the palm of her other hand. "I can't help noticing, sir, that you appear to be on much less formal terms with Nell than with Ellie and me."

"I find it difficult to be formal with any of you," he said swiftly. "Sometimes I forget, particularly when there's no one around to hear the slip." His smile was winning. "I trust you don't object, Livia."

Livia appeared to consider this. "No," she said. "I don't object in the least. But don't underestimate either Ellie or me, Harry. And you should bear in mind that Nell's well-being is close to our hearts. You jeopardize it at your peril."

"I am duly warned," Harry responded with the flicker of an eyebrow. "Ah, here is your escort back from his errand." He rose from the chair and bowed. "If you'll excuse me, ma'am. Strachan . . ." He strode off, aware of Livia's too shrewd gaze on his back. He had promised Cornelia he would never divulge their secret. He hadn't done so, but something had alerted Nell's friends. He wondered if she knew.

Chapter 19

"Hold the ladder steady, Liv," Cornelia said hurriedly as she reached the midpoint on the steps, and they began to shake alarmingly.

"I'm trying," Livia said, "but there's a ruck in the carpet and it's making it unbalanced. Come down, and we'll straighten it."

Cornelia descended the ladder. "It's those damn dogs," she complained. "They were chasing each other under the table last night, and they must have rolled up the rug." She lifted the stepladder while Aurelia and Livia straightened out the Aubusson carpet.

"There, that's better." Aurelia experimentally shook the ladder. "It seems stable enough now."

"Good. Now we'll see if there's anything of interest in that fresco." Cornelia gathered up the striped muslin skirt of her new morning gown and went nimbly up the ladder while her friends held it steady. At the top she knelt precariously on the little platform and tilted her head back to look up at the painted ceiling.

"I don't see . . . oh, yes, I do." She went into a peal of laughter, and the ladder wobbled violently. She grabbed hastily at the sides.

"Good God, what in the devil's name are you doing up there?"

Harry's startled voice from the open door of the dining room distracted Livia and Aurelia, who both turned their heads towards him, their hold on the ladder slackening with their attention.

"What are you doing? Don't let go," Cornelia yelped, as the ladder swayed.

Harry moved swiftly. He plucked her off the ladder just as she was about to lose her balance. He held her in the air for an instant, his hands warm at her waist, then he set her on her feet again. "Dear girl, what *are* you doing? You'll break your neck."

Cornelia, flustered, tried to regain her composure, never an easy task when he stood this close to her and she could still feel the imprint of his hands at her waist. "I was looking at the fresco," she explained finally.

"Why?" He looked up at it himself.

"Because we had a suspicion that there was more to it than meets the eye," Aurelia answered. "Is there, Nell?"

She nodded, her eyes brimming with laughter. "Oh, yes. It's positively lewd in parts. Those cherubims and seraphims are up to all sorts of tricks. Go up and take a look."

Aurelia needed no second invitation. She hopped onto the ladder. "Hold tight."

"Let me do that." Harry gave up thoughts of further protestation and took a firm hold of the struts. Aurelia's skirts billowed as she climbed upwards to put her knee on the platform, as Cornelia had done.

She craned her neck, gazing upwards, and then she too went into a burst of laughter. "Oh, my heavens, what *are* they up to?"

"No good, that's for sure," Cornelia said, her own voice throbbing with laughter.

"Let me look," Livia demanded impatiently.

Aurelia came down and Livia took her place. Harry, resigned to his allotted role, remained patiently steadying the stepladder. Livia's peal of merriment soon joined her friends'. "Oh, that's not physically possible," she gasped. "How could there be three of them doing that at once?"

"All right," Harry said. "I have to see whatever this is. Come down, Livia." He lifted her unceremoniously clear of the ladder and went up himself. There was a short expectant silence, then he muttered, "Good God," and descended the steps.

"I think Aunt Sophia ran a house of ill repute," Cornelia declared, wiping her eyes with a scrap of lace handkerchief. "What with pornographic paper knives, lewd frescos and jelly molds. I wonder what else there is?"

"I dread to think." Harry stood with his hands on his hips, gazing upwards again. "What an extraordinary imagination."

"Maybe it's based not so much on imagination as on experience," Cornelia said, still chuckling. "When did you arrive? We didn't hear the knocker."

"Because I had no need to knock," he responded. "A maid was polishing the knocker, and the door was therefore open. I heard you laughing, and I'm afraid curiosity got the better of me." He raised an eyebrow. "Should I have waited for Morecombe to have announced me?"

"You may as well wait for the last trump," Cornelia said, shaking out the folds of her skirt. "Would you care for a glass of sherry?"

"Thank you." He followed the women across the hall and into the parlor. "Have you heard from your cousin yet?" His casual tone belied his intense interest in their answer as he sat down without waiting for an invitation, crossing his tasseled Hessians at the ankle.

"No." It was Aurelia who answered him, her brow creased in a worried frown. "We've sent two messages to the marquess of Coltrain's house, but apparently Nigel's friend, Garston, has gone out of town and no one seems to know whether Nigel accompanied him or not."

"I'm sure he did," Harry said. There was no point alarming them at this stage with his own less than complete knowledge of the man's present situation. He accepted a glass of sherry from Cornelia, his fingers casually brushing against hers as he did so. He felt the tingling surge go through her matching the current that

electrified him, and for a second their eyes met in a caress as palpable as if it had been a touch.

Cornelia turned away, stifling a smile. "Yes, that's
what we think. There seems no other explanation," she
said, picking up the thread smoothly. "He's probably at
some friend's hunting box."

Harry offered a noncommittal nod and sipped his
sherry. Children's voices rose high and imperative from
the hall. The yapping of the dogs joined in the cacophony and a high-pitched shriek that was unmistakably
Franny's shattered the air like glass.

"It's those wretched dogs," Aurelia said, "They keep
jumping up at her. Excuse me." She hurried to the parlor door.

"I'll get the dogs," Livia said, following her out.

Cornelia stood by the sideboard, regarding Harry in a
reflective silence. "Did you come on any particular business?" she asked finally.

He shook his head. "Do I have to?"

"No." She twisted the wedding ring on her finger.
"But I find it unsettling to be in your company when
we're not alone."

"As do I in yours," he said quietly. "But I should tell
you that I think your friends have suspicions. Livia
obliquely tried to warn me off."

Cornelia frowned. "They've said nothing to me. How
did she warn you?"

He shrugged. "As I said it was rather oblique. She

merely said that your well-being is close to their hearts, and I would jeopardize it at my peril."

"That doesn't sound at all oblique," Cornelia said. "It sounds rather blunt to me."

"Well, they're your friends. You know them better than I do."

"Yes." She opened her hands in a rather helpless gesture. "This is torment, Harry."

"I know." He stood up, took a step towards her, then stopped at the sound of a familiar voice in the hall. "Ah," he said. "You have more visitors it would seem."

Cornelia cocked her head, listening. "I hope it's not Letitia Oglethorpe, the woman's driving us insane."

"I don't hear her voice," Harry said. "And she does have a most distinctive tone."

Cornelia grimaced in agreement, but her expression cleared as she identified the voices. "Several gentlemen at the ball at Almack's said they would call upon us." She added with a slightly sardonic smile, "How fortunate we chose to wear our finest gowns this morning."

Livia came back into the parlor. "Nell, we have visitors. Morecombe's shown them into the salon. Will you come?" Her eyes darted towards Harry, then back to Cornelia, a question in their depths that had nothing to do with visitors.

Cornelia said serenely, "Yes, of course. What have you done with the dogs?"

"Lester has taken them to the kitchen, and Daisy has

taken the children upstairs. Lord Bonham, do you care to join us in the salon?"

He bowed. "Thank you, ma'am."

Livia led the way to the salon where three gentlemen stood before the fireplace. "Lord Strachan, how good of you to call," she said. "And Sir Nicholas." She offered a cordial handshake to both gentlemen and looked inquiringly at the third.

"Ah, Lady Livia, may I present Lord Forster," Harry said with a smile. "I should warn you he's a sad rattle, but good enough company."

"Calumny, Harry," David declared. He bowed to Livia. "Delighted, ma'am. Thank you for receiving me. I was desolated that we were not introduced last evening at Almack's. Fortunately, Nick here offered to remedy the omission. But if I'd known Harry would be so far ahead of us, I would have attached myself to him."

Livia laughed. "I'm delighted to meet you, sir. And you are all of course acquainted with Lady Dagenham. And Lady Farnham."

Harry retreated to a chair at the rear of the salon and watched with some amusement as Livia deftly and without the slightest discourtesy turned aside the obvious attentions of Lord Strachan. He realized that he needn't have worried. Livia was no more likely than her friends to fall for flattery and extravagant compliments.

The door knocker again heralded visitors, two ladies, fearsome leaders of the ton, whose critical eyes took in every detail of the apartment and its occupants while they stored up their opinions for public dissemination later.

Cornelia and Aurelia handled these new visitors with the same aplomb they had shown towards the duchess and Lady Sefton. They were not about to be intimidated, and Harry found hugely enjoyable the way they deflected the frequently impertinent questions that such arbiters of fashion felt they were entitled to ask.

"I understand you have never been affianced, Lady Livia," the duchess of Broadhurst declared in a tone that implied this was some serious flaw on Livia's part.

"I have not as yet received an offer that would tempt me, ma'am." Livia's smile was tranquil.

Her Grace shook her head. "A gal your age . . . once it's said you're on the shelf, you'll be lucky to get any offers at all."

"Lady Livia is far too delicate to go into details of her many conquests, ma'am," Cornelia said. "Such an indelicate conversation is hardly suitable for mixed company." She glanced pointedly to the men clustered in front of the fire.

The duchess had the grace to look discomposed. She muttered, "Tush," and appeared momentarily silenced.

"Have you seen the new species of shrub in the Botanical Gardens, Lady Dagenham?" Nick asked, stepping valiantly into the breach.

Cornelia, somewhat bemused, looked at him in surprise. "Species of shrub, Sir Nicholas?"

"Is it a completely new species, Sir Nicholas, or a variation on an established one?" asked Aurelia with an air of fascination.

Nick looked desperately at David. "Uh . . . uh, I'm not sure. Forster, you're the expert on plants."

"Am I?" David sucked in his cheeks. "No . . . no, m'dear fellow. It's Harry you're thinking of." Having tossed the hot potato, he visibly relaxed.

"Lord Bonham?" inquired Cornelia sweetly. "Are you acquainted with the shrub that Sir Nicholas is referring to?"

"As it happens, I have not the slightest interest in shrubs of any kind," Harry said emphatically. "And now, ma'am, I must take my leave."

"You may escort me to my carriage, Bonham," the duchess announced, rising to her feet, gathering her numerous shawls around her. "Belinda, I'll take you up as far as Grosvenor Square." She beckoned imperiously to her companion, Lady Nielson.

The two ladies took their somewhat haughty leave, Harry escorting them to the duchess's barouche, which stood at the door.

The gentlemen soon followed, and Cornelia said, "Unless that Broadhurst woman decides to bad-mouth us, I think, my friends, that we're now established."

"She *is* odious," Livia said. "How incredibly rude."

"Oh, the greater the sense of consequence the greater the lack of finesse," Cornelia said. "It's a close-run thing, but I think I prefer Harry's great-aunt's species of rudeness. It had some wit to it, rather than simple malice."

"Mmm." Livia hesitated, frowning, then asked abruptly, "Is something going on between you and Lord Bonham, Nell?"

Aurelia looked at her in surprise. She hadn't thought Livia was aware of the strange currents that swirled around the viscount and Nell. She turned her gaze to Cornelia, who, although composed, had a slightly rueful air.

"Is there, Nell?"

Cornelia could see no point in denying it, and in truth there would be huge relief in talking about it. "Is it so obvious?"

"Not to a stranger," Aurelia said. "But to us . . . yes."

Cornelia nodded. "I don't know how to explain it. It's some kind of madness. A lunacy that seems to have gripped us both. I'm sorry," she said helplessly, looking between them, trying to read their faces.

"Are you having an affair?" Aurelia asked directly.

"I suppose that's what you would call it," Cornelia agreed. "But as long as the earl doesn't find out . . . and there's no reason why he should find out. Is there?" The question was a desperate request for reassurance.

"He won't find out from us," Livia said. "Of course he won't."

Aurelia looked at her friend closely. "Do you love him, Nell?"

Cornelia pressed her fingertips to her mouth. She thought she *did* love Harry Bonham, but she wasn't prepared to admit that, not even to herself. Not while it was one-sided.

"I don't know that exactly," she said. "But it's like some kind of possession . . . obsession, if you like." And that was true enough, with or without the complications of love. And she knew that Harry felt that at least as powerfully as she did.

Aurelia and Livia said nothing for a minute or two, absorbing the implications of this. "Are you happy about it?" Aurelia asked finally.

"That's a strange word for it," Cornelia responded honestly. "I'm frightened by it . . . by the possible consequences."

"What consequences?" Aurelia's question was sharp.

"Not that, Ellie. To be blunt, Harry takes a simple precaution."

Aurelia nodded her comprehension. "So what *are* you frightened of?"

"Of being swallowed up," Cornelia replied simply. "Devoured by obsession. Losing myself."

Aurelia whistled. "That's a powerful fear, Nell."

"Why don't you just marry him?" Livia asked. "That would solve everything. The children like him too."

"Unfortunately, it's not that simple, Liv." Cornelia eyes were shadowed. "I don't think marriage figures anywhere in Harry Bonham's future."

"Why not?"

She gave a short and humorless laugh. "If I knew that, Ellie, I'd be a lot easier in my mind. The man's a mystery, an enigma, and so far I haven't come close to finding the key. But it is as it is. I tried to break it off almost before it began, and I couldn't do it."

"But you have such willpower," Aurelia said, frowning at her.

"Not in this," Cornelia said with a sigh. She paced restlessly between the long windows overlooking the street. "I can hardly bear to endure the time we're apart. And it's torment to have to behave in company as if we're bare acquaintances."

Livia was fascinated. It was so unlike the ordinarily serene and in-charge Cornelia. "Where do you meet him, Nell?"

Cornelia grinned mischievously, her earlier gravity abruptly dispelled. "I don't meet him exactly, he plays Casanova through my window."

After an instant's astonishment her friends burst into laughter. "Oh, that's rich, Nell," Aurelia gasped. "He climbs through your window in the dead of night?"

"In a word, yes," Cornelia said somewhat smugly. "Which is one reason why I don't think anyone will ever be any the wiser. We can't be seen in public behaving as more than ordinary acquaintances, not without drawing attention to ourselves. You know what the gossips are like. If it occurs to someone that Harry's at my side rather frequently, there'll be talk, and it'll get back to the earl. But as long as he's in the company of all three of us, the gossips won't see anything special . . . and no one's watching my window in the dead of night," she added with another mischievous grin.

Aurelia stared at her in dawning comprehension. "Was he there, in your bed, that night the cat squalled and Morecombe came up with his blunderbuss and the dogs got loose and . . . he was, wasn't he?"

"Hiding behind the bed curtains," Cornelia said, laughing. "He'd only just crept in, intending to take me by surprise, but he trod on Puss's tail . . . you know the rest."

"I didn't hear about that," Liv said with a touch of indignation. "Why didn't I know about it?"

"Because the racket didn't waken you," Aurelia pointed out. "I thought there was something odd about it all, but I'd never have guessed, not in a million years." She chuckled suddenly. "Aunt Sophia's house does seem rather an appropriate venue for illicit acts of passion, don't you think? I'm sure it's not the first liaison that's taken place here."

"I own I'm very curious about the lady," Cornelia said, more than ready to turn the conversation into a different avenue. "I wonder if Morecombe could be pumped discreetly."

Livia, however, was not ready to abandon the original topic. "It may be very uncomfortable to be possessed, devoured, or whatever you want to call it," she said thoughtfully, "but I envy you, Nell."

"Me too," Aurelia said. "You do have an extraordinary glow these days, Nell. Passion clearly has something to be said for it."

Cornelia smiled, she couldn't help it. "Oh, yes," she agreed softly. "Oh, yes, it most certainly does."

Two days later she was not so sure. Despite the fact that the door knocker was never still, announcing a steady stream of visitors, Harry was not among them. He seemed to have disappeared off the face of the earth.

She made no comment, however, appearing almost not to notice his absence; but Livia and Aurelia were not fooled.

"Where do you think he is?" Livia asked Aurelia on the third afternoon when Cornelia was out with the children. "They haven't had an argument, have they?"

Aurelia shook her head. "I don't know. Maybe he only comes at night."

"No," Livia said firmly. "You can tell that Nell's puzzled . . . upset. She's not really herself."

"Yes, I know," Aurelia conceded. "First Nigel disappears, now the viscount. It's all a mystery to me . . . oh, it sounds like she's back. She's talking to Morecombe in the hall."

"More invitations," Cornelia said as she entered the salon flourishing yet another gilt-edged card. "I don't see how one could possibly accept them all." She added the card to the pile already on the mantel.

"Most people attend each one for five minutes," Aurelia said, busily arranging winter camellias in a vase. "But that seems so rude . . . aren't these beautiful?"

Cornelia glanced absently at them. "Mmm. Who are they from?"

Aurelia squinted at the card. "A Lord Bailey." She shook her head. "The name means nothing. Does it to you?"

"I think so," Livia said vaguely. "I think I danced with someone of that name at the Bellinghams' soirée the other day."

"So casual, Liv," Cornelia accused. "I suppose with so many suitors you can afford to be insouciant." Her smile was strained, and the intended jocularity of the accusation didn't come out right.

She saw the quick glance that passed between her friends and braced herself for the question that she could not answer, but the salon door opened and brought a welcome diversion.

"Them two gentlemen are here, m'lady," Morecombe announced in his dour tones sticking his head through the merest crack in the door.

"What two gentlemen?" Livia murmured.

Cornelia shrugged and shook her head. It wasn't Harry. Morecombe always referred to him as *that viscount*.

"Well, show them in, please, Morecombe," Aurelia prompted.

"They're right here." Morecombe's head disappeared and another hand pushed the door wide.

"I don't think I've ever come across such an eccentric butler, ma'am," Nick Petersham declared, entering the salon, David Forster on his heels.

"I'm surprised you keep him on," David observed. "Isn't he ready to be put out to pasture?"

"He may well be, but my aunt left clear instructions in her will that he and his wife and sister-in-law were to be kept on until they decided to go of their own accord," Livia explained.

"Good Lord, you mean there are two more of them?" Nick exclaimed.

"Yes, and they're every bit as eccentric, but they're also wonderful cooks," Aurelia said, laughing. "Do sit down, gentlemen. What may we offer you?"

"Sherry or Madeira?" Cornelia moved to the sideboard. "Or claret? I discovered a rather fine '92 in the cellar on my last trip down there."

"Claret then, thank you, Lady Dagenham." Nick came over to take the filled glasses from her.

She glanced sideways at him as she poured the wine. "We haven't seen Lord Bonham in a while," she observed. "I trust he's not ill?" It had become clear to all of them after the first introduction to Nick and David that the three men were fast friends.

"Oh, no, not a bit of it, ma'am," Nick said cheerfully. "Harry has the constitution of an ox. You seen him around, Forster?"

"Come to think of it, no," David said, taking the glass Nick offered him with a nod of thanks. "He'll be attending to some family business, you mark my words."

"Oh, yes, of course," Aurelia said with ready sympathy. "Those poor motherless nephews and nieces. The viscount told us all about them."

Both visitors looked bemused. "Harry has a big family, ma'am, but I don't know about motherless nephews and nieces . . . d'you, Nick?"

"Oh, yes, he explained," Livia said eagerly. "Such a sad story. It's why he wanted to buy this house. He said it reminded him of the house where he'd grown up in London . . . the square garden, cricket, hide-and-seek . . ." Her voice trailed away as she saw the confusion on the men's faces.

"Buy this house, Lady Livia?" Nick asked. "He has a perfectly good house of his own."

"No, it wasn't for him, it was so that he could establish the children close to him to watch over them."

"Ah," Nick said somewhat inadequately. To his certain knowledge all Harry's sisters were flourishing, and while he did indeed have a quiver full of nephews and nieces, none was motherless . . . or fatherless for that matter. But if Harry had spun this particular tale, he must have his reasons for it, and it would hardly be a gesture of friendship to expose it for a tissue of lies.

David seemed to have come to the same conclusion. "Ah, just so," he said. "Yes . . . yes." He buried his nose and his confusion in his wine goblet.

"Lord Bonham's business is his own, after all," Cornelia said, taking a sip from her own wineglass. "What do you think of the claret, Sir Nicholas?"

"Oh, excellent," he said, glad to be on solid ground once more. He held up his glass to the window and the thin ray of sunlight set ruby lights glinting. "Lovely color . . . good body," he observed appreciatively.

"I wonder what effect Napoleon's Continental System will have on the wine trade," Cornelia said, moving to the chaise. It was time to turn the subject firmly away from Harry Bonham. When she was alone she could consider the implications of what she'd just heard . . . or rather hadn't heard. "What do you think, Lord Forster?"

David's confusion seemed to deepen. "Well, as to that, ma'am . . . not much for politics, m'self. Not too sure, really."

"It can only have a deleterious effect," Nick said gravely, coming to his friend's rescue. "With the French blockading the ports, all trade with Europe is bound to be seriously affected."

"Yes, and it won't just be wine," Aurelia chimed in. "Nor just imports. Our own products will have no outside markets either."

As other visitors arrived, the conversation continued to hold general interest, and Cornelia, try as she would, could only concentrate with half her mind. The other half would not let go of the conviction that Harry was an out-and-out liar.

He was most definitely *not* responsible for a clutch of motherless nephews and nieces.

But why, then, had he been so insistent on buying Liv's house?

Chapter 20

"I'm going to have a bath," Cornelia announced with decision after supper that evening. "I want to wash my hair and just soak in front of the fire in my chamber."

"That sounds *so* appealing," Aurelia said. "I'm tired of sponge baths. They're neither one thing nor the other, and you never feel really clean all over. Your turn tonight, Nell, mine tomorrow."

"Agreed." Cornelia stood up from the table. "I'll go to the kitchen and see how much help I can rustle up with the water."

"There's Hester, and the new boot boy," Livia suggested. "I don't suppose Lester is still here. I think he goes home at night . . . wherever home is."

"He was here last night," Aurelia said. "I went down to the kitchen to heat some milk for Franny, and he was sitting by the range with his feet on the fender, reading the *Morning Post*."

"Well, let's hope he's here tonight," Cornelia said,

going to the door. "For some reason I have absolute faith in that man's ability to achieve miracles, even one as difficult as getting enough hot water upstairs to fill that copper tub."

And Lester was indeed sitting by the range, a tankard of ale at his elbow, his feet on the fender, and the *Post* in his hands. He looked surprised as Cornelia entered the kitchen. "My lady? You should have rung."

"We all know this household doesn't run along customary lines, Lester," Cornelia said, looking around. "Are you all alone?"

"Mr. Morecombe and the ladies have gone to their own quarters. Hester and that young Jemmy are havin' a bit of supper in the pantry, ma'am," Lester said. "Hester'll come to the dining room to clear the table presently. If there's something you want done now, I can do it."

"Well, as it happens, there is," Cornelia said. "I wish to have a bath in my chamber, Lester. Do you think there's enough hot water on the range?"

"Plenty to be goin' on with, my lady," he said, setting aside his newspaper. "And it won't take more than half an hour to heat up another cauldron." He gestured to the one that already steamed gently over the fire.

Soon after Cornelia returned to her chamber, Hester arrived with the copper tub which she set on thick sheets before the fire. After the maid encouraged the coals to a full blaze, she said, "I've drawn the curtains against the draft, m'lady."

Cornelia glanced towards the window where heavy crimson velvet curtains hung. "Thank you, Hester."

The maid scurried away when she finished her chores and Cornelia went to the window, sliding behind the velvet to look out at the dark garden. *Where was he?*

She felt a prickle of apprehension. Harry was no ordinary London beau. Oh, you could be fooled into thinking he was . . . but there was steel in him. *Was he doing something dangerous? Was he hurt?*

A tap at the door brought her out from behind the curtains just as Lester entered with two steaming jugs. He poured the water into the tub, nothing in his expression indicating the sympathy he felt. He'd seen the way she'd darted out from behind the curtains. He had no idea when the viscount would emerge from his attic office where he'd been confined for three days deciphering a problematic Russian code, and even if he did know, he could not confide in the lady.

"Would you wish Hester to attend you, m'lady?"

"No, thank you. Just bring up enough water," she said, opening a small cedar box on the dresser. It contained cheesecloth pouches of dried lavender and rosemary, a small vial of orange flower water, and a bar of verbena-scented soap. She might not have a lover tonight, but she could at least luxuriate in another form of sensuality.

Two more trips ensured that the bath was filled and three further jugs stood in the hearth, keeping warm by the fire. Cornelia was at last alone. She dropped the pouches into the water where the aromatic herbs would steep slowly. The orange flower water she would use when she rinsed her hair.

She stripped off her clothes, suddenly impatient, suddenly angry. He had no right to disappear without a word. Not if nothing dreadful had happened to cause his absence. Did he count her as nothing in his life?

And why did he lie? Why that ridiculous story about motherless children? Why the interest in this house in the first place? Oh, it would be nice to think he'd seen her by accident, fallen in love . . . no lust . . . with her, and come up with such a scheme as an entrée. But the solicitor's letter with the offer had come to Livia in Ringwood. Long before Viscount Bonham had set eyes on the woman he'd first thought to be a scullery maid.

Cornelia stepped into the bath and slid down into the water, drawing up her knees to brace the soles of her feet against the far edge, splashing the water over her breasts and shoulders. She hated puzzles, but even more she detested being made game of. And it seemed to her now that Harry had been playing with her even before he had met her.

Disillusion swamped her as dirty and greasy as old dishwater, and she reached for the verbena soap.

Ten minutes later Harry stood in the garden looking up at the house. He knew Cornelia's window simply by position, but it was a black square tonight. The window closed, the curtains drawn tight. He couldn't possibly shin up the drainpipe and hope to wake her when she was presumably sleeping like the dead.

She might have been looking out for him, he thought with a touch of resentment. Hadn't she missed him? But he knew that wasn't reasonable, and if he wasn't as exhausted as he was, he would never have been so irrational. But he wanted her. *Now.*

Lester was in the house. But so too, presumably, was Morecombe of the fearsome blunderbuss, not to mention the taciturn twins. He seemed to remember Lester saying something about other servants now, as well.

He moved, stealthy as a hunting cat, through the garden, keeping against the house wall until he reached the steps that led down to the back door to the servants' basement. He could see a line of light along the base of the door at the bottom of the dark stone steps. Someone was still up in the kitchen, and he had to hope it would be Lester. The man, as instructed during Harry's absence, would certainly be on the alert for anything untoward during the hours of the night.

Harry cupped his hands to his mouth and blew gently. The unmistakable call of a brown owl sounded in the quiet. He waited for two beats, and then repeated the call. If Lester was close enough to hear, he would recognize the viscount's call sign.

After a few minutes of straining his ears into the darkness and hearing nothing, Harry repeated the sequence.

And this time, within a minute he heard the scraping of bolts in the darkness below, and the kitchen door swung open.

Lester glanced quickly around, then closed the door at his back and climbed up the steps to the garden. "Anything wrong, m'lord?" He spoke in an undertone.

"Yes, damn you," Harry said impatiently but in the same undertone. "Lady Dagenham's window is closed and dark."

Lester suppressed a grin. "Her ladyship's taking a bath, sir. In her chamber in front of the fire."

Harry did not suppress his own grin. "Oh, is she now? Well, get me in. Lester."

"Aye, sir. The other ladies have gone up to bed, so I'll open up the library window. You can say as how you found it on the latch and managed to slip in."

"What about those wretched dogs?"

"They're up with Lady Livia. Of course, if they hear you in the corridor, they'll set up their bloody racket again . . . and they don't miss nothing," he added somewhat gloomily. "They can hear an earwig crawl."

Harry considered for a minute, then said decisively, "We'll use the *cry wolf* ruse."

Lester nodded his comprehension. "Give me a couple of minutes to get to the library window, sir, then you can stay in there while I go upstairs and set the dogs off. Lady Dagenham's door is the third down the corridor on the left."

He disappeared back down into the shadows of the

basement area. Light flooded from the kitchen for an instant, then it was black again.

Harry crept back around the garden, clinging again to the wall of the house until he reached the library window immediately below Cornelia's. He heard the slight scrape from within as Lester fiddled with the latch, then the window came up.

Harry jumped onto the sill and slid through into the dark room, landing soundlessly on the rug. Lester nodded, lowering the window as quietly as he could, then slipped away towards the hall door at the far side of the room.

Harry crept to the door and stood behind it against the wall, listening. Within minutes the frantic yapping sounded. Doors opened above and he could hear voices. Livia's he recognized, then Lester's deeper tones. Harry couldn't hear what he was saying, but he would be giving a reason for his presence upstairs, one that would ensure no one would take any notice of the dogs if they started up again.

Doors closed again, and the yapping continued although more muffled.

Harry slipped from the library and darted for the stairs. He was up them in seconds, seeking the shadows of the upstairs landing and the passage leading off it.

Lester was waiting for him and as soon as he saw him he coughed loudly. The dogs began their racket once more, but this time no doors were opened, and Livia's somewhat exasperated voice could be heard telling them to be quiet, it was only Lester.

Harry raised a hand to Lester in silent salute and flitted along the corridor, past Livia's door, and paused outside Cornelia's. He laid a hand on the handle and turned it quietly. The door swung open, and he darted in, closing it gently at his back.

"Well, now, if that's not the most enticing sight," he murmured, standing with his back to the door, gazing at the vision in front of him.

Cornelia sat bolt upright in the bath and stared at him in astonishment. "How on earth did you get in? Did *you* set the dogs off?"

"Well, that's not much of a welcome," he said, reaching behind him to turn the key in the lock.

"*How* did you get in?" she repeated, watching almost warily as he crossed the chamber to the fire.

"A window downstairs was unlocked. I was able to pry it open," he said. "And one of your servants set the dogs off, and I was able to slip in here under cover of their noise."

Cornelia was not sure she believed this. It was all too pat. "Where have you been?"

He leaned over the tub and kissed her mouth. "So many questions, Nell. I'm here now." He moved his lips to her damp forehead and licked the moisture from her eyebrows. "You taste wonderful. And your hair smells delicious."

"Which is more than I can say for you, sir," she retorted, the words at odds with the languid sensuality of her voice and the deep blue pools of her eyes that seemed to engulf him. "You don't look as if you've slept for a week, or bathed in as long."

"Probably because it's true," he said, straightening. "But I can remedy one at least of those failings." He began to throw off his clothes.

"You can't get in here," she protested. "There's not enough room."

"Oh, you'd be surprised," he responded, sitting on the end of the bed to deal with his boots and stockings. "That's better." Naked he stood up. "Now, shift your backside, ma'am."

Cornelia made a laughing protest, but she hitched herself up against one side of the bath, and he stepped in opposite her. Water slurped over the rim and onto the thick sheet as he slid down, pushing his feet beneath her bottom as he slipped farther beneath the water.

"Look what a mess you're making on the floor," she objected even as she shifted against his feet, adding to the deluge. His toes were moving wickedly in places where no toes should be, and her objections faded into a soft whimper of pleasure.

Harry smiled, leaning forward to catch the damp fullness of her breasts in the palms of his hands. He played with her nipples, watching her face. "Ah, but I've missed you, love."

"I've been here," she said, touching her tongue to her lips as her nipples peaked hard against his caressing finger. "Where were you?" But there was no sting now to the question, and she lost all interest in an answer, at least for the moment.

Harry moved his hands to her waist and pulled her body over his, his head falling back against the rim of the tub. Cornelia wriggled herself astride him, heedless now of the water slopping onto the sodden sheets. She knelt up, lifting herself to guide him within her.

Harry groaned and held himself still. "Don't move, sweetheart, right now I have as little control as a pubescent boy."

Cornelia smiled, enjoying her moment of power. She knew she could tip him over the edge with the tiniest movement. She could feel the pulse of his penis deep within her. She leaned forward and kissed him, her loins shifting against his belly. It was enough.

Her own pleasure this time came purely from his, from the knowledge of this amazing female power. She sat back on her heels and looked down the length of his body. He seemed thinner, and the lines of fatigue were deeply etched around his black-shadowed eyes.

"What *have* you been doing to yourself?" she asked, running her hands across his chest as she kissed his eyes. "You're worn to the bone, my love."

For an answer, he put his hands at her waist and eased her away from him. "Is there any more hot water? This is getting chilly."

Cornelia accepted that for the moment she was going to get no answers. "There's one more jug. I used the other spares to rinse my hair." She stood up and stepped out of the bath in a shower of drops. A towel was warming on the rack in front of the fire, and she wrapped herself up swiftly, conscious of the cold air on her wet skin. She picked up the remaining jug and poured the contents over his head.

Harry had not been expecting it and spluttered in indignant surprise as it cascaded over him.

"You might as well wash your hair while you're about it," she said, tossing him the soap that was on the floor beside the bath.

He took the advice and Cornelia dried herself before wrapping herself up in her thick nightrobe. She sat on the chest at the foot of the bed and watched his ablutions. Questions ran riot in her head, but she knew she had to tread carefully. She felt she ought to have the right to ask her questions, and yet she knew instinctively that Harry had not conferred that right upon her. But she was going to ask them anyway.

"Towel," he demanded, standing up, clicking his fingers in mock command.

"At your service, sir," she said, running another long, appreciative look along his body. He was a very fine specimen of a man, she decided. Long and lean, muscular without being obviously so, his strength was implied rather than displayed. His slim waist and hips, the length of powerful but equally slim thighs, were those of an athlete.

"Nell, I'm freezing," he said plaintively. "I'm delighted to offer you such a vision of masculine beauty, but the part of my anatomy that should most concern you is shriveling with cold."

Cornelia laughed. "Oh, we can't have that," she said, fetching another warmed towel from the rack. She tossed it around his shoulders before going to rummage in the armoire. "I have another nightrobe somewhere in here. It may be a bit moth-eaten, but it'll serve . . . ah, yes, here it is." Triumphantly, she flourished a velvet robe. She picked a little doubtfully at the rather tatty lace. "It'll probably be a bit short on you."

"I should think that's the least of its problems," Harry said, regarding the garment with disfavor. "If you don't mind, I'll settle for a dry towel."

"Oh, very well." Cornelia took another towel from the linen press and handed it to him.

He wrapped it securely around his waist and surveyed the general disarray in front of the fire. "I think, if I take up those soaked sheets and put them in the tub, I can move the whole thing into a corner, and it'll be a little less messy in here."

"You can blame yourself for the mess," Cornelia said. "If you hadn't insisted on sharing my bath . . ."

"Ah, but wasn't the sharing pleasant?" he said, catching her hand and pulling her swiftly towards him so that she was held tight against his bare chest. He pushed up her chin, running a fingertip over her mouth, his lively green eyes flashing like fireflies as he smiled down at her.

"It certainly was," she said. "Well worth a wet floor."

"Good, then will you find me something to eat and a glass of wine or cognac, or anything, while I try to tidy up in here?"

"Are you hungry then?"

"Famished," he said. "I don't remember when I last ate."

Cornelia decided, despite the opening, to leave her questions until later. "I'll be back in ten minutes."

She heard Harry lock the door behind her and smiled slightly. Harry, of course, did not know that their secret was out, as least as far as her friends were concerned. But perhaps it was a wise precaution, she reflected. Livia and Aurelia weren't the only occupants of the house. What she didn't know, of course, was that Lester would ensure that no one came near her bedchamber while Viscount Bonham was in it.

Cornelia took the back stairs down to the kitchen, thinking up excuses for her presence there at this time of night. The only person there was Lester, still sitting beside the fire with his ale and his newspaper.

He jumped to his feet as she came in. "What can I do for you, my lady?"

"Oh, nothing, Lester, thank you. For some reason I'm hungry." She wandered towards the pantry. "I think there was a veal and ham pie in here. I have the most absurd craving for veal and ham pie."

"Quite so, m'lady," Lester said solemnly. "I'll fetch a tray. Would a bite of bread and cheese appeal too?"

"Uh . . . yes, possibly, thank you," she replied, wondering what on earth he must think of her wanting so much food after she'd eaten a more than adequate dinner a couple of hours before.

She found the veal and ham pie, contemplated cutting a thick slice, then decided to take the whole thing. The raised crust looked so appetizing, and Harry looked as if he needed feeding up.

"You'll be wanting a glass of claret to wash that down with, I daresay, ma'am," Lester observed, setting bread and cheese on a tray and taking the pie from her.

"Well, yes, now you mention it, that would be lovely." Cornelia said. "But I think we need to open a new bottle."

"Right away, m'lady." Lester took a bottle from the rack and pulled the cork. He set the bottle and a glass on the tray beside the food. "I'll carry this up for you."

"No . . . no, I can manage, Lester." Hastily Cornelia picked up the tray. It *was* both awkward and heavy. "I'll take the back stairs, it's quicker."

"Tell you what, ma'am, why don't I carry it up the stairs for you," Lester offered, watching with some alarm as the contents of the tray slipped a little, dangerously unbalancing it.

That couldn't do any harm, reflected Cornelia, relinquishing her burden with a word of thanks. She preceded Lester up the back stairs, wondering how he had managed to become such an indispensable fixture in the house. Even Morecombe deferred to him on occasion, and certainly offered no objections to his presence.

At the head of the stairs, she took the tray from him with a whispered word of thanks. Lester stood at the top of the stairs, watching her somewhat unsteady but at least soundless progress along the corridor. When she reached the door she tapped it with her bare foot and it opened instantly. Only then did Lester return to his paper.

"Ah, now that looks like a feast to invite a man to," Harry said appreciatively, taking the tray from her. "There's only one glass."

"Well, Lester was in the kitchen, and I couldn't very well explain two glasses."

"Oh, no, I suppose you couldn't," Harry murmured with a smile. "We can share a glass." He set the tray down on the table.

Cornelia looked around her bedchamber in surprise. The detritus of her bath had disappeared, and the room was set to rights once more, even Harry's discarded clothing neatly placed on the chest at the foot of the bed. "What did you do with the bath?"

"Behind the fire screen," he said, slicing into the pie.

The screen that ordinarily shielded a sitter from the heat of the fire was now in a corner of the chamber. "You'd make a good housekeeper," Cornelia said, pouring wine.

Harry sat down on the chair by the table and took a large bite of the pie. Cornelia sat by the fire and sipped the wine, before passing him the glass. Nothing was said for long minutes as Harry ate with the concentrated appetite of a starving man. He finished the pie and turned his attention to the bread and cheese. But at last the tray was empty, and he sighed with repletion.

"A bath and food . . . now I'm whole again." He stood up, stretching luxuriously, before turning to Cornelia, holding out his hands in invitation. "Shall we repair to bed, ma'am?"

Cornelia hesitated. She wanted to make love again, it was as if she couldn't get enough of his body, but her mind was finally asserting its independence in this business. She could not . . . would not . . . give herself again without some explanation for his lies.

He looked at her in puzzlement, his arms still open in invitation, while she sat unmoving. "What is it, Nell?" His hands fell to his sides. He appeared relaxed, but the tension in the room would have cut diamonds.

"Was it family business that took you out of town?" she inquired, her hands clasped loosely in her lap. "Something to do with your motherless nephews and nieces, perhaps?"

His eyes narrowed and he rocked slightly on the balls of his feet. He shook his head in irritation. "I might have known that would come back and bite me."

So he wasn't going to deny it. Cornelia felt some relief. "But why would you tell such an obvious lie? Of course you must have known it would come out at some point. Do you really think me so ingenuous, so naive, as to accept at face value everything I'm told?"

"No," he said. "But what you're forgetting, dear girl, is that when I told you that little untruth, I had no idea I was going to find myself in thrall to you. It didn't matter a damn to me at the time whether you believed me or not."

Cornelia considered this. It made perfect sense, but it didn't explain anything. "So why *did* you want the house so badly?"

He looked at her ruefully. "I can't tell you that, my dear."

"Oh." She plaited the folds of her robe, looking down at her fingers. "And I suppose you can't tell me either why you disappear for days at a time and come back looking like one of the walking dead?"

"No," he agreed.

"And I must be satisfied with that?" She shook her head. "I'm sorry, Harry. I can't be. You have to give me something, if we're to continue." She looked directly at him. "Do you wish this . . . this that we have together . . . to continue?"

He came swiftly towards her, kneeling in front of her, taking her hands in his. "More than I have wanted anything in my life," he averred, bringing her hands to his lips.

She felt the antagonism melting away, but even so he *had* to give her something, something that established some private trust between them. Something of himself that went deeper than the charming man, the deeply sensual lover, the attentive friend. Oh, she believed he was genuinely all those things, but she wanted some small share in his soul.

"Give me something," she repeated quietly.

He released her hands and stood up again. He had lived so long by his wits, inhabiting the shadowy corners of secret intelligence, that he didn't know how to offer her even a chink of light. But he knew absolutely that if he denied her now, he would lose her.

He spoke hesitantly. "If I remind you that England is at war, will that be sufficient?"

She looked at him, startled out of her composure. "You're a soldier?"

He shook his head. "Not in the way you mean." He turned away from her and went over to his clothes on the chest.

"No," Cornelia said. "Don't go."

He looked over at her again. "I will not say anything else, Nell. And I have to trust that you will say nothing of this either."

"Of course I wouldn't." She sounded shocked.

"You are very close to your friends," he pointed out.

"Yes," she agreed. "And now they know of this liaison. But I will not betray a confidence. I *never* would."

He inclined his head in acknowledgment. "I believe you. Are we done now, Nell?"

She stood up slowly. "Almost. Answer me just one last question. Is there danger in what you do?"

He laughed a little and prevaricated a little more.

"Not if it's managed properly . . . now, I have a powerful need of that bed, and of you. So, I ask again, are we done with this?"

Her choice was stark and simple. Accept what little he'd given her, or refuse to accept Harry himself. She nodded and went to him.

Chapter 21

"I'M GUESSING CASANOVA HAS REAPPEARED," Livia said slyly as she buttered a piece of toast several days later.

Cornelia poured coffee. "Maybe," she said.

"Stuff and nonsense," Aurelia scoffed. "Maybe, indeed. Have you looked at yourself in the last couple of days, Nell?"

"I look the same as usual," her sister-in-law said, but with a twitch of her lips.

"Not the same as you looked when Harry disappeared," Aurelia said, reaching for the marmalade. "Where did he go?"

Cornelia shrugged. "I'm not entirely sure. Some family business in the country I believe . . . now what?" Her friends were looking at her with undisguised skepticism.

"It's strange that his closest friends appear ignorant of his obligations to his late sister's children," Aurelia observed.

"Did they say that?" Cornelia inquired innocently, taking a bite of buttered toast.

"Yes, yes . . ." Aurelia waved the marmalade spoon impatiently. "Point taken . . . it's none of our business, but don't insult our intelligence, Nell." She licked a gob of marmalade from her finger.

"I wouldn't," Cornelia said with a rueful smile. "But can we leave it there?"

"Of course," Livia said. "And on the subject of Viscount Bonham, what are we going to wear to this excursion he's arranged for us all to Vauxhall this evening? I thought if I wore your green crepe tunic over my cream taffeta, Ellie, no one would recognize either garment."

"That should pass muster," Aurelia agreed. "And I'm going to borrow Nell's blue gauze shawl to wear over the striped muslin."

"You'll be cold," Cornelia pointed out. "It's still only March. You can't stroll nonchalantly through the gardens in gauze and muslin. Try my fur pelisse. The one Claire fashioned out of that old opera cloak."

"But what about you?"

"I was thinking your taffeta cloak over my lavender silk." She sipped her coffee.

"Then that's settled," Livia said. "It's certainly amazing what Claire has done with our old clothes, not to mention the new ones she made up for us."

"And the constant alterations she makes," Aurelia said, pushing back her chair as she rose from the table. "She's quite the cleverest needlewoman."

"That reminds me, if you're going out, Ellie, could you buy me some red velvet ribbon? I thought I'd trim that chip straw bonnet and add a bunch of cherries or something," Cornelia asked, as she too rose from the table.

"Of course," her sister-in-law agreed amiably. "What are your plans for the morning?"

"I have to work with Stevie on his Latin conjugations," Cornelia said with a grimace. "The earl's latest communication demands a progress report on his heir's educational."

"Why don't you ask him to release funds to pay for a governess?" Livia asked.

"He won't do that, not when the Reverend Lacey's curate for a mere pittance is ready, willing, and more than able to prepare Stevie for Harrow," Cornelia said grimly.

"I much prefer listening to my father's sermons," Livia said. "Even if they do send me to sleep. Barker preaches fire and brimstone every Sunday. Even at Christmas."

"Yes, and you can imagine how that translates into his teaching methods," Cornelia said as grimly as before. "I'm not handing my son over to his tender mercies, whatever the earl says."

"I don't blame you." Aurelia sighed. "At least he won't interfere in Franny's and Susannah's schooling."

"No," Cornelia agreed with a sardonic smile. "Girls are fit only for marriage, obedience, and duty. The only tutors they need in those requirements are fathers, brothers, and, of course, husbands." She went to the door. "I'll see you at luncheon."

Despite her apparent nonchalance, Cornelia was, however, concerned about her son's educational progress. It was one area in which his grandfather could accuse her of being remiss. If he sent the curate up to London to test the child, Stevie would probably come up short on some of the more rigorous skills, like his Latin and Greek.

Cornelia could handle a five-year-old's Latin, but her Greek was lamentable. She could manage the alphabet, but little else, and while she was convinced it was unnecessary at this age for the child to be conversant with Greek verbs and vocabulary, she knew that if Markby appealed to his peers, she would lose the battle, and she would be compelled to return with her son to his grandfather's supervision.

She had no desire to leave the life that was opening for her, but if such a move was in her children's best interests, she would go and take her regrets buried deep within her. But she did not believe such a move was in anyone's best interests at present. Her children were certainly not suffering. Everything about their new surroundings fascinated them, and they were cocooned in the stable familiarity of their mother and Linton.

No, she had searched her conscience and come to the conclusion that her own inclinations were not detrimental to her children at this point. They simply condemned her to a morning of conjugating Latin verbs with a recalcitrant five-year-old.

⚬❧⚬

"I don't understand how you could lose him so completely." Harry tried to conceal his anger even though his frustration was close to explosion. "You had him in Billingsgate, you said."

The two agents looked discomfited but also defiant. "We tracked him to those first lodgings, sir. We could have picked him up there, but our orders were to leave him for you."

Harry sighed. "Yes, I know. Forgive my impatience. But what of the second place."

"In Billingsgate, sir," Coles said. "Again we had him, but we still had the same orders. By the time we'd passed on our information, he'd gone again."

"And this time there were no clues," his fellow agent said with a certain laconic satisfaction. "We've scoured the neighborhood, questioned every Tom, Dick, and Harry, begging your pardon, my lord, and we've come up with nothing. Even his tail has disappeared."

Harry drummed his fingers on the tabletop. He realized he should have let these two pick up Nigel Dagenham when they first found him. Once Nigel's tail had been identified as definitely French and it had become clear that Nigel was in enemy sights, Harry himself should have had nothing to do with the business apart from the first tip to Simon. He should have resisted the urge to keep the whole mess in the family, so to speak.

And now Dagenham had disappeared, and Harry was forced to admit that he had for once in his working life allowed personal concerns to cloud his judgment. The essential question now was whether Nigel was still on the run or already in enemy hands.

"Keep looking," he said. "The fault is mine."

"Aye, sir." The two agents nodded their agreement, but with respect. "If we find him again, should we move?"

"Certainly," Harry responded. "Don't delay for a second. Just tell me when you have him safe."

"Right, sir." They turned to go, then Coles glanced over his shoulder as he reached the door. "If it comes down to it, sir . . . ?"

"Do what you have to," Harry said. He might be signing Nigel Dagenham's death warrant, but he could see little alternative.

Personal business did not meld with professional. He had always believed that, but he'd never had to face the conflict before. In two hours he was going to be escorting his lover, who was Nigel's cousin, her two dearest friends, also close friends of Nigel's, at a jolly party in Vauxhall Gardens. The boats would be awaiting his guests at the water steps at nine o'clock, a carefully chosen supper would be served in a private pavilion at eleven. He had wanted to spend some time with Cornelia in a public setting. An absurdly dangerous impulse in the circumstances but one he had been unable to resist. Among the secluded groves and shadowed pathways of Vauxhall Gardens they could inconspicuously find some privacy, and he had planned the excursion with all the care he would have devoted to the planned extraction of an endangered agent in the heart of St. Petersburg.

And he would have this hanging over him.

"So, what do you think?" Livia presented herself in the salon just as the clock struck eight. "Isn't the pelisse perfect? Oh, and you both look stunning."

"We all look stunning," Cornelia said. "And the teacup awaits." She led the way to the front door, which for once was held open by Morecombe.

"Where's Lester this evening, Morecombe?" she inquired, drawing on her silk gloves.

"Said he had summat to do," the retainer informed her. "Ye'd best knock 'ard when you comes back. I sleep like the dead."

"Leave the key beneath the flowerpot," Livia said, gesturing to one of the empty stone Grecian urns that stood sentinel at the front door. "We'll let ourselves in."

Morecombe shook his head. "Couldn't do that, mum, not with all these goin's-on at night."

"There haven't been any, recently Morecombe," Cornelia pointed out. "Leave the dogs loose and the key underneath the urn."

"Right y'are, then. If 'n you knows what y'are doing." Morecombe retreated into the hall, closing the door on his ladies, who merely shrugged and descended the steps to the waiting Berlin.

The new coachman, a very elderly man as dour as Morecombe, who had produced him without a word once the carriage had been made roadworthy, sat on the box, twirling his long coaching whip while Jemmy, who acted as groom when his services were so required, saw the ladies into the vast crimson depths of the ancient vehicle.

"I wish I knew where Morecombe had found Harper," Livia said, settling herself against the faded squabs. "He didn't even offer any references."

"I suspect he was Aunt Sophia's coachman until she gave up the carriage," Cornelia said. "He seems very familiar with its bulk, and it's not an easy thing to drive around these streets."

"Yes, I'm sure they weren't as crowded when all the carriages were the size of this teacup," Aurelia agreed. "He's certainly old enough to have been in Aunt Sophia's service at some point. I'm guessing he's as old as Morecombe."

"And just how old do you think that is?" Livia inquired with a chuckle. "He seems so fossilized it's impossible to tell."

The carriage delivered them to the steps opposite the water gate to Vauxhall Gardens, where a line of sculls jostled, bobbing on the river, the boatmen calling to potential customers. Jemmy jumped from his perch on the back of the carriage and let down the footstep.

"I'll call a scull, m'lady."

"It's already taken care of," Sir Nicholas Petersham called out cheerfully. "David and I are commissioned to carry you safely across the river, my ladies, where our host awaits us."

"That's comforting." Cornelia took his hand as she descended from the carriage. "I have no wish to be pitched headlong into the dark greasy waters of the Thames on a cold March night."

"Oh, never fear, ma'am, such a thing could never happen," Lord Forster reassured. "I've never heard of such a thing happening . . . but ladies do have their fears, I know."

Cornelia laughed. "Indeed, Lord Forster, it was but in jest. I have no such fear I assure you."

He looked somewhat relieved. "We've hired a very stable scull, ma'am. Big enough for all of us."

"You are very kind, my lord," Livia said, smiling from beneath her hat, a frothy creation of lace and chiffon that framed her face beautifully.

Two brawny oarsmen pulled them swiftly across the river to the water gate of the gardens, where Harry stood waiting for them. He came swiftly to the steps. "Good evening, ladies."

His green eyes glittered as they met Cornelia's gaze and he held out his hand ostensibly to help her ashore, but his fingers closed tightly over hers, and for a second his thumb moved wickedly against her palm through the thin silk glove. Somehow he managed to invest the little movement with a deeply erotic meaning, and Cornelia's body responded as always with a jolt in her loins that made her tighten her thighs abruptly.

"My aunt decided to make one of the party," Harry said with a hint of apology in his tone. "She's listening to the concert in the Rotunda."

"Wouldn't have thought Vauxhall would be to Her Grace's taste," David observed.

"No, neither would I," agreed Harry. "But when I happened to mention our little party, she announced that she would be one of its number . . . she and her companion," he added.

"Eliza Cox has been my great-aunt's companion for the last twenty years," he explained to the women. "She's an inoffensive soul, somewhat bullied by my aunt, I fear." He offered Cornelia his arm.

The garden was awash in so much illumination from the many thousands of lights strung from the trees and colonnades, and the supper pavilions, that it could almost have been midday, Cornelia reflected. She had only once before been to Vauxhall Gardens, during her one and only London season, and had considered it rather vulgar then. It didn't seem to her to have improved much.

"I confess, it surprises me that you would choose this as a venue for a party, Harry," she murmured, as they walked up the path towards the Rotunda between displays of what were admittedly magnificent fountains.

"Does it not please you, ma'am?" He raised his eyebrows.

"You don't consider it to be just a little garish?" She glanced sideways at him with a hint of a smile.

"More than a little," he agreed readily. "Indeed, I've never truly understood the appeal at all."

"Then why would you select it?"

"Can't you guess, Nell?" His voice was low and sensual, his eyes glowing with pure lust as they met hers. "This is one of the very few public places where one may withdraw unremarked into the shadows to pursue whatever . . ." He spread his hands in an all-encompassing gesture.

She inhaled sharply, and touched her tongue to her lip. "It's a little chilly for al fresco seduction, sir." Her voice had a strange little quiver to it.

He gave an elaborate sigh of regret. "Alas, I fear you are right, my dear. So much for the best-laid plans."

Cornelia went into a peal of laughter that drew curious glances from those around them on the path. Hastily she withdrew her hand from his arm and dropped back to where Livia was walking with David.

"Isn't it magnificent, Liv?" she called gaily.

Livia gave her a puzzled stare. "Is it?" Then she thought of her host and the possible discourtesy he might see in objections to his choice of venue. "Oh, yes, of course it is. The lights are magnificent, and the orchestra is very . . . very loud," she finished lamely.

"Gallant is probably the *mot juste*, Lady Livia," Harry

said, slowing to wait for them. "No one pays them any heed, and they play on into the night, ever hopeful."

Livia gave him a reproachful frown. "How callous, viscount."

"You're a brute, Harry, to upset the lady in such fashion," David protested. "D'you care to listen to the orchestra, Lady Livia? I'd be happy to escort you to their kiosk."

"Thank you, I would like that," Livia said. They walked off towards the largest of the many groves that made up the gardens, beyond which could be glimpsed the colored lights that adorned the huge kiosk that housed the orchestra.

"I fear I have offended," murmured Harry.

Cornelia and Aurelia both laughed at this. "Liv has a soft heart, Viscount, but she's not sentimental," Aurelia told him. "She was only teasing you."

They walked on towards the Rotunda, where a string quartet was playing. The duchess waved her lorgnette imperiously when she saw them. "Bonham, over here. I require rack-punch." She rose in a flurry of shawls, heedless of the disturbance this caused to her fellow listeners in the rows around her, and sailed out of her own row, trailing in her wake a small lady, brown hair tucked under a white lace cap, who murmured apologies to all and sundry.

"Poor Eliza," Harry muttered going forward to assist his great-aunt as she reached the end of her row.

"Tedious music," his aunt declared. "I dislike Handel."

"You were not obliged to go to the concert, ma'am," Harry said quietly.

"Well, what else was I supposed to do while you were off gallivanting at the steps?" the lady demanded petulantly.

"Hardly gallivanting, ma'am, merely meeting my guests," Harry said. There were times when he refused to indulge his great-aunt. He was the only member of her family to do so, and he knew she liked him for it, even though she would die rather than acknowledge it.

"Insolent puppy," she said, but the petulance left her expression.

"Good evening, Your Grace." Cornelia spoke first, offering her hand. "What a delightful surprise. You remember my sister-in-law, Lady Farnham. Lady Livia is listening to the orchestra. She'll join us shortly."

"Yes . . . yes, of course," the old woman said. "Eliza, these are the gals I was telling you about. My companion, Miss Cox." She waved her fan in the general direction of the lady, who smiled and bobbed her head even as she gathered up her employer's trailing shawls.

"Your Grace." Nick bowed.

"Oh, it's you," she said, raising her lorgnette to peer at him. "Where's the other one . . . Forster, isn't it? You two are always together."

"Not quite always, ma'am," Nick protested as he bowed again. The lady, however, seemed to lose interest in him. "Bonham, if you've arranged a supper box, I'll go there now. I'm in want of a glass of rack-punch. You,

Lady Dagenham, walk with me." She beckoned to Cornelia, adding, "In my opinion, my dear, the only reason to come to this place is for the rack-punch."

Cornelia smiled polite acquiescence and offered the lady her arm. Harry, accepting his place, offered his own to Eliza Cox.

Aurelia said swiftly in a low tone, "I'd like to listen to the concert, Sir Nicholas. Just for a few minutes. I happen to be very fond of Handel."

He was instantly responsive. "Of course, ma'am . . . Harry, you'll excuse us? We'll join you at supper."

"Of course, dear fellow, of course." Harry waved a hand in careless agreement. It was supposed to be his party, but once the duchess had decided to take charge, he might just as well resign his commission. "I believe the box is number six along the main colonnade. You'll find us there."

Aurelia and Nick retraced their steps, and the other four continued down the lamplit path. Cornelia made small talk until she realized that her companion had absolutely no interest in anything she was saying, so she fell silent and was rather amused to discover that since this caused no remark either, she had been right.

Harry directed them to the supper box he'd hired for the evening and himself procured a glass of negus for Eliza, who wouldn't touch anything as strong as rackpunch, while a footman served goblets of punch to Cornelia and the duchess, who without saying anything had somehow made it clear that Cornelia was not to leave her side.

After two glasses of punch, Her Grace announced, "I'll walk a little. Give me your arm, Lady Dagenham." She gathered her shawl tightly around her as she issued her instructions.

"Ma'am . . . ?" Harry began.

"No, no, we have no need of your escort, Bonham. Stay here and take care of Eliza. Come, ma'am." She tapped Cornelia's arm smartly.

Cornelia complied. She couldn't imagine doing anything else, and, in truth, she found Harry's great-aunt rather amusing, although she suspected that a little would go a very long way. She cast a glance towards Harry who offered an infinitesimal shrug and the flicker of an eyebrow, before turning his attention to Eliza.

"We'll walk this way," announced the duchess once they had attained the path beneath the main colonnade. She gestured with her fan to a narrow path that ran at right angles to the broader pedestrian thoroughfare.

It was a much more secluded path that led them to a small inner grove from which other paths radiated. Judging by the whispers and rustles that surrounded them as they entered the grove, Cornelia guessed that this was some kind of lovers' retreat. Perhaps one of the places Harry had had in mind for a quiet walk of their own. Instead of which she was arm in arm with a fearsome old lady who had some kind of reason for this tête-à-tête. It would have made her laugh if she wasn't at the same time somewhat apprehensive. She was convinced that the duchess did not do anything without purpose. In that respect, if not in others, her great-nephew resembled her.

"I'll sit down over there," Her Grace announced, pointing towards a wooden seat beneath the branches of a beech tree, whose winter bare branches were hung with colored lanterns.

"We'll leave the shadows to the lovers," she added. "We're trespassing on their territory quite enough." To her astonishment, Cornelia heard a note of dry humor in the old lady's voice.

The duchess sat down on the seat, arranging her skirts and shawls around her. "Now, m'dear, let's to business."

Cornelia's apprehension came to full flower. But with it came anger. She did not have to subject herself to this woman's bullying even if the lady's own family did. "I don't understand you, ma'am."

"Don't get on your high horse, Lady Dagenham. Sit down beside me." The woman's voice was positively pleasant.

Cornelia sat beside her, but held herself apart. She folded her hands in her lap and waited.

"You have an interest in Bonham," her interlocutor stated.

"What gives you that impression, ma'am?" Cornelia inquired icily before this could go any further.

"Well, you'd be a fool not to," the lady retorted. Then

she said in a rather more conciliatory tone, "But that's not what I meant. Bonham has an interest in you."

"Again, ma'am, I ask what gives you that impression?" Cornelia could feel dread twining around her gut. If this woman suspected anything, just the whisper would be enough for Markby.

"My dear, I've known Bonham since he was a babe in arms. And I probably know him better than his own sisters. He *has* an interest in you. Apart from the way he looks at you when he thinks no one's watching, he'd never otherwise bestir himself the way he has on your behalf. The Bonhams are one of the first families. They can trace their lineage to the Conqueror. Face up to it, Lady Dagenham, you and your friends, while respectable enough, would not on your own gain entrée to the best circles. No . . . no, don't bristle. Believe it or not, I mean this interference kindly. Harry has no need to go to such lengths to assist three women who possess neither fortune nor great lineage to get on in this world."

Cornelia knew this to be true only too well. She held her tongue and waited.

"Therefore, he has another interest in one of you, and I wasn't born yesterday, Lady Dagenham. His interest is in you. And if it was not reciprocated, then why would you accept his help . . . unless you're all social-climbing gold diggers."

Cornelia didn't dignify this with a response. She sat seething, keeping her hands still in her lap with only the greatest difficulty.

The duchess chuckled disconcertingly. "No need to tear my eyes out, m'dear. I know perfectly well that's not the case. Very prettily brought up you all are. A credit to your mothers. And there's nothing objectionable in your families."

"You are too kind, ma'am." Cornelia stared rigidly ahead towards the center of the grove, where some anonymous Grecian statue held court.

"There is however something objectionable in Bonham's. You will hear of it eventually; I'd prefer you to hear it from someone who has his best interests at heart."

Cornelia turned to look at the woman for the first time since this abominable conversation had begun. "Lord Bonham's family?" she inquired incredulously.

"No, not his family. Bonham himself." A hint of discomfort was now apparent in Her Grace's demeanor. Her mittened fingers started to twist the fringe of her cashmere shawl. "Has he told you anything of himself?"

Cornelia laughed, a short, humorless laugh that held more than a hint of bitterness, and averted her gaze once more. "Very little, ma'am."

Her companion sighed a little. "That is ever his way. Even I know almost nothing about him . . . about what he does. But that's for you to sort out, my dear. Either you can live with that, or you can't. I do not consider that to be my business."

And that makes a change, Cornelia thought acidly. She said only, "I assume you mention this objectionable fact because you intend to tell me about it." She felt her companion's eyes on her profile, and she felt them to be uncomfortably penetrating.

"You know that he was married?" the duchess asked.

"Yes, he told me that," Cornelia responded without expression. "And that she died in an accident."

The duchess seemed to take a deep breath as if preparing herself. "His wife was Lady Anne Fairbanks, daughter of the duke of Grafton. She died in suspicious circumstances." The duchess closed her lips in a thin line as she said this.

Cornelia felt as if someone had thrown a pail of cold water over her. "Could you explain, ma'am?"

"They were in the country together." Her Grace spoke briskly now, as if recounting distasteful facts as quickly as possible.

"They were heard quarrelling. According to witnesses at the inquest, Anne left her husband's bedchamber in high dudgeon. Bonham was heard protesting at the head of the stairs as his wife began to descend them. Anne somehow caught her foot. She fell to her death. No one saw exactly what happened, but her father became convinced that her husband had caused her death."

She fanned herself for a moment, before saying, "It came out that Anne had a married lover . . . indeed she and Vibart had been lovers since before her marriage to Bonham, who had known nothing of it. That fact seemed to offer some motive, enough, anyway, for the inquest to pursue the possibility that her death had not been accidental. Nonsense, of course."

She stopped as if to catch her breath, and Cornelia was perturbed by her pallor beneath the carefully applied rouge.

Cornelia said, "Please, don't distress yourself any further, ma'am."

The duchess produced a scornful snort. "I'm not distressed, I'm angry. Even after five years, it still enrages me."

She took another deep breath. "Well, the long and the short of it, Lady Dagenham, is that Bonham, although exonerated at the inquest, carries this shadow and will carry it until his death. The duke continues to believe in his guilt, and there are others who follow his lead. The facts are murky, the witness statements in general muddled. Bonham's own circle stood by him and continue to do so. Society in general behaves as if it never happened. But if he married again, the scandal would become the day's news."

Cornelia absorbed this in silence for a long moment, then she said, "Are you warning me off, ma'am?"

The duchess swung her head slowly to look at her. "Not *off*, my dear. Just warning you of what to expect. I'm deeply fond of Bonham. If you're willing to stand by him, he'll make you a good husband. But it will test you if you can't find a way to manage the scandal. Make no mistake about that."

She rose abruptly in a billow of cashmere and silk. "There, I've said my piece, and it grows cold."

Cornelia got to her feet and offered her arm. She was unsure how to make sense of what she'd just been told. After a minute she said, "Forgive me, ma'am, but while I appreciate your taking me into your confidence, it seems unnecessary. Harry has never given the slightest hint of a marriage proposal."

The lady gave another scornful snort. "Of course not, girl. He wouldn't subject any woman to what he's convinced will happen. As far as he's concerned, marriage is never going to be a possibility for him because he wouldn't subject any woman to the scandal. But he's wrong. I'm old enough, and I've seen enough, my dear, to know that news of his marriage will be no more than a nine days' wonder. I'm not saying it'll be easy, but if you both brazen it out, it will die down sooner rather than later."

Cornelia said nothing, and the duchess spoke again into the silence, "You think me presumptuous, of course, a nosy old woman . . . but as I said, I've a fondness for Bonham. And I like you," she added, almost as an afterthought.

And here was yet another tangle in the skein of Harry Bonham, Cornelia thought, as they returned to the supper box. Did she want to unravel it? Could she afford to unravel it? The taint of murder . . . It would certainly produce the sun by which the earl of Markby, given half a chance, would make hay.

And she supposed it explained why Harry played Casanova at her window. In his eyes, as long as their liaison was secret, she would not be tainted by the scandal. And for the same reason, their relationship could never progress beyond a liaison. Understanding brought a chill of satisfaction, but no pleasure.

Chapter 22

*J*UST WHAT THE DEVIL *had the meddlesome old woman wanted of Nell?* Harry watched the two women stroll down the path back towards the supper box. They were both silent, his great-aunt somewhat grim-faced, Cornelia looking noncommittal.

He had been joined a few minutes earlier by the other four, giving him some relief from Eliza, who was always so pathetically grateful for any attention that she tended to lapse into a loquacious confusion of thanks and apologies. Aurelia was now engaging her in conversation, politely attentive as she tried to find the sense in the muddle.

"Ah, there you are," Harry greeted pleasantly, as Cornelia helped the duchess up the few steps into the box. "Supper awaits."

"So I should hope," Her Grace retorted. "I can't abide eating this late."

"Then, ma'am, perhaps you should have stayed home," Harry said gently, pulling out a chair for her.

She glared at him but took her seat without further comment.

"Ham, ma'am?" Harry proffered the silver salver of wafer-thin ham that the gardens were famous for. He placed two slices on her plate, before turning to her companion. "Ma'am, may I serve you?"

"Oh, goodness me, my lord, you are too kind . . . really too kind. Perhaps the tiniest slice . . . just the tiniest . . . maybe that little piece over there. I mustn't be greedy, must I?" She smiled and bobbed her head as she looked at her fellow guests.

"Oh, stop gibbering, Eliza," her employer demanded. "There's more than enough for everyone."

"Yes, of course, Your Grace . . . I didn't imagine there wasn't . . . indeed I know dear Lord Bonham always provides. . . ." Eliza subsided dolefully under a glare from the duchess.

"How was the orchestra, Liv?" Cornelia asked swiftly.

"Oh, quite a spectacle." Livia picked up her cue after shooting a sympathetic glance towards Her Grace's beleaguered companion. "A lot of couples were dancing, but they all wore masks. I hadn't realized it was a masked ball."

The conversation swirled around Cornelia. She offered an occasional comment when she caught the drift of the chatter, but it was hard to concentrate. She couldn't imagine that the man who was such a tender, humorous, deeply sensual lover had killed someone. And yet she knew shadows concealed his self from her.

He was a master actor, of that she was convinced. Whatever role he chose cloaked the real Harry Bonham. But who and what was the real Harry Bonham?

"You seem distracted, Lady Dagenham?"

She jumped guiltily, suddenly aware that Lord Forster had been talking to her for some minutes. "Oh, I beg your pardon, sir. I was lost in contemplation. There's so much to see." It was such a feeble excuse that it made her feel even guiltier, and she was now very conscious of Harry's cool green eyes appraising her. Had he guessed what his aunt had told her?

She forced herself to focus on her companions around the table, and after a few minutes, Harry looked away.

"I would love to see the fireworks," Livia said, as supper drew to a close. "Shall we all go?"

"Can't abide 'em," the duchess announced, not unexpectedly. "Forster, you may escort us to our carriage."

David bowed his acquiescence to the imperious command. "It will be my pleasure, ma'am."

Harry rose swiftly. "I'll escort you, ma'am."

"No you won't. Forster will do very well," his aunt declared, gathering her shawls about her. "Have a care for your guests, Bonham."

"Yes, ma'am." His bow was ironic.

Her Grace took a relatively gracious leave of the party and departed on David's arm, her companion bobbing along behind, carrying her employer's large reticule.

"Poor woman," murmured Aurelia. "How can she

bear it? Oh, I beg your pardon, Lord Bonham, I know she's your relative, but the duchess is so overbearing."

"Think nothing of it," Harry said with a dismissive gesture. "She's a positive Gorgon and delights in being so. Are we *all* going to watch the fireworks?"

He looked interrogatively at Cornelia and she understood that he was asking her to stay behind. But she was not ready for a tête-à-tête, not until she'd fully absorbed his great-aunt's confidence.

"I would certainly like to see them," she said, ignoring the flash of puzzled disappointment in his eyes. "Are you coming, Ellie?"

"I wouldn't miss it."

Harry gave up. It was always possible that Cornelia was avoiding being alone with him because of her acute concern about appearances. He didn't think there was any reason to worry about something as natural as a couple in clear view in a supper box on the main colonnade, but he knew how worried she was about a whisper of scandal touching her children. It might be an unnecessary precaution on this occasion, but he supposed he could . . . or should . . . understand.

He offered her his arm. "Let us go then."

Amid the noise and dazzle of the spectacle, Cornelia's abstraction passed unnoticed by all save Harry, who could feel the tension in her body as a palpable force as she stood close beside him. He touched her arm, and she jumped almost out of her skin.

"Why so nervous?" he asked quietly.

"You took me by surprise," she responded with an unconvincing laugh. "I was so taken up with the fireworks. Look at that Catherine wheel." She pointed upwards at the whirling circle of sparking colors.

Harry merely shrugged and after another minute, said as quietly as before, "I'll come to you tonight."

He felt her stiffen before she said, "I don't feel too well, Harry. If you don't mind, I'd rather sleep tonight."

"We could do that," he said mildly. "I would like to be with you, making love is not the only pleasure I gain from your company. I would like you to sleep in my arms."

"Hush," she said in an urgent whisper. "Someone might hear."

"Not with this racket going on," he observed frowning. "You can barely hear yourself think."

"Still . . ." she demurred.

"As you wish," he said flatly.

Cornelia bit her lip. She couldn't blame him for being hurt by her abrupt withdrawal, but until she could explain it to herself, she could hardly explain it to him. She didn't know whether his great-aunt's revelations really mattered to her. They were important when it came to the wider question of his possible remarriage, but did that matter to her? Harry had never suggested regularizing their liaison, and his aunt had explained his scruples, although dismissing them as unnecessary. But whether society in general was forgiving of such a taint on his reputation, the earl of Markby would certainly use it.

What Cornelia couldn't decide was whether this strange depression was because somewhere deep in her soul unconsciously she had hoped for this love affair to become permanent, and now there could never be such a hope.

The excruciating evening finally drew to a close, and Cornelia had difficulty hiding her relief as they walked down to the water steps. David had rejoined them halfway through the fireworks display and he walked now with Livia, who chatted as animatedly as Aurelia was chatting with Nick. Only Harry and Cornelia walked in a strangely deadened silence.

Harry went with them in the scull, and together with Nick and David escorted them to the waiting Berlin. He held Cornelia back for a moment with a hand on her arm as the other four made their farewells at the carriage step.

"What is it, Nell?" His eyes raked her face, looking for some clue to this sudden tension.

"The time of the month," she lied in desperation. "I really don't feel at all well, Harry. It will pass in a day or two, but . . ."

"I understand," he interrupted almost brusquely. He didn't believe her, although he had no evidence for disbelief, but if she was so anxious to sleep alone that she would produce the one excuse no gentleman could ignore, then he must accept it. He handed her into the carriage, raising her hand to his lips for an instant before releasing it.

"May I call upon you in the morning?"

She could hardly refuse such a request, although she knew she would have to have come to some resolution of her feelings before she saw him again. "Of course," she said lightly. "You are always welcome, Viscount . . . as indeed are you all." Her smile encompassed all three men. "Thank you for a delightful party, Lord Bonham."

"It has been my pleasure." There was no disguising the sardonic tone. He bowed and stepped back, closing the carriage door upon them.

"Well, that was an entertaining evening," Aurelia said, grabbing on to the strap as the carriage suddenly lurched forward over the cobbles.

"Yes, your Casanova is certainly an exemplary host, Nell," Livia remarked. She looked across the carriage, catching sight of Cornelia's expression in the light from a gas lamp, and said with concern, "Are you ill, Nell? You're very pale."

"Actually, you've been pale all evening," Aurelia said, joining Livia in her examination of their friend's countenance in the uncertain light. "And very quiet."

Cornelia sighed. "I was buttonholed by the great-aunt, who insisted on a private chat."

"What about?" Livia leaned forward intently.

"Harry. What else?"

"Does she suspect something?"

Cornelia shrugged. "She was kind enough to inform me that she believed Harry had an interest in me because why else would a Bonham bestir himself for three women with so little to recommend them to the Upper

Ten Thousand. She thought I should know that such a union was impossible." It was close to the truth, she comforted herself.

"What a witch," Aurelia declared in disgust. "I hope you put her in her place."

Cornelia was now on the horns of a dilemma. It wasn't strictly fair to the lady to paint her as black as she'd implied, but neither could she so much as hint at the truth. Not yet at least. She settled for another shrug and a dismissive, "Oh, I didn't attempt the impossible. It's immaterial anyway. The idea hadn't occurred to me."

Her friends regarded her doubtfully. The ring of truth was absent here, but they were both too sensitive to probe further.

The great iron key was underneath the Grecian urn beside the door, and they let themselves into the darkened house. Morecombe had remembered to leave one lamp burning in a sconce in the hall, and three carrying candles stood on the table beneath. They lit the candles from the sconce, and Cornelia blew out the latter before following her friends to the stairs.

She produced a convincing yawn as they reached the landing. "I'm dead on my feet. It must be all those Latin verbs this morning. Are you coming to the nursery, Ellie?"

"Yes, of course," Aurelia said. "Good night, Liv." She kissed Livia.

"Good night, Liv." Cornelia kissed her too, and they parted company, Cornelia and Aurelia heading for the nursery stairs.

Aurelia tucked Franny's blanket tighter around her and kissed her daughter's smooth brow. "She looks so peaceful when she's asleep, it's hard to believe what a tempestuous little creature she is." She smiled down at the sleeping child.

Cornelia smiled her agreement as she moved between her children's narrow beds, adjusting coverlets, smoothing back errant locks of hair.

"Ready?" Aurelia moved to the door.

"In a minute," Cornelia whispered. "You go on down."

Aurelia nodded. "Good night then."

"Good night, Ellie." She stayed looking down at her son, his face a little flushed with sleep, his long dark eyelashes, his father's eyelashes, resting in half-moons on his pink cheeks. She could not lose him. Not even for a lifetime of joy with Harry Bonham.

Stevie had his ball and was kicking it in front of him as the little party came through the iron gate into the seclusion of the private garden.

"Daisy, will you play ball with me?" Stevie asked in his childish treble. He was much less importunate than his cousin, who instantly shrieked her own claims to the game.

Susannah merely plopped herself down on the grass beside the border and picked a crocus.

"All right, Lord Stevie, just a minute," Daisy called, bending to wipe Franny's nose.

Stevie kicked the ball onto a path running away from the lawn, and Franny pulled herself free of Daisy's ministrations and chased after her cousin as he followed the ball. There was a slight slope to the path, and the ball rolled of its own volition, gaining speed.

Stevie ran after it, Franny shouting excitedly behind him. And then the little girl caught her toe against a tree root and went sprawling on the path. She howled, and Daisy, clutching Susannah's hand, came running.

Stevie continued after the ball.

"Stevie . . . Lord Stevie, come back here." Daisy's voice was distracted as she tried to soothe the wailing Franny even while holding on to Susannah.

Stevie halted his pursuit of the ball for a second, glancing back as if considering whether to obey the summons or not. He turned around again, and seeing his ball heading rapidly towards a curve in the path, chased after it.

Franny's frantic howls were now joined by Susannah's in sympathy, and the nursemaid, on her knees on the path as she mopped the blood from Franny's scraped knee and tried to reassure Susannah, didn't look back again.

Stevie rounded the bend in the path and didn't hear the man stepping out behind him. Then he was suddenly enveloped in a suffocating blackness, something wrapped tightly around his head. Something pressed hard against the back of his head forcing his face into his abductor's shoulder. He kicked and struggled, but his efforts were no match for the strong arms that held him as they set off at a fast lope heading for the far side of the garden and the gate on the other side of the square.

His captor ran from the garden to where a horse was tethered to the railing. He swung up, still holding his blind and stifled burden tightly against him, and kicked the animal into a fast trot out of the square.

Daisy finally managed to quieten Franny's frantic yells, but by then Susannah was crying in good earnest. She stood up, holding the three-year-old on her hip, jiggling her rhythmically while she looked around for Stevie. She called and listened. But there were only the quiet sounds of the garden, a rustle of a squirrel, the trill of a thrush in the privet hedge.

She called again, her voice rising with panic, then she began to run along the path to where she'd seen him last, Susannah bouncing on her hip, Franny clutching at her skirts.

"Where's Stevie? Where's Stevie?" Franny chanted repetitively.

"Oh, hush yourself, Franny," Daisy demanded, her desperation giving way to angry frustration. If it hadn't been for this child, she would not have lost sight of the other one. She bent and shook the little girl, not hard, but for a child who was totally unaccustomed to anything but patient responses, it shocked Franny into unaccustomed silence.

Daisy ran around the outside path that circled within the railings, calling Stevie. When the circuit produced nothing, she plunged down the various paths that all emerged into the grassy lawn in the center of the square. Stevie was not a particularly mischievous child, and he would never torment her in this fashion. He might hide for a few minutes, but then he'd bounce out laughing at his cleverness.

She stood still in the center of the square, tears pouring down her cheeks at the utter futility of the quiet and the absolute conviction of the truth.

Little Viscount Dagenham was not in the garden.

She grabbed Franny's hand in a viselike grip and ran almost blindly out of the garden and across the road to the house. She hammered on the brass knocker, and the door was opened by a startled Cornelia.

"Whatever . . . ?" Cornelia took in the nursemaid's tear-streaked countenance, the shock on Franny's face, Susannah's hiccuping little sobs, and the color drained from her face.

"What's happened to Stevie?" The question came through bloodless lips, then, without waiting for an answer, she pushed past Daisy and ran across the street to the garden.

Chapter 23

Harry walked into the storm an hour later. The front door was ajar, and he didn't trouble to knock, instead pushing it wide and stepping into the hall. It was immediately apparent that something was badly wrong. He could almost smell the panic in the air.

Daisy, the nursemaid, was a sodden tear-stricken heap on the stairs, the two little girls wailing beside her. An ashen Linton was berating the sobbing Daisy in a voice edged with hysteria. The twins, for once showing emotion, were trying to comfort the children with gingerbread, while Morecombe stood, clearly at a loss, to one side of the little group muttering to himself.

"What's going on?" Harry demanded, tossing his hat and whip onto the bench and drawing off his gloves.

"Lord Stevie," Morecombe stated in sepulchral tones. "Such goings-on . . . I knew things would come to a bad end after my lady passed away. I told our Ada and our

Mavis so, didn't I just?" He appealed to the twins, who murmured assent.

Harry didn't respond. Instead he strode towards the parlor where he assumed he would find the women. Cornelia's voice rose above the rest as he entered the room without ceremony, but he couldn't make out what she had said. She was standing in the middle of the room, a sheet of paper in her hand, her face set in stone, pale as alabaster, her eyes oddly blank. To Harry it looked as if she was holding herself together by an act of supreme will, as if at any moment she would fly apart in a thousand pieces.

"What's happened?" He went swiftly towards her. "What is it, Nell?"

She looked at him for a moment as if she didn't know who he was, then she shook her head impatiently and returned to her intent scrutiny of the paper she held. "I have to go at once," she said in a strange detached voice. "They won't hurt him if I go at once."

"Stevie's been kidnapped," Aurelia told him swiftly. "He was in the square garden with Daisy and the girls, and he disappeared." She opened her hands helplessly. "Gone . . . not a sign of him."

"But then Nell got this letter," Livia put in. "It arrived just a few minutes ago." She went over to Cornelia. "Nell, let us see the letter. Or at least tell us what it says."

Cornelia folded the letter and thrust it into her pocket before saying adamantly, "No. No one's to see it. This is my business and only mine. I'll deal with it in my own way. I have to go now." She took a step towards the door.

Her voice did not sound like her own, and Harry could hear beneath the brittleness how close she was to breaking. He went over to her, taking her shoulders gently. "Whatever this is, love, you can't manage it alone. Give me the letter."

She jerked herself away from him, saying vehemently, "This is *nothing* to do with you. It's a family matter."

"I understand that," he said with deliberate calm. "However, I can help you. I want you to give me the letter."

She stared at him. "How could you possibly help? Someone has taken my child. Do you understand that? I know what I have to do to get him back, and that's what I'm going to do. Just me . . . no one else can be involved. Now get out of my way, Harry." She attempted to push past him, but he remained where he was, once again taking her shoulders.

"Nell, give me the letter. *Now.*" He made his voice almost harsh in his need to break through the carapace that prevented her from understanding anything beyond her child's disappearance. "There's little time to waste. I need to see what they want you to do."

And now she looked at him with sudden awareness, hostility and mistrust bright in her blue gaze. "What do you know?"

"More than you think," he returned grimly. "Now give me the letter." He snapped his fingers imperatively.

He turned suddenly to where Aurelia and Livia stood staring at him. "Leave us."

It was a command they couldn't imagine ignoring. This was not the man they knew. This incarnation of Viscount Bonham was almost frightening. Without a word, they left the parlor.

"Now," Harry said, "the letter, Nell."

She felt numb, powerless to resist him. But still she protested. "They'll hurt him if I show it to anyone."

"That's not going to happen, love." His voice now was gentle and cajoling. "I won't let it happen. Trust me now and give it to me." He held out his hand.

She reached into her pocket for the letter and handed it to him, unsure why she trusted him but knowing that she did.

Harry took in the contents of the letter in one quick sweep of his eyes. His mouth hardened, his nostrils flared with a surge of anger, as much at himself as at the idiot Nigel Dagenham. It had to be Dagenham's handiwork, even though he was only a tool in a much broader game. It was pathetically amateur, but Cornelia wouldn't see that. How could she when she thought her child was in danger? How dared that stupid, self-indulgent, weak-minded *dunderhead* cause Cornelia this agony.

Harry handed her back the letter. "Leave this to me, Nell. Just stay here, don't leave the house. Do you understand?" He looked at her closely, seeing the flash in her eyes, the set of her mouth. "I mean it. Stay here and wait for me. I'll bring Stevie back, I promise."

Unable to bear her stillness, the terror and confusion in her eyes, he pulled her against him and kissed her hard on the mouth, holding her tightly trying to impart his own strength to the suddenly fragile figure in his arms.

She let him kiss her, but it was as if she didn't feel his lips upon hers. She remained stiff in his arms, then finally pushed him away.

He stepped back, looking at her uncertainly. He didn't know whether she'd heard him. And even if she had whether she would follow his instructions. But there was no time to waste. He had to get to the child before Dagenham's masters did. He was confident Nigel wouldn't hurt the child, but Nigel was a puppet, a cat's-paw. And those who used him wouldn't give a fig for the health and welfare of a five-year-old boy. If Cornelia took matters into her own hands, she would only get in the way, endanger herself as well as the child.

He spun away from her and left the parlor. The tableau in the hall had changed, and only Morecombe and the twins stood at the foot of the stairs in some kind of confabulation.

"Where's Lester?" Harry demanded as he crossed to the front door.

They didn't seem particularly surprised by the question. "Went out, when the letter come," Morecombe informed him.

Lester would have gone after the messenger, and he would have caught him soon enough. Harry picked up his hat and whip and left the house. As he'd expected, Lester appeared at a run from the far side of the square.

"I hoped you'd be along, m'lord," he said, panting slightly. "I caught the lad, but he didn't know anything, said a cove had given him a message and a penny to deliver it to the house."

"Where did he get the message?" Harry had hold of his horse's reins now preparing to mount.

"Just a few streets away," Lester said. "Did you read it?"

"Aye." Harry nodded, swinging onto Perseus. "He's got the boy at a tavern on Gray's Inn Road, at least that's what I'm assuming. I don't think he has the wit to hide the boy somewhere different from where he's expecting the ransom. It's the Greyhound Tavern. Follow me there. It may take two of us if he's got reinforcements."

"I'm on your heels, sir."

Harry raised a hand in acknowledgment and urged Perseus into a trot.

The child struggled against the suffocating folds of the blanket. A voice, a familiar voice, told him that it would be all right, that he should lie still and be a good boy. The blanket was lifted and he opened his mouth to scream. Before a sound could emerge a spoon went between his lips and his mouth was immediately filled with a vile-tasting liquid that made him choke and splutter. From a distance he heard the same voice, soothing, telling him it was all going to all right. He'd see his mama soon.

Cornelia waited only until she was certain Harry had left the house before she looked again at the letter. It was badly printed and misspelled, but the message was unambiguous.

> *If you want to see the lad agin, bring the thimbel with the ritin on it to the Greyhound Tavern at Gray's Inn by tomorrer forenoon. Don't tell no one or else.*

How did these people know she had a thimble? What if she hadn't found it in the flour barrel? Cornelia shuddered, hot and cold alternately. *Why* the thimble?

But what did it matter? They wanted the thimble. And she had it. She opened her workbox and took it out, turning it around, trying to make sense of the engravings. They didn't strike her as writing, although the note described them as such. *What if it is the wrong thimble?*

No, that wasn't to be thought of. She dropped the object into her pocket with the note and hurried upstairs for her pelisse.

Aurelia and Livia were waiting in the hall as she came out of the parlor. Aurelia had dispatched the wailing children and their frantic attendants to the nursery, and an eerie silence had settled over the hall.

"Cornelia, what can we do?" Aurelia reached a hand for her as she brushed past her on the way to the stairs.

"Nothing . . . nothing, Ellie." Her voice was impatient, her desperation clear. "Please, just let me go."

Aurelia fell back, exchanging a helpless glance with Livia, and Cornelia ran upstairs.

In her bedchamber she stopped, forcing herself to think clearly, to calm her fast and shallow breaths. What would Stevie need when she found him? He had a coat and hat. . . . Linton wouldn't have let him out of the house without those. Would he be hungry . . . thirsty?

Oh, God, what had they done to him?

She grabbed up her old cloak and rushed to the door. Then remembered she had no money for a hackney. She found her reticule and rushed back downstairs, hatless, her hair coming loose from its pins.

She raced past her friends who still stood at a loss at the foot of the stairs, and headed for the front door, which still stood ajar. Outside in the chilly sunshine she paused for a second, trying to decide where she had the best chance of finding a hackney.

She headed for Mortimer Street, trying to control a little whimpering sob of panic at the time she was wasting. Then she saw one, the horse between the traces a broken-down nag, the driver looking as if he'd be more at home in Newgate Gaol than plying his trade in Mayfair. But he pulled over for her.

"Greyhound Tavern, Gray's Inn Road," she gasped as

she wrenched open the door into the greasy, evil-smelling interior.

The jarvey stared at her in momentary stupefaction. Gray's Inn Road was hardly a common destination for the ladies of Mayfair. Then he spat a juicy wad of tobacco onto the road and cracked his whip.

The cab started off with a jerk, and Cornelia sat bolt upright on the torn, stained squabs. Despite her desperation, she was still too fastidious to allow herself to sink into their depths, which she was convinced were infested with a colony of fleas.

She felt for the thimble in her pocket, closing her fingers around it as if it were a talisman. And now while there was nothing else she could do, the questions she hadn't had time for flooded in. What did Harry know of this business?

More than you think? She heard his voice as he had said that, saw again the cold light in his clear green gaze. He had told her he would bring Stevie back, but he hadn't asked for the thimble. If he was going to rescue her son, why would he not take the ransom with him? Not that she would have let it out of her sight, but why hadn't he mentioned it?

She took out the thimble and looked at it again in the dim, swaying interior of the frowsty carriage. Icy certainty gripped her. There was only one explanation. Harry had known, or guessed, that this, or something like it, was going to happen. He'd known about the thimble, knew what secrets it held. And for some reason, despite the ransom demand, he had considered it irrelevant. He had known, and he had made no attempt to protect them, prepare them even. He'd stood to one side and watched as the trap had closed around them. And she could think of only one reason for that. It had suited his purposes to use the little household on Cavendish Square to bait his trap.

Maybe she was being melodramatic, but Cornelia didn't think so. She knew enough about what she didn't know about Viscount Bonham to be certain he was somehow responsible for this horror. Maybe he hadn't orchestrated it, but something he had done, an omission if not a commission, had brought this upon her.

And only she could get her son back.

Impatiently, Cornelia grabbed the worn leather strap and leaned forward, thrusting aside the strip of leather that formed a curtain across the window aperture. How far had they gone? Were they getting close? It was a part of the city she knew nothing about. A grimy downtrodden street of tumbled houses, kennels overflowing with filth, the carriage bumping over uneven cobbles.

Harry rode past the Greyhound Tavern as if it was of no significance to him, but his swift appraisal had taken in the narrow alleyway to the left of the building, barely separating it from the decrepit hovel next door. He could see no sign of unusual activity, no indication of anyone on the watch from the tavern. But that didn't mean that there weren't eyes watching the street for unexpected visitors.

Lester's support would be reassuring, but Harry decided he couldn't wait for him. He rode about a hundred yards farther down the street and saw an urchin kicking a stone in desultory fashion through the muck in the kennel, splashing the cobbles with dirty water and unnamable refuse.

"Hey, you!" Harry called to him in peremptory tones, and the lad paused and looked up at the tall figure riding towards him.

"You wan' me, guv?" He looked alarmed, glancing around him, clearly ready to flee.

"Yes, I do, if you want to earn yourself a sixpence," Harry said, drawing rein beside him. "Take my horse and hold him here." He dismounted and examined the boy closely. "Do you hear me? Don't leave this spot. Just hold him and wait for me to get back. Is that clear?"

The boy looked up and down the street again, licking his lips nervously. Then he nodded and reached up for the reins. "Awright, guv."

Harry looped the reins around the filthy, clawlike hand, and closed the scrawny fingers tightly over the leather. "Sixpence," he said. "And you're to be right here in exactly this spot when I come back."

The boy nodded, but he looked scared rather than delighted at the prospect of the coming largesse. There was nothing remotely benign about the gentleman, and the threat, while unspoken, was clear enough to the boy. Failure to perform this task was not an option.

Harry fixed him with a hard stare for another second or two, then nodded, and strode away, back towards the tavern.

There was still no sign of Lester. Harry ducked into the alley beside the tavern. It was dark and barely the width of his shoulders. He sidled rather than risk brushing against the slimy walls, trying not to breathe too deeply of the fetid air.

The passage opened into a tiny, high-walled courtyard with a well in the center, a noisome privy in the far corner, and empty ale barrels rolled haphazardly across the unpaved ground. Harry stepped into the yard and examined the back of the building. There were only two windows, one above the other, and a narrow door.

He approached the door and listened. Raised voices, the clatter of pots and pans, the squawk of a chicken in distress. Nothing untoward, he decided, reaching down into his riding boot for the knife he always kept tucked out of sight. The knife and his riding whip were his only weapons, but he was adept with both.

He raised the latch on the door, then kicked it open so that it banged against the inside wall. He entered the small, smoke-filled kitchen, knife in one hand, whip hand raised in menace. The room's inhabitants, a slatternly woman flourishing a ladle, an ancient man hunched on a stool by the open range, and a man holding a flapping chicken by the neck stared openmouthed at the intruder.

"Good morning," Harry said pleasantly. "Would you all be so good as to stand over there in that corner." He gestured with his whip to the far corner of the kitchen beside a Welsh dresser and well away from a door that he guessed gave access to the taproom.

Still staring at him they shuffled into the corner, the man still holding the flapping chicken.

"Thank you." Harry turned and swiftly dropped the heavy bar across the door he'd just come in by, then crossed the kitchen in two strides and closed the other door, standing with his back against it. He wanted no surprise visitors in the next few minutes.

"Now, ma'am, perhaps you would tell me who else is in the tavern." His voice was quiet, even, and deceptively amiable. His mouth smiled, but his eyes were as frigid as an arctic blizzard.

For a moment no one answered him. The chicken let out another despairing squawk, and, with a reflex movement, the man holding it wrung its neck with a swift and efficient twist of his hands. The bird dangled inert.

"Who else is in this building?" Harry asked again, a slight edge now to his voice.

It was the woman who answered him. "There's two in the taproom, an' them upstairs."

Harry's gaze sharpened. "Them? How many?"

The woman, who seemed to have recovered from her surprise, demanded, "What's it to you?"

"Rather a lot as it happens," Harry said, tapping his whip against his boots. "Oblige me, if you please." The edge was sharper.

The woman shrugged, and her tone was sullen. "Don't rightly know. Sometimes there's one of 'em, sometimes more. I don't keep watch on the street door." She shrugged again. "Better things t'do with me time."

Harry frowned, and the man with the chicken volunteered hastily, "They pays regular, sir, fer the use o' the chamber, and they comes and goes as they pleases. We don't ask no questions if'n they pays regular."

Harry accepted that he'd received all the information he was going to get. He raised the latch on the door leading to the taproom. "Where will I find this chamber?"

"Top o' the stairs, on the left," the woman told him, still sullenly.

Harry gave her a brief nod, and left the kitchen, closing the door softly behind him. The two men in the taproom, raised their eyes incuriously from their ale pots as he crossed the floor, the soles of his boots sticking to the clotted sawdust. He ignored the drinkers and softly climbed the narrow staircase at the far end by the street door.

At the head of the stairs he paused outside the door the woman had indicated. It would be locked, of course. How many of them were in there, waiting for Cornelia to bring the thimble? He glanced back down the stairs, wondering whether to wait for Lester. But then he saw again Cornelia's anguished eyes, and he knew he couldn't wait. He needed to get to her child.

He heard footsteps on the stairs and spun around, the knife poised in his hand. A girl, no more than twelve, stopped on the stairs and stared openmouthed. The slop jar in her hand shook, threatening to deposit its malodorous contents on the floor. Harry put a finger to his lips, then came lightly to the stairs. He pointed downwards and made a shooing gesture with his hands. She hurried down again, and he followed her.

He took a gold sovereign from his pocket. It glimmered in the dim light of the narrow hallway at the foot of the stairs, and the girl gazed at it as if mesmerized. "Listen carefully," he said in a bare whisper. "This is yours if you do exactly as I say." He explained what he wanted of her, and she nodded, her eyes never leaving the glittering gold. "Can you do that?"

She found her voice. "Aye, sir." She held out a grimy hand.

"I'm going to put it here," Harry said, balancing the coin on the newel post at the bottom of the stairs. "You may pick it up when you come down, when you've given the message."

She nodded eagerly, setting down her slop jar before running up the stairs again. Harry followed her, knife in hand, and pressed himself against the wall beside the door.

The girl knocked timidly and when there was no immediate response knocked harder. "Who is it?" a strongly accented voice demanded from within the chamber.

"Beggin' yer pardon, sir, but there's a lady what wants to talk wi' you," the child said, sticking to her script. "She's belowstairs, sir. Says she's got summat fer you."

They heard the sound of the heavy bar being raised and the door opened a crack. "Send her up," the same accented voice growled.

The girl shook her head vigorously. "She don't want to come up, sir. Said fer you to come down. Said she's got summat fer you." She turned tail and ran down the stairs, scooping up the gold coin as she passed, heading for the street door as Harry had instructed.

There was a murmured exchange in the chamber, then the door was pushed wide and a lean, dark-visaged man stepped onto the landing followed by a much burlier companion who commanded brusquely, *"Allons-y."* They hastened down the stairs.

Harry reckoned he had maybe three or four minutes at the most before they realized there was no one waiting for them. He stepped swiftly into the chamber, his gaze sweeping the room.

Nigel Dagenham was tied to a rickety chair, gagged with a scarf, an ugly cut bleeding above his eyes. Eyes that regarded Harry with anguished terror. His face was bruised and swollen, his clothes torn.

Harry took a step towards him, then he saw the small shape on the sagging cot in the corner of the chamber. He took two strides to the cot.

He bent over the blanket-wrapped bundle. The child was unconscious, his breathing stertorous, complexion pasty, the lips a little blue. Harry put a finger against the pulse beneath the boy's ear and exhaled slowly. The pulse was strong and steady, but he could smell the telltale sweetness on the child's breath.

Laudanum. How much? But there was no time to speculate. He straightened and moved to cross the room to release the bound and gagged Nigel. Then he heard footsteps on the stairs. No time for Nigel now. He crossed to the still open chamber door. He slid behind it, flattening himself against the wall as he nudged the door half-closed with his foot.

The door was pushed wide open concealing the man behind. *"Merde,"* one of the men cursed as he stepped into the chamber, his shadow falling long across the floorboards from the flickering candle in a sconce by the door.

He stepped quickly across to Nigel who tried to shrink back against the chair, his eyes wide with silent terror. "You think to make a fool of us, *mon ami.*" He raised a hand and struck Nigel across the mouth.

Harry remained behind the door, barely breathing.

"Laissez-lui, Michel," the second man said, coming into the room. *"Il n'est pas vaux l'effort."* He spun quickly towards the door again, just as Harry pushed it closed again with his foot.

Harry smiled. *"Bonjour, messieurs."* He stepped away from the wall, his knife in one hand, the lash of his whip curled against the palm of his other.

For a moment, nothing was said. The three men assessed the situation, each swiftly calculating possible moves in the confined space. The two Frenchmen appeared unarmed, but Harry was not prepared to rely on appearances. He reckoned he could handle both of them in a knife fight, but if one of them produced a pistol, then he'd be in trouble.

Where the hell was Lester?

Silver glinted as knives appeared in the Frenchmen's hands. The wicked shining blades of stilettos. They stood shoulder to shoulder facing Harry. He could only pray that they didn't think about using the child. A knife at Stevie's throat, and Harry would be rendered helpless.

His hand moved swift as lightning and the lash of his whip snapped, catching the knife hand of the man closest to him. The lash curled around his wrist, and he gave a cry of surprise and pain. Caught off guard he stumbled, and Harry sent the whip curling again, snapping against the man's cheek.

The other Frenchman took a jumping step towards Harry, his knife raised. Harry feinted, then came in low, driving upwards with the knife. It caught the man's thigh but without sufficient force to penetrate deeply through the cloth of his britches, leaving little more than a scratch on the flesh. But it was first blood, and they both jumped back, taking stock.

The sound of feet racing up the stairs broke the taut concentration. Harry's gut sank. It was a woman's feet. *Cornelia.* He stepped backwards in front of the door. He couldn't bolt it or stop her from opening it without taking his eyes off his opponents, and they were both lined up again, shoulder to shoulder, and the one he'd caught with his whip had a most unpleasant gleam in his eye.

"Cornelia, stay where you are," he yelled, but with only the faintest hope that she would obey him. He felt the door shiver as she seemed to hurl her entire weight against it and his two opponents pounced on him at the same time. He ducked sideways, dancing towards the far wall, and the door crashed open.

Cornelia stood on the threshold, looking wildly at the scene. Two men with drawn knives. Harry by himself against the wall, a smeared knife in his hand. Some huddled body on a chair. Nothing seemed to make any sense at first, then it did. She made a move to back out of the room but an instant too late, as one of Harry's opponents, realizing his advantage, leaped at her.

Cornelia didn't think. She drove her knee upwards into his groin as he grabbed her arms, and twisted to drive her elbow into his belly. He let her go with a grunt and Harry jumped on him, his knife slicing deeply into the shoulder of the man's knife hand. The knife clattered to the floorboards, and Harry bent and swept it up, discarding the whip as he did so.

Nigel groaned. Momentarily distracted, Cornelia looked towards him, and the second man grabbed her from behind, spinning her back against him. He held her with one arm a tight band across her breast, his knife pressed against the side of her neck. She felt a prick and a sticky wetness on her skin.

And silence fell. Harry's face was without expression, his eyes almost blank, showing nothing of his feverish calculations. He had two knives now and one wounded and disarmed opponent. But the other had Cornelia.

There was one possibility. "Give him the thimble, Nell," he said quietly. He didn't know how long it would take for the man to realize the thimble was a counterfeit, and a clumsy one at that, but there was a chance he might be fooled long enough.

"Not until I have Stevie," she said, her voice clear and steady. "Where is my child?"

"Stevie's all right, love. He's sleeping," Harry said, still quietly. "Give him the thimble. It's what he wants."

Cornelia didn't immediately respond. If she refused to give her captor the thimble, then it seemed likely he would try to wrest it from her. If she put up enough of a struggle, it might give Harry an opening. But then, of course, the man at her back could simply drive the knife into her throat and take the thimble that way. The grim reflection was punctuated by another prick of the knife against her neck.

She looked bleakly at Harry. Did he really know that Stevie was all right? How could she really trust him? He might be deceiving her for his own ends. He'd been doing that, after all, since first they met.

As she stared at him, trying to read his soul, she sensed a change in him. A sudden stiffening, imperceptible, and yet she who knew his body so well could sense the subtle tension in his muscles. His eyes never left her face, his mouth showed nothing, but he was as alert as a panther scenting the hunter.

She stamped hard on her captor's foot, bringing her full weight to bear, heedless of the threatening prick of the knife, aware instinctively that Harry needed the man to lose focus, even for a second.

As she did so, Lester hurled himself from the doorway. Her captor made a surprised little sound, halfway between a grunt and cry, and the press of the knife was no longer against her neck. The imprisoning arm fell away, and she felt his weight brush against her back as he crumpled to the floor.

"Where's Stevie?" Her voice sounded thick and hoarse.

"Behind you," Harry answered. "On the cot." He wanted to look at her neck, but he knew it would have to wait.

Cornelia saw the cot for the first time, or at least registered its presence for the first time. And she saw the small, curled, blanketed bundle. She ran to her child, kneeling by the cot to gather him against her, tears now flowing as she cradled his head against her breast. She was aware only that he was breathing, and his body felt the same as it always did. Holding him tightly, she inched herself onto the bed, positioning herself in the angle of the wall so that she could hold him in her lap, rocking him gently, while her eyes now roamed the miserable chamber, taking in everything she had not noticed before.

Lester. What was he doing here? But, of course, he was

connected to Harry. His employment in Cavendish Square, such a useful man to have around, had not been in the least serendipitous. Harry had planted him there. It was all too clear now. She watched as the two men conversed swiftly in an undertone, heads together with the ease of those who knew each other of old, who trusted and relied upon each other. Who would each give his life into the other's hands.

Another melodramatic thought, Cornelia reflected, amazed at the return of cynicism after the scrambling terror of the last minutes. It would be melodramatic in the ordinary world, she amended. But not in this shadowy universe in which she now found herself. The rules by which these four men played bore no relation to any she understood.

No, not four, five. Harry had moved to the bound figure in the chair. He sliced through the bonds with his knife before reaching behind his head to untie the gag.

Cornelia stared. The figure moaned with pain as the blood returned to his arms. *"Nigel."* She spoke his name incredulously, clutching her child closer to her. What had Nigel to do with this?

Nigel spat blood. His voice was thick and muffled. "I didn't do it, Nell . . . I couldn't do it," he said, confusing her even more. "They tried to force me . . . I tried to stop him from being scared . . . I swear—"

"Don't try to talk," Harry instructed curtly. "You can explain later, when Nell has the time to listen to you. You're the least of anyone's concerns at the moment."

He went over to the cot, and sat beside Cornelia. He caught her chin, turning her head to one side to look at the cut on her neck. "It's not too bad, but it needs cleansing. Lester is going to take you and Stevie home." He touched the child's cheek, relieved to note that a smidgen of color had crept into his complexion and the lips were less blue. "He's taken what I suspect is a fairly large dose of laudanum, and he'll have a headache when he wakes. He'll probably be sick too. But there'll be no lasting ill effects."

"You would know, of course," she said bitterly. "Did you calculate the dose precisely?"

Harry looked shocked. "You can't imagine that *I* . . . Nell, I didn't do this."

She gave a short laugh. "No, not with your own hands, I'm sure. But you were responsible for it." She stared at him, her eyes as hard and blank as blue stone. "Deny it, if you can."

And he couldn't.

He rose from the cot, his face closed. "Lester has a carriage downstairs. I must finish up here." He gestured briefly towards the physical debris on the floor. One man was surely dead, Cornelia thought with strange dispassion. The other rocked on the floor clutching his shoulder, from which the blood oozed thickly. Nigel sat slumped, his hands over his face.

"Coles and Addison'll be along shortly to help with the cleanup, sir," Lester said in his stolid fashion. "I'll be taking Lady Dagenham and young Stevie home now."

He came over to the cot and gently but firmly took the boy from Cornelia. "Come on, ma'am. The sooner the lad's in his own bed, the better he'll be, I reckon."

Cornelia as always found Lester's calm competence reassuring. Whatever his involvement in this shadow world, he was not directly responsible for what had happened to her son. She knew where that responsibility lay. Nigel must have had something to do with it, but God knows what mess he'd found himself in. She did believe him when he said he'd tried to help Stevie.

Harry Bonham was another matter. He had used her, used her children, her friends. But most unforgivable of all, he had taken her soul.

Chapter 24

A HACKNEY CARRIAGE stood in the street outside the tavern, a much more salubrious-looking vehicle than the one that had brought Cornelia. She climbed in and impatiently held out her arms to Lester.

"Give him to me."

"Here you are, ma'am." Lester leaned in and placed the child on her lap, then called an instruction to the jarvey as he climbed in after her. He took the corner seat opposite and sat back, folding his arms with an air of placidity that seemed extraordinary to Cornelia, given that he'd just killed a man.

But presumably that was not a noteworthy occurrence in the world that Lester and Harry Bonham shared. Her mouth hardened.

Stevie stirred, and his eyelids fluttered a little, but he didn't wake. She drew him closer to her, hoping that her familiar scent and warmth would penetrate his drugged stupor and chase away the fear that must have been his last waking emotion.

"How long have you worked for Lord Bonham?" she asked, glancing across at Lester.

"Around twelve years, give or take," he responded serenely. "Since his lordship joined the service."

"What service would that be?" She couldn't help the sardonic edge to the question.

"Why, the Crown's, ma'am," Lester answered, as if it was obvious.

"Ah, yes, of course, the Crown's," Cornelia said as sardonically as before. She should have known. Harry had told her rather obliquely that he worked for the government when he'd reminded her that England was at war. She just hadn't really absorbed it.

So she and her friends and her children had been conscripted in the same service, without their knowledge. Was that supposed to excuse Harry's actions? Was it supposed to make her feel better? Was she supposed to be grateful for the compulsory opportunity to serve her country?

Well, it didn't and she wasn't.

She was simply enraged. And if she could hold on to the purity of her fury, then she could ignore the tangle of emotions swirling beneath.

She reached into her pocket for the thimble and drew it out. "So what is this, Lester? Why was my son's life risked for this?" She tossed it disdainfully onto the seat beside Lester.

He picked it up. "You should ask his lordship, ma'am."

"I'm asking you," she stated flatly. "What's the significance of those engravings?"

Lester for the first time looked uncomfortable. He turned the thimble around between finger and thumb. "Actually, there's no significance to *these*, ma'am." He held the thimble out to her.

Cornelia stared at him. "What? I don't understand." Absently she took it back, enclosing it in her palm.

Lester pulled at his chin. "His lordship will explain, my lady."

"In his absence I see no reason why *you* shouldn't," she insisted. "As it happens I don't intend to give myself the opportunity to ask Viscount Bonham anything, but I would like an explanation from you."

Lester frowned. "I don't fully catch your meaning, my lady. His lordship will explain everything, I'm sure, when you see him next."

"Let me be quite frank, Lester. I do not intend to see Lord Bonham again. So, will you tell me why those engravings have no significance?" She thrust the thimble back into her pocket.

Lester felt himself shrinking from the ice blue darts of her eyes. This was the viscount's mess, not his, and he wanted nothing whatsoever to do with it. "It's not for me to say, ma'am," he stated, fervently hoping that she'd leave it at that.

Cornelia continued to regard him in the dim light, a

deep frown drawing her arched eyebrows together. Then Stevie gave a little cry, and she forgot all about Lester, the thimble, the viscount.

"It's all right, love," she murmured. "Everything's all right now. Mama's here." She lifted him up against her breast and kissed his damp forehead. His eyelids fluttered open, and he gazed up at her dazed and uncomprehending. "Go back to sleep," she said softly, kissing his cheek. "Everything's all right now."

Stevie settled again, his eyelids drooping heavily as he burrowed against her breast. She held him tightly within her arms and rocked him, crooning a lullaby, feeling him slide back into a deeper sleep.

Nothing more was said until the carriage drew up in Cavendish Square. Lester jumped down and reached in to take the child, but she said sharply, "No. I can manage."

He helped her down with a steadying hand under her elbow and ran up the stairs to bang on the door. But it opened before he reached it, and Livia and Aurelia came rushing out.

"Do you have him . . . oh, thank God. Is he all right?"

"I think so," she said, carrying him carefully up the stairs. "He's drugged, but he'll come out of it soon. He's already beginning to stir."

"Who the devil did this?" Aurelia demanded, outrage shaking her voice as she looked at the inert little body in her sister-in-law's arms. "Who on earth would do such a thing?"

"You won't believe it when I tell you," Cornelia said grimly as she entered the house. "I must take him upstairs. Linton will help."

"The little lad's safe?" Morecombe stepped out of the shadows of the staircase. "Thank the good Lord, m'lady." He called over his shoulder, "Our Ada . . . our Mavis, the lad's back, all right and tight."

The twins emerged from the back regions at a near run, wiping their hands on their aprons. "Oh, mercy me," Ada said, flinging her arms wide. "The poor little lamb."

"Poor little lamb," Mavis reiterated, fluttering around Cornelia and her burden. "I'll make 'im a junket. 'E likes my junket, 'e does, bless him."

"Aye, but I reckon 'e'll need a spot o' gruel first," Ada declared. "Looks right poorly, 'e does, the poor lamb. I'll get it goin' right away."

"Thank you both." Cornelia managed a fleeting smile despite her anxiety to get upstairs to the nursery. She hurried up the stairs, Aurelia and Livia in her wake.

Linton gave a cry of joy as they came into the nursery and rushed across to Cornelia. "Oh, he's safe. Oh, merciful heaven." She flung her hands in the air and behind her, Daisy, still sodden, threw her apron over her face and burst into another flood of tears. Instantly Susannah and Franny, who'd been sitting by the fire solemnly sucking gingerbread, joined her in tearful wails, and Susannah hurled herself at her mother's knees.

Once order was restored, Cornelia sat with Stevie in

the rocking chair by the fire, refusing to relinquish him. Susannah sat at her feet, sucking her thumb, resting her head on her mother's lap, her eyes drooping after the exhaustion of the long morning.

Linton, once more in command of herself and her domain, kept a sharp eye on them even as, wisely, she left mother and children to themselves.

When Stevie finally stirred with more purpose than before, Cornelia felt a surge of relief so powerful she realized how terrified she still had been that he wouldn't come out of his drugged stupor.

He opened his eyes fully with a cry of protest, and threw up.

"That's better," Linton said briskly, coming over to them. "Let him get rid of that poison, my lady . . . Daisy, girl, bring a basin, hot water, and cloths. Jump to it now."

Stevie vomited miserably for what seemed an eternity to Cornelia, who held him close throughout, rubbing his back and murmuring soft encouragement. But at last he lay back against her ruined gown and gazed up at her. "My head hurts, Mama."

"I know, sweetie. I know. It'll pass soon, I promise."

"He needs a nice warm bath and some hot milk," Linton said authoritatively. "And then a proper sleep. Then he'll be right as rain." She reached down to take the child from his mother. "Give him here, my lady, and you go and get yourself cleaned up. I'll look after him."

Stevie allowed himself to be relinquished to the familiar arms of his nurse, and Cornelia stood up, gingerly holding her skirts.

"Take off your dress, and I'll fetch your nightrobe," Livia said. She and Aurelia had remained in the nursery throughout.

"Thank you, Liv." Gratefully, Cornelia accepted Aurelia's helping hands with her gown, then sponged herself roughly with hot water and a cloth before slipping into the robe that Livia brought up for her.

Linton was bathing Stevie in a bath in front of the fire, and the child seemed to have regressed to babyhood, offering none of his usual protests or comments. Cornelia knelt by the tub, wondering if it was wise to remind him of what had happened. But then she decided it couldn't be ignored. It might frighten him more if it wasn't acknowledged.

"Can you remember what happened, sweetheart?" she asked, reaching for the washcloth.

Stevie shook his head.

"Did you see who took you?"

The child shook his head again. Then he whimpered. "My head still hurts."

"That's because you drank something nasty," Cornelia told him. "It'll be better soon, I promise."

Stevie nodded again, as if reassured, and his eyes started to droop. Linton scooped him out of the water, wrapping him in a thick towel. "Let's tuck you into bed, my sweet. Mama will read you a story."

It was an hour later before Cornelia left the nursery, satisfied that her son was sleeping a natural, healthy sleep. She needed a bath herself, but was not surprised to find Livia and Aurelia waiting for her in her bedchamber.

"So, who did this?" Livia asked without preamble.

"Well, Nigel's in there somewhere. Although I really don't think he had any truck with Stevie's kidnapping." Wearily Cornelia sank into the chair by the fire. "I don't know the whole, but I'll tell you what I do know."

They listened in an incredulous silence and when she was finished, Aurelia said wonderingly, "So this house is the key to all this. Harry wanted to buy the house from the beginning, presumably because of the thimble . . ."

"Except that Lester said the thimble had no significance." Cornelia leaned down to her stained dress that she'd dropped in a heap on the floor. She found the pocket and took out the thimble. "Actually, what he said was *these* engravings have no significance." She held it up. "What did that mean?"

"That there's another thimble?" Livia suggested.

"And because Harry knew this was not the thimble they wanted, whoever they are, he didn't bother to take it with him when he went to rescue Stevie." Cornelia leaned back against her chair and closed her eyes. It all made some weird sense in a world that bore no relation to the ordinary one she and her friends inhabited. Somehow they'd strayed into another one.

"How did Nigel get involved?" Aurelia asked after a minute. "It seems incredible."

"I imagine he found himself in a terrifying nightmare," Cornelia said rather dully. "Somehow he found himself in the company of people for whom a life means nothing." She thought of the dead man on the floor of the tavern and shuddered. A life meant little enough to Viscount Bonham and his cohorts.

"And what of Harry?" Aurelia leaned forward on the window seat where she was perched. "Do you think he'll tell you everything now?"

Cornelia laughed shortly. "He'll not have the chance, Ellie. I don't intend to set eyes on him again. And as soon as Stevie's fit to travel, I'm going home with my children."

"Yes, of course," Aurelia said quickly. "We'll leave by the end of the week."

"No . . . no, you don't have to come with me," Cornelia said. "Of course you don't. You and Liv stay here. You're enjoying yourselves. I'll take Linton, if you can spare her. Daisy can stay here with Franny. She's perfectly competent with one child."

Her friends exchanged glances that she couldn't read, but before either of them could speak, there was a knock at the door. "My lady, that viscount's here," Morecombe announced from the corridor. "Wants t' see you summat urgent."

Cornelia stiffened. "Tell him I'm not at home, Morecombe."

"Oh, aye. Likes as not he'll not believe me."

Cornelia got up and went to open the door. "It doesn't matter whether he does or not, Morecombe. I won't see him. Tell him that if you wish."

"Oh, aye." Morecombe shuffled off towards the stairs again.

Livia and Aurelia rose as if they both heard the same summons. "We'll leave you to bathe, Nell, and get some rest," Livia said. "Shall we have dinner in the parlor, as we used to before we became so grand that we had to dine in the dining salon?" She attempted a light laugh, but it had a somewhat hollow ring.

"Yes, I'd like that," Cornelia said with a warm smile. "I'll probably take a short nap after my bath. Dinner at six?"

"Six o'clock," Aurelia affirmed, leaning in to kiss her sister-in-law. "Poor love, you've had a rotten time. Are you sure there's nothing else we can do?"

Cornelia shook her head, trying to hide the sheen of tears in her eyes. "No, but thank you both. I don't know what I'd have done without you."

"Seems to me you did rather well on your own," Aurelia said briskly. "Disarming some knife-wielding thug." She touched the scratch on Cornelia's neck. "I think Linton should look at that."

"It's nothing. It doesn't hurt." Cornelia moved her head gently aside. "I'll bathe it with warm water and use a little witch hazel. It's a mere scratch."

Her friends offered no further comment and left her

alone. And once she was safely alone, the key turned in the lock, Cornelia allowed the tears to flow. Relief mingled with despair, joy with grief. She had her child safe, but she had lost the possibility of a happiness that, without considering how it was to be achieved, she had insensibly begun to consider her due.

Harry listened to Morecombe's uninformative denial in tight-lipped silence. He'd heard from Lester what had transpired in the carriage, and he knew he had but one chance to put things straight. And that one chance was a mere thread at best. But he would not give up. It was not in his nature to accept defeat. He knew what he had done, and he could guess what and how Cornelia was feeling. But she was a reasonable woman, a highly intelligent woman. She would see both sides. She would consider his position. Once her hurt and anger had died down, she would see things clearly.

He accepted that now he had no choice but to tell her everything. And if that confidence compromised his service, then so be it. He had given twelve years to that service, and much as he loved his work, if continuing meant losing this woman, then he would retire.

He shook his head impatiently as Morecombe made to close the front door on him, and before it shut, he put his shoulder against it and heaved. His second unceremonious entrance in one day, he reflected dourly, following his own momentum into the hall.

"My apologies," he said perfunctorily to the dazed butler. "Where's Lady Dagenham?"

"You can't see her," Aurelia said from the stairs as she came down to the hall.

"No, she's not well enough to see you," Livia corroborated from behind her.

Both women regarded him with unconcealed hostility as they stood at the bottom of the stairs. "I'd have thought you'd have the sensitivity to leave her alone after what she's been through," Aurelia said in frigid tones.

Harry sighed. "I don't think any of you fully understand—"

"What is there to understand?" Livia interrupted furiously. "We understand that a five-year-old child has been vomiting uncontrollably for the last hour. We understand that our friend has been pushed almost to the brink of insanity with fear for her child. And we understand that if not for you, none of that would have happened."

Harry took an involuntary step backwards at this tirade. Livia, usually so soft and gentle, was a veritable termagant, her gray eyes blasting fury, her black hair springing out around her face as if infused with her rage.

He looked in appeal at Aurelia, who stood in stony silence, her brown eyes cold. Then he recovered the initiative. "Where is she?" Even as he asked the question he headed for the stairs. It was a reasonable assumption that if her friends were coming downstairs, Cornelia would be upstairs.

"You can't go up." Livia planted herself in front of him.

"Oh, yes, I can," he said, firmly putting her to one side. "This lies between Nell and me." He took the stairs two at a time, leaving Livia and Aurelia staring after him.

He went first to Cornelia's bedchamber. If she wasn't there, he'd head for the nursery. The door was locked.

"Cornelia, please let me in." He kept his voice even, the demand couched as a request.

"Go away, Harry. We have nothing to say to each other." She sounded weary.

"Oh, but we most certainly do," he declared, aware that the other two women were now standing behind him. "I'll break this damn door down, if I have to. Now, let me in."

Cornelia stood irresolute in the middle of her chamber. She had little doubt that if Harry was determined, he would indeed break down the door. Or find some other way to get to her. And in truth she knew that there was no point running away from this. It needed to be finished, once and for all. She went to the door and turned the key, then walked away from it, back to the fireplace.

Harry opened the door and came in. Livia and Aurelia stepped forward at the same time. "I appreciate your concern, but believe it or not, Nell doesn't need protection from me," he stated, closing the door in their faces and turning the key once again.

He faced her as she stood in front of the fire, holding the robe closed at the neck. She looked ineffably tired and he longed to take her in his arms, to kiss the fatigue from her eyes, to stroke the tension from the tall, slender frame. There was an emptiness to her eyes that filled him with sorrow.

"Oh, my dear love," he murmured, coming quickly towards her. "I will never forgive myself for this." He tried to draw her close, but she stepped away from him, warding him off with upraised hands.

"What is it you'll never forgive yourself for, Harry?" she asked with a cold detachment. "For pretending to love me, pretending to be my friend? For using me? . . . No, let me have my say," she demanded fiercely as he tried to interrupt. "You've forced this upon me, and by God you'll listen to me."

Harry acknowledged this with a faint inclination of his head and moved away to stand in front of the window, his hands loosely at his sides, his clear green eyes filled with pain as he gazed unwaveringly at her.

Bitter anger, the knowledge of betrayal, wretched hurt, and humiliation at being duped fueled her eloquence. She made no attempt to modify her denunciation, instead allowed the most powerfully hurtful words full rein, and Harry stood and listened in silence.

When finally the eloquence ran dry, he said, "I dispute only one accusation, Nell. You say I never loved you. That's not true. I have loved you for many weeks now. I cannot imagine not loving you."

There was such quiet confidence in the statement that Cornelia was unable to voice the scornful dismissal that rose to her tongue. "How can you say that?" she asked. "If you loved me, you would not have put me, my family, my friends, into this position."

He sighed and felt for words. "Lester was here to protect you. I was here, all the time. We were looking for Nigel. I truly didn't believe that there was any real danger for any of you. Once I'd retrieved the thimble—"

"You knew that Nigel was somehow involved?" She stared in disbelief. "And you didn't say anything to any of us. And what do you mean, 'retrieved the thimble'?" She pushed her tumbled hair away from her face with a distracted air.

"I saw no need to tell you about Nigel," he said. "I thought we had the situation well under control. I couldn't risk jeopardizing an operation—"

"Oh, of course, your operation . . . your mission . . . or whatever you want to call it." Blue flames enlivened her previously dull gaze as she interrupted him. "And just what was that mission, Harry? I would like to judge whether it was worth the agony my son went through."

"Hear me out then." His tone clipped as if he were giving an official debriefing, he told her everything from the moment the thimble disappeared from his house.

Cornelia listened and even though she wanted to dismiss his words as feeble excuses for the inexcusable, her rational mind reasserted itself through the tangle of angry emotions. There had been lives at stake, many lives. It was sheer misfortune that she and her friends had walked unknowingly into the midst of a web of espionage. All that was true.

"You had no need to involve *me* . . . my heart, my soul, in this operation," she said when he'd fallen silent. Her voice sounded thick to her ears, thick with hurt and disappointment, and mortification. "You made love to me, I made love to you. Was that necessary in order for you to retrieve your damnable codes?"

"At first I wanted you," he said simply. "And then I realized I loved you, and the reason for getting involved in the first place was no longer relevant." He took a step towards her. "Nell, my love, please . . . you must believe me, there was nothing deliberate or manipulative about the times we shared."

He reached for her hands, but she jerked them away and he let his hands fall helplessly to his sides again. "I never expected to fall in love. But I want . . . no need . . . to spend the rest of my life with you. Without you I will have no life."

"What are you saying?" Her eyes were still cold, her voice expressionless as she refused to acknowledge the first faint stirring of an emotion that was not anger or hurt.

"Will you marry me, Nell?" The words were blunt, but in his eyes doubt warred with conviction, despair with hope.

Cornelia simply stared at him. "You know that's impossible. Even if I wanted to . . . after all this . . ." She gestured widely as if to encompass the whole canvas of their history. "Even if I could forget that you put my *children*, my friends, myself in danger for some mission that meant more to you than our safety, I couldn't ally myself with a man who's been accused of murdering his wife. A man with that stain upon his reputation . . . I would lose my children. You must know that."

Harry inhaled sharply as if trying to catch his breath after a blow to the solar plexus. "Who told you?"

"Your great-aunt. But what does it matter who told me?" She shrugged, shaking her head in exasperation.

"I would have found out one day, and you can be certain that my father-in-law has heard the story. And he would use it to get Stevie, make no mistake. Of course I can't marry you. The only hope I have of recovering from this *episode* is to go home to the country and hope that no whisper of this reaches the earl."

"Do you believe I killed her?" he asked quietly.

She shrugged again. "What does it matter what I believe?"

"It matters to me." His face was very white beneath the weathered tan, and his green eyes rested on her countenance with an intensity that unnerved her.

"If Lester hadn't killed that man this afternoon, *you* would have killed him," she said.

"Yes, I would have," he agreed as quietly as before. "Rather than risk his hurting you, I would have killed him. But that is rather different, don't you think, from killing one's wife for having an affair?"

Cornelia bit her lip. "No, I don't believe you killed your wife," she stated. "I never did. But that doesn't alter the situation. I couldn't marry you even if I wished to."

"And you don't wish to," he declared flatly. "Well, there's no more to be said." He gazed at her for a long moment, then moved towards the door and reached for the key. "Good-bye, Nell."

The door closed behind him with a decisive click.

Cornelia picked up the first thing that came to hand, a pewter candlestick, and hurled it with her all her force at the closed door. It hit its mark with a splintering crash that did little to relieve her feelings.

"What on earth . . ." Aurelia put her head around the door, her eyes a little scared. "Nell, what happened?"

"Oh, I don't know," Cornelia declared on a sob of part fury, part anguish. "I have never been so miserable in my life, and I can't see any way that's going to change, Ellie."

Chapter 25

"I WISH YOU'D LET me go with you, Nell." Aurelia carefully folded one of Cornelia's evening gowns before laying it in the half-filled trunk.

"There's no need, Ellie. And Liv needs a chaperone if she's to stay here," Cornelia pointed out for the tenth time as she put her hairbrushes into her dressing case.

"Liv would go back too, you know she would."

"Yes, but it's not necessary." Cornelia closed the dressing case and turned the little key. "Everything's going so well now. Liv's established in society; she has enough men dangling after her, one of them will declare himself soon, I'm sure of it."

"Maybe, but are you so sure Liv will take one of them?" Aurelia turned to fold another gown. "She hasn't expressed any preferences."

"Give her time." Cornelia took petticoats out of the linen press and began to fold them. "Before the season's over, she'll have more than one offer, I'll wager you."

"I wouldn't take the wager," Aurelia declared. "Of course she will, but I still say she might not take any one of them."

"What might I not take?" Livia asked from the doorway. "Morecombe's put a hamper of food into the chaise, Nell. And the twins made gingerbread for the children, so it should keep them sweet on the journey . . . What might I not take?"

"A husband," Cornelia told her. She tried an accompanying chuckle, but somehow it didn't work. These days it seemed as if she'd forgotten how to laugh. "We were discussing your marital prospects."

Livia made a little moue. "I'm not exactly sanguine about those myself." She sat on the edge of the bed. "In truth, I'd be happy to go back with you, Nell."

"No," Cornelia stated definitely. "The object of this exercise was to find you a husband, and that's what's going to happen." She became aware of her friends looking at her as she said this and felt her cheeks warm. Neither of them would be tactless enough to point out that only Cornelia thus far had received such an offer.

"We'll see," Livia said pacifically. "Are you nearly ready? Shall I tell Morecombe to send Jemmy up for the trunk?"

"Yes, thank you, Liv." Cornelia closed the lid of the trunk and bent to lock it. "Linton has everything in hand from the nursery. Are you sure you don't mind if she goes with me, Ellie?"

"Hardly," Aurelia said, shaking her head in mock exasperation. "Linton's your nurse, Nell. She's in your employ, I'm not about to poach her. Daisy will be fine with Franny. Although Franny's going to miss Stevie and Susannah."

"I could take her too, if you'd like," Cornelia offered, although she knew the offer would be refused. Aurelia was no more willing to be separated from her child than Cornelia was from hers.

Aurelia smiled and shook her head again. "If she gets too fractious, I'll bring her home for a few days."

"Mr. Morecombe says I'm to take the trunk, m'lady." Jemmy appeared in the doorway. "An' Hester's here for the rest." The kitchen maid bobbed up behind him.

"That's it then." Cornelia surveyed her denuded bedchamber with a pang of loss that she was coming to accept would now be a permanent part of her self. Puss, curled as usual on the end of the bed, appeared unperturbed by the disturbance around her. Cornelia scratched the cat between her ears and was rewarded with a flick of whiskers. She turned resolutely and went downstairs.

The hired post chaise waited at the curb in the early dawnlight, the driver on his box, mounted outriders in place, the postillion supervising the loading of the trunk onto the roof while Tristan and Isolde yapped in ecstasies of excitement, straining at leashes resolutely held by Livia. Linton and the children were already inside the chaise when Cornelia bade farewell to the household before kissing Aurelia and Livia good-bye.

"Write to me," she enjoined them both. "I want to know everything that happens."

"Oh, we'll tell you every piece of tittle-tattle," Aurelia said, her eyes suspiciously bright. "And Liv will give you a detailed description of every suitor."

Cornelia climbed into the chaise and settled herself on the seat opposite her sleepy children and the ramrod-straight Linton. She leaned out of the window to wave as the chaise pulled away and she stayed waving until the vehicle had turned the corner out of the square, and she could no longer hear the yapping of the silly pink dogs.

The watcher on the far side of the square waited only until the carriage had disappeared before he nudged his horse into a fast trot towards Mount Street.

They were crossing Wimbledon Common by eight o'clock. It was a gloomy April morning, heavy rain clouds gathering low on the horizon. The weather suited Cornelia's mood, but she endeavored to show a cheerful front to the children, entertaining them with stories and games of I Spy, while Linton, unable to hide her satisfaction at the prospect of a return to the regular routines of home, allowed her charges to indulge in gingerbread and the apple tartlets supplied by the twins, who had seemed genuinely dismayed at their departure.

When the carriage came to an abrupt halt, Susannah nearly fell off her seat and set up a wail of protest. Cornelia leaned out of the window to find out what had happened, then gazed in horrified astonishment at the scene that met her eye.

A phalanx of men sat their horses in a line across the road, barring their progress. The outriders were fumbling somewhat belatedly with their weapons while the coachman cursed up hill and down dale in a futile tirade.

Highwaymen were hardly infrequent on the commons and heaths around London, but Cornelia had never heard of them being active in broad daylight on such a well-traveled road. Besides, these horsemen didn't really look like they were interested in highway robbery, just rather set on preventing the carriage's progress. She leaned farther out of the window, wondering why she felt no sense of menace at all. But she knew why almost immediately.

Lester's jockeylike frame was unmistakable, and the identity of the lithe, lean figure on the familiar chestnut needed no guesswork.

She pushed open the carriage door and jumped down to the ground without the help of the footstep. She was astonished at how calm she felt, as if somehow she'd been expecting something like this. Which was, of course, ridiculous. Only a lunatic would have expected this. Only a bedlamite would be doing such a thing.

"Gentlemen?" She raised her eyebrows interrogatively as she looked directly at Harry Bonham. "I suppose it didn't occur to you that you could be swinging from the gibbet at the crossroads for this?"

He laughed. "No, my lady, it didn't. Highway rob-

bery is not my object. Although I admit to the holdup."
He swung off his mount and handed the reins to Lester.

He came swiftly over to her, caught her chin, and
kissed her. She raised a hand and dealt him a ringing
slap, and he laughed softly, taking her hand and kissing
the palm.

"Well deserved, I grant you. And you shall do it again
as hard and as often as you choose once we get where
we're going."

Still holding her hand he leaned into the carriage,
where the children sat gazing wide-eyed on either side of
the rigid Linton. "Good morning, Stevie . . . Susannah,"
he greeted them with a smile. "Good morning, Linton."

Linton gave him a stiff nod that did little to disguise
her confusion. The children, on the other hand, beamed
at him. "We're playing I Spy with Mama," Stevie said.
"Susannah's not very good at it because she doesn't know
how to spell yet."

"I am . . . I do," his sister cried indignantly.

"I'm sure you can," Harry soothed. "Now, I'm going
to take Mama with me, and you're going to follow in the
carriage. I have a big surprise for you both."

Stevie shrank back against the seat, immediately suspicious. "Don't like surprises," he muttered.

With instant comprehension, Harry said seriously,
"This surprise is nothing to be afraid of, Stevie. Nothing
like the last one. I promise you'll like this one. Mama will
tell you so." He stepped back to make room for Cornelia.

She had little choice but to reassure her son, even

though it appeared as if she was agreeing to whatever madness Harry was indulging in. "It's all right, Stevie. We'll be on our way in a few minutes."

She stepped back and away from the carriage. "Now, for heaven's sake," she said sharply. "Stop playing games, Harry. And let me get back inside and on my way."

He gripped her hands tightly. "Please, Nell, indulge me for half an hour. And then I give you my word, if you insist on continuing your journey, I'll not stand in your way." His eyes begged her, and there was a catch in his voice that told her how desperately he was making this play.

She had thought she would never see him again, had resigned herself to a long future with only memories of those transcendent moments of pure bliss. She would remember his voice, his green, glowing eyes, his strong, deft hands. And she would be strong for her children, live only in her children, feeding off her memories.

And now, as she stood there on the cold common and read the desperate need in his eyes, she knew that that would not be enough . . . never would it be enough. She could at least hear him out.

She said nothing, but he read her acquiescence, and joy flooded his countenance. "Come then." He lifted her onto his horse, mounting swiftly behind her. He encircled her waist, holding her against his body, as he reached round for the reins.

"Lead them in, Lester," he called as he nudged Perseus's flanks, and the horse broke into an easy canter.

Cornelia said nothing. There seemed nothing to say. Once again she seemed to be caught up willy-nilly in the strange and mysterious world of Viscount Bonham, but this time she was a willing partner, fully conscious of what she'd agreed to. And capable of walking away. *Or was she?*

They turned through a gateway flanked by two stone gateposts, and Perseus cantered up a long, curving driveway beneath the overarching branches of still-leafless beach trees. The driveway opened into a gravel sweep in front of an imposing mansion.

"What is this place?" Cornelia asked, breaking the silence that had become strangely companionable.

"Gracechurch Hall," Harry answered, drawing rein at the foot of a wide flight of shallow stone steps leading up to a pair of double doors. He swung off his horse.

"Ah." Cornelia nodded. "And is Her Grace in residence?"

"But of course," he responded, his eyes sparkling with an anticipation that had banished his previous anxiety. He reached up to lift her down. "I would hardly bring you here without a chaperone in residence."

Cornelia almost laughed, but then she sensed an underlying seriousness to the comment, and she looked at him sharply. "What's going on, Harry?"

"Wait and see," he said, setting her on her feet, keeping his hands for a moment at her waist as if reluctant to let her go. "All I ask is half an hour of your time. The carriage with the children will be here shortly."

He offered her his arm, and, with a tiny shrug, she took it and allowed him to escort her up the steps, past two liveried footmen who stood at the now-opened front door, and into an elegant, high-ceilinged hallway.

She drew off her gloves and gave her pelisse to one of the footmen. Then she looked inquiringly at Harry, who gestured towards a door on the far side of the hall.

"Would you care to go into the library, ma'am?"

Cornelia merely followed the direction of his hand and found herself in a paneled, book-lined apartment comfortably furnished with heavy leather armchairs and massive reading desks.

She took up a stand in the middle of the room. "So?"

"So," Harry said, going to a sideboard where decanters and a coffeepot reposed. "Coffee . . . or something a little more potent?"

"It's barely eight in the morning," she protested. "But coffee, if you please."

He poured and handed her a cup. "My great-aunt keeps to her room in the morning, but she will be down by noon. Eliza, of course, is up and about. She's made provision for Linton and the children. Breakfast and such like."

"That's very thoughtful. But could we stop this charade now? What's going on?" She put her coffee cup down on a table.

He reached into his pocket and drew out a document. He tapped it against his palm. "This is a special license. I would like us to be married this afternoon in the chapel here. It's all arranged . . . No, please, love, let me finish." He spoke in a rush as if desperate to get the words out before she could interrupt him.

"I understand the difficulties with your father-in-law, but if they can be got over, would you marry me, Nell? Do you love me?"

He took a step towards her, holding out his hands, his face somehow naked, his eyes vulnerable. "I know you wouldn't say it before, but now, please . . . tell me the truth. Do you love me?"

She looked at him and spoke the simple truth. "Yes." There was no earthly point in denying it.

His expression cleared, the anxiety left his eyes, and he seized her hands. "I knew it, but I didn't dare hope . . ."

"It alters nothing, Harry," she said, hearing the desperation in her voice. "I can't lose my children just for love."

"You won't," he promised, drawing her towards a sofa. "Listen to me now as I listened to my great-aunt. She's convinced it can be managed, and . . ." He smiled rather ruefully. "She's convinced me too."

He took her hands again and leaned in to kiss her eyelids. "She convinced me that I never wanted to be convinced before. So here's what we do. We present the world with a fait accompli . . . announcements of our marriage in the *Gazette* and the *Morning Post.* They're already prepared." He reached for a piece of paper on a side table and held it out to her. "It's only a rough draft."

On April 15th, Eighteen Hundred and Seven, a marriage between Viscount Bonham and the Viscountess Dagenham was celebrated in the private chapel of Gracechurch Hall, in the presence of the Duchess of Gracechurch.

Cornelia read the formal announcement and shook her head in bewilderment. "How does this help?"

"Afterwards, we go away for an extended honeymoon to Scotland. I have a grouse moor, an estate, trout streams . . ." He waved a hand expansively, his voice warming persuasively to his theme as if he would sweep her away on the tide of his logic.

"No one will find us there, it's almost inaccessible by road. Markby isn't going to set the Bow Street Runners onto you just because you've made an impeccable marriage, and believe me, Nell, without undue modesty, an alliance with the Bonhams *is* an impeccable alliance. And whatever gossip the old scandal produces, when we come back to London in the autumn, in time for the winter season, it will be old news that we can easily weather. Your father-in-law can't contest the marriage, and if you've had the children with you the entire time, he won't stand a chance at contesting custody in the courts."

"How can you be sure of that?" She didn't want to hope, it sounded too glib, too easy.

"My great-aunt's lawyers," he said. "I've not been idle these last wretched days, my love."

"And they say he couldn't take them from me?"

"Not if you don't leave them behind. As long as they stay with you . . . and with their stepfather . . . there's not a court in the land would side with him."

Cornelia closed her eyes. For the first time she really allowed herself to think that perhaps this glimpse of a future could become reality.

"I should tell you too that I've resigned from the service," Harry said, his voice a little stilted now. "If that will make any difference to your answer. I know you probably can't forgive—"

"Oh, I can forgive," Cornelia interrupted, putting a finger on his lips. "I have already done so since that dreadful day. I understand now that at first you couldn't have told me the truth, and I can see how things became more and more twisted and tangled." She gave a tiny laugh. "A litter of kittens in a basket of wool couldn't have made a knot so impossible to unravel."

He grasped her wrist hard, pressing his lips into her palm. "I have been so terrified that you wouldn't be able to forgive me."

She leaned over and kissed the corner of his mouth. "I won't forgive you if you give up your work. Or, at least, I won't be able to forgive myself. Give us your undivided attention this summer, and we'll begin anew in the autumn."

Harry gave a shuddering sigh as if a massive burden had been lifted. "We'll leave that issue for the moment . . . ah, there are the children."

The sound of childish trebles came from the hall.

Cornelia jumped to her feet and headed for the library door, Harry on her heels.

Eliza Cox appeared from nowhere and bustled over to the little party. "Miss Linton, isn't it? I'm Eliza Cox. So happy to make your acquaintance . . . and these are the children . . . such pretty little dears. Let me take you to the nursery . . . I've ordered soft-boiled eggs for the children, and I'm sure you'll be glad of a nice hot cup of tea, Miss Linton. There's a good fire going, and a kettle of hot water . . . such a tedious journey from London . . . I do so hate it."

"Aye, well I thank you kindly, Miss Cox," Linton was heard to say as they disappeared onto the first landing. "I'll not say no to a cup of tea, and the children could do with a wash."

"Now," Harry said softly, "there seems but one more task to accomplish. You have need of attendants at your wedding. If you'll write a note, I'll send a carriage to Cavendish Square to bring Livia and Aurelia here."

"I can do that," Cornelia said, a slight smile flickering on her lips. "But after that, I think there's one more task to accomplish."

"Oh? And what is that?" Sparks of fire flickered in the green depths of his eyes as he traced the curve of her mouth with a forefinger.

"You may need to remind me why you went to the trouble of holding me up on Wimbledon Common." Her tongue darted, catching the tip of his finger.

"Oh, I believe I can do that," he promised, a half

smile playing over his lips. "In fact, let me do that now, then you can write your letter."

"Perhaps that would be best," she murmured. "I need to be absolutely certain, you see."

His eyes darkened. "You'll be in no doubt, by the time we're finished," he promised. He took her hand and led her up the stairs.

Much later Cornelia stretched languidly as she lay along the length of his body, kissing the hollow of his shoulder. "I appear to be reminded," she murmured.

His hand stroked down her back, coming to rest on her backside. "And absolutely certain?"

"Oh, yes," she affirmed, wriggling slightly so that their hips were aligned once more. "Never more certain of anything in my life."

She lifted her head a little to look down into his eyes. "I love you, Harry Bonham, whatever you are."

He took her hair between his hands and drew it back from her face. "I will be a good father to your children," he promised.

Cornelia smiled languidly. "How's your Greek and Latin?"

He laughed a little. "My love, I deal in codes. My grasp of the ancient languages is impeccable."

"Well, that's good," she murmured. "You can take on Stevie's preparation for Harrow, and his grandfather won't have a thing to complain about."

"I knew I could be useful." He reached up and ran his hands through the buttery fall of hair. His voice was low and intense as he said, "You will never regret entrusting your children to me."

"No, I know that." She kissed his eyelids. "And you will be a good father to any others who might happen along." She reached down for him, guiding him within her. "I think I need one last little reminder, my lord."